195732

1st Ad
4 —

NOBLE ROT

STORIES 1949–1988

BY RICHARD STERN

Golk

Europe, or Up and Down with Baggish and Schreiber

In Any Case (reissued as *The Chaleur Network*)

Teeth, Dying and Other Matters

Stitch

Honey and Wax: The Pleasures and Powers of Narrative

1968: A Short Novel, An Urban Idyll, Five Stories, and Two Trade Notes

The Books in Fred Hampton's Apartment

Other Men's Daughters

Natural Shocks

Packages

The Invention of the Real

The Position of the Body

A Father's Words

Noble Rot

NOBLE ROT

STORIES 1949–1988

Richard Stern

GROVE PRESS

NEW YORK

The name Grove Press and the colophon printed on the title page and the outside of this book are trademarks registered in the U.S. Patent and Trademark Office and in other countries.

Published by Grove Press
a division of Wheatland Corporation
841 Broadway
New York, N.Y. 10003

"There came a Wind like a Bugle," "Apparently with no surprise," "As imperceptibly as Grief," by Emily Dickinson reprinted by permission of the publishers from *The Poems of Emily Dickinson,* edited by Thomas H. Johnson, Cambridge, MA: The Belknap Press of Harvard University Press, Copyright © 1951, 1955, 1979, 1983 by the President and Fellows of Harvard College.

Library of Congress Cataloging-in-Publication Data

Stern, Richard, 1928–
Noble rot: stories 1949–1988/Richard Stern.—1st. ed.
p. cm.
ISBN 0-8021-1056-8
I. Title.
PS3569.T39N63 1989
813'.54—dc19   88-19156
CIP

Designed by Irving Perkins Associates

Manufactured in the United States of America

This book is printed on acid-free paper.

First Edition 1989

10 9 8 7 6 5 4 3 2 1

These stories, written over a forty-year writing life, aren't arranged in chronological order. (The collection isn't meant to display literary development or decline.) The arranger thinks of the reader as a story lover looking forward to his nightly story fix. Such a reader is comparatively disinterested in the towns and times of composition, the recollected fusion of experience and invention. Fascinating stuff that, but uncooked fiction, more or less cooked fact. Actually, the chief point of this note is its own superfluity.

It pleases me to set down the names of some friends who were around during some or all the years in which these stories were written: Don and Jean Justice, Tom and Jacqui Rogers, Hugh and Maryanne Kenner, Jeff Hayden and Eva Marie Saint, Mark Harris, Norma McDaniel, Mike Zwerin, John Wallace, Paolo Cherchi, David Malament, Guity and Gary Becker, Bob and Carole Morgan, Andy Austin, Peter Kovler, Jim Schiffer, Doug Unger, Susan Albertine, Jonathan Hall, the Rollings and Heiserman families, my sister Ruth, and my cousins Bob Lewin and Ruth Tishman. A special pleasure and a special—if fragmentary —sentence for my wife, Alane Rollings.

Richard Stern
August 1988

Contents

Contents

NOBLE ROT

ROT

STORIES 1949–1988

Ins and Outs

*Why not the quite simple effort to touch the
other, to feel the other, to explain the other to
myself.*

—FRANTZ FANON

1

HOLLEB knew the meaning of his respiratory trouble, but
what could he do? For him, outlet was intake. When some
strong reply to the world sailed up to his lips, he drove it back
toward the respiratory tract. Summer, winter, spring, and fall,
Holleb hacked, spat, and blew. He was thought by most Hyde
Parkers to be a drinker. No such high romance. Their sign, his
nose, bulbous, rosy, capillary map agleam, had been burnished
not by Scotch and rye but by a million handkerchief massages.

"Why Dads blow nosys?" The first remembered question of
son Artie.

The remembered response of May, the ever-yukking wife:
"Brains, Art. Dad's got so much brain, he's got to relieve the
pressure. Why Dad's handkerchiefs"—she let no routine drop—
"have higher I.Q.s than most guy's heads. There's people running governments today'd swap their minds for one of Dad's
blowers."

If Holleb's inner tract marked repression, May's shimmied day-in-and-out with that other form of evasion, yuks. Her big laughs. Wasn't laughter, with tears, the easiest form of human action?

That her laugh capacity should dwindle, that she would actually get up and do something else, was last year's surprise. A note on the pillow; she had not been up to talking it out with him. "I'm taking off for the Coast. See you in the funny papers."

Amazement, fury, relief, suspicion, jealousy.

The suspicion lit on Kruger, the Grove Press salesman whose rounds seemed to include the tiny Book Nook every other week. Though all salesmen went for her. She'd kept her looks, was taken for his daughter half the time, though she was less than a year younger. Up close, she didn't look so young. The laugh lines had trenched her mouth and eyes. But remoteness, a kind of snoot, kept her from close scrutiny. That and the routines. Still, forty, he'd guess she was taken for thirty.

Apparently it was not Kruger or anyone else. At least when Artie went out to stay with her in July, the only one around the bungalow was the woman she shared it with, a German geneticist at UCLA. "Kind of a lady," reported Artie. "With these thigh-high silver suede boots. And whiskers, real Franz Josef mutton chops. I mean, they were *there,* you could *see* them. Sideshow stuff."

Sideshow was a category of Artie's mind, though God knows he was a foot, at least, from midget class. Five-one anyway. But height had brought him much misery for years. It was the Great Age for Uglies, but shorties still made out poorly. Holleb, at five-nine, stooped, slouched, sat, and lay low before Artie's sad smallness.

What also surprised him was that Artie didn't stay out on the Coast. May was his favorite, also a shortie, though bigger than Artie. And she'd made Artie a yukker, they amused each other for years. "Give Mom my love," he'd told Artie, expecting not to see him for a long time.

"You got some to spare?" yukked Artie.

In a month, though, he was back in Chicago. Seems the bungalow had a bed and a couch; he'd slept on the floor, using Gisella's boots for pillows. Beverly Glen, called Swinger's Canyon in Westwood, was full of musicians, starlets, animators, younger technicians, assistant profs from UCLA, but, said Artie, while music rumbled up and tumbled down on them from every side, he, May, and Gisella sat in front of Johnny Carson and the Late Show night after night. The talk was whose turn it was to have the rocker. "Mom wasn't getting too many laughs out there. It was like living inside a fish." May worked in the UCLA Library. "The laugh meter there was broken too," said Artie.

"She probably couldn't adjust to a structured work environment." The Book Nook's famous charm was chaos. Holleb had to go in every few months to straighten out the inventory.

These days, Artie didn't do much laughing himself. In September he'd started college in Urbana. One semester, and he was back in Hyde Park. "I can't finish a book. And those lectures." So he bagged groceries forty-four hours a week at the Co-op. He had six months of grace before he turned nineteen and fodder for General Hershey.

His problems were turning him hippie. He had his own mutton chops, two brown trunks of hair edging toward each other across his cheeks. And, on top, fuzzy-wuzzy. Perhaps the intent was not to erase the boundaries between men and women but between animal and vegetable. In addition, his chin and what could be seen of his forehead simmered with boils. Little Artie was a beautiful sight.

Holleb said nothing, did nothing. He felt Artie's misery.

The most expressive part of his son was his room. This sight hit Holleb each time he left his own. A trash can of Artie's life, or not a trash can, because that suggested assemblage; a frozen tornado, a planless exhibit of his son's bafflement. Shirts, shorts, socks, pants, newspapers, letters, record jackets, crimped tubes of Derma-Sil, cylinders of Man-Tan, orange rinds, hardened gobbets of toothpaste like marble droppings—for Artie was an ambulatory toothbrusher—what else? Anything. Cans of Fresca and Tab—though weight was not one of his problems—even soil and leaves scuffed from his shoe soles.

Unbearable, though Holleb bore it, and then, one day, cleaned it up, hung up the pants, knifed gobs of Gleem from the shag rug, stacked the books and records, piled the garbage into bags, and took the laundry down Fifty-Seventh Street to the Chinese.

If Artie remarked the change, he found no words for it. So, every week or ten days, Holleb cleaned it again. As well, that is, as any room in what May called their "Battered Five" could be cleaned.

Nine years ago they'd sublet the place from Willard Lobz, a singer. Illicitly, for the University, which owned the place, didn't permit extended sublets. Lobz kept it to save storage on his grand piano and record collection while he sang in Europe. The Steinway was tuned twice a year, the collection was locked up in a cedar chest. They took up most of Room Five, Holleb's study.

The rest of the place went to pot. And the University was not to be called when the toilet fell in or wires strayed from the walls. Lobz would "take care of everything." Yes, while he had Puccini up against the wall in Palermo or Bad Nauheim.

Lobz was one of these *beaux laids,* fierce, chesty, full of operatic presence. Leonine, except it was not a lion's head but a monster catfish's, chinless with spears of pale whisker fanning out from enormous lips, nickel-colored eyes, a mat of yellow hair arranged on the great dome in the shape of Florida.

The voice was something terrific. It started below the shoes in a rumble that lasted seconds before words issued. Said May, "We could get the oil-depletion allowance if we bought him." What a diaphragm. What a chest. And an Adam's apple which, said May, he could rent as a box at the opera.

When Lobz appeared in Chicago, Holleb would present him with the latest crisis in plaster or wires. Lobz was an operatic listener. He listened louder than many yelled. The body throbbed with rumble, then moved with gigantesque motion, charged the telephone, dialed with furious strokes of a thumb-like pinkie, and then, a great piece of fortissimo lip; his technique, the Multiple Threat. "You got a damage suit on your hands, Simmons. We got hot wires sticking outa the walls here, one of these kids get toasted, you've had it. Ninety-nine to life for you, Simmons. Criminal negligence. I'll take out full-page ads, your name in a black box. I'm sitting right here now with a man on the *Herald.* Don't tell me that, I called you nine times myself, you better get you a secretary knows something beside Polack. I got me a lawyer's itching to crack your skull for a jury, we know what you Mafiosi electrics been givin' the people of

4

Chicago." Followed some Italian curses, or perhaps *Rigoletto*, and the phone was crashed into itself; once Lobz cracked the casing. "These jaybirds got to feel the color of your whip, Holleb. Finesse they don't hear. That's why you're getting no service."

Of course no electrician showed up. Either Lobz had dialed Weather Report or he underrated the insensitivity of Simmons Electric; men who service the homes of midcentury cities were no virgins when it came to abuse.

By the time Holleb got an electrician himself, Lobz was fighting Donizetti to a draw at the Sud-Deutscher Rundfunk.

He tried deducting from the rent, but Lobz was a master of epistolary violence; it wasn't worth his static. Holleb wrote the repairs off. There were very few cheap apartments left in Hyde Park, and, for all its defects, the Battered Five was convenient, steps away from the Book Nook, a grocery, the laundry, the few restaurants and coffee houses spared by Urban Renewal. In a dying neighborhood, the few live coals were here. Besides which, he could walk to the *Herald* office in ten minutes, it was even closer for Artie and May to school and work. And what could you expect in a modern American city anyway, Arcadia?

2

Holleb was the business manager of the neighborhood weekly. He also wrote a column about anything which struck his fancy. Such freewheeling columns were a Chicago newspaper tradition, from Lardner and Hecht to Mabley, Harris, and Royko. Holleb's dealt with everything from neighborhood gangs to comments on books and University lectures. It was a popular column, Holleb's picture appeared above it, he was a minor neighborhood celebrity.

He was not a bad writer, and though not ambitious, his desk was filled with sketches and notes for longer essays, even books. He'd published one long piece in the *Southwest Review*, an essay on the conventions of newspaper reporting, the subject which interested him more than any other. He had a working title for a book he might write about it, *The Fictions of Journalism*.

Holleb distrusted his profession. May said it was sour grapes because he was at the rim of it, but he didn't think that was the case. The journalistic situation was, if anything, worse on metropolitan dailies. If a neighborhood reporter couldn't get a story about his own neighborhood straight, how could men sent to the four corners of the world without language or social lore come up with anything but bilge? It was hard writing up what one knew. When you wrote up what you didn't know, it was professional insanity. Or so thought Holleb. He went at the subject in frequent columns. One of his favorites was called "Reflections on Malinowski." "What do we learn," it went

> from the journal kept by the great anthropologist during his pioneer field work among the Trobrianders? Here he is, the European student of language and customs, living month after month cheek by jowl with his subjects, and what fills his notebooks but reveries of lust and murder. How does he divert himself from "the savages"—as he calls them in one of his gentler references—but by reading detective stories. Mostly he broods on his disgust, nay, his hatred for "the brutes."
>
> Shades of his fellow Pole, the novelist Conrad. But this is a scientist, a super-reporter, a model for anthropologists from Mead and Benedict to Leach, Geertz, Powdermaker, and Fallers.
>
> Can we wonder at the turmoil of the world when men without a tithe of Malinowski's learning or genius are sent to report the political opinions of Asian villagers? Diplomats or reporters, these are the men whose muddled accounts inform the world's decision-makers. (Cf. the *Herald* column of Sept. 17, '63 on Hughes's *Ordeal of Power.*)
>
> Is this what Scripture means by Evil Communication?

May especially disliked this column. "More show, less tell, Billy. You sound like the Court of Appeals. Judgments, judgments. Less schmoos, more delivery," with four or five other variations. Hers was the tenacity of old composers; give her a theme, it was mangled for an hour. A pretty woman with such brilliant eyes, most people couldn't remember their color— blue. She had the stiff nostrils and high cheekbones of snoot, yet she was not snooty. If anything, she was the reverse, crawling before anyone classed beneath her in the organization tables she'd grown up with, janitors, Negroes, workers below the craftsman-shopkeeper class. The word, even the concept "class" was alien to her; which, of course, meant her sensitivity was riddled with it.

"It's no joke turning out quality on a deadline."

"You bet your life. I wonder how Lippmann managed." Her voice was rough, thick, from childhood diphtheria before antibiotics made the disease a strep throat. Without that voice, she might have been a Milwaukee cheerleader, married an inspector at Schlitz. Instead, shy, she read and got a scholarship to the University, where they met in freshman, married in junior year. Twenty years, minus the one in Beverly Glen, an easy year for him once the shock had worn off, once he'd stopped dreaming of running her down in a car. It was relief to be away from that tongue which grew rougher each year. In a long marriage, what is unthinkable at the beginning may come to seem a caress. As in any form of human degradation. The first years, his columns might have issued from Olympus; she quoted them to friends. The last years, he was relieved at her attacks; it showed she still read him.

"Lippmann's got top-level sources. And what's he do but hand down judgments?"

Lippmann, though, was Holleb's model, and Holleb knew how much more Lippmann did. He'd had a fortunate lifetime of observation and literary practice, and he'd worked out comprehensive principles. He, Holleb, only scratched at the surface of things. He had not even put together the little he knew.

"If you don't know what a tree is, you can't describe a branch." Holleb had used this reproof of Erasmus to Dürer as epigraph for one of his favorite columns, "The Question of Coherence." It had come out a month or so before May's taking off. "When do we know," it began

that something really counts? When do we know a true conclusion, how differentiate it from a "Fading into the Sunset" convention?

We force events to cohere for us by stuffing them into old containers, old story patterns. Three meals a day, funerals, graduations, how true are these to the life surge? Isn't our very sense of life deformed by such false stages, false expectations, by violated senses of fulfillment?

It ended, "Readers, don't look in next week for the solution. Holleb doesn't know it."

3

A week before the anniversary of May's departure, a cold, late-March day, Holleb, having cleaned Artie's room and cooked himself some liver and onions, was half-dreaming in an armchair by the window, when the doorbell rang. Through the speaker system, Holleb asked who was there and heard some response about Biafra. People in Hyde Park were always collecting signatures for petitions, money for causes. (Sops for violent Cerberus.) Holleb pressed the admission button and waited by the stairwell.

A young Negro in a blue dashiki came up the stairs. "I'm collecting for Biafra," he said. He had no can for money or clipboard for petition signatures; odd, thought Holleb, but he subdued his uneasiness. In these times, it was a white burgher's obligation to suppress suspicion of Negroes. Of—correcting himself—blacks.

The dashiki was some reassurance. When a man wears what sets him apart—and these tunics were still uncommon in Hyde Park—it means self-consciousness has found an outlet. Such a man is not one of those stymied anonymities who are transformed by sudden rage into assassins.

"I'll get my wallet. The situation is frightful."

The fellow followed him into the living room; Holleb supposed it was all right. In fact, he was thinking he would offer him a cup of tea—they might have an interesting talk—when the fellow asked, "You got the money?"

That did unsettle Holleb, but again, he calmed himself; manners weren't the man.

The fellow was about twenty. He had a large head, the hair was bushed in the natural style, though the coiffure wasn't natural. The sides were trimmed low, the bush rose only in the middle, a camel effect. The mouth was large, the teeth were big, though Holleb remembered no smile. The skin was almost fair, a dark gold. Holleb remembered thinking there was less melanin in that skin than in that of some Caucasians, strange in view of the hair. This while he drew out his wallet, said cautiously he never had much money around, and handed over a dollar.

It was then the fellow clouted him with his fist, and something more, brass knuckles, coins, something that flashed and caused Holleb to move enough so that he was caught not in the face but the neck. It was terrific, he couldn't breathe, couldn't call. "No," he must have tried, maybe "Help," and the fellow punched him again, low, in the stomach. The fellow's face was near his, bunched in excitement and cruelty. It was then Holleb must have seen the teeth, heard the heavy breath, smelled and felt a hot, vinegary discharge from the leaping body. He was down, his wallet grabbed, he grabbed for the fellow's shoe, a blue suede, a Hush Puppy, which arced out of his hand and then drove into his chest. It was all Holleb remembered of that.

He came to on the floor. Artie, kneeling and crying, "Dad, Dad, Dad," was putting a washcloth to his face. Holleb rang with ache, so much he could not localize it. It made him distant from the room, from Artie, from his, yes, tears, from his strange sideburns, from his voice, "Are you O.K.? You poor, poor Dads. What happened? I called the police. Easy, old Dads."

The apartment, it turned out, had not been so much burgled as assaulted. The man had taken a hammer to Lobz's Steinway, the keys were cracked, the mahogany case was pocked and splintered. Chairs had been knifed, their stuffing bled into the room. Glasses and cups had been smashed and trampled; there was a glass icefall in the dining room.

Holleb spent three days in the hospital, and there looked through thick mug books, page after page of Negroes with records. Local Negroes, local records.

The sergeant, an alert-looking fellow in civvies, eyeglassed, neat, nervous, pointed to pictures as Holleb turned pages. His tone was studious, even loving. "Got this one with a baby carriage full of hardware over on Sixty-Third. Here's a fine one. Dumped lighter fluid on his momma and lit up. This one here hoists Impalas. Only Impalas. Fourteen years old. An Impala's missing, he's on the street, I don't think twice." The pictures which looked so much alike to Holleb were for the sergeant intimately different. "We been hunting this mother a year. His trick's carving initials on girls' cheeks."

Holleb's man was not in the books. At least, he didn't recognize him.

"We'll keep after him." The sergeant got up, a small man with the large books, a C.P.A. checking out company records. "I think we've got a chance. He'll be going up and down the streets with this Biafra. We may well get him. Then, Mr. Holleb, I hope you'll stick with us."

"What do you mean?" Holleb lay in his white hospital wrap-around, his sides taped, his face bandaged. With his almost white hair, he looked like a piece of human angel food—but smeared, battered—an odd extension of the antiseptic cubicle with its air of formaldehyde and the terrible histories of the mug books.

"Charge him. See it through the court."

"Of course. Why not?"

"You'd be surprised. People lose their lumps, they lose their interest. They get lazy. Scared. Or, in Hyde Park, they start thinking, 'These poor . . . these guys . . .'—who beat their brains out, remember—'they got no chance in life, why should I make it hard on them?' and so on. You'd be surprised."

"Foolish," said Holleb.

4

Two weeks later, Holleb was more or less back in shape. There were a few welts on his body, he had a small scar on the base of his neck, but he wasn't in pain. The apartment was cleaned up also, except for the piano, about which he hadn't dared write Lobz. At seven he got a call from the sergeant. "Mr. Holleb, we've got a line on your boy. We think he's one of that nest of dopies that hang out in the Riviera Hotel over your way on Dorchester. We're going to go in there about eleven o'clock, eleven-thirty, so your bell rings late, don't be scared. It'll be me with somebody for you to look at. I hope."

Though he usually went to bed after the ten-o'clock news, Holleb waited up in the armchair. Or tried to, for he woke to the humming buzzer. One o'clock. Fuzzy, he put a bathrobe over his shirt and tie and went downstairs.

In front of the glass door, between the sergeant and a patrol-man, stood a black man in a violet turtleneck and orange pants, head hung low, regarding his shoes. Holleb, following his look, saw untied shoelaces, strung like lax whips from brilliant black oxfords.

The sergeant motioned Holleb to stay put behind the door, then cupped the man's jaw in his palm and raised it into the hall light. A horsey, huge-eyed face flowered toward Holleb's in terror and imploration.

It was, of course, not his man. This fellow didn't even have a bush, didn't the sergeant remember his description? Besides, the man was his own age, if younger looking. There was a raw cut on his cheek, a puffy, active, furious rose. In a week he'd have a Heidelberg *Schmiss*. No, not his man.

He shook his head. The face in the palm leaked relief, the eyes closed, the dark flesh sank around the cheekbones. Holleb wasn't thanked, he no longer existed.

Upstairs, unable to sleep, Holleb sat in the dark and watched the whirl light of the patrol car raise blue welts on Fifty-Seventh Street. It was heading off, east. Were they taking the man home, or down to the Twenty-Third Street Station to dig out a congru-ence between his life and their tally sheets? Search long enough, they should be able to come up with something. That *Schmiss* hadn't been earned at the barber's.

They would, thought Holleb, have to do subtler research to line up *his* life with their sheets. He too had a *Schmiss*, though it had been earned on the right side of the law. But his own tally sheet was nothing to carve on granite: Marriage: over. Son: miserable. Apartment: in bad shape. Work: third-rate. Books: unwritten. Victimizer: uncaught.

He was able to tabulate it himself, he was at his own immedi-ate disposition, he hadn't inflicted any visible scars, personally. These were his pluses.

Against what, in the morning, he would call better judgment, Holleb suddenly understood and almost forgave his attacker. The dashiki and nutty coiffure hadn't been enough for him. The money wasn't enough for him. Conning wasn't enough. His terrible rage, his fierce sense of himself, had wanted something more. To inflict on a Holleb an unearned pain. To make the secret welts of a Holleb visible.

Holleb knew the weakness of this fatigued exoneration, knew

the evasiveness of easy pardon, but tonight, as the sergeant had predicted, he wavered.

Tout comprendre, tout pardonner.

Though who comprendred tout? Of May? Of his victimizer? Holleb had been abandoned without a word by a yukker, he'd been knocked around by a cruel man. Where did they sit on the spectrum of cruelty? With the farcical basso Lobz? With the poison-hearted Malinowski? But Malinowski described his savages, did not stomp them. And Lobz's basso soothed thousands.

If you didn't have the brain of the one, the Adam's apple of the other, weren't you even more obliged to hurt minimally? To bag groceries, grow sideburns, drive rage back to your lungs and blow your nose the year round?

In this world of opulent expression, where even soup cans were given voice, who was Holleb to advocate self-repression? Were not such chains being struck off in daily celebrations?

It was not clear.

The world, where action was loved beyond truth, beyond the full report, insisted Holleb had to fish or cut bait. He could forgive and forget, remember and pursue. In the great holes between, truth fell through.

It was not clear.

But, as of fuzzed head hitting soft pillow in this early morning, Holleb thought that, yes, if they caught his man, most unlikely, but if they did, he would, yes, probably, reluctantly, see the darn case through.

The Ideal Address

1

EVERYBODY close to Winnie's center was in motion.

Fred, no kid anymore, was doing what he'd been doing for three years, crisscrossing the country, following—he told her in collect calls from Phoenix or Fargo—"leads." That is, friends—often met the week before—who had houses to build, acres to plant, jobs to offer, places to crash. Then it was arrival, and weeks, or days, even, *hours* later, departure. For every amical ointment, a fly. "Ma, the guy lies around all day getting wasted. Good drugs is all there is here. It's one bad scene." Failure of mission reported to Chicago, Fred would be on the road again, thumb cocked, life's accumulation in his rucksack, the Ideal Address summoning him from a few miles, a few states away. "I'm down to twelve bucks. But I don't want anything, Ma. This low, I'll have to stick somewhere."

Twenty-four.

At twenty-four, Winnie had two children, two degrees and

supported four people selling Southside Chicago lots. Supportee Number Four was the Greater Frederick, rounding the last turn of his eight-year doctorate. The Great One had passed to his namesake blond charm, the gift of living off women, and— might as well face it—a deep tract of sheer dumbness, a power of self-delusion from which contempt or dislike washed easily. (The Fredericks couldn't be snubbed.) "Stick anywhere, Freddy. Build up a stake before you move on. You have to eat lots of dirt before flowers bloom in your face. The planet offers no perfect situations."

"I stuck New York, Ma."

Six months in the *Newsweek* morgue, long enough—to the day—to qualify for battered New York's Unemployment Compensation. Eighty dollars a week, which, with his girl's salary, gave him the life of not-Riley, but Oblomov.

An Oblomov who discovered the Off-Track Betting parlors. And won. Spectacularly. Twenty-three thousand dollars, fourteen on one daily double. "You know the way accountants look at a sheet of figures and see the shape of corporations. Ma, I look at those dope sheets and I *see* the race."

Close to six-and-a-half feet, a hundred and ninety pounds, the green eyes glistening with this *Dummheit.* Yet, the pudding had proved out: twenty-three thousand dollars. "Freddy, now it's time to take the journalism course. Go up to Columbia."

"It's not time for that, Ma."

"Look, Fred, it never hurts for anyone to talk to a counselor. Why not spend a few bucks and get your head cleared? Find out what you'd be best doing, why you're not doing it."

"I'm doing it."

She sensed he was going to stick the money in a hole, not report it to the IRS. "Fred, the tax men are everywhere. They get reports from the OTB every day. Don't conceal anything. Every dollar lights up those computers in Virginia. Don't wiggle."

Was she trying to subdue the divinity of idleness, she who'd burnt offerings to its opposite number since she was nineteen? All those mortgages and leases smoking in the golden nostrils.

Fred went to Aqueduct, he'd never seen the track itself before; the actuality needled his balloon. "All these bums in funny hats coming up to *me* for tips. I'm standing around in my Kenyon sweatshirt, and they're asking *me.*" It was another sliver of his pride that no one in New York dressed as badly as he did. In New York! It was like the man in Chekhov who was identified as "Lubov, the one who lost his galoshes at the Balan-offs'."

A month later, in a manner hidden from—and hardly credible to—her, Freddy was down to seven thousand dollars, six of which he put into a mutual fund. "I've been studying the Street, Ma." (He watched "Wall Street Week" on the educational chan-nel.) "What baffles people?"

With the seventh thousand, he "cleared the post," left girl, apartment (the lease had two months to go), and a phone bill, which she, his permanent address, paid. And headed—*tailed* was a better verb for Fred—west. "I might have a day with you in Chicago, Ma. But Jack's in a hurry. He's got a pad in Sonoma County, he says there are millions of jobs in the wineries. And it's more beautiful than the south of France."

He did stop for a day, but she was just moving in with Tom. Fred never liked her boyfriends, and he missed the old apart-ment, so he and his two pals (the third was picked up in Ohio, a Marx-bearded dreamer who ate one of Tom's plants) stayed only a night. "There's no place in Chicago for me anymore, Ma."

"It's a big city, Fred. You can go down to Hyde Park with Dad."

"Dad doesn't see where I'm at."

Fourteen inches shorter, plain and dumpy as a muffin next to this green-eyed giant, Winnie couldn't bring herself to ask where he was. He was so hugely *there.* Besides, she had all she could handle now with Tommy.

2

The reason she'd moved in with him after twelve years in her own place was his desperation. A month ago, he'd been "dumped" by his analyst, and had imploded, collapsed. He couldn't get out of bed. The black pearl eyes which sat out on his gold cheeks dropped tears down them. "Why did he do it to me, Winnie? What did I do wrong? Was it the writing? He knew I was writing the book."

Tom was finishing a doctorate, writing on the nature of evi-dence in psychoanalysis. One section recorded his own reactions to fifteen analytic sessions and was to be followed by Dr. Culp's notes on the same sessions. It would be a unique document, real material for students of the profession. But Culp slammed the door. The impassive, lunar face which had dominated Tommy's dreams for two years, burned with rage. While Tom was on the couch, Culp called Dr. Fried and told him he thought it was time to turn Mr. Hiyashi over to him. Tom fainted, was revived, staggered up the hall and found two doctors and three cops—"with guns, Win"—would he sign himself in or did he prefer to be committed by Culp? "You were signaling you wanted to be hospitalized," Culp said when he finally agreed to talk to Tom.

Winifred got Tom out. She went to Professor Klugerman, he found someone to sign for Tom, then gave her the word on Culp: Chicago was littered with his wrecks, he'd been a promising young man, but his own problems had ruined him; he was O.K. when the transference was rosy; when it got rough, he abandoned ship, hospitalized the patients and told them he couldn't work with patients who'd been hospitalized.

Psychoanalysis is the best-protected fortress in the world; its stones are invisible; even with a Klugerman on one's side, a malpractice suit was next to impossible.

Anyway, Tom was too low to think of litigation. For two years, all the feeling in the world was held by the four walls of Culp's office. Now he'd never see him again. "Analysis may not have the power to cure, it sure has the power to hurt." Tears dropping on the gold cheek flesh. "I can't think of anything else, Win." Even now, two months after Winnie had moved in, five weeks after he'd started with Dr. Fried, Tom's head was a Culp museum. He parked near Culp's house, gawked at his wife and children, took pictures of the garden, the cars. "Win, yesterday I wanted to steal his garbage. A big sack of garbage, and I wanted it."

"Oh, Tommy."

"Maybe because I was his garbage. And I gave him all mine. I gave him all the crap in my head, and he told me to get out. He's supposed to take it. An analyst is an incinerator. No, a recycling plant. But he cycled me out. How would you feel, Win?"

"I know, Tommy, I know," stroking him, the handsome little black-top head, the beautiful little shoulders.

She knew a little anyway, she'd been dumped as well, and not by a passing stranger. The Greater Frederick had finished his dissertation, acknowledged "its essential ingredient, my wife," and four years later, just starting to make enough money so she could stop making it and concentrate on her poetry, he discovered that "everything on this earth has a term," they "had had the best of marriage, the worst was coming," it was "time to think of 'fresh fields and pastures new,' old Win."

Of course he'd been plowing the new pasture for a year. Stroking Tom, Winnie remembered her own obsession with Rosanne, looking her up, what a shock, a scrawny kid, rearless, breastless, with a nose that hooked wickedly toward her teeth. A classic Frederickan delusion. (Line up, Rosanne.)

Eight years they lived five blocks apart. So the move to Tommy's had the relief of that separation as well. And maybe some of the relief of Freddy's moving; moving for its own sake, though she believed what she'd quoted at him from Donne, "For there is motion also in corruption."

"Corrupt, Ma?"

"No, Freddy, it's just that motion isn't necessarily healthy."

"You could sell it to Weight Watchers. I always lose five or six pounds a trip. You should try it for that alone, Ma."

She didn't need that. Her weight was what she had. "Lose enough, you can fit in an envelope, mail yourself to yourself. You'd never catch up. Ride round the earth for the price of a stamp. Need the dime?"

"You're some punkins, Ma." Harshness slid from him. (He always gained his five pounds back.)

The move did occupy her, and it blurred some of Tom's first shock and the brevity of Freddy's stay; and then Nora's hysterectomy, which came ten days after Freddy left.

She had "never been close" to Nora was what she told friends, what she thought, but of course that was too easy. Nora had been in her belly and at her breast, she'd loved her wildly, as she'd loved Freddy. But when Frederick took off, Nora, though she stayed with her mother, took off too. Eight years old, and Winifred would see the green eyes flashing chill at her, the unvoiced indictment: "You let what counted get away, you weren't good enough to hold it. Are you what I have to be? Is that what a girl is? Someone left?"

But over the phone, Nora wept, she was never going to have

her own child, and Winnie took off for Denver and held Nora's blond head on her breasts, she mustn't worry, she and Francis could adopt ten babies, it was the right thing to do in this 1970s world, the hysterectomy was a sign her system would have trouble with babies, she would have all the joy—and almost all the difficulties—of children, the genetic part was insignificant.

She stayed two weeks, doing chores, keeping cheer, even had the first good talks of her life with Nora, it looked as if at last they would be friends. But toward the end, the new grievance must have revived the old, she looked up to the green eyes flaming at her. "You don't know your own nature, Momma."

"Maybe I'd run away from myself if I did."

"No. If you knew where you were, what you are, things wouldn't happen *to* you all the time. You'd happen to them." Nora, white as a bathtub, with only her green eyes for color.

"I'm not much on all this knowing thyself. That's what our Fredericks are after, or say they are. 'Where's that Great Phone Book in the Sky with my number in it?' What's the point, Nora? Look at Tom." Nora never wanted to look at Tom. "Ten years on the S.S. Couch, and what's his America? Shipwreck. 'I'm too busy for that,' as Pat Nixon told Gloria Steinem. Right on. And if you want better authority for burying the self, go to Jesus. Or Buddha. Or Jane Austen. George Eliot. Did they squat around asking who they were?" But Nora would write no book, adopt no child. "I'm just dodging, Nora. You're right."

It was time to go. Francis took her to the airport. "I can be back in hours if you need me, Francis."

"You're a brick, Win." Endless, vague, unbricklike Francis.

3

Solid, maybe dumpy Winnie, yes, a bit of a brick, but, on her own, had put two children through Lab School and college, had moved more Southside noncommercial real estate than anyone in the city, could have had her own firm, been a rich woman, if she hadn't hated being a boss (firing people, fighting the IRS). She was a brick, and then some, a lot of bricks, and some windows, doors, and not a bad interior, ask Tom, ask a few discriminating human beings.

But in need of tuck-pointing, chimney work.

Mornings, waking up next to Tom (unless he was out casing Culp's garbage), her head was full of nutty projects: she'd form an Effluvium Corporation, market the leavings of the great (Picasso's shaved hairs, Elizabeth Taylor's sweat, a bottled ounce for eighty bucks); or she'd discover Jesus' *Autobiography*. *The Word first? No. Words come from throats. I was born in almost the usual way. In a backwater town.*

Breakfast up here was nice. Tom's place was across the street from Wrigley Field, and in the morning, or on days there was no ball game, the neighborhood felt as if it had fallen out of the present tense. The streets zoomed up to the great oval and died; the silence was spectral. There were lots of Koreans and Japanese around—they'd come from California after World War II—the small business streets had a special feel, old ladies bowing to each other, Shinto shrines and rock gardens behind standard Chicago threeflats, the kanji script on the hardware and grocery stores suggesting intense messages from the clouds.

Ball game days, the morning silence thickened into noise, vendors wheeled their carts, the pennant men and car-parkers warmed their throats for the crowd as it poured in under the windows.

What was that crazy mass they celebrated in the oval? (The little white grail pounded and pitched.)

She sat in Tommy's "greenhouse" room, doing her accounts, reading poetry, or just dreaming of something happening, something working, Freddy settling in, Nora taking care of a baby (knowing what feelings you couldn't allow yourself in the depth of that dependence), Tom shifting the hump of trouble from Culp to Fried.

A stillness in others so that her own motion would count.

She didn't want ease, she was even tired of not being tired, of trouble washing too easily out of her system. (Inside, she was brick.)

She wasn't ready to hit the road. (What road was there?) Down the street was far enough.

> . . . Green Chill upon the Heat
> So ominous did pass

We barred the Windows and the Doors
As from an Emerald Ghost—

That childless lady in white who never left her room.

> The Doom's electric Moccasin . . .
> The blond Assassin passes on . . .
> imperceptibly . . . lapsed away

For Emily D., the motion of the world was sinister.

But poems didn't do the trick today. They handled too much, stood for too much. (As the accounts stood for too little: Illinois Bell Tel., Consolidated Ed.)

The Oval burst. Home run.

She'd left home, but not arrived. Hidden in Tom's green world, little insectless, birdless, snakeless jungle, so much less jungle than his mind.

Or hers.

Born? In the usual way. Not knowing. Daughter, mother, but alone. Without ideal address.

Good Morrow, Swine

THE doors swung open, and a small, gray-haired man strode to the platform, jumped the two steps and slammed his briefcase on the desk. The class rose and called, "A good morrow to thee, Mistair Perkins."

"Good morrow, swine," said Mr. Perkins.

The class sat down. Mr. Perkins unhooked a yardstick from the blackboard, raised it as high as he could and slammed it on the desk.

"Vun," called the class and, to the yardstick's slash, "two, tree, four, five, seeks, seven, hate, hate prime, ten."

When the counting finished, Le Quillec raised his hand. "Alleviations of ze bowel, sair."

"Pity," said Mr. Perkins and waved Le Quillec from the room.

Mr. Perkins scratched his nose, and the class divided into two groups which spaced themselves single file at opposite sides of the room. Mr. Perkins took a child's coloring book from his briefcase and held it before the first boy in Group One. The boy examined the picture of a massive turtle.

"Igle," he said.

"Precisely," said Mr. Perkins, and he called for the translation of "Igle" from the first boy in Group Two.

"*La tortue,*" was the response.

"Acceptable fiction," said Mr. Perkins, turning the page. The picture was of a boy feeding sugar to a horse.

"I forgets," said the second boy in Group One, and he held out his palm, which Mr. Perkins slapped with the yardstick.

"Ze lovair," called the third boy, and the translation from across the room was, "*Le cheval.*"

Group Two triumphed, eleven to eight.

"Conquerors up," called Mr. Perkins. "Massachusetts."

Group One went down on its hands and knees, and Group Two leaped over the desks, first to straddle the Conquered and then to reassemble in a circle around Mr. Perkins's platform.

"Pang," went the yardstick.

"Vun," called the prostrate Conquered.

Boots stamping, heads jerking, the Conquerors raced around shrieking, "Oodirtydad, oodirtydad, oodirtydad, oodirtydad."

"Vun, two tree, vun two tree, vun two tree, vun two tree," pounded the prostrate Conquered.

"Pang," went the yardstick, and the Conquerors froze, arms extended, sweat tickling their stillness.

"Massachusetts," said Mr. Perkins, "a bloody state." The class resumed their seats.

"Ahgony of ze bladduh," called Rigobert, the smallest boy.

"Your sentence, Rigobert," said Mr. Perkins.

Clutching his right side, Rigobert recited, "Shane ze catupilluh, sad my oncle, so hees weengs cahnt grau. . . ."

"Mangle the coral and its blood will show," finished Mr. Perkins, and he waited for the translation.

"*Quand on lit trop vite, on n'entend rien.* Shokespierre."

Rigobert left the room, passing Le Quillec on guard at the door.

"Sentence, Pinot," said Mr. Perkins to a pale, fattish boy in the first row.

"Ze barbair scrimed and waved ze bloody shears," and before Mr. Perkins could add the coupling line, Pinot went proudly on with "Tinking ze infant's blood its mudder's tears. *Le mal est aisé, le bien presque unique.* Calvin Coolitch."

He drew back quickly, just dodging Mr. Perkins's spittle.

"Arrogant whoremaster," said Mr. Perkins, and he walked slowly to the windows and looked out. "The minor villainies are weighed with the major, my dears. Look at the sky, *la terre,*" and, with the yardstick, he indicated the rows of bare trees along the banks of the hidden river while the class followed the motion, wide-eyed and silent. "It's made up of a trillion tentacles which, each minute, draw up our villainies to the heavens, *l'enfer,* and drop them into the destined receptacles of our blood. And, one day, our lives, *nos erreurs,* are gathered up, the vats overflow, and the sky runs with our blood." The yardstick arched slowly down to the dusty planks, and Mr. Perkins walked back to the desk.

"Strethman," he called.

A rickety form arose, trembling, in the back row.

"Strethman, you look ravishable today. Hast thee on a new frock?" Mr. Perkins was quivering.

"Sair?" asked Strethman softly. He fingered his old brown sweater and shrank back toward the seat.

Mr. Perkins waved him down with a gesture of blessing. Strethman sat and put his head on top of his crossed arms.

"Il pleure, monsieur," called the class.

"There are times for weeping as for mirth, times for fronting, times for birth," chanted Mr. Perkins, and he walked back to Strethman and pulled his hair till the weeping stopped. "A new elegance today, my dears," he said, walking to the blackboard.

He printed, "A child's tears are the devil's pearls. *Le cœur pleure quand les vices triomphent.* Waldo Emerson."

"We will violate the vision drop by drop. *Nous répéterons la phrase mot à mot.*"

Mr. Perkins led the class through the sentence. They repeated it individually and in small groups. He assigned the English to the Conquerors and the translation to the Conquered. The class chanted in round fashion, Mr. Perkins guiding the repeats and phrasings with the yardstick.

"Ze bahbee's tairs are ze davil's pairls. *Le cœur pleure quand les vices triomphent.* Valdo Emairso."

When the bell rang, there was instant silence on the words

"tairs-*vices.*" Mr. Perkins erased the blackboard, took up his briefcase and said, "Pleasant dreams, swine."

"Pleasant dreams, sair," called the class, on their feet.

They continued to call "Pleasant dreams" until Mr. Perkins disappeared down the hall on the way to his next class.

Mail

At least it doesn't count as much as it used to: the day saved because of what's in the little steel cave. Age? Resignation? Or is it I care more for what *I* mail?

Still, it's still nice to get nice letters. Out of the unblue blue where people we're not thinking about are thinking about us. Yet not transmuting themselves (and us) into electric pulses in a vast system of immediacy. Just hes and shes, people with individual calligraphy, personal styles.

Even the salutations are special: "Dear Marcus"; "Dear Tuck"; or (one fairly recent style) "Dear Marcus Firetuck." Which is how the letter from Quito started.

The one from Sandra Lukisch began

> How I wish I could begin with "Dear Marcus." But I can't.
> You will always be the one who guided my first scale lines,
> reshaded my first chloropleth map. So, "Dear Mr. Firetuck."

Sandra is director of the Lukisch Cartographic Service in Melbourne. I haven't seen her for twenty years but remember her better than people who worked in this office last year. In the mid-Fifties, girls wore soft sweaters, cashmere, alpaca, lamb's wool. (So much memory has to do with clothes, what's inside and what issues from them. Legs, eyes, sweet—unmappable— hills, ridges, thickets; rough trapezoids, astonishing spheres; eye-brightness; smiles: Sandra's was—is?—a dolphin's deep serene; earlobes; nostrils; waists.) I remember Sandra's beautiful maps. They fuse in memory with her delicate roughness. (No standard beauty.)

In my head there are thousands of maps. My dear gone father said he remembered every mouth he ever worked on. To which hyperbole, Fred, my middle son, responded, "Lucky you aren't a proctologist, Grandpa." On the other hand—as it were—who is to gainsay those cavy regions? To any true investigator, every variation of the studied genotype fascinates. Nothing there can be beneath study, if not devotion.

Sandra writes she is getting married. "At forty, Mr. Firetuck. Imagine." Not difficult, Sandra. Hundreds must have thought of spending years beside—and inside—you. (I myself.) "I had to tell you, dear old master. Who first showed me what an isopleth was." (A line which represents a constant value.)

Those who have stayed in our heads live there as isopleths; though often unrepresentative of anything but themselves. They are their own color, flag, fruit and meat, the country of Their Self. Sandra stands for Sandra. And for the feelings rising as she re-enters the lit part of my head with her two sheets of typescript. Bless you, Sandra. I will send something or other to Melbourne for you and your fortunate air force colonel. (Did he use your maps?)

The letter from Ecuador was something else. Last March, a fellow called me at my hotel there. I'd flown in from the Cartography Congress in Buenos Aires to give my little spiel on Andean mapping in relation to the new high-resolution photographs we'd been getting from a hundred thousand feet. Joachim ("but called Jock") Fopper had seen the notice of my talk in *El Comercio*. (The good newspapers of that splendid little town may not have sufficient news to fill their local pages.) He wondered if the speaker could be

the same man who'd written *Reliefs*. I did not think "Marcus Firetuck" could be so common a name in your country.

It is the only time in my life that this has happened. In a foreign country—and not one of the world's most populous or worldly—someone who is not a cartographer, textbook publisher or military man has not only heard of me, but knows me in that tiny—if intense—part of my life of which *Reliefs* is the only—can I say?—monument.

A forty-four-page chapbook printed by a West Virginia press which "split the cost of printing" with me, *Reliefs* received two reviews (that I've seen, for there's no clipping service which hunts down the places in which reviews of such books appear). Yet Joachim—Jock—Fopper of Quito, Ecuador, not only owned a copy of *Reliefs,* had not only read and apparently found it— I can hardly credit and won't repeat his compliments—but he'd located—"through friends in New York whom I commission to send me little magazines from the Gotham Book Mart"—eleven of the fewer than twenty other poems I've published in publications, only one of which, *Poetry,* in my own hometown, prints more than two thousand copies an issue. Most of these journals bear the names of small animals—*Raccoon, Marmoset, Gnat*— and print fewer than five hundred copies. Yet out of this black hole of literature, Joachim Fopper had fetched a couple of hundred lines of Marcus Firetuck. "Your work meant something to me from the first three lines I read," he'd told me on the phone last March. And, no dispenser of vapor, he cited—I assume from memory—three lines from "Scratches on the Record": " 'They do not mean to hurt the music / They were not made by a mind / And no one will ever try to reproduce them. . . .' "

These lines had "spoken to" Mr. Fopper. Mr., *Herr,* or *Señor* Fopper. There were tiny Germanic tilts in his close-to-perfect English. Yet, as his letter informed me, he'd lived "twenty-odd years" on "this God-forsaken continent." I had asked him on the phone if he was a poet. "No. Unfortunately." He did not say then, nor does he say in his letter what he was (or is). He had just seen the notice in the newspaper; he was astonished, then thrilled at the notion that it might be "the very man" who had given him "such immeasurable pleasure." (Do I detect a stylistic influence of Firetuck in Fopper? The love of internal rhyme, verbal repetition, the mix of stiffness and idiom?) He did not dare to ask me to have a drink, he had hesitated a long time before telephoning, he did not want to be one of those importunate "voice-tremblers" who "intrude" into the lives of those who had "already done so much" for them.

I was travel-and-lecture weary, and also low: Ethel had flown back to Chicago from Buenos Aires and the cartographers here assumed that I was being taken care of by "someone else." (Sweet Quiteño modesty.) So, after our seminar, I was deposited at the Colon Internacional in a heap of weary loneliness. I suppose I should have asked Fopper to have dinner with me—the hotel food was terrific—but, who knew, intelligent as he seemed, and surely as sympathetic, wasn't it better to let well-enough be enough?

I did tell him how much his call meant. "This isn't an everyday occurrence, Mr. Fopper. I am not exactly Lord Tennyson or T. S. Eliot. You've cheered me up considerably."

I don't think he was set on meeting me. I believe Fopper is one of those true readers whose truest passion is literary. To encounter the actual flesh of authors (or their characters) would be a gross intrusion on their perfectly adjusted mental life. His phone call was, then, very daring. His letter is only slightly less so. Perhaps if I were a more prolific poet, Fopper would not try to drill for epistolary firetuckery.

The letter—about two thousand words long—is almost entirely literary. It begins by quoting

> one of the three French poets born in Montevideo, Jules Laforgue. The others, as I do not have to tell you, are Jules Supervielle and the astonishing Isidore Ducasse, the self-styled Comte de Lautréamont.

(He did not have to tell me, but I would have gone to my grave—not necessarily less happily—not knowing.)

> I know a small master's career is, as Laforgue writes, "decked out with rags and praise" (*"un train pavoisé d'estime et de chiffons"*), but I could not resist trying to sew in my rag. I hope it did not disturb you.

From this variation of his oral apology for "intruding," he goes on to the most intricate and subtle criticism I have ever had (and I include reviews of my professional—cartographic—publications). There are comparisons of my poems to ones in four languages, including poems by Americans of whom I've never heard.

An amazing performance by a true amateur of poetry. An amateur of Firetuck. An extraordinary letter. An extraordinary pick-me-up. (How I wish it could be sold in the drugstores between Valium and Mepro-probane. *Fopper's Uppers.*)

But who is or what was Joachim—Jock—Fopper? I wonder now, and in Quito, a bit nauseous and dizzy from the height disease they call *soroche,* I wondered then. (Sucking the nausea-fighting barley sugar candy given me by an English salesman, my seatmate from Buenos Aires.) Once I even wondered if Fopper's call were not a distortion of my dizziness. And later, over pickled *camarones* (the local shrimpy shrimp) and some *sopa quiteño* (egg and white cheese in a rich soup), served in the white and silvery dark elegance of a Colon Internacional dining room, I pursued the hints of vertigo to conjure up careers for Herr Señor Fopper. One was shaped by decades of reading mystery and spy novels. So: Joachim Fopper, the only one of the two hundred million people living on the enormous continent who knew Marcus Firetuck as a poet, one of the, say, fifteen? ten? human beings who had been enriched, expanded, *pleased* by my poems—the strangest and most beautiful of mental handshakes—this fan of mine was some Nazi-dribble who'd crawled out of Europe via the Odessa Network to South America where his brutal talents went underground to emerge only in such perverse passions as admiration for the obscure poems of a North American—and *for repentance*—Jew. Didn't such careful study of the obscure bespeak training, say, on Admiral Cana-ris's Counter-Intelligence staff? Indeed, might Fopper's "intrusion" be a subtle way of establishing an American contact?

"Tell me about yourself," I will write back to Fopper.

Or should I? Here in Chicago, with the day's rich mail, his four single-spaced typewritten sheets create an island of international lucidity on my desk. Between matt-finished cellulose plastic, calipers, T squares, nomographic charts and cartographic journals, Fopper's letter is a grail of communion. Why should I test it for fool's gold?

* * *

For five or six years now, my steadiest correspondent has been another man with whom I've had next-to-no physical contact. In the spring of 1973, I got away from a tumultuous house party my older children were throwing in our house in Door County and lunched myself in a restaurant in Sister's Bay. At the next table was an enormous young fellow whose head, I remember thinking then, could have been put up almost intact alongside the four Presidents carved out of the South Dakota mountain. As I was marveling at this stony, eyeglassed immensity, it turned my way and asked if it could borrow the sweetener in my sugar bowl. That began a monologue which ended with an exchange of addresses, and this, in turn, became an epic correspondence, the most intense and one-sided correspondence of my life (excluding a shorter one with my first fiancée, Mary Joe Weil— pronounced "wheel"—of Durham, North Carolina, back in the early months of 1952). It is certainly the most peculiar.

Vernon Bowersock.

Is he out of his mind?

I think not. Vernon is just out of your mind, at least out of mine. Or was then. By now I'm used to him. Vernon is one of the very few people who very early on is hooked by a life project. His project is self-reflexive. That is, Vernon is concerned with Vernon. Or, at least, with a kind of vernonization of the world. Vernon wishes to make sense of everything he has seen, heard, or can think about. His tools are numerology and epic poetry. Vernon is always thinking "Where will this or that fit into the *Vernoniad*?"

There is a lot of *this and that.* Vernon runs up and down the United States getting a degree in one thing here, a degree in something else there. He marries, he separates, he divorces. He reads, he carries on his Napoleonic correspondence, and he supports himself wherever he goes as a computer programmer. (Knowing such work was useful in any city, Vernon took it up in high school.) Vernon is not a careless man. Indeed, a theme of the future *Vernoniad* is that there is nothing accidental; everything belongs in the great scheme called Vernon.

Vernon was born in the only Mississippi county which seceded from the Confederacy (or does one say, "stayed loyal to the Union"?). His grandfathers have been the county sheriffs.

"As close to being dictator as humans can get in this country," says Vernon. So it is out of this singular world of authority and pride that the future epic poet comes.

Future poet. There's the rub. Vernon has only prepared to write his epic. What's written now is introductory matter. Perhaps Vernon, dazzled so by the possibility of the *Vernoniad,* will write nothing but Introductions. But if one includes the letters to his four chief correspondents—"my four compass points"—Vernon's prose already constitutes an epic, a kind of Epic of Introduction.

I answer one in ten or twelve of Vernon's letters. (He doesn't require answers from his Easts and Wests: the three others are a preacher in Binghamton, Alabama, an undertaker in Lompoc, California—"picked because it's the setting for W. C. Fields's *Bank Dick*"—and a "beautiful seventy-year-old librarian in Lima, Ohio, so I can begin her letters, '*Ohi-o*'—'hello' in Japanese, I'm told—'Lovely Lima Lady Libe.' ") Why do I answer them at all? Because through Vernon I see much of the country and encounter a mentality my small, skeptical intelligence habitually rejects. I suppose too that Vernon's numerology is a wild form of that impulse which made me both cartographer and "lisper in numbers," a desire to achieve clarity by reduction.

Vernon, always in "financial holes bigger than canyons," "thrown out by three wives, all of whom I love and will always love," always working, reading, moving on and writing about it all, is, I suppose, my own Odysseus, the moving part of my essential inertness. I have been in fifty or sixty countries, but almost always in ways which eliminate their strangeness; Vernon has never left this country, but every inch of it is different for him.

> 163 Farrell Ave.
> #19
> St. Paul, Minn.

Dear Mr. Firetuck,

It is 6:18, and I have consumed the day's second thousand calorie. I took a four mile walk, jogged two, did ninety push-ups, forty kneebends. Tomorrow, I go for my weekend at the Sunfare Camp. I go twice a week. Erections are forbidden. Joke: "When do the Japanese have elections?" "Before

bleakfast." I am twenty-nine years, three months, four days,
six hours and thirty-one minutes old. I was conceived when
George Marshall was making his Marshall Plan speech at
Harvard University. Or close to it. You were conceived
when Babe Ruth was hitting the twenty-seventh or eighth
of his record-breaking sixty home runs. Lindbergh was en
route to Paris when your—excited?—parents conceived you.
"Le hasard infini des conjunctions." (Mallarmé, *Igitur*—I
know only this quote which is scrawled on the backflap of
Irma Rombauer's *Joy of Cooking* which work I slobber over
as I eat my broiled turbot—120 calories, 200 with Tartar
Sauce and catsup. How about the infinite romance of conso-
lation to balance the infinite chance of conjunction?)

I owe twenty-one thousand, nine hundred and seventy
dollars, eight thousand of them to Rosaleen who will let me
pay back the others first. (She is in Spokane, earning good
money in a carob and soybeanery.)

Your friend,
Vernon Bowersock

Imagine. I was spawned in a heroic time. My loving progenitors
were excited by Lindbergh's flight. (Had they come out of a
newsreel theater? Did they exist then? Or had they news on the
radio? Did they own one in 1927? No. Too new.) Still, the excitement was in them, the market was good. What a grand time to
be conceived. Does it account for the essential peace of my
unheroism?

My own son, Frederick Gumbel Firetuck, was, I'm almost
certain, conceived the night Ethel and I went out to Midway
Airport with other lost-causers of 1957 to greet Adlai Steven-
son's plane. Carl Nachman was there, and he was paying lots of
genteel attention to Ethel; much as I liked him, my old jealousy
was roused, and, that night, her body roused me like a new one.
Fred sprang from that passion. Which explains—why not?—his
blue eyes, his exceptional strength and height, his sweet reserve. Why not?

3126 Walnut Street
Evansville, Indiana

Dear Mr. Firetuck,
You'll note I've moved again. A bit of trouble in Sunfare.

A forty-year-old blond-headed, brunette-pubed lady from Milwaukee. Someone with such prodigious endowment should not be allowed the good clean health-fare fun of the colony. It was not before breakfast, *mais* I was elected. Bad show. The saintly Mr. Carmichael was taking his matutinal walk in the sun and nearly tripped over the barrier. He is like Voltaire's Jesus, "an enthusiast of good faith with a weakness for publicity." I was summoned, marked—though within terrible half-seconds my guilty member had resigned its office—and asked to remove it and its base. Life here in the besummered north is not for such as I anyway. I am part-Floridian—"oh, Florida, venereal soil,"—and I don't have the manners of you northerners.

I weigh 179, though I have not eaten today and on the road was down to fifteen hundred greasy calories.

I'm on page 134 of three books, pocket jobs. I will now advance to page 184 of each. The books: *Back Swing,* a novel; *The Arnheiter Affair; My Days with the Mafia.*

Do you realize what half a century of life means? It eases my terrible approach to the *mezzo del cammin.*

Your friend,
Vernon Bowersock

There is only one other real letter in this day's mail. (I don't discount the documentary value of dental bills, charity appeals, advertising flyers, and treasure packages, expected—subscriptions, say—or unexpected—perhaps forgotten; but they are not the essence of mail.) The letter is from my old pal, Lester Doyle, whose father was my teacher in Ann Arbor. (Working for the State Department in 1942–44, Prof. Doyle mapped the boundaries which became the three—later four—zones of postwar Germany.) Lester, a poly-progenitor, has not otherwise been as productive as his father. Nor has his life been as serene. Almost every Lester-letter contains at least one piece of bad news. Yet so considerate a person is pale, tiny Lester that he manages to find some countervailing sweetness to enclose with the month's misfortune. He has so large a family—five boys, three girls—that there is always a supply of each on which to draw.

Lester teaches musicology at a remote branch of the University of Arkansas. As the only faculty member who has published an article, he has become a figure of both awe and exoticism. "I am their Paris and their Greece," he wrote me once. "But they are so remote. And so, it appears, am I." I've wondered if Lester's incessant progeniture is an attempt—like his letters—to people solitude. Today he writes that William, his second son, has had a leg amputated. "Soft-tissue sarcoma, I'm afraid, and the prognosis is not good." I hardly know William Doyle, remember only a frail, shy, small-chinned young man, a young edition of the professorial grandfather for whom he was named. William, like all Doyles, is very intelligent. He got scholarships to Milton and Williams where he was a brilliant student of something like Provençal. A pro football freak, he knows the lifetime won-and-lost records of every professional team. He must be about twenty-two and works for the Atlanta Braves baseball team (doing something with season subscriptions). "Eileen has gone to stay with him." Eileen is his oldest sister.

> I was there for several days after the operation. William was very brave. I cannot bear the thought that we might lose him. Yet just that, we have been told, is what will soon happen.

There is other Doyle news, busy news, grandchildren conceived and jobs changed; then there is a paragraph about his research.

> I am trying to complete an article on Delphine Potocka, the randy countess who had an affair with Chopin. Chopinologists are most exercised about the subject. A lady in Warsaw discovered a cache of letters in 1945. Or did she? You can imagine what life in Warsaw was like then. Is it unreasonable to see a starving lady scholar filling her belly with the invention of her head? I don't think poor Mme. Czernicka capable of forging them. For instance, there's a line from "Chopin" about wanting to set "something precious in D flat." That is a pun on the most intimate part of a woman's anatomy. Human beings surprise, but I would be very surprised to see Mme. Czernicka making this up.

Little William Doyle prepares to leave the world, and his loving father Lester works to fill the gap with a perhaps-affair of the melancholy genius. Giving Chopin this bit of postmortuary life, does Lester somehow provide for his son?

Mail

* * *

The word "mail"—I've looked it up—derives from the Old High German *malha,* a wallet. Its homonym, the woven metal rings used for armor, derives from Old French *maille,* link, and the Latin *macula,* stain.

I like to think of the lexic-twins in Siamese unification: so in these small sacks, these envelopes, we inscribe our little *maculae,* the spots and stains of our individuality. Some we show to one correspondent, some to another. And the result is a mesh of strands from all parts of the world and of our lives. Against the day's brute fact, the fatigues and routinage of *now,* this mesh armors us.

Sandra Lukisch, Joachim (Jock) Fopper, Vernon Bowersock and Lester Doyle, and even you, Frédéric Chopin (or your letter-writer, Mme. Czernicka), though none of you has met or will meet except in my head, on my desk, you are citizens of the country of correspondence, the soul of commerce across time and space; you are society itself.

Beloved correspondents, blessed institution, may the terrible convenience of speedier linkage never triumph completely over your clumsy, difficult frailty. "Very sincerely yours, Marcus Firetuck."

Wanderers

THOSE Jews sure did travel." Miss Swindleman reflecting, as
the bellhops carried away her glowing Collection, the four hundred and fifty post cards which memorialized the wanderings
of Hotel Winthrop guests for a quarter of a century. A wild
shuffle through the world Miss Swindleman herself knew not
otherwise. Unless one counted the scenic provision of a quadri-
annual locomotive between New York City, her place of permanent exile, and Synod, Missouri, her detested point of origin.
Some provision. The green pudding of southern Ohio, the
hoarse red gullet of southern Indiana, and that scab of ambitious
hummocks called the Ozarks. One week there with the surviving Swindlemans, and she was ready for another four years of
New York.

Though less and less ready, thanks to the Jews. When she'd
first come, the Winthrop and the Depression were as new as she;
they broke into the New York world together. The clientele was
quiet: widows, widowers, bachelors, spinsters, a few small families, the ex-rich, learning to adjust their wants to their con-

stricted means, as she learned to adjust hers to the constrictions of New York loneliness. A quiet, respectable, learning time.

Then as the Depression slid away, and the quiet goyim died, the Jews began moving in. They too were bachelors, spinsters, widows, widowers, and small families, but they had not been broken by hard times. Decades of finagling, deception, complaints and theft had hardened and renewed them. Behind the three bronze staves of her cashier's den, she regarded their great noses twitch with the strain of hoping that she would overlook the delinquent quarters in their monthly settlements. She never did, but the strain of guardianship showed in her face.

The Winthrop too showed strain: the rotting plaster showed it, the bursting water pipes, the splintering toilet seats, the ripping carpets. And the management! No more the quiet little Jew, Oppenheim, who'd moseyed noiselessly in the corridors her first twelve years, and then, fifty if he was a day, and weak as the cocktails the surviving goyim drank in the Peacock Room at five o'clock—shoring their ghetto within the ghetto—he was drafted away in forty-five to be replaced by a perfect 4F, the hunchback and supreme yeller, Nagel, a black Jew, oily, welching, eavesdropping, and mean-eyed as the skua bird Doctor Mochus had mailed her ten years ago from the Faroe Islands. Board Six.

With the onset of the Jews, though, Miss Swindleman had conceived her life's mission: their assimilation. Assimilation to the ways and manners of the older stock which she represented, and which gave names to the invaded hotels of Eighty-Sixth Street, the Peter Stuyvesant, the Governor Brewster, the Dorchester Arms, the Winthrop. Every check she eyed, every sum she re-added, contributed to their education, to the enforcement of the rules of western life, rules to which no amount of traveling could educate them.

They were great travelers. Great post card senders. She'd started her Collection one day after Roosevelt beat Landon, when they'd sent her three post cards from three different continents. Board One had gone up, and the Jews traveled to fill it. Over the years, war or no war, the boards filled with twisted, six-word cards from Sfax and Borneo, Tarsus, Rhodes, Rio, and Auckland. The fjords ran a blue storm down Board Three; the statuary of Board Five made up a great museum; and

Board Two carried enough exotic, mean-eyed animals—they loved killers—to stock a Bronx Zoo. If she'd used "repeats," the Taj Mahals alone could have replaced the slums of New York, but the eye which spotted the delinquent fifteen cents in Milton L. Bungalow's monthly was ruthless about filtering repetition from the world's views and could spot a repeat bend of the Trondheim fjord more quickly than a native. There were few places on the traveled earth to which Miss Swindleman lacked some sort of key. Even the Arab countries were well represented. Not only had the Jews traveled there before the war, but the Winthrop's few voyaging goyim liked to visit there, if only to flaunt the experience before the excluded yehudim.

Miss Swindleman understood the desire to flaunt experience before these wanderers. Experience was a fact, like family, like money, which had to be respected. Not that it marked superiority. Miss Swindleman didn't believe in superiority. There were only greater or lesser collections of fact. She was concerned with the arrangement of the few facts under her control, because that was the human task, to fend off the disorderly, the ugly, the crooked. It was why she never turned her back on a Jew when she was in her den. "Get thee before me, Israel, I'll keep thee orderly." And she surveyed their avaricious disorder through the peeling bronze staves which never vouchsafed them more than partial views of her.

It was why she classified her own partial views, those nickel four-by-sixes, classified them by area, type, color—the blue fjords, the checkerboards of Scotland, highland, lowland. They were not an altar, but a demonstration that the world would be put into shape, and, too, that there were things beyond unsteady checks, paid-up phone bills, change for a clanked quarter thrown like an insult under her staves. Stability and place were there amidst the wild shuffling, amidst the packed suitcases, the scarred trunks, the taxis to Pier 40.

Miss Swindleman could spot traveler-types as they signed the Register. They signed both easily and wearily. Half the few couples who stayed in the Winthrop traveled; about a third of the widows, three-eighths of the widowers. Under forty didn't count. She'd probably not received more than ten cards from guests under forty, usually children who had lived with widowed parents (not more than twenty regulars in her more than thirty years). She once got a Blenheim Palace from a pock-marked Mettenleiter, and had discarded a repeat of Sugarloaf Mountain from a Baer twin, but that was all of the memorable.

Nothing of course from the two boys of Harvey Mendel, though they had lived in the Winthrop for fifteen years. She was the only person in the hotel—probably including Mendel—who remembered their mother. Ina Mendel, a name like a sigh, a nice Jewish woman who talked to her in a fluty little voice. No traveler, but nonetheless had once bought her a post card of the Roman Forum before being told that only mailed post cards were pasted up. Ina took plenty from Mendel and the two nut sons. Sonny, who, at fourteen, was nearly arrested for lowering an armchair out of the eleventh story to an accomplice on the ground in full view of Eighty-Sixth Street. He'd been hauled in to Nagel by Lester, the cabbie, who looked up from examining one of the pigeons he liked to grab by the throat and pick at with his penknife. Just last year, Sonny, now known as Harvey, had proved his early promise by being jailed for three months in Phoenix, Arizona, on a charge of taking pornographic pictures. The second nut was Burton, the railroad buff, who spent hours in the lobby memorizing the timetables, but couldn't figure out change for a quarter. Ina lasted six years, then went on the operating table to be knifed to death by some Lester of a surgeon. With her passing, and Oppenheim's, the reign of half-decent Jews ended, and the Mendel-type took over.

They were too mean-spirited even to travel, too cheap to live. Once she'd called him the monk of Eighty-Sixth Street. "Are you related to Gregor Mendel, the monk?" she asked him.

He never smiled. Baby lips in a cranium the size of a great soup bowl. Between it and abnormality—water on the brain—was scarcely a hair's breadth of dispute. "What monk?"

"Invented genes," said Miss Swindleman.

"A monk in skirts invents jeans. Crazy," said Mendel.

He was a designer of men's suits, and knew nothing else. An odd man; an odd looker. Under the perisphere of a head was a fat little body, maybe five-feet-five, and then two midget's feet. He wasn't a black-looking Jew. In fact, with eyes so blue they were sometimes hard to see and a nose like a soap bubble, he looked as Irish as the policemen who patrolled the streets and held their annual brawl in the Peacock Room. Mendel had once

been involved in their brawl and fitted right in. Involved because he was, as usual, staring at people, from the lobby armchair where he spent half his life. Staring with those snow-blue
eyes, this time at one of the Irish cops who'd staggered out of
the brawl, highball in hand, and, seeing Mendel, in overcoat and
fedora, staring up at him, had removed the fedora and poured
the highball over the great dome. Mendel had risen, sixty-six
years old, five-feet-five-inches tall, wrenched the standing lamp
out of its socket, raised it over his streaming head, and started
after the cop. The cop ran, Mendel followed, the old ladies
screeched, Gelb, the cigar man, ducked under his counter, and
she, safe in her den, waited for Irish brains to go flying down to
Seventy-First Street. Only half a squad of uniformed micks leaping out of the Peacock Room preserved the cop. And then they
made Mendel a hero, took him into the Peacock Room, shot him
full of whiskey, and then elevated him upstairs in triumph.

There weren't many triumphs riding armchairs in the Winthrop lobby, not many triumphs anywhere for Mendel. And the
only other thing she could think of in this line was his escaping
indictment after pushing Lepidus out of the window; you might
as well count not catching flu a triumph.

What did she object to in Mendel?

It wasn't idleness. He worked, went downtown three or four
times a week till Lepidus's death. He'd once been a success
according to Ina, had managed a whole men's department in
Buffalo till he'd punched a customer who'd tried to return a suit
from another store. Not idleness.

Nor was he particularly crooked; only particularly cheap. The
number one Jew for cheapness. The Winthrop never collected
a penny more from him than his rent. To telephone, he came
down to the lobby, day or night, using the pay phone and saving
a nickel; he never went into the Peacock Room except to use
the toilet; he never bought a cup of coffee in The Nook, and he
avoided Gelb's cigar stand so conspicuously that despite twenty-
five years of sharing the same lobby, the two never exchanged
good mornings. When sick, he sent for borsht with a hard-boiled
egg from Sheffrin's, the delicatessen on Columbus Avenue
where he ate every day of his life but Yom Kippur and Rosh
Hashanah, when he took his trade to Chock Full O' Nuts. This
according to the young thief Sonny, who also told Lester—his
confidant after the armchair heist—that except for these two

restaurants, the Yorktown Movie Theater—forty cents before one o'clock—and the annual Thanksgiving Dinner downtown with Ina's brother, his father hadn't been inside another place of entertainment since—big leer—his mother had died.

Miss Swindleman was aware of the Thanksgiving Outing. Next to Macy's Parade, it was the surest sign of the holiday. Mendel and the two nut sons washed their faces, put on clean ties, and paraded out of the hotel as if they were on the Number One Float. Two hours later they'd be back, soiled with blots of stuffing and cranberry sauce, their faces bloated with self-satisfaction at having a Family Dinner at a Downtown Hotel.

"Mr. Mendel," she said to him after one of the expeditions. "You should try our Thanksgiving Dinner here some day. Forty-six birds they cooked this year." (Jewish syntax had crept up on her twenty years ago, and she relaxed into it. She wasn't interested in self-preservation.)

Mendel had sent one of his blue-blank stares through her staves. "Family obligations, Miss Schwindleman. Nothing to do about it," and he floated upstairs, followed by the nuts.

Miss Swindleman objected to more than Mendel's cheapness and third-rate vanity. She objected to his fixity. There he'd sit in the lobby, three sofas, six armchairs, stand-up lamps, Gelb's cigar counter, bent Jews going up and down in the two elevators night and day, the blue and gold elevator men, her bright post cards, a little tropical island in the Eighty-Sixth Street cold, plunked down there for no reason but to allow amphibious transients to crawl across it before they dived back down into the ocean. Shelter? Home? Reservoir? A sour little hotel whose only real distinction was her flash of the world and her disciplined hand on the financial wheel. In the midst of this discipline sat that unsmiling, waiting, staring Mendel, isolated like a monk in a burlesque show. It wasn't until the day Lepidus went out of the window that she understood all this about him.

Lepidus was one of Mendel's two visitors. The other was Mrs. Minnie Schlag, a hirsute, muscular woman who for years was thought to be the unlikely means of satisfying whatever passion resided in him. It turned out, however, that Mrs. Schlag and Mendel did nothing more passionate together than play pinochle. A bellhop looked in through a hole in the plaster and saw them humped over the coffee table, Mendel in suspenders and Mrs. Schlag in a blouse which showed an arm like the ones on the statues in the Oslo gardens. Board Five. Every other Saturday, Mrs. Schlag turned up for pinochle at the Brewster, and once a month on Thursdays, as Sonny told Lester, Mendel went to the Schlags for poker with Doctor Schlag, the bone man, Simon Gabrilowitsch, a bassoonist and reputed cousin of the pianist, Mrs. Schlag, and two other refugees from Vienna, one of whom sold perfume atomizers door-to-door. Lester further reported—what she was certain was a lie, until Schlag's obituary confirmed it—that as a young bone man in Vienna, Schlag had rented rooms and lent money to an unpromising young man named—"you guessed it," Miss Swindleman would say wickedly to whatever black Jew she passed it on to—"Adolf Hitler. Ha, ha, ha. Old Schlag could have saved you an ocean voyage, eh Mr. Rappaport? A little arsenic in the chicken soup, doctors aren't suspected, and Schlag would have had a place in history."

"Wouldn't have been no history then," the paling Rappaport or Goldhammer or Mochus would say.

Though not Mendel. His response when she offered him the homicidal suggestion was a simple, "I wouldn't have much of a poker game then, Miss Schwindleman." A hard man, a bit of a Hitler in his own right. She could see him in the seat of power, bombs instead of stand-up lamps in his angry little arms.

Lepidus, Mendel's partner, was a more frequent visitor. As small as Mendel, but wiry, blue in the face, a scowler, a rapid man, cigar crunching. A stormer, of elevators, candy counters, her den. Like the last day. "Gimme change fifty," he'd said.

"You a guest of the hotel?" As icy as the roughneck deserved.

"Change of fifty. I'm a guest a guest." Meaning, "a visitor to a hotel resident."

"Who, may I ask?"

"Mendel. Harvey. 11C. You seen me a hundred times. I'm here five times a month. You got fifty bucks in this cage?"

"You'll have to get the manager's signature. And he's out. I can't be expected to remember every visitor to the hotel. It's hard enough keeping track of the guests."

An oath, a sneer from the penny-colored eyes, he slung himself into the elevator.

Five minutes later, a call from 11C. "I'm coming down to change fifty dollars, Miss Schwindleman."

"Swindleman."

"Next time Mr. Lepidus requests a service, I'd greatly appreciate it, Miss Schwindleman."

But Lepidus would never again request a service, and apparently her exchange with him had something to do with it. Her proper invocation of a proper regulation. What was the world without rules, she asked the detective, not adding what was appropriate in this instance, that the trouble with the Jews was that they fled rules, claiming that rules had rigged the world against them? That's why they'd had to wander since Christ's time, evading the rules, and then trying to make up for evasion by sending nickel post cards back to those they fled, the enforcers, hoping for a more than even break the next time. Could she cash checks for everyone who walked in off the gutters? The Puerto Ricans stood six deep between Columbus and Amsterdam. Give them an opportunity like that, and they'd make the Jews, who were clever or mean enough to be pikers, look honest. She'd worked nearly thirty years around other people's money, and nobody had ever suspected that her purse held one cent that didn't belong there. She personally had nothing to lose or gain by enforcement of the rules. Rules were what she went and lived by. Did Lepidus think she was a country girl waiting for wool to be pulled over her eyes? So his temper was riled. What did that have to do with rules? What did what happened have to do with anything but the breaking of rules?

According to Mendel, he and Lepidus worked as usual. When he, Mendel, was indisposed, they worked at the hotel. It was just as convenient as the closet they worked in on Fourth Avenue. Gotham Fabrics and Designs. A big name for a small enterprise. Two men, two desks, cardboard patterns, sample materials, drawing paper, colored pencils. Not enough for a child's Christmas. That's all they needed to carry off twelve to fifteen thousand a year. "I've been with lots of outfits, big and small," said Mendel up in his room where she'd never been before. "There was nothing more efficient in the world than Charley Lepidus and myself. I designed. He marketed. That's all there was to it. I had pencils, he had a mouth. Three or four days a week was all the time we needed to put in. Didn't matter where, down on the Avenue or here in the hotel."

That was the Lepidus-Mendel history. But every history has

a history, and who more than the wandering Jews—barnacling themselves onto the histories of every nation on the civilized earth—would know that? A squad of Irish cops, Annalee Swindleman, and assorted old ladies, half of them under the earth now, had witnessed Mendel going berserk with a metal stand-up lamp. Other incidents made longer history. The punched customer in Buffalo, and a doorman in Minnie Schlag's building who, according to her, had the habit of stepping on Mendel's small foot until the latter, after years of the abuse, had one day grabbed the fellow by the voice box, toppled him, and tried to throttle him there in the snow of Lexington Avenue. Yes, the huge woman went on, in some ways, he reminded her of a man she'd known in Vienna, also a docile young man till seized with rages. Luckily she mentioned the young man's name, and the detective wrote her off as a nut. Miss Swindleman, who had listened to her along with Mendel, shook with anger. There was more history to come, this time from Sonny, the ex-furniture mover and photographer, recently returned from his stay in the American Southwest. Yes, moaned Sonny, his father had raised him and his brother on a diet that would have done in a robot; by the time he was twelve, he'd eaten enough cabbage soup and kreplach to have felled a horse. Also, his father entered into frequent altercations with a waiter named Bungmeier in Sheffrin's Delicatessen, capped one day when his father stuffed Bungmeier's gray head into a plateful of borsht after being rightfully accused of dawdling over his meals.

After all this, Mendel's own story of the day did not look strong. The story was that Lepidus had been riled by the behavior of the good Miss Schwindleman. Never was Lepidus a cup of tea, but fired up, he was a terror. They worked hard, in shirt sleeves, though it was drafty, a Christmas cold driving through the peeled window frames, never strong since the no-goodnik, Sonny, had pushed the armchair through them. Lepidus talked, he, Mendel, was all concentration. When he designed, he was lost in his materials. Lepidus had started on Miss Schwindleman: piss-cold anti-*semitischer* virgin-whore were the easiest things he said. (Blushing, head averted from her stricken head.) Then he was on to the Winthrop, the fleabag where he, Mendel, too cheap to waste piss in a pot, had holed himself up for thirty years, killing his wife with the cold and inflicting two loonies, the junior Mendels, on the world. "A Hitler with his mouth, he was," said Mendel to Detective Milligan. "A marketer, he had talent for the mouth." But he, Mendel, could take it. He was small, he was old, but he could take it. He kept on cutting his patterns. Not from cowardice, he was afraid of nobody. He took where it did no good to do something about it. Years he had taken guff from Miss Schwindleman. Why not? What could she do, poor old girl (head averted, lost in his materials), poor old cold bag, full of hate, collecting her post cards from a world she understood nothing of. Years he had taken insults from family, wife, bosses, sons, doormen, policemen, waiters, inhuman cabbies, but now and then, once in a great while, he had to strike out. The Jews had a history of taking it. Nevertheless, sometimes, they turned. The Maccabees. Suez. Jews were not Hindus, not cheek-turners. For humanity, for peace, for an end to persecution, they rose up. Lepidus wouldn't stop; he got hotter and hotter. He, Mendel, caught fire and gave him a push. One push. The window frames were weak, Lepidus was small, and solid. Out he went into the middle of Eighty-Sixth Street under the nose of Lester knifing a tail feather from a pigeon. Out he went, like garbage from a Puerto Rican window. Unpremeditated, unintended, the victim victimizing, and being victimized thereby.

Miss Swindleman, looking up at the detective without the protection of her staves, minus the glowing backdrop of her Collection, smaller, chaired, sworn—though without Bible—to honesty, a gray girl from the Ozarks, up in the bejewed city, thought back thirty years. Every morning she walked through Central Park to the Hotel. Every year it seemed bigger to her. This morning, all the familiar trees were there, branched in snow, imploring the New York sky to spare them. Bushes and shrubs were turned into crystal chandeliers, the buds alive somewhere in them, unseen but living in the icy beads, waiting. Walking in her furred galoshes around the Reservoir, she'd looked through the crackling trees toward the General Motors sign flashing "8:23," and thought that she had not one single post card in her Collection from New York. It would have been perfectly all right to send herself one, for, after all, she'd traveled from her home and was still a visitor in this place, as much a wanderer as the poor black Jews she served and governed.

Mosaics from Ravenna, bark-colored farmers from Sierra Leone, twisted statues from Rotterdam, skyscrapers from Brazil, mountains, rivers, pyramids, but nothing of this city where she and almost everyone else she knew was a wanderer. Her stopover, Mendel's stopover, this old line hotel was rotting, façade intact, but pipes going—a geyser had burst from a flushed toilet only last week—and the wanderers were the only thing that sustained it, deprived people, harboring their small-time leisure, their miserable quarters. Mendel was one of the best. Polite, quiet, he hurt no one that didn't hurt him much more. The wife had seemed a good one, but who knew? Behind the flutter she could have given plenty. After all, she let her boys grow up in this hotel, went gladly to restaurants, avoided kitchen work. Maybe Mendel had not had much from her. He hadn't much period. A monk in the barrage of Eighty-Sixth Street. Cheapskate, but no quibbler. As for Lepidus, he was the blackest of the black, yes, nasty, cigar-chewing scoffer, crook, a hurrier and worrier of others. If she had riled him, well and good. If Mendel had pushed him, he deserved it. She spoke the truth, always had, had no reason not to.

So it was over, and Milligan wrote it up. *Accidental.* Miss Swindleman went back to her den.

Things were not the same. No. An opening had been made. What does one do about an opening? Send a post card of the Empire State Building to oneself? Go to Mendel's room and say, "Mendel. I saved you. Now save me. I'm yours. Be mine"?

Or even, think more gently, speak more kindly ("Blank cold, anti-*semitischer* virgin-whore." "No, Lepidus."), cash checks more readily, make up delinquent quarters from one's own purse?

Possibly.

The opening was a wound in Miss Swindleman. Days passed, and embarrassment at defending Mendel was all she could stuff in to stop the raw ache. She was altered, but alteration had nowhere to go.

The incident had altered Mendel much more. He grew thinner, whiter. He no longer sat in the lobby. More and more frequent were the calls to Sheffrin's for borsht and pastrami. Two or three times he came down for coffee and English muffins in The Nook. He bought a TV set, and the bellhops reported that it was on from Garroway to the Anthem. There was no more work, and no visitors except a monthly call from Burton, the timetable son, who, like his father, never frowned nor smiled, and whose only nonambulatory motion was the Adam's apple popping up and down in his neck as he swallowed unuttered words. So Mendel passed on in his own den—pneumonia, TB, heart. Everything hit him at once.

The day after he died, she took the first notice of her Collection that she had taken since the "hearing" six months before. It was in wretched shape. The pasteboards were rotting: gnarled scabs of string dripped from the edges, odd swellings humped the boards where drafts and radiator heat had gnawed the fiber. She called the bellboys and told them to take it out to the garbage heap. Her wandering was over.

Gaps

1

WHEN a gentleman is out of sympathy with the times, he drifts with the wind. So Lao-tzu is supposed to have told Confucius, who sought instruction in the rites from him. "Rid yourself of your arrogance and your lustfulness," continued the sage, "your ingratiating manners and your excessive ambition. They are all detrimental to your person."

William McCoshan, a gentleman out of sympathy with the times, had no such guidance. And though he did not exactly drift with the wind, he was a travel agent. (Who had never traveled.) He descended from a New England aristocracy whose authority had disintegrated in the rise of an urbanism and federal power managed by the sons of immigrants. William had not taken the aristocratic option of waiting on the sidelines until the rulers invited him into a decorative spot. Instead, he sank slowly until he found a level which supported him. That is, he left the University of Connecticut in his sophomore year and took a job with the American Express Company in Hartford. Six years later, he transferred to the Dayton office, where for fifteen years he was the assistant manager of the Travel Department. He married his landlady's niece and fathered a daughter.

What William appeared to care about was schedules. From Dayton, "the cradle of aviation," he sent fellow citizens to Lima and Melbourne, Portugal and Paris, working out for them intricate fusions of tour and pocketbook.

At home, to Elsa, his life's only confidante, he exposed the deeper side of his nature. William, the schedule maker, distrusted the apparent order of things. Beyond human contrivance lay terrible blanks. Planetary schedules and galactic shifts, these bubbles of human dream could pop in a blink. The world's Newtons and Einsteins, convinced they'd uncovered threads of the Real Fabric of Things, were, for William, life's prime dupes. Nothing he'd read infuriated him more than Einstein's remark that God was not malevolent but subtle. If God—whatever that meant—was so subtle, how could such a piece of mathematized dust dare to believe it could touch the least of His contrivances. Closer to William's view of the True Grain of Things was Einstein's wife, also an Elsa, who carried the ashes of her cremated daughter in a sack next to her heart until forced by her husband to give them up. William's own day-to-day truce with Appearance was unmarked by fetish, but such confessional gestures of human incompetence gratified his heart. The world's vacancies had to be stuffed with bilge. The human job was to see bilge as itself, not wisdom.

His Elsa was a true listener, no debater, no echo. Space probes, Korea, cancer, revolution, civil rights, civil riots, William uncovered for his wife the terrible configurations beneath the newspaper facts. The wars of the Chinese periphery were the conversions of peasant societies into industrial markets at the hidden service of the same force that destroyed a thousand of every thousand and one eel eggs. As for industry, it was a less conspicuous form of the diversion he provided his customers; Chartres and automobiles were made to stop people from thinking about actualities. "People start thinking about the way things really are, the only manufacturers who'll stay in the black will be the rope-, knife- and gun-makers." The Birchers, Minute

Men, Mafia, Neo-Nazis, and the NRA were far more useful than
the planners, utopians, and think-tankers. Why? "Because they
take care of civil roughage. They're the national excretory system."

William's breakfast seminars came to an end one winter day
when Elsa drove their 1961 Pontiac into a low retaining wall and
was decapitated by the windshield.

This death, whatever it was, pricked bubble, discharged syn-
apse in some monster's bloody brain, whatever, drove William's
fears into the depths of misery. Almost, almost, he had Elsa's
ashes saved for his own heart, but no, that was naked unreason.
There was no decent human option left but that animal reason
which brought food to mouth, head to pillow.

William had never been close to his daughter, Winnie. Elsa
had absorbed all the feeling he had in him. Winnie grew, was
hugged, grew more, and found her own life. Yet in the months
after the funeral, they spent time together, cooking, doing
dishes, cleaning the apartment. One day, apropos of nothing,
out of the blue, he mentioned to her the possibility of a vacation
in Europe, then, on her birthday, reaffirmed it with the gift of
a suitcase.

So they drifted into a three-week European excursion.

In July, Winnie and William flew to Milan, and took the train
to Rome. The idea was to stay in Rome a week, then fly to Nice,
hire a car, and drive west along the southern coast as far as
Spain. In Rome, though, Winnie ran into one of William's customers, the boyfriend of her best girlfriend, and with the flirta-
tious power of adolescent treason, encouraged him. In two days
they felt themselves in love. Winnie begged William to let her
stay alone in Rome while he went off to France.

At first it seemed out of the question. The very fact that
months of closeness had not brought him truly closer to her
increased William's feeling of paternal responsibility and simultaneously deepened habitual fears about her safety. (Whatever
that really meant beyond scheduled change.) Yet, after all,
she was not his type, their lives depended on becoming in-
creasingly separate; true responsibility would be to give her her
wish.

"All right," he said.

But anxiety dominated the night before his takeoff. He went

to his daughter's hot little room and studied her curled in regression, legs around the stuffed cylinder which misserves Europeans for pillows. Her breasts, oddly full, glazed with silver sweat, rose and sank in her nightie. Looked at quickly, she seemed like Elsa, but the temperament was a sport. This was a passionate little girl, fed on wild rock music, on the pointless violence and anarchic farce of American pop culture. He forced himself to touch her forehead. "No," she said loudly, though not to him. "No, no." Her life wasn't his.

At breakfast William gave copies of his itinerary to Winnie and Robert, her friend, told them how to place an Emergency Traveler's Notice in *Figaro,* cautioned them to eat sensibly, not stay out late, and remember they were being treated as mature young people.

A Roman summer day. Tufa walls sweated orange dust, the heat close enough to feel internal. William took off in a bus for Fiumicino. For France.

Twenty years of reading had prepared him for it. But had also prepared him to show no excitement, prepared him not to expect and not to be disappointed. In the plane, he read *Le Monde,* drank Seven-Up, and ignored the pilot's invitation to look down at Corsica and Sardinia.

At Nice, a blue Citroën waited for him in the lot.

Two P.M.

William made for Saint-Tropez. Why not? Since Bardot's first films, he'd dispatched hundreds of Daytonians there; he himself was not averse to seeing such things. Who knows?

But what a route. Travel photographers must hang from clouds. How else omit the snack bars, gas stations, motels, bulldozers, house frames, the wads of hotel cement pasted into the hills. Though, now and then the sea showed up between cypress trees and one understood what had brought people here for three thousand years.

At Fréjus he ran into an endless spine of cars. Four o'clock. With this mob heading down the peninsula, he'd never get a room. He broke from the line, made a U-turn, took a side road, and drove southeast for four kilometers.

A chunk of glass and cement rose out of a pine grove. He circled a floral driveway, entered a lobby, and for eighty francs, thirty more than he'd planned to spend, got a room with a

terrace, overlooking a slope of pine backed with marine glitter.
The bed was large, it had normal pillows instead of the murder-
ous cylinders, and the bathtub was good-sized, important to
William, who was six feet and liked to loll.

He stripped, ran in place in front of a closet mirror, breathed
deep to force an outline of ribs and broaden his narrow shoulders. God knows, he was no body fetishist, he didn't even care
about being in good shape, but why should a man provide comic
relief on a beach? Why offend? He took a bath, wrapped himself
in a towel, and snoozed. When he awoke, the room was filled
with an emerald light. France.

2

Next to the hotel was a small *brasserie* with four tables outside
under a string of unlit bulbs. A woman, barefoot, pushed a
little girl in a swing. There were no diners, apparently no
other staff. William went over and asked the woman if one
could order dinner. Yes, indeed, though the cuisine was a simple extension of what they themselves ate. What would he
like?

The woman was about thirty, high-browed, her flesh a gold
tan, her eyes deep blue, large, and set back, her nose narrow,
straight, wide-nostrilled, her mouth full. She talked beautiful
French, her manner that ease one thinks to find only in the rich
and usually finds only in the beautiful. He proposed *potage,* an
omelette fines herbes, and wine, but his unsieved thought was
"You."

William was used to driving such spasms of desire out of mind,
but this innkeeping princess going off to cook his meal stayed
there, the gravity of rump in a green miniskirt, the length of
neck where the hair parted into braids at the nape, the solidity
of her legs.

It had been six months since he had been with Elsa, and there
had been no one else. His dreams, his reveries, his sheets bore
the marks of abstinence. Yes, there was another side of the
pretty world. The age boasted liberation, but millions were
chained by need, could scarcely admit it even to themselves.
And to break out wasn't easy. Firstly, it might involve one with

tenacious, ignorant people who could permanently infect tranquillity. Still, one knew there were millions of fine women,
needy as oneself, waiting as one waited. Every other story was
about them.

But he didn't know them, nor even how to meet them. Dayton was a place like another, bigger than most, there were
stylish women there, long legged, sympathetic. But not in his
life.

And now to this young Frenchwoman who carried his tureen
of soup and extracted the cork from a bottle of wine with a smile
that nipped the tan base of her cheeks, to this woman, if widowed, divorced, separated, if somehow available, he could surrender himself.

The mental release enriched the soup, the omelet, the agitat-
ing wine.

William constructed a French approach and two or three
contingent follow-ups, and was, perhaps, on the point of resolve
when a black hound loped out of the restaurant followed by the
little girl running and waving to a vegetable truck bumping up
the road, around the driveway, into a space in the pines. A squat
little fellow got out, flicked a switch which lit the colored bulbs
above the tables, lifted the little girl, cuffed the hound, nodded
to William, and went in. In a minute William heard the rage of
family argument.

Life's harsh ecology.

In his room William read the news magazine, *L'Express*: de
Gaulle, *Roi de Quebec;* Castro and Stokely Carmichael in
Havana; the Pope in Turkey at the Virgin Mary's death house;
the film director Godard married to the granddaughter of Mau-
riac; the death of a ninety-one-year-old poet named Birot, inventor of the word "surrealism." Yes, exactly. The human
bubble glistened like a maniac's dream.

The next morning William was on the road at seven, tearing
along as if he had a mission. A second's decision brought him
past the turnoff for Saint-Tropez. Why break his stride?

There were lots of hitchhikers, and at Cogolin, he stopped to
pick one up, a girl who waited motionless with a rucksack at her
bare feet. She stuck her head in the window. "Toulon?" Young,

perhaps sixteen, with a long, horsy face, yet pretty in a stupid way.

"Yes," said William. "To Marseilles. Maybe farther."

She threw her rucksack in the back on his suitcase and got in. She had on tight, grass-green pants and a yellow sweater. Very well built.

—You going to Toulon or farther?

—Béziers.

—Where's that?

For response, she made an expression he believed peculiar to French girls. The chin went forward, the mouth dropped, the eyes widened. It signified, "Beyond me."

—Maybe you're on the wrong road.

The expression was modified by a shrug and pouted lips: "Could be." He handed her the Esso map of Provence. After a minute she said, "It may be after Montpellier."

—I might not get that far.

This didn't even call for a shrug. Well, she was no orator. Or perhaps questions violated the hitchhiker's code. Still he persisted, he'd picked her up for company.

—You visiting people in Béziers?

The facial telegraphy signaled the unseen hitchhikers of the world that she had been picked up by a real lulu, but as William sustained his air of expectancy, she said, "My aunt."

—How far have you come?

—Antwerp.

—Are you Flemish?

A shrug, as much "Perhaps" as "Yes."

—My name's William. What's yours?

Another telegraphic Waterloo, then, "Christine."

Did she like music?

She supposed she did.

Who?

Armstrong. The Beatles.

No, she did not know the names Monk, Miles, or Ornette, nor did he say from whose album covers he knew the names.

Did she read?

No time.

Hobbies?

No time.

Did she swim?

Yes, it was why she came to the Riviera.

—If we spot a beach, we can take a dip.

The telegraphy went wild.

In Marseilles William pulled up before a wall on which was scrawled in charcoal, "*U.S. Assassins. Viet Cong vaincra.* Johnson = 卐 ." He reached for his Instamatic and asked Christine if she'd pose in front of that, he needed a foreground object. She made a bovine facial shrug, but got out and stood in front of the yellow cement. William studied her through the lens. She was large, very well developed, though her feet were those of an adolescent, soft, large, tan, the toenails faintly silvered. "Frown," he said. "I want to show how America is detested." The Flemish droop hardened into a tiny smile. Well, they were a bit slow in Wallonia, but they came around.

They went to Montpellier, had a sandwich and a glass of wine in a snack bar—William's treat—then drove south toward Béziers. The country turned to scrub and then dunes. The Gulf of Lions opened at their left, a piece of blue plate touched with crumbs of white sail and foam. Long, spiky, wild grass bearded the road's edge, and every mile or two, paths sliced through it to the water.

William pulled up on the edge near a path, and said it was hot, he was going to take a swim. Christine's eyes, little blue fish, scooted around in suspicion.

Still, while he changed in the car, she took off her pants and sweater in the high grass.

When he got out in his trunks, she was in a bikini. "I had it on underneath."

She was terrific.

Between the grass and the great basin of water were a few yards of brown sand. From it, Christine hung a probing foot, then dived shallowly and swam a full-armed crawl fifteen yards out. William flexed himself and walked in. The bottom was marshy, the water warm. He swam in her direction.

She stood, the waterline at her breasts. William tried to think of something to say, to do, but settled for a smile, which he directed at her till her eyes opened and became part of her answering smile. "I'll race you," he said. She made her "beyond-me" shrug but plunged off, swimming hard. He followed, caught up, and when she kept on, followed again and caught her ankles. She kicked loose and stood up, her eyes bluely puzzled, afraid, excited. He smiled doubly wide, and splashed her gently. She flicked water back at him, he splashed her face, she turned on her stomach and kicked water at his. He dived, his nose an inch from the marsh bottom, turned, and came up under her, his chest touching hers and his legs her kicking legs. She was still a second, then pushed off from his shoulders and swam. William, very excited, swam after her. "Surrender?" His voice cracked between embarrassment and desire.

She stood, blushed, smiled, and for want of something to say, splashed him. At which point he came up to her gently, and, without lifting his arms, kissed her mouth. Only for a second. Her mouth stayed open, her eyes shut. When she opened them again, William put his arms around her, kissed her very hard, and felt her kissing him back. They fell into the water. With his right arm around her bare waist, they crawled to the sand.

She was virgin, there was enough obstacle to cause William to discharge on her stomach. Pained, pleasured, absorbed, she turned over, a hand reaching back for his. They lay this way for a few minutes, then William leaned into the water, washed the dried seed from her stomach, and handed her the bikini, the little flag of sexual liberty. "Don't worry about anything. There's nothing inside you."

She shrugged, not a girlish shrug, and followed him through the spiky grass up the slope.

The outskirts of Béziers are blocks of factories and apartment buildings. He needn't drive into the center, said Christine, she could take a bus to her aunt's. He stopped on the corner she indicated and said, "I wish we could stay together for a while, but it's best not to."

She shook her head. "It doesn't matter. Thank you for the ride." She hoisted the rucksack to her shoulders and walked off.

William found the route to Narbonne, and drove very fast, relaxed and happy. Ahead, off the road, a truck lay on its side with a line of police around it. Cars slowed to a cortege for half a mile, then spread and zoomed. *Christine,* thought William.

The tight grass-green pants walking down the granular white street in Béziers. Why couldn't two human beings with common needs and common culture (Armstrong, French, swimming) service each other in such a countryside?

But that long bent head walking away down the sidewalk out of sight forever. Out of eyesight.

There was something at the edge of his mind, a buzz of sorts, but not in his mind as much as his chest, a hum of feeling—what was it?

Christine did not walk off with his stuff in her, but her body held what was not just air, not in the clownish human treasury. He, William, was part of her wherever she would go, whatever do. And she, of him.

He thought he might make it to Perpignan, but when the Narbonne signs multiplied, he felt his fatigue and turned in to Centre de Ville, past walls of aperitif posters into a polygonal fortressed heart of rose and silver, then past shops to a canal flanked with plane trees. He pulled up by a hotel and got a room.

Oddly, for the first time in Europe, he felt like going to a museum. In Rome he'd gone only to the Campidoglio, but the gigantesque marble feet in the courtyard only confirmed a harsh view of what survived.

The *patronne* directed him to the medieval polygon he'd passed on the way in, he walked over, found a courtyard full of Roman fragments, hesitated, then rang a bell for the guard, followed him up a stone screw of stairs into a huge half-frescoed hall with tiny medieval windows and case after case of museum stuff: Neolithic potsherds, Volgae statuettes, Gallic shields incised with boars, "the oldest Roman inscription on French soil" commemorating the victory of Ahenobarbus at Valadium, and then, what William might have been looking for, a bust of Mark Antony, governor of the Narbonne province after Caesar's death.

Antony's tiny bronze forehead wrinkled with puzzlement. The bronze leaked stupidity. This was the soldier to whom Cleopatra, dolled up as Venus, had come in the barge with purple sails, the fellow who'd laughed at Cicero's severed head. This world-shaker was a dope. William's heart trembled with renewed confirmation.

The guard was already asleep, chin on his sternum, huge key in his fist: the new Frenchman, descendant of the men who'd carved the shields and broken the pots, who knows, container of genes that had passed through Cleopatra's royal corridors. The old stupidity, Gaul to de Gaulle. William put a silver franc on the inert knee.

At dusk, by the plane trees, William drinks light beer and smokes a twist of black tobacco barely as thick as its smoke. The wind in the gleaming trees stirs up odd clicks. Mysterious telegraphy. The Canal Robine quivers in its pilings. William thinks vaguely of a grand French dinner, *pâté, saucissons, moules, mouton, petits pois, fraises, vin de pays.* It will be in his body by nine. Then, alone, he will do what he has sometimes done in Dayton, walk the streets, go into bars, looking quietly for someone with a face unenameled by commercial fury. As usual, he will go to bed alone.

A woman at the next table is handing a dish of brandy to a Pomeranian. William finds himself saying, "I should be glad to take nourishment from such hands, Mademoiselle."

The woman looks up. She is fat-nosed, scraped; what had seemed blond hair is silver. "Were you addressing me, Monsieur?"

"I too have a dog." He puts six francs on the table. "*Au revoir,* Madame."

Tomorrow.

Tomorrow he will drive back to Béziers, will cruise the streets. At a corner, around a turn, by an alley, he will spot the grass-green pants, the rucksack, the lowered head.

But the next morning, William drives back to Marseilles, turns in the car at the airport, and flies to Rome.

It is four when he reaches the hotel. Signorina McCoshan is out. He waits by the window. At six there is talk outside the door, then a knock. It is Winnie, and beside her, a flushing Robert.

—What a surprise, Dad. Something wrong?

She raises her face painfully for a kiss. William cannot put his lips there. He smells an unscheduled knowledge.

"I felt I was running out on you," he manages, glaring at them, at their blushes.

Teeth

*In the multiplied objects of the external world
I had no thoughts but for the teeth. For these I
longed with a phrenzied desire.*

—POE, "Berenice"

1

AH, MISS WILMOTT, how did you come to think what you did?
Is all your interpreting so askew, so deformed by self-interest?
And is your self-interest so unbroken a pup that any street
whistle seems its master's voice? To think that you were misled
as wisdom itself was being certified in your aching jaws? Those
third molars, so long held back, and then so painfully emergent,
fangs and cusps clinging savagely to the gum flesh. "Impacted,"
said Dr. Hobbie, and despite the kind, soft-beaked, confident
face behind the metal glasses, you shuddered. You remembered
the last one, also impacted, eight months before, also in the
Bank Building, though two flights up on the ninth floor in a large
office afloat in the strawberry light off the lake. Dr. Grant, the
extractionist, Miss Blade's recommendation, a strong fellow
with white moustache and a post on the Executive Council of
the American Dental Association, just back from a downtown
committee meeting to have a go at your trouble. A lovely May

day, the creamy air swimming over the IC tracks, enough to make you forget the pain, until Dr. Grant, eyes asweat under his speckled horn rims, leaned over your open mouth and blocked out the view. And then, the tugging, the hammering, the cracking, chiseling, wrestling, blood squirting into the cotton gagging your mouth, blood dripping past it down your throat, your heart pumping, your great brow streaming, your wet palm grabbed tight by the fierce little nurse, Miss Romeyne. Afterward, on the couch, another blow, Dr. Grant sitting beside you, your long legs dripping feet over the edge, hand to your swelling jaw. "How does a hundred dollars sound, Miss Wilmott? Pretty fair? Including postoperant care, anaesthesia, the works. I know you're a teacher."

The pain lasted twelve days, unabated by Miss Blade's late revelation that she had been charged a hundred and twenty-five dollars. For this omission, Miss Blade would not get to know about Dr. Hobbie. Not that she'd appreciate him anyway. Miss Blade favored all the weak sisters in the department, the students with the loudest line of gab and the worst minds who took so long with their dissertations that they completed them and their scholarly life simultaneously.

Miss Wilmott learned of Dr. Hobbie through her once-a-week cleaning woman, Mrs. Spiders, whom she passed in the lobby of the Bank as she was on her way to request it to honor Dr. Grant's hundred dollars, although her balance was zero until the first of June. Mrs. Spiders was on her way to Dr. Hobbie. "Yeah, Miss Wilma, mah Hobbie's a grand tooth man." Mrs. Spider's syntax obscured identification, but she spoke of him now and then throughout the year, so that when Miss Wilmott's second tooth began cracking her head open the night after Epiphany, the vision of the great dental surgeon soothed it till morning, when she phoned him up and got a noon appointment. Dr. Hobbie was seldom too busy to squeeze in a sufferer. Half his business was "street business" anyway, delivery boys feeling pain between the first and fifth floors, taxi drivers from the Yellow Cab Stand, salespeople from the local stores, even receptionists from other dentists' offices in the building. A good sign. Not that Miss Wilmott needed confirmatory signs.

Except for that first day. An initial visit to Dr. Hobbie was disconcerting, especially if your appointment came on Wednes-

days. Every Tuesday, he danced at the Tall Girls' Club till three
A.M., and Wednesday was one long yawn for him. An unrepressed yawn, for Dr. Hobbie repressed no habit that any normal dentist would. No dentist with a smart practice walked
around with his smock so loosely tied that a skinny, peppermint-
colored back exposed itself to his patients' gaping faces. No
normal dentist worked in a shelfless closet which barely enabled
his movements, and certainly no nurse's. As for answering the
phone, tucking it between shoulder and jaw while continuing
to drill, or taking long looks at Educational Channel Spanish
lessons while working in a silver filling, these were procedures
which—Miss Wilmott imagined—might lead to dismissal from
the A.D.A. Yes, there was almost no limit to the external defects
of Dr. Hobbie's practice.

But Hobbie was a dental genius. In thirty years of agonized
dental visits, Miss Wilmott had never known such not-only-
painless, but even pleasurable sensations. Dr. Hobbie's office
did not face the strawberry-colored lake air but the west wall
of the Bank Building; there were no couches, no magazines, in
fact nothing at all in the scarcely redeemed cave of a waiting
room but a kitchen chair and a coat rack. But you almost
never had to wait, and when you were in the chair, there was
almost no pain. The fees were ludicrously small, even for her,
a low-grade instructor in the History Department. Ten dollars
for her impacted wisdom tooth, and for that there were
sound-wave drills, the best Swedish steel, a lecture on her
lower jaw, Mantovani playing Cole Porter on the hi-fi, and the
sweetest of all analgesics, Dr. Hobbie's account of his personal
troubles.

These came out of him as naturally as his pale, thin back out
of the white smock. They were not unlike Miss Wilmott's own
troubles, at least his implicit ones. They had to do with Suzanne,
his tall, expert-dancer of a wife, who'd left him last June to live
with the Bank Building florist, Mr. Consolo, but who still somehow or other extracted money from him, though they had no
child to support. Which led to another trouble: here he was,
forty-two years old, the only fellow he knew who had no children, as well as the only one who had to spend half his time
looking for girls with whom to dance the samba and the twist,
though he had a perfectly good dancing wife of his own. The

implicit troubles were, she knew, those for which she had female equivalents.

It was her early insight into their equivalence that made her think that Dr. Hobbie could help her with more than teeth. He wasn't the world's most attractive man, God knew, not even the most attractive she'd known, which said a great deal; for her timid six feet, popped eyes and no-nose face—she'd overheard someone say she looked as if she'd been blotted—were no powerful magnet for men.

In her entire life, there were very few times she'd gone out with half-decent men. She'd come to think that perhaps it didn't matter, that she could make it without a man. If only people would stop pressuring her. Thousands of small pressures: salesgirls calling her Mrs. when she bought her father's birthday shirts; people being introduced to her at parties; being the extra girl and getting tied up with the miserable extra man, more miserable when he saw her; the hundreds and hundreds of self-pitying hours in her two rooms, Jack Paar jabbering maniacally on the twelve-inch screen while she shared him with *Middlemarch,* its pages stained with the peanut butter she sometimes supposed was more faithful to her than any person on earth.

She had yens, God knows, though not as many as two-bit Freudians would think. She'd even had a little experience, a summer at Truro where her six feet and impressive learning had substituted for a movie star's chest and model's face. There'd even been a marriage proposal, from a Wyoming historian at the American Historical meetings in Fifty-Eight. It turned out that he wanted introductions to the scholarly Big Chiefs at Chicago. At least, though, it was on the books, her chance at the middle-class nirvana.

As Hobbie's big-beaked, sandy face, a good-hearted parrot's, leaned over her open mouth, even that first day, Miss Wilmott felt a kind of root tremble in her heart. A sweet man, a poor troubled fellow. Not a cretin either, though naïve and uncultured. In dentistry, he was actually a scholar, full of the history of instruments, surgical procedures, technical advances. He spent weekends reading the journals, and while Dr. Grant was in A.D.A. executive sessions, he listened to papers. He was so enamored of his profession that she began to pick up toothy tidbits for him, things she'd come upon in her ubiquitous browsing in the stacks.

"Ever read ahhh Poe's 'Ber-ahhh-niece'?"

"Nope. Spit out, Miss Wilmott."

Then, after rinsing with the sweet, violet water, "It's about a man so insanely fond of teeth that he breaks open his former fiancée's grave ahhh, pulls out all her teeth ahh and keeps them in a box."

"Oh, my Lord," eyes furry with astonishment. "And I thought I liked teeth. Little wider there, Miss Double-U."

Miss Wilmott read the *Britannica* on Teeth and Dentistry, soaked up tooth lore, began to think in tooth metaphors, and felt the root tremble in her heart whenever Dr. Hobbie leaned over to pass a steel shaft beneath her strong, white crowns. "There's a tribe called the Ndembu in Rhodesia which has a tooth ceremony called the Ihamba, ahhh. They pull out the premolar incisor, and their troubles are supposed to come out with it. Then they have a tooth dance."

"That's really something. Not much longer. Good girl. Where do you find such things out?"

She puffed her cheeks with the violet water and spat as daintily as possible into the bowl's soft whirlpool. "Periodicals."

"Periodicals?"

"Magazines. That was in the ahhh *Rhodes-Livingstone Journal* last month." Into her mouth and out, a silvery tool. "Dahhhhh."

"Just a little bit more now. There we are, almost out. I envy you book people. Myself, I can't . . . here we are," holding up an enamel needle bloodied with nerved dentine. "That's the old troublemaker. I think you're going to be all right for a while now."

"I might as well get everything cleaned up, Dr. Hobbie. As long as I'm making real progress. I'd miss my visit anyway."

With the hand that held the silver forceps in which her troublemaker lay, he brushed the soft tip of his beak back and forth, as if to sniff out a proper response. "Might work a little on that back bite then if you really want to go ahead and spend the money. It'll run you thirteen, fourteen dollars." He opened the child's notebook in which he entered all appointments and payments. "That'll be three-fifty today, and we'll set you down for next Thursday. Four-fifteen, O.K., right after Mr. Givens. He's my other book patient."

Thursday, she came a few minutes early and sat on the kitchen chair listening to Dr. Hobbie tell Mr. Givens that he had this fine teacher from the University coming right in, he wanted Mr. Givens to meet her.

At 4:14 the door opened, you never had to wait, and a short, good-looking Negro of forty, dressed in house painter's stained overalls, was introduced to her by Dr. Hobbie and said he was very glad to meet her, was she a Marxist like the other teachers up there at the University, and to her "I'm afraid not," said he was disappointed, he having been a Marxist for twenty years, the Manifester and the Working Day being his favorite books of all time.

Dr. Hobbie's other book patient. After this, most of her appointments coincided with Mr. Givens's. She wondered if Dr. Hobbie also brought his salespeople together. At any rate, she exchanged a few words each time with him while a beaming Hobbie stood by. Once she recommended Herzen's *Memoirs* to him, and another time she told him that she'd just reread the *Manifesto* and not only the "Working Day," but the whole first book of *Capital*. At this, Mr. Givens struck a great hand to his fine brow. "You mean to say there's a whole book of that, and I don't know it? Give me the name there, Miss Wilmer. I'm ashamed of myself. I'll go git it today if I got to go to every bookstore in Chicago." Miss Wilmott gave him the name, told him it was readily available, and recommended the Everyman Library Edition, one sixty-five for each of the volumes. "God," said Mr. Givens, "they could charge three or four dollars for them, and I'd git them as quick as I'm going to now." He held out his hand, and she put her own great one into it. Dr. Hobbie said, "What'd I tell you, George?"

Today Miss Wilmott's tidbit was that biologists regarded fish teeth as migrated scales. "I suppose our ancestors may have masticated on the skin," she said, as he placed her head back into the rest.

Dr. Hobbie said that that sure would make dentistry easy. Then, a large shape darkened the office door, a gray fedora pulled nose-level on the head. " 'Night, son," it said.

" 'Night, Dad," said Dr. Hobbie.

Though she'd not seen Hobbie's father, a doctor from the floor above, she knew that the glass cabinet of unfinished bridges and tooth sets over by the television aerial was due to him, or rather to the dying patients whom he felt would be comforted by his son's diverting skill. They often died in the midst of their absorbed interest in refurbished mouths, and Miss Wilmott's Dr. Hobbie kept their work, as if, in some odd turn of the world, a mouth would appear just right for one of the unfinished bridges.

"That your father?"

"Yep. That's the old man. Been in this building since they put it up. He's a real good doctor if you need one." He was washing his hands, and she studied his reflection in the dark window. He took off his smock, and she saw his skinny, harmless back, white and pink, a rabbit scooting into a green shirt. "He helped me out with Suzanne last week. She hit a car. Two hundred bucks. I've got to pay her lawyer. That doesn't seem fair, does it? I mean Consolo is no poor man. They do well, even in winter. Three-fifty a dozen for irises." She put on her coat. "What do I owe you today?"

"I put my book away. I guess I can't charge you, or they'll be getting me up for not reporting income."

"I won't think of that," she said, and laid out a five-dollar bill on top of his sterilizer.

He took out his wallet and gave her two dollars. "I'll drive you home. It's another cold one."

"Lovely," said Miss Wilmott. She drove a fifty-two Pontiac which hadn't started for most of January and February.

Out on Fifty-Third Street, the wind was knifed for murder. People passed like thugs, scarves pulled over mouths, hats down like old Dr. Hobbie's to the nose. Ridges of steel ice humped the streets, and every third corner had its famished crocodile of open car hood, whining for life.

"I'll offer him supper," thought Miss Wilmott, though there was nothing in the kitchen but two cans of roast beef hash, eggs, and a loaf of Pepperidge Farm bread. Nor could she take the chance of asking him to let her shop. He'd not let himself be invited then. "I'd like to give you a little supper, Dr. Hobbie. If you're free, I mean."

"Gee."

"I don't get too many chances to cook for other people."

"That would be something, Miss Wilmott," but he was turning round, looking for something. "Darn," he said. "Guess what? I don't have the car today. It's in the garage. I am sorry, Miss Double-U. I'll put you in a cab. Let me take a rain check on that supper, O.K.? It's real nice of you." And he opened a taxi door, put her in, spoke to the driver, and said, "So long." Turned out he'd paid the fare.

But Miss Wilmott had a bad night. The heat was low, her bed was cold. She got up, put on a sweater and the furry bathrobe her father'd sent her for her birthday. Feb. 2. Thirty-one. She turned on WFMT. Buzz. It was three o'clock. Dr. Hobbie'd be coming home from the Tall Girls. She sat back in the terrible green armchair she'd gotten at Carmen the Movers for eight dollars. A troglodyte. The only arms that ever held her. How long was it going to go on like this? She couldn't even get a man over for supper. For talk. For an exchange of troubles. The enamel crown was off, the pulp cavity cut away, and the tiny, mean, piranha nerves of the dentine sang out in the iron cold of February. Today's *Sun-Times* remarked that a marine had pole-vaulted sixteen feet, twenty years to the day after another man had pole-vaulted fifteen. A photographer, rapacious for a shot, had knocked down the bar and the record might not be official. Dr. Hobbie had said he'd come for supper, but the garage had his car. The grain of the world was wrong. What could she do? She was a Ph.D. in English history, a low-grade instructor at a high-grade university. If she wrote a few more articles and a good book, they'd give her six years as an Assistant Professor and then maybe tenure. She could get a tenure job right now at lots of women's colleges. Down south, where the streets didn't look like an illustration of the Inferno, where women were loved. But she wouldn't live down south again. She'd gone a year to W.C. in Greensboro, and she wouldn't live in a place where Mr. Givens would have to sit in the back of a bus and drink from a different water fountain. Maybe she'd go back east, nearer relatives, nearer the marrying girls of her class at Wheaton. But she'd left such dependence and such competition behind. She was a scholar. She knew her stuff. She loved to work, to find out what happened, to read two-hundred-year-old periodicals, to trace in detail the rise of sentimentality, the alteration in attitudes toward children, toward women, toward pain, toward dirt. But now, now. Tonight. She could not read, not listen to the radio, not steam a kettle. She stared at the arrested chaffinches in her stained rug border, the bricks and boards which held the books she'd dragged around for years with her, east, west, south, her swelling paunch. It was a terrible night. Only self-consciousness kept her going. She brooded on until the room turned fuzzy with fatigue, and then she went off to sleep in the troglodyte's arms.

2

Miss Wilmott did not see Dr. Hobbie again until spring. She was writing an article on the use of opium in England during the first two decades of the nineteenth century, and it took up every minute of the time that she did not give her classes, committee meetings, papers, meals, and pillow. Weekends, nights, vacation days found her in Harper Library or downtown at the Newberry reading account books, newspapers, doctors' diaries, the works of Coleridge, De Quincey, Bramwell Brontë, and other well-known users of the drug. Her fingers bore dots of yellow where the dust of the old accounts bit into the curious, living flesh: her addiction marks. When she got to the use of opium by dental surgeons, she was brought up short.

It was May, a year from her terrible encounter with Dr. Grant. Walking home from the bus stop one evening, facing the strawberry light off the lake, she felt the root atremble in her heart. "Your liking and your lust is fresh whyle May doth last,/ When May is gone, of all the yeare the plesaunt time is past." *Carpe diem,* Miss Wilmott. Old time is swiftly flying. "Oh dear," she said, taking her long, slow strides into the fading light. "It isn't simple."

But the next morning, she telephoned Dr. Hobbie and asked if she could come in to have her teeth examined. No, there was nothing special wrong except that her jaw ached when she ate ice cream, and her bite was a little unsteady. Dr. Hobbie told her to come in on Tuesday.

Monday night, he telephoned and said he was awfully sorry, he couldn't see her tomorrow. "The old man kicked the bucket today. This afternoon. I'll be real busy tomorrow. How about Friday?"

"Of course," she said, "and I'm awfully sorry about him."

"Three-thirty, right in his office." For a moment, she thought it was her appointment time, and that he was moving into his father's office. "Had his stethoscope on a patient and kicked the bucket right there, listening. Seventy-eight years old."

Miss Wilmott could not think of opium that May night. There was a burr stuck in the evening: Dr. Hobbie's mortal phrase, "Kicked the bucket." It was not worthy. Offhandedness had limits. Distaste helped blunt her disappointment at the postponement. By Thursday, however, she could hardly wait to see him.

It was ten-thirty. She must have been his first patient, for she had to wait outside the locked door. When he arrived, he said, "Don't have to work so hard now. The old man left me eighty-four thousand bucks. Never thought he was within fifty of it. Suzanne would hit the deck if she knew how much she lost out on. I'm going to New York, take in some shows and restaurants before she gets the word and tries to get her hands on it. I don't think she's given up on me. Every so often, she gets soused up and calls me on the phone, gives me a good chewing out. You don't do that if you've given up on somebody. Maybe you can give me a list, Miss Wilmott." A list of what—girls? "I don't know the restaurant situation too well there."

Ah. She said she knew very little about New York.

Dr. Hobbie's hands at her mouth were sure as ever, but Miss Wilmott did not feel comfortable. He talked a blue streak. "People been calling me day and night asking about the old man. They can't figure out why his phone doesn't answer. Think they'd read the papers. That's a nasty one you have back there." He touched her with a silver prong.

"I'm on the run every minute. Have to shut off his phone, sublet his office, the apartment. Papers, you have no idea, writing relatives, the funeral. Dying is harder on the relatives than the dead man. I'll bet getting born is easier. Not that I know much about that. You ever had a child, Miss Wilmott?" He'd run on too fast, and blushed. Miss Wilmott's file turned up a sentence, "A blush is a primitive erection." Her own face chugged with capillary action. "Of course not," he was saying. "Excuse me. I was just shooting off. The old man's kind of thrown me. Never had a bad word for me since I was a little tyke. Helped me through school, helped me furnish the office, helped with Suzanne." Had his old man given him the kitchen chair, the TV set, the glass case?

Miss Wilmott nearly invited him to dinner on the spot. But held back. This time she'd prepare. There'd be another appointment in a week. She'd invite him then.

Two days before the appointment she went down to Halstead Street and bought a fine roast, a Greek cheese and olives, baklava, and a beautiful eggplant which she would transform into a marvelous Greek dish she'd read about in an eighteenth-century cookbook. It took two days to make, and Miss Wilmott turned to it from her opium with the energetic passion she knew great cooks must have.

So there she was, the day of her appointment, ready to show her stuff. But oh how foolish was Miss Wilmott. The most untutored person would not prepare so elegantly for an empty chair. If she'd telephoned even one day early, Dr. Hobbie might have canceled his plane tickets to New York; for that's where he was going, one hour and ten minutes after finishing up her mouth.

Her disappointment was immeasurable. Back she walked along Fifty-Third Street, hardly looking at the colors which the sun stirred up in the chubby western clouds, hardly aware of the birds singing good night to her from the cottonwood as she pushed her legs past each other down Harper, Blackstone, Dorchester, Kenwood, and then up Kimbark toward her apartment.

Nor did she see Mr. Givens, the house painter, till he was practically at her feet. "Hey there, Miss Wilmer. How ya doing this fine evening?" He'd taken off his cap, was in coveralls, and he carried a paper bag. Miss Wilmott's heart, which had jumped with fear, calmed in recognition. And then in a brilliant flash, she remembered the beautiful dinner waiting twenty feet up from where they stood. The rest was simple. "Mr. Givens, I couldn't be more happy to see anyone. Guess what just happened to me," and she told him about someone being called away from the dinner she'd cooked, an emergency. Could he help her out and share it?

"Why Miss Wilmer, that's really something. I'm just going on up to Blackstone Library with a couple of hamburgers and a jelly doughnut. I'm reading that Memoir book you told me about. Best thing I ever looked at. I'd like to come up, it's real nice of you. I'll read at it tomorrow night."

So Mr. Givens came and sat down at the table she'd set the night before, between her green troglodyte and the TV set, with her complete supply of Wedgwood picked up in the corners of State Street pawn shops and Maxwell Street stands. It was a wonderful dinner, praised by Mr. Givens as the last word in a lifetime of good eating.

He was not bad company, either. He had strong opinions about everything. There were the rich, who always argued about bills, never paid you what they'd agreed to, always trying to cut your throat; there were the sports-crazy people of Chicago, blowing off the air raid sirens when the ball team won the darn pennant; there were the "jawbreakers" (whom she didn't identify with John Birchers till he lumped them with the Boond and the Ku Kluxers) out to loot everybody by scaring them out of their brains, not that there were too many around to be scared out of; there were these Careoaches and Milers, beat writers who were full of more hot air about colored people than Talmadge and Bilbo; there was De Goal sitting up in a French cloud while everybody in Paris killed themselves with these plastic bombs; there was the Russians, more boojwa than the capitalists, never thinking beyond their own bellies, not that he should be thinking about anything else after such a wonderful meal, for which, Miss Wilmott, I never will git to thank you enough.

With which he was up, a handsome man with a fine moustache, gray at the temples, a high forehead, a very distinguished-looking and intelligent self-educated man, probably unmarried, though she didn't know and wouldn't dream of asking, and if the world wasn't the way it was, and if he could possibly get interested in her, who knows if despite everything that separated them, she would not enjoy cooking for him and taking his praise and affection every single remaining evening of her life. If she could take anyone that much, there being, after all, much to be said for freedom, one's own time, doing one's work at one's own speed, so good night, Mr. Givens, it's been a real pleasure, mutual, yes, some time again, and I certainly would like to go out with you, no absolutely, I'm not in the least offended by the offer, I'm proud you asked me.

The next week Miss Wilmott began writing her article. It

flew. Never had she written so fast, so well. In one week, she laid out a thirty-nine-page first draft, and she knew that there wouldn't be more than a handful of changes. Still, she distrusted compositional euphoria, remembered Horatian maxims, and laid the article aside for a few days before turning to the final draft.

Fatal delay.

The evening Dr. Hobbie was due back from New York, she sat in the troglodyte's arms, fingering her reference cards, thinking about plunging ahead. On the very first card, the terrible equation, "Picul=133 1/3 lb." swooped toward her eyes. "Oh no," she said out loud. "No, no, no." But there it was. Her calculations about imports had been pegged at a hundred and sixty-six and a third pounds to the picul. She'd misread her skewered threes. An absurd error, yet an easily corrigible one. But, no, those thirty-three false pounds lodged in Miss Wilmott like splinters she was too fearful to dig out of her tender article. Infection set in. Her beautiful account of opium consumption, rich in psychological insight, economic analysis, social theory, and literary allusion, rose rankly to her nostrils, a festered lily.

That night her jaw throbbed in sympathetic misery. Her knowledge, her research, her opium, what were they now in the dark, stranded by her needs, errors, miscalculations, her muddled self-interest? In agony, Miss Wilmott reached for the phone and called Dr. Hobbie's home number. Four, five, six rings. The receiver was on its way down when she heard his "Hallo."

"Oh Dr. Hobbie. Thank goodness. Forgive me for calling you. I wasn't even sure you were back. It's Miss Wilmott. I'm in awful pain."

It was right to call him, said Dr. Hobbie, he'd just gotten in, he was barely asleep. He'd meet her in twenty minutes at the office, no, better, he'd pick her up in fifteen minutes. Yawn. That too quick?

"I don't want you to have to do that. I'm just being nervous. It probably was knowing that you'd come back that made me tooth conscious. If you were in New York, I probably wouldn't have noticed."

"We'll take a look anyway, Ethel. See you in a few minutes. Bye now." Click.

He'd called her Ethel. Bye now. Bye now. By now he was

taking pajamas off his long, pale body, slipping into underwear, pants, shirt.

She dressed in a flash, a blue cotton with her initials figured in the lapel, EAW, an unfinished word. Downstairs, she waited at the door, her nose blob flattened further against the glass, waiting. The first car brought her out to the stoop, but though it paused in midcareer, it was not Hobbie, and went on. Few neutral cars would stop for Miss Wilmott.

There was a bite to the air. Miss Wilmott was starting up the stairs for a sweater when Dr. Hobbie's open Dodge pulled up in front of the house. She ran down and climbed in beside him. Oh, how gay she felt. "It's wonderful of you to do this."

Behind his glasses, beaked the soft face. "I'm kind of proud to get a night call. Doesn't happen more than twice a year. Makes me feel like the old man."

Suddenly, Miss Wilmott was in a stew: there was not a splinter of pain left in her body. Nothing. Yet it had been genuine. Her whole head had gone out on strike with pain. There was no question of that. There may have been a psychic trigger, but the somatic twinges were genuine. Now there was absolutely nothing. Could it be that sitting beside this gentle fool, this *beau sabreur de la bouche,* was enough to soothe her uproarious gums?

At the Bank Building, all was dark. Dr. Hobbie's keys got them into the elevator and his office. He lit up his little workshop of analgesia, put a smock over his short-sleeved shirt, flipped a few switches, and before she'd summoned the strength to tell him how fine she felt, he'd sat her in the chair and stared into her mouth. "Whew. Good thing you called me. This must have been killing you. Can't remember a worse-looking abscess. We'll lance it and see what we can do."

Sir Percival. He was over her, touching, spearing, dabbing, in-and-out of her mouth, his beaky head swimming in a kind blue light. There was music—the hi-fi—"Is It True What They Say about Dixie?" Time flew. It was bitter dark, bitter cold, the iron February cold; she was lying down, face up, staring at the wicked ice smothering the earth. Above her head, the whacking, cracking blade opened up the ice. Hobbie's terrible lit face, a starving bird's, gleamed in the white air. His talons, fierce Swedish tools, reached for her mouth. "Berenice," he screamed,

"Berenice." And out, out they came, one by one, her thirty glorious crowns, roots, rapt from her yielding jaws. Oh it was over. She lay back, vacant, depleted, fulfilled.

Dr. Hobbie leaned over, a bloody three-pronged crown caught in his silver forceps. "There's your troublemaker. He won't bother you ever again. How do you feel, Ethel?"

She nodded. Her face felt shot away by the Novocaine. The nod was like lifting a boulder.

"We'll pick up a little painkiller and Chloraseptic for you, and I'll take you home."

She raised his good dentist's hand and patted it for thanks. For more than thanks.

In the car, she asked him if he'd seen some good shows.

"Not a one. Went dancing most of the time. Those places that sell you tickets. They're not bad. You get some fine dancers. And then last Saturday who showed up at the hotel but old Suzanne. I knew she'd smell out the old man's dough."

It was wickedly dark out. They were on Cottage Grove. The May night blew cold on Miss Wilmott's brow. Struggling through the rocky, cotton-lined resistance in her mouth, she said, "Well, well. And what did you do?"

What a question, Miss Wilmott! Where do you come off to ask such a question?

"She's not so bad, Ethel. You get used to a certain person, and then you take her faults with her better parts. Flags." Indeed there were, on stores. "Decoration Day."

"When May is gone, of all the year the pleasant time is past," said Miss Wilmott.

"I like June," said Dr. Hobbie. "I was born in June. I graduated in June. I got married in June. Of course, Suzanne ran off to Consolo last June. Every month has its good and bad times."

They were outside the drugstore. He ran in, and she waited alone in the car, her head back on the seat, aching.

"I don't have my purse," she said when he came back.

"Forget it," he said, and put the package in her lap. "They give it to me cut-rate. I'll stick you next time."

Oh stick me now. Her great head leaned against his shoulder, and without warning, large tears bloomed and fell in her face. "Oh dear," she said.

Dr. Hobbie took his hands off the steering wheel and put

them around her. "That's all right, Ethel. Just what you're supposed to do after an operation. You're going to be O.K."

She was not going to be O.K. The Ndembu's troubles left them when their teeth were pulled; not hers. The Ndembu danced to celebrate; Dr. Hobbie had not taught her the twist.

The Good European

1

MR. Weber was mad, a pleasing shock to most of the office staff, but for Harry Pfeiffer mere confirmation of a painful commonplace.

Pfeiffer was Mr. Weber's "New York end," had been ever since coming to work for D-J International barely a year after he'd stepped off the boat from Hamburg. For fourteen years he had listened to the stories told about Weber without being at all amused; as a German refugee, he had had enough of eccentricity in power. His job was to read Weber's turgid official reports, and it soon became clear to him that he was also responsible for attending to the personal requests appended to each of them. Every month he sent his secretary to the newsstand for the comic books which the Weber children wished to read; and twice a year, he telephoned Bloomingdale's to order the twenty-four jars of peanut butter and the two kegs of saltines which the Americans in St. Germain-en-Laye phenomenally consumed. These, and less regularly requested items—jars of Sanka, crates of Kleenex tissue, Emerson radio tubes, Sunbeam razor cutters, nylons, cigarillos—would be parceled by company help on one side of the Atlantic and unparceled by company help on the other.

The Webers had lived in Europe for nine years, and before that in Buenos Aires for ten. All this while, their passion for American products grew until it displaced every other affectionate sentiment connected with their native land. The situation was not modified by annual New York visits.

It was during these visits that Pfeiffer had had his views of Arnold Weber, views which had sent him home to his wife muttering, prophetically, as it turned out, "The man's mad."

Now that events had certified his assessment, Pfeiffer sat back triumphantly in his small office watching the clerks outside spread their varied distortions of the story. He had heard what appeared to be an accurate version from Mr. Crain who had talked with Chanteloup on the transatlantic phone.

The story was that Weber had returned to the office looking particularly despondent and saying something under his breath about Europeans. After an hour in his office, he had sent for Chanteloup and de Roubain. They entered to find him swinging naked from the parallel bars. (His office was fitted out like a gymnasium.) As they came forward to ask if they could help, he had shouted, "Lousy frogs," and leaped onto de Roubain's shoulders, rolled over on him, and bitten him in the throat. They called for help, and in a minute, the room filled with pacifying assistants. Weber's chauffeur was summoned, and he and Chanteloup had gotten Weber dressed and carted off to the doctor's. The diagnosis was that he had suffered a complete breakdown. He was to be confined for an indefinite period in an institution, an American one in view of his obviously paranoid feelings about Europe and Europeans. Plane reservations for New York had been made, and two nurses hired to accompany him back to the States.

At three-thirty, Pfeiffer's secretary made a twirling motion with her forefinger. Pfeiffer laced up his special shoe and limped down the hall to Bellman's office. The talk, he well knew, would have to do with Weber, but this was not his chief concern. Indeed, for the past hour he had been considering the Weber affair only as it might affect the execution of his resolve to smoke a cigarette in Bellman's presence. On the way up the hall, he decided that Bellman might be so distracted by the news that he might not notice anything.

Miss Pinney waved Pfeiffer into the office, and he drew a pack of Chesterfields from his pants pocket. Mr. Bellman's head was poised over some papers. Pfeiffer sat down and struck a match.

"Take a seat, Harry," said Mr. Bellman, not looking up.

"Thank you," said Pfeiffer, lighting it despite the initial disadvantage. He held the smoke in until he felt he'd be consumed by it, then puffed it away from the desk toward the window.

Bellman's big blue stare was on him. "You've heard about Arnold?"

Pfeiffer nodded, and took another puff, his face white with the effort to keep his hand steady.

"I'm going over tomorrow to see what I can do. One thing I cannot do, Harry, and that is stay there." Pfeiffer blew a load of smoke toward his lap. "Crain and I have been talking about it. We think you're the man to take over." He pushed an ashtray over the desk, and Pfeiffer stubbed out his cigarette. "I know it's hard to decide such matters overnight, but we've got to have a quick answer, Harry. Can you give us one this weekend? If you decide against it, cable me at the Georges Cinq. Otherwise we'll book the passage for you next Thursday. Your family can join you later. Do you have a passport?"

"An old German one for souvenir," said Pfeiffer.

"Yes. Why don't you start on that right away? If you decide against going, the company's only out ten dollars." He opened a Damascus mosaic cigarette box. "Try these. They're Roumanian, I think."

"Thank you," said Pfeiffer, taking one.

"Two hundred in francs there, three hundred here, and expenses in francs or whatever local currency you need. Have a nice weekend, Harry. I hope you're going to decide to help us out. It might only be for six months or so. Arnold's a hard man to keep down. And I think you'll have a nice time. You and your wife have never gone back over there, have you?"

"No," said Pfeiffer.

"It'll be a lark for you then. Seeing Europe as Americans."

"Yes, that would be something," said Pfeiffer.

"Shipley's horsing around over there," continued Bellman. Shipley was an old-time company man whom Bellman had been trying to insult off the payroll for a decade. "You're a friend of his, aren't you?"

"He brought me into the company."

"Perhaps he can earn some of his keep by entertaining you."

"I'll talk it all over with my wife, Mr. Bellman. I appreciate your confidence in me."

"I hope so, Harry."

"And meanwhile, I'll do something about the passport."

As Pfeiffer opened the door, Bellman called out, "There's no one who can do the job like you, Harry. If it's 'Yes,' Gilly will make you reservations at the Castiglione. It's a nice place, much quieter than the Georges Cinq. I think you'll prefer it."

Pfeiffer put out the Roumanian cigarette in Miss Pinney's ashtray. At least he had done that.

"Leopold," he called to his accounts assistant who sat in the main clerks' office at a table piled with immense ledgers. "Tell Gilman to book me a passage for Paris next Thursday. I'm going down to the Passport Bureau now."

"Sie fahren nach Paris?"

"Thursday."

"Und zurück?"

"Who knows?"

Pfeiffer put on his suit coat and limped to the elevators. He had never seen Paris. He'd been in Strasbourg but never in Paris. Within three months, within a month perhaps, he might be seeing it again. And he would see Germany: there was a D-J office in Frankfurt. He might even see Bebelshausen again. Or Hamburg, although he never wanted to see Hamburg again, not even stone detached from stone with veils of dust between it and the sun.

2

Hamburg was the last Pfeiffer had seen of Europe. Fifteen years ago. He was Heinz Pfeiffer then, and he had walked the streets of Hamburg for five hours unable to take a seat in a restaurant or hotel lobby, to go to a movie or to sit in the park where the benches too were *für Hunde und Juden Verboten.* He had walked with his head bent away from the looks, curious or embarrassed, until, near the wharves, he had bought two sweet rolls from a peddler and eaten them leaning against a wall.

Withal, it was still Europe, rather than Germany, he was leaving, and, therefore, the tremendous relief of departure was coupled with regret, regret for that sweet condition which had enabled him, the small, club-footed son of a German-Jewish grocer in Bebelshausen-am-Rhein, to consider himself, and to be considered by his fellows, *ein guter Europäer.* He had gone to school in Munich, Geneva, Strasbourg, Heidelberg, and Bern, and everywhere his role had been the same, his humor and intensity composing the ideal temperament for the European bourgeois student of the twenties and thirties. Everywhere he was a success. Men liked him, and, despite his foot, so did women.

There had been almost no trouble, no sign of what was to come. Pfeiffer remembered only one incident, and that largely because it had a startling, if, happily, brief sequel. It was in the spring of 1930, and he was on a Rhine cruise with a group of his friends. They drank a lot, and there was singing and dancing. Pfeiffer danced fairly well, all things considered, and it was while he was dancing with one of the prettiest girls on the boat that he felt himself pushed, and, a few seconds later, pushed again. At the third push, he turned to see a large boy from another party whom he knew as a member of the young Nazi group at Heidelberg. "Once more," Pfeiffer had told him, "and I'll punch you in the nose." Laughter from the boy and a punch from Pfeiffer. His friends stepped in, threatened to throw the other into the Rhine, and toasted Pfeiffer's heroism.

The sequel came five years later. Pfeiffer stepped off the train one evening in Düsseldorf where he was making the contact which resulted in his getting an exit visa. He was alone on the street when he saw walking toward him, in uniform, pistol at hip, the same fellow. "I'm dead," he thought. "It's all over. The *Schwein* will shoot me in the head and kick me into the gutter." He closed his eyes and heard the footsteps thunder up and pass him.

The year before, he had returned to Germany from Bern. He had not planned to come back until the political situation changed, but an aunt had written him that his mother was dying. At the border, he was stopped by two policemen and asked, "Where are the papers, Pfeiffer?" Pfeiffer replied that there must be a mistake, he was only a law student in Bern. They didn't bother to dispute this, but took him to the station house, stripped him, poked around in his mouth and anus, sliced open his special shoe and examined his deformed foot saying that it would be an excellent place to hide something. He was detained at the border for two days, but never learned for what papers they were searching. When he got to Bebelshausen, his mother was already buried, and the house with the grocery on the ground floor was sold for one-twentieth its value.

During the next two years, Pfeiffer lived with his aunt. In that time, he never left the house, not even to sit in the backyard, until he made the trip to Düsseldorf, and then, at the end, the trip to Hamburg.

3

During his first three weeks in Paris, Pfeiffer worked from eight o'clock in the morning until nine at night. He thought of nothing but fighting his way through the labyrinth into which Arnold Weber's incompetence had maneuvered the European affairs of the company. The incompetence went beyond even conscious irregularity: Pfeiffer's most difficult hours were spent deciding when the madman had strayed into accuracy.

By the fourth week, he saw his way clear. Weber's stranglehold was loosed, though at a large price. Pfeiffer's review of the accounts indicated that Weber's nine-year reign had cost the company close to eight hundred million francs for the French market alone. He drafted a long cable to Mr. Bellman, and, after dispatching it, took to his bed in the Castiglione for three days during which he did nothing but sleep, read Agatha Christie, and order immense dinners from La Crémaillère which were wheeled to his bed on tables covered with embossed silver and flowers of the season.

The evening of the third day, Shipley telephoned to ask him over for a drink. "I'd've called before, Harry, but we just got back from Rome. How are you? I hear you've been doing a number one job filling in for Arnold. I'm going to cable Dolph the good word. Get here at four-thirty, will you? Belle and I eat at six."

To his surprise, Pfeiffer found himself looking forward to seeing Shipley. The only person with whom he'd talked socially in Paris was Chanteloup. Half his lunches had been ruined by the Frenchman's stories about Weber, stories of personal mania which matched those which Pfeiffer was digging out of the company books, stories of the gymnasium (dismantled by Bellman on his visit), of the tiger hired for "publicity shots," but kept in an adjacent office so that Weber could go in to stare him down, until one day he had had his arm clawed after punching the sleeping animal in the nose through the bars of the cage. "You crazy Americans," Chanteloup had come out with after telling this one. "Americans," exclaimed Pfeiffer, but held back from saying either that madmen were international or that, at any rate, he was scarcely more American than Chanteloup himself.

After such stories, even Shipley seemed a relief. He opened the door himself, resplendent in a Floridan outfit of purple sandals, green slacks, and mauve sport shirt. "Let me show you the works, Harry." The works were five enormous rooms in which magnificent lounges, beds, tables, pictures, and tapestries bloomed like subtly acclimatized natural growths. In a far corner of the largest room sat a white-haired woman who didn't look up as they came in.

"Belle," screamed Shipley. "Belle."

The woman smiled and came over. She was dressed in black and wore a chrysanthemum over each ear. "You know Belle, Harry, don't you?"

"I don't think I've had the pleasure," said Pfeiffer, taking Mrs. Shipley's hand.

"She don't hear you, Harry," said Shipley.

"I'm sorry, I don't hear well," said Mrs. Shipley. "Did you tell him about the accident, Billy?"

"She got her eardrums burst by an explosion in a Rome laundry. Ripped some of the ear off," and he raised one of the chrysanthemums to give Pfeiffer a glimpse of some blasted flesh. Mrs. Shipley stepped out of reach. "We were having tea next to this place, when 'Boom,' " and he slammed a fist into his palm. "They'll bust no more eardrums in that place. I'll tell you that."

"I'm very sorry, Mrs. Shipley," said Pfeiffer.

"She can't hear you," said Shipley. "Call her Belle."

"I'll get you something to drink," said Mrs. Shipley.

"Like hell you will," said Shipley, and he shouted, "Annetta!" and to Pfeiffer, "We pay the slut seven thousand francs a month."

The maid appeared, and Shipley said, "Scotch and water. Two," and he held up two fingers. "Lemonade. One," and he held up one.

Mrs. Shipley went to a corner with a magazine. Pfeiffer sat on a couch opposite Shipley on another.

"See this picture?" asked Shipley, pointing over his head to a small Utrillo street scene, dark under an unlit display light. "Comes with the place. It's by the modern Rembrandt, one of the reasons this damn place is costing me six hundred thousand francs a month. You know what? I had to draw on my New York salary twice last year. What do you think of that? I wrote Dolph about it. I said, 'Dolph, if you want the company to stay big over here, if you want your top men to give up their country and their homes and their friends so that the company can survive, then you got to treat the big men in a big way.' Expenses here won't cover a dog's cubbyhole, let alone the slut and a quack for Belle's drums. What are you making?"

Pfeiffer told him, adding a hundred each way.

"Not bad for a starter. Though I remember when I picked you up out of the gutter—" Pfeiffer had been on a fellowship at Columbia—"and put you into the office at thirty-five dollars a week, and you were so happy, you kissed my butt." Pfeiffer saw the warning signs of reminiscence, and settled back mournfully to shepherd his drink through it; he would not be offered another. At six, the maid came in to announce that dinner was served.

Shipley stopped in the middle of a sentence, shouted, "Belle," and when his wife looked up, jabbed a finger toward his open mouth. "Sorry you can't stay, Harry," he said, walking Pfeiffer to the door, arm around his shoulders. "Yes," he said just before he closed the door, "a man shouldn't have to leave his country just to save a few bucks to retire on. The old roots sting when they're cut. You stay over here a while, and you'll see, Harry."

Pfeiffer walked down the Champs Elysées, letting the music of a European dusk ease Shipley out of his head.

The next morning a cablegram came from Bellman: "With all his faults, Arnold Weber's good will, generosity, fairness, and great spirit quadrupled both financial and spiritual assets of the company. We are looking to you, Harry, to maintain the position he won for us. We believe you will do a grand job. Come home and take your family back with you. We will speak further in the office. Fondly, Dolph."

4

If he were to have reviewed his own accounts six months later, just before his first inspection tour of the Frankfurt office, Pfeiffer would have noted an ease he had not known since his student days. Established with wife and son in seven lovely rooms above the Etoile, served and guarded by a brisk French couple, he left for Germany without the trepidation he had felt at his departure for Europe. Watching his wife in her new Persian lamb coat standing by the car with little Henry to wave him off, Pfeiffer felt a confidence which would have steeled him for a trip through hell. Before he stepped on the plane, however, his wife called him back, clutched his arm, and said, *"Pass mal sehr gut auf, mein Lieber."*

"For what?" asked Pfeiffer sharply, "and anyway, Henry hears," for they never spoke German around little Henry. He kissed her goodbye again, and then bent to his son who jabbed at him with the little model of the Empire State Building which Bellman had sent him as a going-away present. "Goodbye, darling," said Pfeiffer, pushing the model away and kissing him.

His wife's warning had done something to Pfeiffer's confidence, and he could not help trembling as the plane circled over Frankfurt and came down at Rhein-Main. On the ground, he stared at the blue-coated officials who examined his traveling case. One of them said in better English than he himself spoke, "There are taxis over there, sir."

"Damn you to hell," thought Pfeiffer in even better English than the official's.

The German office turned out to be in fairly good shape, but not so good that within a week everyone in it didn't tremble when Herr Pfeiffer sounded the buzzer, for, though he was always polite, he harrowed the tiniest error and lashed the least culpable of its perpetrators.

At night, Pfeiffer went back to the Frankfurter Hof, had dinner, sat around the lobby for an hour reading the Paris edition of the *Herald Tribune,* and then went upstairs to bed. The second evening he had gone to a movie, but it was a comedy, and when he heard the audience laugh, he walked out. "Why should they laugh?" he asked himself.

He spent some time walking along the river down by the great Dom where the Emperors of the Holy Roman Empire had been crowned for centuries. Damaged, it stood alone amidst the rubble of those half-timbered Roemer houses which Pfeiffer remembered as the prettiest in Frankfurt. He was not unpleased by the destruction. On the other hand, he was not displeased by the construction projects going on over most of the city. "They can begin again too," was his notion.

During the second week of his stay, Pfeiffer began to eat dinner with his Frankfurt secretary, Fräulein Uta von Bensheimer, and her American boyfriend, Jimmy, who worked for Hicog, the State Department apparatus in Germany. They spoke German, for Jimmy spoke it better than Pfeiffer English, although he hadn't known a word when he'd come over three years ago.

Fräulein von Bensheimer was a German type Pfeiffer had never known, a most charming aristocrat, restrained, yet witty, and splendidly at ease. Sometimes, however, the ease became a kind of looseness Pfeiffer wouldn't have believed possible in a girl of her type and training. Once she reminded Jimmy that he had failed to buy a new bed for them. "The one we have now is so hard, and it squeaks terribly," she explained to Pfeiffer.

Pfeiffer began to feel that such looseness was an important element in the new Germany. Everywhere he looked there were signs of it. The newsstands were crowded with Physical Culture magazines in which nudes flexed themselves for prurient cameras. The conversation along the Königstrasse was often ripped by smutty hilarity, and not just from the numerous prostitutes—harder faced than any he'd ever seen—who strutted there with GIs from the casernes around the Farben building.

Despite the many augurs and present signs of material prosperity, this looseness helped Pfeiffer decide that the Germans were really finished; he saw the laughter and smut as the marks of their uneasy presentiment of the end.

He began talking frankly about these matters to Jimmy and Uta. They were understanding, sympathetic. Indeed it was Uta who suggested that he make the trip to Bebelshausen before he returned to Paris. "Who knows that this will not provide an antidote to your discomfort. Maybe it will help heal the awful scars that are making you so unhappy. If you can only bridge the terrible years, who knows what you will think then?"

She and Jimmy offered to drive him down, but he decided to go with the company chauffeur, and that Saturday he found himself in the Mercedes speeding down the Rhine and into the Würtemberg hills to Bebelshausen. He had returned in somewhat this fashion in not a few dreams.

Although it had been shelled, Bebelshausen seemed basically unchanged. Many of the houses and stores were completely familiar to Pfeiffer, and once or twice, he felt the fearful excitement of recognizing a face. He passed by his old school—it was a shell—and the woods—half-stripped—where he used to play and where he had first made love. He directed the driver down the road to his house.

It was no longer there, just a bare lot he might have missed if it hadn't been for the pair of oak trees which had shaded the west side of the house, and where, in summer, they had put up, American-style, a great hammock. "Thank God," he thought, seeing that the trees had been spared. He climbed out of the car, limped up to them, sat down facing the river, and looked between the hills where knots of smoke from the thermometer factory untied themselves in the Rhine breeze. Then, in the smaller tree, he saw his initials, HP, carved four feet from the ground. The strain of fifteen years eased suddenly from his heart, and Pfeiffer burst into a kind of teary groaning which caused the chauffeur to look first toward and then away from him.

That night he tried to tell Uta and Jimmy about what had happened to him; he managed to say enough to enable them to pronounce his experience an important one.

That he knew. He had come back home, and what counted

was still there. His country's misery was a version of his own; he saw in her looseness and silly posturing the awkward attempts to atone for the misery she had madly inflicted in her fifteen-year exile from European sanity.

He returned to Paris with a confidence he had only masked before his trip. When he told his wife about his discoveries, she said that she would go with him on his next visit, and they even decided to take little Henry. During the conversation, they slipped into German, even though the little boy was in the room building the Tour Eiffel with his blocks.

The next weeks in Paris were the happiest of their lives. They went to the theater and found they could follow it with ease. De Roubain introduced them to some French and Spanish friends with whom they traded dinner parties, and they began planning all sorts of trips around their recovered Europe. It was at the summit of pleasure that the cable came from Bellman.

> Arnold Weber in full recovery of his full powers after elec-
> trotherapy (shock treatment). Wishes to join me, and whole
> company, in thanking you for holding the fort in his absence.
> On return to New York you will find more tangible expres-
> sion of our gratitude in weekly envelopes. With sincerest
> best wishes to you and entire family, Adolph Bellman.

It wasn't until he was two days into the Atlantic that Pfeiffer thought to himself, "Maybe I should have stayed," but by then it was too late, and a little later he even wondered whether he had meant "stayed in Europe" or "America."

East, West . . . Midwest

*Alas, we Mongols are brought up from
childhood to shoot arrows . . . Such a habit is
not easy to lay aside.*

> —CHINGHIS KHAN, March 1223

a small thing, lightly killed

> —AESCHYLUS, *Agamemnon*

1

BIDWELL, a man like many, woefully incomplete and
woefully ignorant of it, was, this Christmas Day, worse off than
usual. Hong Kong flu. "The latest installment," as his usually
quiet, usually uncomplaining wife put it, "of Asian vengeance."
Bidwell's single scholarly contribution to her domestic arsenal:
an essay on the Pendulum of Revenge which had swung between East and West since the thirteenth century.

"One more trip up these stairs"—carting iced grape juice to
his bedside—"and your Genghis can notch up another casualty."

"Chinghis," corrected Bidwell, part-time historian of the
Mongols. Their second-oldest exchange.

"Historian, journalist, translator," as he listed himself in
Who's Who in the Midwest, Bidwell was functioning in none of
these roles when Miss Cameron called that Christmas afternoon
four years to the hour since she'd first shown herself to be what
she'd had to be put away for. Not up to Chinghis, not up to

Christmas games, and certainly not up to Miss Cameron, he was reading old letters in bed when the phone rang at his elbow.

He identified the dead voice between "Mis" and "ter."

"Mr. Bidwell?"

"Speaking."

"This is Freddy Cameron."

"Miss Cameron. Goodness me. How are you?"

"Better."

"I'm so glad."

"How are you?"

"Not too great. Got the flu. Can't shake it. Been in and out of bed for two weeks. You get it, you get over it, and you get it again. They call it the camelback."

"I'm sorry." And oddly, the voice, rising from death, was full of sorrow, no formula. Bidwell had her narrow, foal's head in mind, could see it narrowing more in genuine, illegitimately genuine sorrow. He was still the unwilling usurper of feeling which belonged to those who had denied her. These victims of deniers. How many millions had suffered for that cangue the fifteen-year-old Chinghis-Khan, Temüjin then, had dragged from yurt to yurt month after month. "Thank you."

"I wanted to talk to you."

"Yes."

"I mean." The pause which asked him to say her piece, but only the wronged dead could make such wordless demands. "See you."

"Would that be right, Miss Cameron?"

"I don't know."

"Mightn't it trouble you again?"

"Yes."

"Shouldn't you ask your doctor?"

"All right. If it's all right with him, will it be all right with you?"

"I think so. Soon as I shake this flu. Though it looks like a bad bet. You're up, you're down, you're up, you're down."

"Thank you. When?"

"When?"

"When can I call you about it?"

"I should be O.K. in a week or ten days. Maybe two weeks. Say three. You can call me at *Midland*."

"I'm sorry I called you at home."

" 'Tsall right. I'm glad to know you're better. And while we're at it, Merry Christmas, Miss Cameron."

"Yes. You too."

"So long, then."

"Yes. So long."

Thirty feet up on the third floor of the old brick house, Bidwell opened window and storm window, scooped snow from the cottonwood branch he'd failed to trim that fall, and brought it to his boiled forehead. Could all relief be so simple.

This Christmas week, the astronauts Anders, Borman, and Lovell were looping the moon in Apollo Eight, but down here, thought Bidwell, down here, even the fish are begging us to let up. Featured in Sunday's *Midland,* the coho salmon loaded with the DDT washed from its plant-louse-killing jobs in Indiana and Illinois. The pendulum of ecological revenge. Oil, bled from underwater shale, burst its iron veins and ruined the shores where the stockholders of Gulf and Humble lay on their dividends. Pigs and cattle, murdered for their chops, loosed lethal fat into the arteries of their eaters. Chicago, named by a smell-shocked Ojibway sniffing the wild-onion tracts, stank with the sulfurous coal palmed off in arm-twisting contracts. The air, the lake, where a trillion silver skeletons rotted forty miles of shoreline (the starved alewives washed in with the opening of the locked interior by the St. Lawrence Seaway). Out Bidwell's windows, north, south, west, the locked slums, leaking vengeance on those who'd locked them there. "A fifth of American color television sets are dangerously radioactive," last Sunday's feature in *Midland,* and there, sucking poison into their cells with Garfield Goose, his little boys, Josh and Petey. In fury, Bidwell called Sears, threatened them with a follow-up story in *Midland,* and in two hours, a redheaded engineer, Swanson, zoomed up from the Loop, in hand two thousand-dollar boxes, scintillators whose needles reported his boys safe. Safe, that is, said Swanson, until the gaseous regulator tube broke down, and the voltage soared to transmit reds, greens, and blues.

The classic hang-ups of the twentieth-century burgher, and they were Bidwell's; in spades, for they were also the staff of his Sunday supplement's life.

And now, his very own pestilence, Miss Cameron. Obsessed, frenzied, the great mechanism of perception wild with unreality. A pair of legs, a pair of ears, a pair—he supposed—of breasts, all the paraphernalia of a reasonable woman, and then, above the neck, behind the eyes, between the ears, a loose nut. Back to the factory. But no, the factory turned her loose, and now so did the repair shop, and once more she was after him who had nothing, next to nothing, to do with her.

This Christmas week, between bouts of chills and fever, Bidwell worked on the Christmas Day of 1241, when Batu, Chinghis-Khan's grandson, crossed the iced Danube and battered the town of Esztergom. Europe, a small island of feudal civility, hung by a thread. Batu's armies had wiped out Kiev, Ryazan, Moscow, Bolgar, Vladimir, and Pest. There was nothing to stop them but the immobile, tanklike knights of Hungary. Then, Christmas Day, Batu got the news his uncle Ögödei, the Kha-kan, had died, and back he turned. Europe was saved, as it would be saved by such threads for three centuries, until its sea power flanked the masters of the Eurasian landmass and began that great rise of the West, which, this very Christmas week of 1968—as its feet were chilled by Eastern threat—reached the moon itself. A distance which should annul the old divisiveness of the world. A great story.

For years Bidwell had published bits of it in the *Harvard Journal of Asiatic Studies,* the *Abhandlung für die Kunde des Morgenlandes,* and the *Journal asiatique.* Austere, careful stud-ies, but Bidwell had literary ambition, and in mind a fine book like Mattingly's on the Armada or Runciman's on the Sicilian Vespers, a work Josh and Petey would see on general reading lists, not merely in footnotes. This ambition went against the grain of his graduate training, but there it was, a desire to shape data into coherent stories which would serve men who counted as models and guides. All right, such stories were formed by fashion and lived by style, but they were what deepened life. Didn't Chinghis, didn't all heroes, live and die by them?

Sweat poured into the blue clocks of his flannel pajamas; he pulled the great quilt about his chilled bones. Mind adrift be-tween the Mongols and Apollo Eight, Bidwell felt the Great Divide in things. The lunar odyssey had its elegant technology and its political-commercial hoopla. Its heroes were no Hectors, no Chinghises, only burghers like himself, bolstered by exercise and the great American confidence in mechanic triumph.

Where did he, Bidwell, stand with these Moon Loopers?

They were the stuff his sort made sense of, the titles of books his sort wrote. Their risks were somatic, his mental; they moved in space, he time.

They lived like finely tooled nuts in a great machine. And how would they die? They had no choice. Bidwell's subject, Chinghis-Khan, had constructed his death, had planned the extermination of the Tanguts, chosen his successor, and then moved north of the Wei to the cool air of the Kansu mountains. No wonder the Mongol bards rose to their great epic; Chinghis had worked his life out as a poem.

Yet the astronauts too were controlled by story. Christmas Eve, they read Genesis to earth as sunlight poured on the lunar crust. Bidwell, fever rising, back troubled by a mattress button he was too weak to rip off or shift away from, felt their voices fuse with the racket of his children.

Human buzz.

What did human enterprise come to, great or small?

Commotion.

The fever drifted him, Bidwell scraped bottom, felt himself buzzing off like an old bulb.

They were all going to have to make it on their own. Ethel, Batu, Chinghis, Josh, Petey, Shiffrin (his boss at *Midland*).

They'd feel the void he left. Yes, but then augment their own emotional capital with it. Functioning men wasted nothing. What could be more ornamental than young widowhood, the loss of a father, a friend?

Sig Schlein would look through his manuscripts, decide what could be salvaged for articles, and wrap up his bibliographical life with an elegiac paragraph in the *HJAS*. A few sheets of paper, a few feet of earth, a few real, a few crocodile tears, and Farewell Bidwell.

And for years, maybe, Farewell Batu and the other Mongol chiefs whose ghosts he'd animated. Though they could take it better than he. Their bloody deeds were on record, his own lay mostly hidden, some in his boys' heads, to be disinterred on couches fifteen years from now (if people were still buying that paregoric). "My descendants will wear gold cloth, feed on tender meat, ride proud horses, press the most beautiful young women in their arms . . . and they will have forgotten to whom they owe it all." August 18, 1227: Farewell Chinghis. Buzz and bitter lemons. December 24, 1968: Farewell Bidwell.

A bad night.

But somehow, by morning, he'd outflanked the flu-dazed grip on his life. A silver band showed beneath the shade. Christmas morning. "Time, Daddy."

Weak, but clear-headed, Bidwell in his sweat-damp clocked pajamas, led Ethel and the boys toward the Scotch pine on their green *tayga* of carpet, where lay, scattered like Chinghis's victims, packages of every color and shape.

The geometry of burgher dreams.

2

Back in 1964, Bidwell was translating extracts from the *Secret History of the Mongols* for the University of Minnesota Press. The *Midland* typing pool sent up a girl who did extra work at home.

Miss Cameron. Five and a half feet of long-faced timidity, hands crossed before her parts, eyes down, though sneaking up when she thought his weren't. Yes, she did extra typing, she would be happy to do his manuscript.

He gave her a short section about the kidnapping of Temü-jin's wife Börte by the Merkit warrior who impregnated her. Miss Cameron brought it back the next day, a fine job. He gave her the rest of the manuscript, about a hundred pages.

A week, ten days, two weeks, and there was no word from her. The typing pool said she hadn't called in and, furthermore, had no telephone. They assumed she was sick. She lived on the edge of the Lawndale ghetto. The Friday before Christmas, Bidwell drove fearfully on the shattered rim of the slum and rang the doorbell of her apartment.

She came downstairs, and when she saw him through the glass, a small hand went to her small chest. "I'm very sorry," she said, opening up. "I've been sick."

He told her not to worry, he'd been concerned about her as well as his manuscript.

A smile showed a half-second on raw lips. Physics had cloud chambers for such short-lived states. What self-distrust killed such smiles? Miss Cameron's long hair, a dull red, shook about her narrow shoulders. Cold? Fear? Negation? "I'm almost done with it. Do you want what I have?"

In her dead voice, these words hung all sorts of interrogation before Bidwell. He wanted nothing from Miss Cameron but what he'd paid for.

"I'll wait till you finish. Can I bring you anything? Food? Medicine?" There was a deep barrenness in the stairwell. Miss Cameron was as stranded as the old moon. "No, thanks," she had everything. "Goodbye," and sorry she caused him so much worry. "I can't remember why I didn't call. I didn't know so much time had passed."

Monday she brought in the typescript. There were hundreds of mistakes in it, omitted paragraphs, garbled sentences. He had the whole thing redone by another girl in the pool, but said nothing to Miss Cameron, only thanked and paid her.

That Christmas afternoon, he answered the phone.

"Why did you?" asked the dead voice.

"Excuse me."

"You had no right."

"Miss Cameron?"

"You shouldn't have done it."

"Please tell me what's wrong."

"You know." Sly and accusatory, new sound in the monotone. "You know."

"Look," said Bidwell, "let me get a doctor for you. You're not in good shape."

"No." A wail. "No. Tell me why you stood at the window. Naked you were. Pudgy you are. Yet had your way. With me." Then fiercely, "It's you should see a doctor." The phone banged.

Bidwell rang up his analyst neighbor, Spitzer, told him what happened, asked if the girl sounded suicidal or homicidal.

"Probably not," said Spitzer. "She's having an episode. Happens frequently on Christmas. Or Sundays. The routine's broken, there's nothing to intrude on the fantasy. Can you get hold of her parents? Or some relative?"

Bidwell knew nothing about her, he'd have to wait till the office opened in two days, then he could check with Personnel.

"You could call the police," said Spitzer, "but I don't advise it. The girl's called you because she's got it into her head that you're important to her. If you bring the police, it'll confirm the worst of her fears. Don't worry. She won't hurt anyone. And she won't throw herself out the window."

(False prophet Spitzer. Though it was four years off.)

That night, the phone jangled him from sleep.

"St. Stephen's Day, Mr. Bidwell."

"Oh, Lord. Miss Cameron. What?"

"I must see you. You came again. The scale fell from you. Devil. At the window. Yet it can't be. I'm so, so, so mixed up. Please see me?"

St. Stephen's Day. Every year they went to Sig Schlein's Boxing Day party. "Today?"

"Please."

"Where? Not at your place. Wouldn't be right."

She would come uptown, they could meet at Pixley and Ehler's on Randolph opposite the public library. It would save him miles.

This was rational, she was aware of him. All right, he'd be there at ten-thirty. Pixley and Ehler's. How did she pick it? Chicago's Olympus of the radical thirties. His boyhood. Thick buns frosting in the windows, bums mixing with scholars from the Crerar Library upstairs, the filthy classic hulk of the Chicago Public Library across the street.

At ten-thirty there was no one at the round tables but a bum dipping a cruller into coffee.

Bidwell waited at one of the tables with a pot of tea till Miss Cameron swung open the doors. In a cloth coat which didn't seem up to stopping frost, hardly enough to contain her, and hatless, the red hair like thread laid over a counter to be woven for something more useful than itself. The long face, beak-nosed, chapped, pale, eyes a clouded blue and looking as if stuck in at the last moment, full of haste and hurt. Her progress to his table was a drift. Then, arriving, head down, she said, "Thank you."

For coming? For existing? For not being something contrived by her brain and found nowhere else?

"Miss Cameron, I came to persuade you to let me take you to a hospital."

The raw face slapped against her palm. "God," it said. She sat down.

"Miss Cameron. Tell me what I can do for you."

The face faltered, thickened, grew inward, the eyes cleared, lit with what he had not seen there before. "Have you not killed the devil's warrior for my bed, Temüjin? What a question."

Wednesday morning. Chicago. Nineteen-sixty-four. Women pouring out of the IC tunnel where Capone had had Jake Lingle, the diamond-belted go-between, shot to death, the news dealers calling out Lyndon Johnson's Christmas menu on the ranch, the bum lapping his cruller, and here this frail cup of girl's flesh thought itself the bride of Chinghis-Khan, eight hundred years and fifteen thousand miles away.

"It's just me, Bidwell, Miss Cameron. It's nineteen-sixty-four, and you're Miss Cameron, somewhat unwell, and you typed the manuscript about Chinghis and Börte for me, and I think it's confused you."

Her face blinked. Bidwell could make out the present taking over her face, a hard march through swamps, but she made it, she nodded. Up and down went the foal's head. "I know," and as he was about to welcome this with "Good," the face blinked again, the smashed eyes said, "But he told me."

"What?"

"At the window," she said with her small wail. "He said you'd take me back, though Jaghatay was in my belly. Here," and a thin hand came from her lap to the brown middle of the coat to show the unlikely presence of Börte's son.

Bidwell, a weight of misery in his own stomach, found nothing to say. Her head rose and fell, his went from side to side.

"Yes," she said, the face blinking again. "I know it's in my head." Which now pendulumed like his.

Bidwell, knowing, even as he did it, that a risk was in it, covered her small hand with his gloved one.

"Gawd," she moaned. The head twisted away from its stem, her body, rising, followed it. Before Bidwell could get his bearings, she was into Randolph Street, red head down, ramming the cold air.

3

By the time he'd gotten her personnel file and located a mother who lived in Evanston, she'd called to apologize and request another meeting.

"All right," he said, his campaign formed. "At the same place."

Where, not Bidwell, but mother and mother's priest came with a car. Miss Cameron was wrapped up and taken to the Sisters of Mercy in Milwaukee, "not," said Spitzer, "a great center of treatment, but they'll be kind to her, and she'll be off the streets."

Eight months later, Bidwell received a letter in green ink.

Dear Mr. Bidwell,
    I know I caused you trouble. My mind troubled. The man at the window—was it not you? I would say it was real, though I know you could not have been at such a place. But did you not mean it for me? Sitting there with your glasses, so kindly, why not? The world thinks Genghis a monster, but you showed me how in bad times, he drank his saliva and ate his gums, slept on his elbow and saved his Börte. Did you not mean me to know I was to you what Börte was to him? I cannot quite straiten it out. But remain
Very truly yours,
(Miss) Frederick Cameron

4

Monday, January 15, 1968, three weeks to the day after she'd called, Miss Cameron rang him at *Midland.* He was having his weekly fight with Shiffrin, the editor. His junior by ten years, a classic Chicago newsman out of the City News Bureau and the *American,* Shiffrin had married meat money and put some of it into the sinking *Midland.* Hard, thin, a board of a man, Bidwell called him Giacometti. "A face like a cheese knife," he said to Ethel. "When it comes at you, you think it'll slice you in half. And his ideas are narrower than his face."

Shiffrin was on top of whatever was on top, but for him that meant what appeared in the newspapers of St. Louis, Milwaukee, Minneapolis, and Chicago, with dollops of *Time* and *Newsweek* for intellectual debauches. "You should be reading the tech and business mags," Bidwell told him the first week, but Shiffrin was unable to detach the text from the ads in *Avia-*

tion Week, and besides, the mere sight of a technical word blanked him out of consciousness.

When Miss Cameron's call came, they were having a shouting match about a piece on the students. Bidwell had listed twenty different issues raised by the world's students, the lighting system at Prague Tech., the language question at Louvain and Calcutta, football at Grambling, political issues at Hamburg and Berkeley. To this he'd attached a tail of explanations from commentators, Aron, Howe, Feuer, McLuhan, and a handful of college presidents. A rapid, agitated surface, but it covered lots of ground and let the pancake-sodden readers of the supplement get an idea of the complexity of the matter.

To Shiffrin, it was Bidwell's usual academic glop which turned every second piece he touched "into the *Britannica.*"

Of course, he was right, was always right. To most of their readers, Joey Bishop was Einstein, the amount of information that could be ladled out in any one story should not exceed a recipe for French toast. If Bidwell hadn't been there since the Year One, and if he didn't do good rewrite jobs, Shiffrin would have bounced him.

"Look, find some little spade chick on the Circle campus, let her yack away half a column, then get some yid prof to yack up the other half, a few pictures, and we got our story. Save this truckload of cobwebs for the *Atlantic Monthly.*" Which is more or less the way it would work out, and another issue would be ready to wrap Monday's fish.

Bidwell took the call from the switchboard in middispute. "Mr. Bidwell?"

The whirl in the office subsided, hung. "Oh, yes, Miss Cameron. How are you?"

"I'm fine. You said I could call you."

"That's right."

Shiffrin's black eyes bounced off his cruel nose and moved skyward. Then finger-snapping.

"I'm afraid it's not a good time, though. I'm in conference."

"Finish up," said Shiffrin. "Nail the nookie, and let's get shaking. It's sixteen to press," meaning sixteen hours till their press roll.

"Call in half an hour," said Bidwell and hung up. "If you had nookie like that, you'd turn monk."

Shiffrin's wife weighed in at a hundred and sixty pounds, all vocal, he ran through the secretarial staff with his agitated wand, overpromising, underperforming, he understood women trouble. "Professors like you working me to the grave, I'm ape now."

This last week, Bidwell had been writing up Ye-lü Ch'u-ts'ai's revelation to Chinghis that it would be better to regard towns as resources rather than pools of infection, a great moment of generous truth in the Mongol world and the never-ending education of the Khan. All right, he, Bidwell, would make the best of Shiffrin.

He arranged to meet Miss Cameron in Pixley and Ehler's.

Four years later, the Crerar was gone to I.I.T., but the buns and the bums were still there. And Miss Cameron too, about the same, the long face bent over two cups. No smile to meet his, but her look was relaxed, even intimate.

He shook hands, his bare, hers gloved. Their flesh had still not touched. Which Bidwell knew counted, though not how. "And," weeks later, "what could I have done?"

"Thank you for coming."

"You're looking well."

Which brought blush and smile. The body gets simpler near the surface. Its economy there offers small variety to register the terrific feelings beneath. Bidwell could but guess the recrudescent girlishness of Miss Cameron's smile, not coyness, no, only simple pleasure in the situation which the inner time of derangement had kept from the years. "You haven't changed," he said, meaning the standard compliment.

"I hope I have." A remark in clock time, and its own evidence. "It's why I wanted to see you. To show you I understand how wild I was."

Was this all?

He sat down to a cup of tea, continuation of the cup he'd drunk four years before, but bought by her for whom his taste was absolute.

Bidwell, fleshy head given jots of youth by the frost, civil tonsure indulged at the sides and back in concession to style and barber's prices, had now a vagueness of feeling, seeing in this half-smiling, pale person not only an old trouble but also a not-bad, if thin, woman's body.

"Your trouble seems to be over."

"Mostly over."

"Still have bad times?"

"Now and then. I don't drink now."

"I didn't know you did that."

"Once a week, I'd really lush up. Now I sit tight."

Bidwell eased off his overcoat, stuck his scarf in his sleeve. Like most Pixley customers, Miss Cameron kept on what she'd come in with. Who knew when quick hands would grab? He should have seen this as trouble.

"What can I do for you?"

"You are," said Miss Cameron. "Seeing you. That's all. Just this. And to talk to you every once in a while."

The strange creep of human feeling. Unable to stay put. Could he find pleasure on that thin chest? What would pass between Pudgy and Miss Giacometti?

"I suppose that's all right, Miss Cameron. It's not a hard way to help someone."

"You're a good person."

"Not really. It's habit. Laziness. Though, you know, I probably can't see you once a week. But we can certainly talk on the phone. Maybe on Thursdays. That's an easy day at the office. Then, every once in a while, we can meet here."

Which created her schedule, her life.

Every Thursday after he came back from lunch, Bidwell would answer the phone and talk with Miss Cameron about her health, her work—she did part-time secretarial work at Northwestern—and her reading—she was going through Will Durant, had been in *The Oriental Heritage* since the day after their first meeting. Once a month, they met in Pixley and Ehler's at five o'clock and drank tea for an hour.

The Thursday after their fourth and last meeting, the telephone did not ring. Bidwell waited uncomfortably, felt its silence, felt the absence of that dead—though somewhat revived—voice. Ah, well, she was out of town, sick, at a movie, or, true revival, she'd faced down her madness, seen through the old delusion.

The next day's *Sun-Times,* though, showed something else. At the time of her usual call, Miss Cameron was jumping out of the tenth-floor window of the Playboy Building on North Michigan Avenue. The first such occurrence there, clearly a dramatic one, for Miss Cameron had, as far as was known, no business in the building. Other than the melancholy one therein reported. She'd been seen by an elevator operator at lunchtime, "While most came down, she went up," and then, when the rest came up, she took the quick route down.

The famous owner of the building couldn't be reached for comment, but a spokesman said the girl was a mental patient, perhaps the building was chosen as a deranged protest or symbol, but, of course, there was nothing to be done about that. Most of the building's windows didn't even open; the woman had found a janitor's storeroom and even then had to climb up on a trash can and smash the window with the nozzle of a fire extinguisher.

A small thing, lightly killed.

Bidwell was, of course, very upset, but the week passed, he worked on Chinghis-Khan's eradication of the Tanguts and did not think of Miss Cameron; except the next Thursday, when the silence of the telephone stirred him, and that night, when the garage door shut behind his Pontiac and he was alone the usual few seconds in the dark.

What a death the poor narrow thing had constructed for herself. No campaign, no successor, no trip to the cool mountains, only an elevator ride, a smashed window, an untelephoned farewell: "This is it. I can't ask you anymore. Let alone by phone."

In Return

WALTERS had been in Kyoto four or five times, but only one time counted for him. The other times he'd come for conferences and stayed in the hotels—the Miyako, the International —and hardly got outside. There'd been tours of the Imperial and Nijo Palaces, a walk through the Katsura gardens and an hour at Gion Corner for snippets of puppet drama, tea ceremony, *gagaku* music, and flower arrangement; there'd also been a couple of hours in a nightclub where girls dressed as apes mounted each other. He'd been too tired for curiosity, let alone excitement. What tired him, what counted then and always, was serious business seriously conducted. Even failed business succeeded as part of larger schemes: definition of ends and relationships as they altered from administration to administration.

Walters had worn several hats: Assistant Secretary in the Commerce Department; negotiator for Bechtel and the Chase Bank; and, for the last six years, Assistant Secretary for Economic Affairs in the State Department. In four decades of professional life, there'd been fifty-odd conferences in Japan alone.

Almost never, though, had he spent time there on his own. The *almost* was accounted for by five days in the summer of 1973. By himself—with next-to-no official assistance—he'd stayed in a small Japanese inn near the Kodaiji Temple in Kyoto. He couldn't remember now who had told him about the place or who had made the arrangements, but he remembered that he'd taken the *shinkansen* from Tokyo Station and called Mrs. Fukuma from the one in Kyoto. A slender woman with thick black hair and a smile so full of sweetness he'd remembered it as well as anything else, she had met his taxi at the temple and led him through small streets to her small inn. It was why, fourteen years later, he was back, once again taking time out of a life in which there was very little time to be out.

Walters was most at home at work. (His wife Dorothy's explanation for this was "Some people look better frowning.") A problem solver, problems were Walters' pleasure. (The more impersonal the problem, the better he liked it.) A bit of paternal and connubial motion persuaded even those who counted that he was a good father and husband. He was, he knew, a lucky one. (Walters disliked confessions but had heard enough to know how lucky.) Dorothy was charming, civil, amusing, brave, loyal, and loving. What he most loved about her was the similarity of her public and private selves. "She's of a piece," he told their daughter Laura. *"Integer vitae.* Is that the Latin for it?" One reason their marriage functioned well—both felt this —was that unlike many official wives she didn't come with him on business trips. Or on the rare occasion when she flew with him, she'd sight-see, shop and socialize on her own. Their schedules were distinct; they might see each other at breakfast or at supper, but there was no pressure to do that. If they did, it was—usually—a bonus. "We don't lean on each other," was their boast. He told Laura, "We're parallel lines, which make a track on which your life has rolled along reasonably well. Is that too fancy?" (Laura herself had had less luck: her second marriage had just gone off the track.)

"I'd like to see that Kyoto *ryokan* of yours," Dorothy said out of the blue when he told her about the next Tokyo conference. "Would you have time or shall I go myself?"

It came out that she thought she better go while she was still spry enough to sleep and eat on the floor and to rise without cracking her joints. Fifty-four, and no athlete, she was limber, walked miles, swam, lifted things, and worked in the garden.

Walters hadn't thought of going back to the inn. He wasn't much on sentimental returns, preferred to keep his better memories untested. Still, bits of fatigue floated in him; it had been a difficult winter, why not take a few days off? Kyoto was a good place to do it.

He had the Embassy find out if the *ryokan* was functioning, and if Fukuma-san was still there. It was, she was.

Even in the Department, there were opposing views about the Japanese. Products of several thousand insular years, their contradictions—arrogance and humility, courtesy and rudeness, generosity and niggardliness, originality and lack of it, xenophilia and xenophobia—signaled to some a mentality incomprehensible to Westerners or even other Easterners. There were people who had spent thirty years in Japan who said they had no Japanese friends and no idea what went on in a single Japanese head; there were others, some who knew the language and some who didn't, who felt the Japanese were exactly the same as everybody else with the same problems; Westerners would understand them as soon as they understood the problems.

The contradictions were also topographical, architectural, and physical. There were the glass, steel and concrete skyscrapers, and there were the little shrines with their curling roofs, the wooden plaques with the kanji inscriptions, the trees filled with blossoms and white prayers knotted on the branches. There was the terrific noise, the loud public announcements and police commands, and then the quiet of gardens, the small, carless streets, the noiseless electronics of light and motion. There was the bulky male strut and the demure, in-turned delicacy of the traditional woman.

The country had survived the endless eruptions whose deposits were its ubiquitous mountains. No wonder the holiest holy place was Fujiyama. Walters and Dorothy saw it, perfectly symmetrical and snow capped, from the hotel room, and for much of the trip to Kyoto, they'd seen it swell and spread, green beneath its creamy top. Dorothy had bought a book of Hokusai's, *Thirty-Six Views of Fuji,* full of charming scenes from Edo markets, Shinto prayer wickets, and the mountain itself. The most beautiful was one called *Red Fuji,* the mountain a triangular ember in the clear air. To convert the fearful—climbers were still regularly killed in Fuji avalanches—into the sacred, a subject of lithographs and *haiku,* wasn't that *pure Japanese*?

Whatever that was. That it was *something,* though, most Japanese believed. Department experts were full of this subject. *Nihon-jin-ron,* the theory of Japanese uniqueness, was related by some to the mastery of the difficult language and the complex cerebral work this required. Some Japanese intellectuals, the *hyo-ronka,* carried the theory around Japan's dangerous new prosperity. Their chief antipathy was the *shin-jen-ron,* the *new human being,* the soft Westernized idler adrift in a floating world whose key word was *tsu-kei-sute,* "disposable."

Erikson, a Japanese deskman, had written out these words for Walters and given him this brief course in Japanese singularity. Walters took it, as he took much expertise, skeptically. Without knowing a word of Japanese and next to no Japanese history, he'd negotiated with Japanese officials and businessmen for decades and had come away with hundreds of agreements on everything from whaling rights to silicon chips. Of course, there was a special style of negotiation, many levels of authority and deference, there were "concessions" that weren't concessions, "agreements" that weren't agreements, there was even the excitement of a signed agreement which was sometimes a systematic postponement. Still, once you got used to all this, it had an agreeable, piquant quality, as special as bonsai trees or a Japanese inn.

The conference finished late, but the fast trains from Tokyo Station left every fifteen minutes. When he and Dorothy arrived in Kyoto, it was dark and cold. Walters showed Fukuma-san's address to the taxi driver. Still there was some difficulty finding it; it was not well known. The driver circled blocks and finally called Fukuma-san for directions. A cold rain started. They drove a block and saw Fukuma-san running under an umbrella. She was in kimono, slippers, and white socks. Walters remembered the sweet, barely lined face. She did not—of course—appear to remember him. Why should she?

The de-robing and de-shoeing at the entrance were complicated by bags and overcoats. Walters had forgotten how low the
ceilings were, how fragile the walls and floor. He and Dorothy
were upstairs in two rooms, one filled with their sleeping pads
and quilts, the larger with the almost-legless table beside which
were the *zabuton* cushions and low-backed legless seats. Each
room was more or less warmed by a gas heater.

The cold was the first problem. The Western bath and toilet
were downstairs. Dorothy could do without a bath, but she did
not like the Japanese toilet. A hole in the floor asked her body
to do what it wasn't used to; disgust followed discomfort. If she'd
been in the woods, she would have adjusted, but she wasn't and
didn't. To go down the cold corridor and stairs to the Western
toilet disturbed her.

Then too, Fukuma-san was noiselessly in and out of rooms and
bathrooms. At least parts of her were. A kimonoed arm, towel
draped over it, would appear. After a knock they barely heard,
Fukuma-san entered with bows, smiles, bowls of tea, and small
dishes of soaked rice and fish. "I suppose the idea is that service
is invisible," said Dorothy. (This was her form of complaint.)

In 1973 what had counted for Walters was the inn's tranquillity. Sitting cross-legged in his kimono on the tatami, back
against the *tokonoma* alcove, he'd looked out at a twisted
gingko tree abloom with gold flowers. It had seemed part of the
room. After a hot bath in the steep tub, he'd been profoundly
relaxed. Fukuma-san would bring him newspapers, maps of
Kyoto and Nara, tea, fish, biscuits; she'd adjusted the fan, shown
him the radio, the English books. The feeling was that he could
have anything he wanted.

It had been a long time—no, more than that—it was the first
time he could remember being actively contemplative without
a specific problem. He'd logged time on beaches, rocking chairs,
and hammocks, but the leisure of the *ryokan* was different.
He'd thought it might have something to do with the room's
subtle bareness, the interaction of outside and inside.

For that ease, and for the courtesy and grace which created
it, he'd come back. Now, though, it was March, not August.
Paper shutters screened them from the dark exterior. They
were enclosed with gas heaters, bag racks, and clothing hooks
(had these been here in 1973?); and between their rooms was the

cold corridor. There was still beauty, the *tokonoma* with its blue vase, a mural screen of cicadas on a blooming branch, the tatami; and there was Fukuma-san who plied them with delicate constancy. More tea? Biscuits? Hot bath? Shower? And what time would they like breakfast? Did they prefer Western or Japanese?

Walters hadn't remembered her asking anything in 1973.

Their reservation was for four days. When he turned out the light in the sleeping room, Dorothy said, "I think we'd better leave tomorrow."

"I suppose so," he said. ("Oh, my," he thought. "What will Fukuma-san think?") Her last appearance had been with the house guestbook. "Would prease sign?" She held the large book for them with the inquisitive deference that seemed an apology for existence. For Walters, the gesture conjured up that diplomatic delicacy which he admired even when it frustrated negotiations. Under the last name in the book, "Toby Jenkins, Hong Kong, Jan. 15, 1987," Walter wrote, "Mr. and Mrs. H. L. Walters. March 8, 1987." Unless there were guests who didn't, wouldn't or couldn't sign their names, the Walters were Fukuma-san's first guests in almost two months. "I'm sorry it didn't work out, Dorothy."

"I too, dear. I'm sure the place is wonderful in summer. And I'm glad I've seen what you loved."

Walters was up before seven. He washed up downstairs in the bathroom, where a kimonoed arm appeared with a fresh towel and a fluty "Good mooring. Hope srept we'?"

"Very well, thank you, Fukuma-san." Though he was a bit startled by the be-kimonoed, vocal arm.

"And missus? Eat now?"

"I think she'll sleep a while. *I'd* love some breakfast."

When the trayful of boiled eggs, rice gruel, dishes of vegetal and doughy oddities and tea appeared, he said, "I'm afraid we have to cut short our stay in Kyoto, Fukuma-san. It's a shame to have had so little time, but it's been lovely to see you again. Did you know I was here back in 1973?"

He saw not the slightest sign of perturbation in the delicate, gentle face. If anything, her smile was exceptionally deep. "Oh, thank you," she said. Was it for the fact that he'd returned to her house? Or, if she doubted that, for the graciousness of his invention? Whatever, her graciousness concealed the embarrassment of the broken reservation.

"I hope we'll return before long."

"Thank you, thank you. Sha' core taxi?"

"That would be very nice. I would like to walk around the neighborhood for an hour or two first. I remember how lovely it is up here."

"Taxi ten o'crock?"

"Thank you, Fukuma-san. That would be fine."

Upstairs, he told the waking Dorothy he was going to walk around for a while. "She'll give you breakfast in the other room. I told her we had to go back. She was perfectly understanding. I said I'd been here before, and that we both looked forward to returning. I think that saved face."

It was bright and nippy. The tiny wooden houses with their black and white wooden signs in hiragana and Roman letters looked like old guild shops. Crooked trees twisted in tiny yards. Here and there were hydrant-shaped stone shrines, Buddhas, bodhisattvas. Quiet, remote, graceful. At the end of the street was the arch of the Kodaiji Temple. In front of the central shrine, an old woman in black *tanzen* kimono pulled the bell cord, clapped, and bowed for the spirits. Downhill was a sign, "HOTEL US-YASAKA." It stood over a six-story concrete affair with glass doors and plants. Inside was a small marble lobby; behind the reception desk, a man in a blue blazer.

"Do you speak English?" Walters asked him.

"A rittle."

"Do—you—have—a—room—for—myself—and—my—wife?" Walters held up two fingers.

The man handed him a sheet with a price list. After ten minutes of slow talk and pointing, Walters made the man understand that he and his wife would be back at ten o'clock, and that if they liked the room, they'd take it for three nights. The man wanted him to pay now for all three, but Walters walked out saying he'd be back shortly. (Dorothy might not want to stay in Kyoto.)

At ten, Fukuma-san walked them to the taxi, and, smiling, waved goodbye till it turned the corner, where Walters handed the driver the US-YASAKA flier and indicated that they wanted to go there, not the station. The driver showed no surprise or disappointment that they were going only two hundred yards.

The room at the US-YASAKA resembled the cockpit of a spaceship: lights, music, drinks and snacks were governed by a large keyboard between their beds. This wasn't the Japan that Walters sought. Still, Kyoto was Kyoto, and there was more to it than contemplating a gingko tree. Outside the spaceship were temples, castles, villas, gardens, museums, lovely old streets, the Kamo River, the hills. As if to compensate their defection from the *ryokan,* the next days were radiant with spring. The Walterses took to the back streets, walking toward the hills down lanes coddled with blooming fruit trees. Everywhere were beautiful surprises, little spreads of quiet: rock gardens, brooks, tiny bridges, prayer trees, sacred nooks and pagodas tucked away in groves. Gilded devils guarded recumbent gods; bells and drums erupted from closed shrines, old men contemplated rocks, uniformed high-school students played soccer and baseball; adorable infants smiled and laughed at the tall Americans. "This is the idea," said Walters. "Don't you feel splendid? Rested? Better than rested?"

"Yes."

The third day Dorothy, a bit under the weather, stayed in bed. Walters said, "I think I'll go see Kinkakuji. The Golden Pavilion. Would you mind, dear?"

"I want you to, dear."

Across from the Yasaka Shrine, he took the Number 12 bus. He followed the route on his map. It went down Shijo-Kawarama-chi, crossed the railroad tracks, turned north on Horikawa-dori, went past Nijo Palace, then west again on Kitaoji-dori. A half-hour trip, full of interest. Walters tried not to squirrel away calculations about traffic, commerce, the mix of old and new; he tried to bathe in the impressions. Still, he had to be alert for his stop. Just behind him sat three young women, university age. He turned around and asked, "Do you speak English?" There was some giggling, then a pretty girl in spectacles said, "Can I he'p you?" Walters showed her the map, pointed to Kinkakuji and asked if she'd be kind enough to tell him when to get off. "I te' you, with pressure."

Relaxed again, Walters fell into thinking how happy he was, how precious the world's offerings, how lucky he was to be able to enjoy them. And Dorothy, true-blue Dorothy. How lucky to have the self-melting love for and trust in another human being. In his entire life, he could not remember having such a thought. Bad luck to count blessings. It could be a forecast of loss. A year ago, he'd come home early and heard his own voice saying, "I'll be home by nine, darling." When he came in, Dorothy blushed, then told him she'd kept messages recorded on their answering machine. She had the equivalent of a long-playing record of his messages. Now and then she played it. Would he forgive her? This fear of loss was an element now of the deep love the aging couple had for each other.

"Prease, sir, Kinkakuji now."

Walters walked up an oak-lined alley. Men in coveralls swept the gravel with long brooms. As Walters approached, one of them, a short squat man, stopped sweeping and came up to him. "Excuse, Kinkakuji repair. Crosed indefinitry."

"Oh, dear, what a shame. I've come a long way. Could I just get a glimpse of it from the fence?"

The man bowed twice and said, "Very sorry. Crosed indefinitry. Nothing to see."

There were times when Walters would have been angry. He had his share of the American temper, that perpetuation of infantile anger into adulthood, but decades of diplomatic frustration had taken the starch from the temper. Frustration was not only expected, it was almost welcome; it made his services more valuable. Today he'd prided himself on taking the bus, not a taxi (let alone a car from the American Center). He was playing the ordinary man and enjoying it. There might even be rules against upper-echelon people using public transportation. Walters was playing hooky. That counted more for him than Kin-kakuji.

On the Walterses' last Kyoto day it snowed. They made their way through slosh down Higashioji-dori to the National Museum, where, visibility poor, they turned too soon and found themselves in front of a huge bronze bell. Flake after thick flake piled on the dark gold bronze. It was very quiet. Snow piled on their hats and coats. For a second they looked at each other and, without saying anything, acknowledged the loveliness of the moment. It was the best of their stay.

While Dorothy took a shower, Walters decided to take pictures of besnowed Kyoto. The air was silvery with bits of evening dark. He walked uphill from the hotel to the Kodaiji Temple. Snow fell in the groins of crooked trees and on the curled struts of the shrine. By the square "n" of the Shinto archway, he snapped pictures of a woman pulling the bell cord, clapping and bowing. She was a sporty little figure in red jacket, pants, and woolen cap with a pink ball. Sporty but dignified. As he put the camera down, she came toward him. It was Fukuma-san. A surprised but fine smile spread in her face. "Herro. Herro," she said merrily. He spread his own face with a smile. "How good to see you, Fukuma-san," and, bowing, moved past, the jam of deception smeared on his face.

About fifteen years ago, Walters had made a public fool of himself. He'd had the bad luck to testify before a Congressional committee on a slow news day. Two days before, he'd crossed the Pacific, and though he was a quick recoverer from long flights, he hadn't completely recovered from this one. In addition, he hadn't adequately prepared for the hearing, and so the witty subcommittee chairmen had forced him into a trap: he'd had to expose a presidential position which had been carefully veiled. It earned him and the congressman a minute of evening news time. It was the equivalent of having one's weakest moment painted into the Sistine Chapel, and Walters had never entirely recovered from it. The only comparable humiliation of his life had occurred when he was ten years old. He and his prettiest cousin, Jeanie Walters, were inspecting and caressing each other's more intimate parts when the supposedly hooked door was pushed open by Walters' father. Years later, Walters senior had told his son what a laugh he'd had about it, but there was no laugh that day. These memories went through him as he walked downhill in the dark, silvery air away from Fukuma-san's smile.

He didn't tell Dorothy he'd seen Fukuma-san until they were back in Washington. She'd known something was wrong but thought it was anxiety about ending his rare vacation. From the taxi to Kyoto Station the next day—a beautiful, summery one—they saw a grove of flowering trees. Dorothy said, "How lucky to see cherry blossoms."

Uncharacteristically, Walters said, "All these years in Washington, I'd think you'd know cherry blossoms."

"I am a dodo. These must be avocado or persimmon." All the way back to Narita, she endured his uneasiness.

It was almost two weeks later—his uneasiness gone—that he told her about the encounter at the Temple. He'd had a long afternoon with the Far Eastern deskmen and the Deputy Secretary. (It dealt with ways of softening—and using—Congressional anger about US-Japanese trade imbalances.) In one of the easier moments, Charlie Okhosa told them how his Kyoto-born mother had handled his Kobe-born father. "Kobe people are supposed to be excitable and pushy, port people, quick to take in, quick to dispose. Kyotans are supposedly confident ironists who've seen everything and know it passes. Mother was a good Japanese wife, but she handled my father the way the President handles his prima donnas, with jokes, smiles, letting him wear himself out. She never expressed her will, but we were all controlled by it. A great natural diplomat. I take after the old man."

At supper, Walters passed Charlie's remarks on to Dorothy and, with an apropos, told her about running into Fukuma-san at the Kodaiji Temple. "I don't know which of us was more surprised. I didn't want to upset you by telling you."

"I hope she blames me for our decamping. And for the little deceit."

"That would be just," said Walters with a smile. "I'm glad we moved. I'd have just stuck it out there—and been miserable. It was stupid to go back there anyway," meaning "Back to Fukuma-san's." But remembering that he'd gone there more for Dorothy, he threw in, "Back to the temple, a hundred yards from her house. Her own shrine. My *papparazzi* madness."

"We do have some wonderful pictures, though," said Dorothy, who had caught her husband's unusual indictment of her but, in the habitual diplomacy of their long marriage, ignored it.

Gifts

I was not come to do any harm but actually gave presents of my own substance.

—HERNANDO CORTEZ
September 3, 1526

WILLIAMS had allowed himself six hundred dollars for a Mexican week, five days in Mexico City, two in Yucatán.

Round trip to Mérida was two hundred and twenty dollars, the hotels ran him about sixty pesos a day—he preferred third-class—meals were cheap, and that gave him a few hundred dollars for special pleasures. He usually spent fifty on presents for his wife and his son, Charley. It took him lots of time to find decent presents, but he didn't write it off. It was one of his inroads into Mexican life. Which was one of the objects of his annual excursions—cultural, historic, and scenic accumulation. And then, whatever came in the way of pleasure.

It invariably came in the same way.

On each of his little annual trips, Williams ran into someone who counted for him, sometimes intensely enough to involve months of further contact (usually epistolary), sometimes only in the imaginative transfiguration of his wife.

"That's the way it goes," said Williams to his sixteen-year-old son, his only confidant. "I don't advocate it, but that's my way. You make your life, I'll make mine."

Years ago Charley had overcome uneasiness at his father's confidences. It was odd, but there it was, he was his father's closest friend.

The Mexican confidence, however, did him in. Giving ear wasn't giving absolution.

Apparently the business had begun as usual. At the University's Olympic swimming pool, where Williams—in excellent shape for a forty-year-old—had picked up a girl guide, Rufelia, an Indian girl working for a doctorate in economics, "bright as a fish, heavy-thighed, thin-armed, beautifully torsoed," and so on, his father filled in detail en route. A mestiza from Yucatán, she hadn't been back to see her family in two years and jumped at Williams's offer, full fare and expenses to Mérida in return for two days' companionship. *Muy bien.*

September's the rainy season. In the capital this meant a fat cloud sailing in front of the sun at four-thirty, then breaking into rain for five minutes. In Mérida the cloud arrived on schedule but flooded the town, turned the streets into canals, with garbage instead of gondolas. The lights and fan went off in the pathetic little hotel they stayed in three blocks off the *zócalo,* they were "forced inside," and had gone at it in the heat, debilitating despite "rather exceptional joys." (This was about as far as father went with son.)

The girl hadn't been a virgin since thirteen, had had a child at fourteen who was raised by her mother's sister in Campeche. The child regarded Rufelia as a mysterious relative wafted by supernatural gifts to the capital, there to work out reforms for family and *pueblo.*

Rufelia did not regret, indeed felt herself steeled by this early history. She saw herself as another stage of the revolution, the feminine liberation that had been in Cárdenas's original plan.

The village had tried to break Rufelia at thirteen, but the revolution had made her literate, and modernity had dripped in through French and American novels and films to soften the bondage of class and sex. A national scholarship did the rest. When the students had rioted in the spring against Rector Chavez, Rufelia had whacked off the bronze head of Fra Miguel and been awarded its metal ears.

This history became part of Williams's. On the plane ride from Mexico City, her story, its blunted English beveled and angled by Spanish insertions, took the weight from her nose, cheeks, and jaw, lit the raw black eyes, and turned her, in his expert view, into one of the love goddesses who queened it in the Anthropological Museum. That miracle world of collection and instruction culminated in this fine-breasted, small-smiling talker, on, under, and beside him in the Hotel San Luis. And yet, in the unfanned woolen air, with the sweat flooding the harsh sheet, and his heart slipping beats, Williams felt he'd been forced into wolfing his pleasure, felt unusual indigestion, and then, in a postcoital gloom, felt that he'd had all that this Indian girl would ever give him.

Never had he been so divided from one of his intimacies.

It was partially language, for Rufelia's intelligence could not vault her limited English and his more primitive Spanish, but more, he felt he was playing parts in her story: He was the childhood rapist, the purchasing *yanqui gringo,* the bargain maker who never lost. In the hot room, forty hours more in hand, despite the revival that would surely come in several of these, Williams began preparing the cultural pleasure that might ease this indigestion.

The night was the fifteenth, Independence Day. No accident, of course, for Williams's intention had been to see the Mexican President hail the anniversary in Mexico City; now he would do with the provincial version.

The water had seeped into the earth; by dinner time only a few streets were impassable. He and Rufelia walked the white-walled streets to the green square ringed by the colonial church and the yellow mansions. The square was filled with more than the usual taxi drivers, kids, and loafers; the band was there, Indian ancients in blue caps and the beautifully pleated white shirts of Yucatán. He and Rufelia ate in an air-cooled box in the loggia, papayas and *mole,* tacos and fried eggs, four beers and coffee, and then walked the market streets, loud with preholiday pitch. Williams bought a fake antique (a two-inch clay goiter sufferer), a three-dollar watch inside a gleaming Swiss face, and, for ten pesos, a bejeweled bug held by a chain to a perforated perisphere, "for you, Charley, if it didn't crawl out of my coat."

At the square, a blue, winy night relaxed the heat grip, the soft gold of the church and administrative palace leaked over palms and pepper trees. The band worked toward a few of the same notes, singers ground out local specialties, the benches were filled, couples strutted, minute children peddled Chiclets, grizzled Indians allowed themselves annual shoeshines, and soldiers set off fireworks from the palace roof. Small-town excitement. The mass of Indian faces, the lucent shoddiness of festival, brass bleats and tropic momentum, a whirl of sensuous information in Williams's head that altered the fatigued ease in his legs and groin, the capillary strain in his rear, the slight, coronary hop in his chest.

In their fifth slow round of the square, he saw in the eyes they met that they'd become a couple, memorable, identifiable. He belonged, he could notch Mexico into his life.

Eleven o'clock. The mayor would repeat Fra Hidalgo's cry at midnight, the bells and Catherine wheels would tip the celebration.

"Let's go to bed," said Williams.

Around the corner from their room was a ten-by-twelve-foot swimming pool, open to the sky and ringed by live trees and vines. They got into bathing suits, the way they'd first seen each other the day before. Alone, they swam back and forth in the hot pool, brushing each other's bodies, working up for the amorous nightcap.

In their room, the fan, a great-winged adjustable bat, revived. They dried off naked beneath it. Rufelia's cherry-tinted body gleamed from shards of street light broken by the shutters.

—You been often in hotels with men, Rufelia?

—*Jamás.*

—Come on, now. You didn't learn everything at the University.

"Never in hotel." Unembarrassed, though not at ease.

Williams was the sort who asks whores their history. More, he almost never failed to love the women he stayed with, one night or twenty. This meant their story was important, and not only their body's story. He wished to know thoughts, hopes, pains, how they met what seemed to him one of the world's three great problems (that of subjugated woman, the others being the population mess and the earth's relationship to the universe). He was a writer for a business newsletter, he relished the trends and numbers of manufacture; nights, he stayed up speculating over Beacon, Anchor, and University Press lists.

Williams never finished any books but novels, yet he regarded himself as the equivalent of a Ph.D. in several subjects. Without ambition, hating little but other men's, he threaded his burgher ease with these annual weeks of experience, drawing on them to translate his nighttime reveries into the facts of flesh.

He lifted Rufelia, no easy matter, onto the great double bed. They lay, arms coursing each other's sides.

The account, at this point, veered for Charley into a realm that seemed at least in part formed by fantasy or by some symbolic fiction. His father, long-headed, the burned brown hair grizzling to silver at tips and clutches, framed his full smile into a mockery of meditative remembrance. Or was it all tale teller's contrivance? Was the mockery in the facts or the telling? Was its motive pain or boast?

Charley heard about the next day's trip, the narrow road razoring the flat, furzy fields, the hills, the thatched *pueblitos,* the doors open to the filthy yards, the hammocks, the chickens, the bony black cows, the spurts of mangrove jungle, the asparagus-thin roots tangling with each other into million-legged beasts, the maize and *henequén* fields asleep in the rising dew, the sun jeweling them while the dusty Studebaker whanged along at sixty, his father wordless, working out some connection between the simmering Indian girl beside him and what he was about to see, the empty priest state in the limestone hills.

"Took us an hour or so," a wonderful trip, though the country didn't change, just the harsh grass and the fronds with their glass-sharp fringe, boring terrain with the villages plopped every now and then along the road, surely the way they'd been for fifteen hundred years. "God knows none of these big-hatted farmers had ever come within any but market distance of Uxmal."

Uxmal now was palaces, pyramids, gorgeous nunneries and temples, gray and pink magnificence, mathematical and masonic genius, "what carving, what symmetry. And it was absolutely still. We were alone. The guard slept at the table, we didn't even buy a ticket, just left the car and walked over a ragged path to the Governor's Palace, built on one of these scary staircases, not so tall, but steep, and eighty feet long, the entrances trapezoidal cuts, all scored with these stone mouths and twists." They heard odd noises, scuffing, scurrying, then saw the iguanas' little dragon tails whisking into cracks in the stones. In the air, red flies pecked at their sweat. "Just the two of us, the animals, and this dead city."

The girl climbed the staircase and stood in front of the frieze, arms akimbo, while Williams sat at the bottom below her summoning face. "The place turned you into an actor." Her hair fell back, "the blackest black in nature," and the full, Chinese eyes, "You can see how the Indians came across the Bering Strait," her fine, solid legs like mangrove roots, "leguminous," a dark Indian remembrance of hierarchical glory, "and I remembered some miserable book about sacrifice to the knife and blood redemption, and, kind of joking, I climbed up to her like a victim. The white god Quetzalcoatl, though a bit unplumed"— hand touching the bald inlet to the burned, grizzled hair— "crazy, you know, but we act all the time, the place called for it." On the plane from the capital, she'd recited a Mayan poem about the body's gift to the furious god. "Yet a human being looked mighty good in that dead city, even if she was only imagining a razor blade tonguing your heart."

So Williams mounted the stairs, receptive, and then, at the top of the flight, not quite kidding, Rufelia pushed at his chest. "I grabbed at her arms, we pulled and wrestled around, sex in it, but fight too, and maybe some of what had gone before us. I was excited, I tell you, scared and excited, and full of love-hate for that crazy little Indian."

Which confused fooling led to her rolling down twenty stone steps.

When Williams got to her, an army, "literally, an army of ants in two columns, twenty feet long, black ants with scouts and generals and ordering sergeants, was crawling over her thighs. There were lakes of blood from her knees. And she couldn't move, her arm was bent over, the nose looked broken, there was blood in her mouth and her eyes, her face was glued into hysteria, and there I was, knowing you can't move a broken person. Scared out of my head."

And had left her there.

For the next batch of tourists or the guide or whoever. Had torn off in the Studebaker and, back in Mérida, had paid his bill, and left a note for her with her ticket, an envelope of pesos, and instructions to see the doctor as soon as possible, forgive him, and *adiós.*

"Which is how come I got back yesterday instead of tomorrow."

"Whew."

"Whew is right."

"I hope she's all right," said Charley. "Can you get in trouble?" He was sunk in the ugliness of it.

"They know my address. I guess I'd hear if anything happened."

"Maybe you should call the hotel down there, see if she picked up the ticket."

Williams regarded this pared-down replica of himself sitting up on the bed, and rubbed its hair.

He went to his study and telephoned, and was back twenty minutes later carrying the jeweled bug chained to the perisphere. "The manager said she'd only broken her arm. What luck. I forgot to give you this."

"Alive?"

"Sure it's alive. It eats those leaves there."

Charley thanked him, and accepted thanks for his advice.

It was, however, the last advice he was going to give his father. And, if he could manage it, he had heard the man's last confession.

Troubles

1

TROUBLE, Hanna knew, seldom came labeled. And her trouble was not simple sexual confusion. Everyone she knew slid up and down the sexual shaft, getting off first at this floor, then at that one. She herself was one of the straightest of straight arrows. (If there were sexual continents to explore, she was no sexual Captain Cook.)

The confusion was deeper. Certainly deeper than what diverted her or with whom she slept. Troubles were deep structures. Or structural defects. Deep, confusing, hard to assign. Cagey. Uncageably cagey.

She thought keeping a diary would help. It had helped Kafka (a pillar of her marooned dissertation, *The Dissolving Self in Braque and Broch, Kafka and Kandinsky*). Instead of burrowing into it, she bought a Woolworth notebook and began burrowing into herself, her life with Jay. It went slowly.

Kafka observed himself dissolve, described the dissolution,

and put another version of himself together. That was caginess. Her first entry in the speckled, Rorschach-y book dealt with him:

Kafka's lodestone was his father. Is mine Jay? Or myself with Jay? I only know I'm bottled up. But is he the bottle or the bottler?

Or was it the rodent life they led on the periphery of lofty mentality?

They lived like anchorites on the last fifteen hundred dollars of their Peace Corps savings and half-time jobs (Hanna in the law library, Jay tutoring Javanese and Arabic). They ate like health-freaked Saint Anthonys: raw carrots, cottage cheese, cabbage, Bran Buds, fruit, dried milk, beans, soy-substitute "meatoids" (a Jayism) frozen into "tomatoid gunk." " 'Poor, forked creatures,' yes," said Jay, "but not poor, forked, *constipated* ones."

They had spent two years among people who owned next to nothing; yet here, in their little white apartment over the Midway, Hanna felt an extraordinary barrenness. If only she had a few plants, something alive to care for.

Hanna was mad for flowers. Nights she got to sleep walking her memory through the forest near Sadjapaht: mangrove, sesamum, cinnamon, palm, banana trees with their edible hives, the casuarinas with whip branches, their sides bunged with vermilion fungi ("jungle whores," Jay called them).

He was no plant lover. "Not in Chicago. Not here." (Their dumbbell-shaped slot tipped over the asphalt-split greens of the Midway.) "A goldfish would crack our little ecosystem. We can't import the jungle." Waving at their walls—puffed and wattled as old Caucasian skin: "We fight the dust for breath."

"Plants would freshen the place."

"Nights?" (When he worked at home, moated by monographs on social stratification, village bureaucracy, shamanism, and apple cores, note cards, dictionaries, the green vase from which he drank decaffeinated coffee. The sacred circle of his absorption.)

He's not cruel. He just hates what he has to do so much, he armors himself against anything that would tempt him from it. As far as he can love anyone, he loves me. He needs insulation. I'm insulation. He's so fragile inside he doesn't want to know about it. He doesn't want to think about himself. This turns out to be more selfish than selfishness. The egocentricity of damaged egos.

For her birthday—the funereal twenty-fifth—he brought home an African violet. He'd scooped and sieved dirt from the Midway—"In Chicago, dirt has to be cleaned"—and planted it in a washed-out jar of Skippy.

"When we get the doctorates, we'll settle in a garden. You can start a vegetable state. Every plant in creation can have its own municipality. You'll be Mother Shrub."

"Oh, sweetheart." Looking at the little purple blossoms.

Which soon curled off. But, eyes to the leaves' small fur, Hanna conjured up Java, the silver alang grass outside the kampong, the ferns, pitcher plants, orchids. Pods, spikes and glumes burst, and fragrance poured over the valley. Transfixed by fatigue, loneliness, heat squatting on every bone, she took in the aromatic ecstasy like some great work of mentality.

Twenty miles away lived the polite, handsome boy she'd met during orientation period in Jakarta. One afternoon, she hitched a samlor ride to the paddies where he was pointed out to her (he was shaded by the nipple-tipped straw hat which, from the road, made him look like an ambulatory mushroom). "Hey, there. Jay. It's Hanna. From Sadjapaht."

How could I tell? I'd have fallen for Dracula if he'd spoken English. Life was so nutty. All that Java courtesy that made you feel transparent. They looked through you. Not even Pua or Madame Charwa talked to me those first weeks.

She and Jay met once a week, hitching samlor or bullock-cart rides until they bought bicycles. The meetings were the week's beacon. On their first three-day leave, they bicycled to Borobudur and, in a hotel near that old monument to release from world and flesh, they worked out their own release.

Oddly, it was Madame Charwa who first sensed their division. Jay had bicycled over to Sadjapaht the day Pua, the old coffee stallman—her first Javanese friend—died. Everyone in the kampong went to Pua's house. Jay told her to make a bowl of rice and go too, it was their chance to see a funeral *slametan*. She sat with Madame Charwa, Jay with the men. Priests recited Arabic prayers, Pua's black body was undressed, washed, and stuffed with cotton pads. Hanna cried. The Javanese tried to ignore this impropriety. Jay looked icebergs at her, she managed to stop; but confusion had crept into the ceremony, the *santri* hurried the prayers and carried Pua off, Jay after them. Elegant Madame Charwa, more worldly than the others —she was the local representative of the yam-and-pepper cooperative in Surabaya—walked Hanna back to the hut. "One acts as one is trained. Your friend was severe with you. The two of you are not alike. Despite your mutual affection. He is less *djava.*" (*Less Javanese,* which meant *less human.*) A peculiar criticism to which Hanna was too far gone in love to attend. Her fear was that she had offended Jay; he would see how badly she acted, how silly she was, and would stop seeing her.

But Jay returned full of what he'd sought. The Javanese temperament suited his own. *Iklas,* the disciplined unfeeling which the funeral *slametan* was supposed to induce, had less assertive snobbery than British "indomitability," less military callousness than Spartan-Roman stoicism. It was an attitude that would do for much of life. *Another mask for his fragility,* she would write in her diary account of these memories.

In their second Indonesian winter, they took three days off and were married in Jakarta. Her parents sent a hundred dollars —probably their vacation money—and Jay's father, a cultural affairs officer with the State Department, wired them twenty-five through the embassy.

They returned to their assignments, still seeing each other only one day a week, until, at the end of the tour, they took a four-day honeymoon in Bali. It was the first time they had been together knowing they would not be separating.

Which may have accounted for their first deep uneasiness with each other. *He didn't know what marriage would mean,* she wrote in the diary.

Even less than most people. Companionship itself is hard for him. He didn't go into the Corps for adventure or idealism or experience. He went in to be a foreigner, the way he was when he grew up. He was escaping intimacy; then he was trapped by it. Maybe he opened to me in Java because I was a foreigner too. Of course, he needed me physically.

Like many secretive, baffled men, Jay was an extraordinarily intense lover. He relished the depths and special silence of the sexual waters. Lovemaking was his release and his attainment. He was a generous lover. Only during exam weeks did he lose sight of her. Then he labored grimly in her body to unlock himself for his work.

He never talked about sex. It was one of the first things that turned him against her new friends. When she told him what they'd told her about their amorous problems, he said the reason they had problems was that "they liked problems more than love and they think frankness certifies authenticity. Nothing is more of a disguise than that kind of openness."

"I don't see how honesty can be dishonest."

"Too much light blinds. Those who feel love can't talk about it."

She was unwilling to certify this self-praise. He was not malicious; he had the assertiveness of those who fear uncertainty. Why make him still more uncertain? "I passed your pal Vanessa in the library. She was chattering like a maniac. Why is she so noisy? To convince herself she exists? There ought to be a bank for shallowness. Your pals could deposit their daily slivers of self. After a few years, they might have enough for a genuine moment or two."

"I think they're genuine."

"You have a certain solidity which gets reflected in them. You supply what you think you see in them."

Even for this rare compliment, she could not betray her friends. "I wish I had enough for myself, let alone to pass around."

At first, her friends said he was beautiful. Then they decided there was something wrong in his looks: not the features, not the snow and strawberry complexion, or—when they knew her better—"that beautiful tight ass." Maybe the eyes, which looked "like mud with fog caught in it," said Wanda, or the extra centimeters of forehead, which always caught light. "That portable nimbus of his. What a strange saint."

What really got them was his distance, his conspicuous restraint. Wanda said he looked at them as if they were sick and he the only available suppository—"one that isn't all that happy about being inserted."

Jay converted them into caricatures: Wanda was "Mount Fat," Clover Callahan was "Mouse," Vanessa was "the Tongue," and Nora, who had nothing on which he could fix, became his own incapacity to fix her, "the Slitherer."

"What's that mean?"

"She has no fixity. It's why clothes are so important to her."

"They are to me too. I just don't have anything to spend on them."

"It's different. She has nothing underneath. She's a flag without a country. She's slither. The Guccied Slitherer." Proclaimed with a discoverer's triumph.

"And you're the Archimedes of slander," said Hanna, but under her breath.

Still, abuse was better than silence. Most nights, silence piled around her. It was like the first months in Java, except that there she knew her tour would come to an end. Jay would study five or six hours without saying anything. Or he would call out, "Why are there no apples?" in such despair that the question was almost metaphysical—amazement at nature's astonishing omission of such an item.

Jay would not discuss their relationship. "It works or it doesn't. Ours mostly works. Discussion kills." He pointed across the Midway to the Gothic stretch of the University. "There's discussion for you. The mausoleum of the real."

The most assiduous of graduate students, never missing a class or an assignment, he hated the idea of the University. "For scholars, the world exists in order to be explained," he explained. He hated anthropology, his field, its "patronizing tolerance." Morgan, a young assistant professor, *la plus noire* of his *bêtes noires,* had made fun of the green revolution. "Of those thousands of hours you and I put into the paddies. Because the new seeds require petrochemical fertilizers, and oil prices are ruining them. As if we were responsible for oil prices. The world's just a collection of props for his notions, mutters his structuralist honey while eighteen mammary glands quiver at him. What are we doing here, baby? Five hundred million people turn into compost while we pay thousands to listen to theoretical snot."

Jay had grown up inside the coziness which compensates foreign service officers for living abroad. He had lain on a couch while a servant five times his age bent down to serve him iced drinks. At prep school, back in the States, he'd turned against his class. His senior honors thesis on American writers was a fiery tract.

Like Henry James, who wrote, "Everything costs that one does for the rich," Fitzgerald saw the rich up close, saw the murder in their charm, their totalitarian need to wipe out individuality and talent. All great American writers have known that, the Hemingway of A Moveable Feast, *the Melville who created in Captain Ahab the warning not to convert nature into commodity.*

The headmaster had written an amused alert to Jay's parents: "One of our brightest boys, though he needs more steering than we've been able to supply. Maybe Stanford will do better." But Jay's parents were pleased with him; his visits to them in Brussels or Karachi were affectionate and brief. He visited less often while he was in college. When his mother died in Bangkok, he wrote his father that he would attend a private service, he didn't have to travel around the world to mourn her. Hanna, thinking of this, wondered when "love had died in him."

Does he love me? Do I love him? I don't know. Know only that my world is too jayed. *I used to be confident, happy. If I had to draw myself now, I would draw a zero. Except zero's useful.*

2

"I don't see why you miss the jungle," said Jay. "You've got your pals."

There was something in it. Her friends were messed up, and somehow overgrown. Each day she saw how troubled they were.

Clover, Wanda, and Vanessa suffered terribly. Yet they were remarkable, gifted girls.

Clover was a math whiz who'd published a paper on set theory as a college sophomore ten years ago.

Wanda was a physical monster with Leonardo-like gifts: she sculpted, embroidered, made furniture, repaired watches, radios, toilets, played the guitar, painted, made beautiful lithographs.

Vanessa couldn't look a dog in the eye, but in class she scorched inferior analysis, and leaped from language to language as if Babel had never been. The intellectual blaze burned connectives from her speech; she spoke a code it took months getting used to. In the Grotto, where they met for lunch, she felt less pressure. The light, submarine and bluish, did not make her feel "on stage"; she was coherent, fluent, sympathetic. Her talk, all their talk, wound in and out of anger, bafflement, flight, odium, fear, and disguise, but its mode was farce. They sat in a corner on facing benches, eating thick, meaty soups and talking out each other's troubles. Trouble was their subject, their poetry.

Clover would have been beautiful except for a dermal scurf that was the façade of a wintry interior. Until a breakthrough in her analysis, she had thought of men as statues, dignified and untouchable, women as sluttish hunks, stuff for centerfolds. With the analyst's help, she was able to see the relationship between such distortion and her anorexia: she'd starved herself in order to make her flesh disappear. At eighty pounds, she felt monstrous, overblown. The year before, she'd nearly starved to death. Influenza saved her life; she'd gone in for a flu shot and was put in the hospital. Now, stronger, she could see, literally see, that women were worthy and men approachable. Although she still sometimes felt like "a pea in an invisible pod," she also believed in herself and even hoped for some kind of physical relationship with someone. "I used to have nothing but numbers. A freak, like someone who can whistle with her knees."

Mathematics was not her only gift. She had an extraordinary sense for other people's suffering. "She knows before you do," said Vanessa. "It's like the sixth sense some animals have for warmblooded creatures." Clover was always on call. People who didn't know her well telephoned at midnight, and she went to talk them back to life.

Wanda's trouble lay under more layers than Troy; enormous energy piled fat, wit, manual genius, and a sense of spectacle over it. Caped to the throat, hair in a great bush, Wanda was the center of any room. She had a lovely, subtle voice which spun the gossip of Hyde Park into manic catastrophes. No one had ever been in Wanda's rooms, though she told Clover—who told Hanna—that she had an intimate friend there. No particulars. (Jay said Wanda had only personified a layer of fat.)

Vanessa was married to a biologist who was driven wild by her hypomania. She knew it, was helpless with the knowledge and the condition. "Knowing, doing, different kettles, different fish." Vanessa had a beautiful body, a harsh, ugly face, tiny nosed, huge lipped. Her husband was handsome, and she was terrified of losing him, but driving him away was better than being left by him. She showed him up, interrupted him, read papers which challenged his—and hated herself. She lived on Valium, had nightmares so awful that after them she'd come close to killing herself.

Compared to the other girls, Nora and Hanna were untroubled. They'd been loved, embraced, encouraged. The Grotto patrons took them for sisters. Both were tall and had dark hair which fell over their shoulders. Nora's was thicker and more lustrous; when she was nervous, her hands ran through it.

Nora's small troubles came from excess: she did lots of things well, painted, wrote poetry, was a good athlete—she ran two miles a day at the gym—did honors work in Romance languages. But she was terrified of criticism, and ran away before it came. Her plan was to finish her master's and become a talk-show hostess. "Hard questions are easy to ask. And Barbara Walters is wearing out." She was also looking into government internships, law school, Vista, Fulbrights to Guatemala, museum training courses, the Sarasota Clown School. "Why not? I love the circus." No notion outlasted the required follow-up.

Her love life was equally serial. She'd lived with eight or ten boys since she'd been in school, the last a "beautiful Nigerian" who'd finished an economics degree and just left to work for OPEC. "It's a relief to lose him. He was heading so straight for the future, he could hardly remember where we lived."

"I envy that," said Hanna.

"I envy you. You've got the toughest decisions behind you."

Hanna said it wasn't so at all, and told her how she'd become a prisoner of Jay's moroseness. "He's dear, but he hates life. It's impossible to reach him."

Nora said every relationship with a man had more censorship than expression. "The sex is so important, you sacrifice give-and-take for it."

Hanna said that wasn't what she feared. She did fear Jay. "He's never laid a finger on me, but I'm afraid of him. Physically afraid. Anger's burned the fat off his bones, and I think it has nowhere to go now but on mine. It's not just a few knocks. I'm not that afraid of pain. It's the anger itself. I guess I shouldn't say it. I love him, he's remarkable in his way. But to be squeezed so is awful. To feel your nature so reduced. I'd always hoped marriage would give me space, energy, desire. It hasn't."

"Try getting out of it more. Don't bury yourself in him. He's become your tomb. Get out. On your own." Nora told her to come over for supper, Jay could manage without her. "It would be the first time," said Hanna.

"She didn't invite *me*?"

Jay was assembling the evening's fortress: apples, books, ballpoints, the vaseful of Sanka.

"She thinks I ought to get out on my own once in a while."

"Fine. Just don't come back on a broomstick."

"Meaning?"

The long face tilted, peering over a celestial ledge. "Witchery's contagious."

"Nora's no witch."

"Wait till midnight. I stood behind what's-her-name, Mount Fuji, the one that sounds like a stray. Wanda! In the Co-op. She was adding her groceries on a pocket calculator. Batting her pig eyes. Not at me. The groceries. Six bags full. And none for my master, or for any dame but you know who. At least the Slitherer has a streak of generosity in her."

"You and I don't exactly keep a great salon."

"All we're trying to do is get out of here quick as we can. We're not the Salvation Army."

"I don't mean to criticize," she said.

"I don't know what you mean."

"It's been my fault too. Our life's too airless. The girls have been a fine thing for me. I feel human with them. You pick at them. I know it's a kind of game for you, your way of being social with me, but sometimes it's too hard."

He opened a book, looked at it, drank from the vase. "O.K. I won't say anything about them. If I have an opinion you don't share, I'll shut up. But Hanna, I can't have those psychotic shrews around here. Sorry."

That night, asleep beside him, she dreamed she was at the top of the Buddhist mountain, Borobudur. Out of the stone bells rose old teachers, her sister, her mother, a boyfriend from Oklahoma who had hit her for not making out with him, girls from grade school and high school. One by one they asked her to forgive them. "We're sorry, we didn't know." *"Mai ben rai,"* she said. "Never mind"—and then was ashamed, for it was Thai, not Javanese. Which brought her to a river, a kayak going down the klongs. Jay lay dead on the struts, the boat headed for the cremation pyre. She was crying. "The others' don't mean anything without yours," she said, meaning the petitions for forgiveness, and now she would never have his. The body moved next to her. Jay. She moved away. In the channel between sleep and waking, she knew she was going to leave him.

3

The next night, before Jay got home, Hanna left a note for him and walked across the Midway to Nora's. She'd taken a shower, and put on her best jeans, an openwork blouse over a bra that lifted her breasts, and a blue blazer that was the nicest thing she owned.

Nora lived on Dorchester in a large attic room with a kitchen off one side and a bathroom off another. The furniture consisted of mattresses covered with shawls and cushions. There were lots of plants, books, a stereo, and knickknacks. The walls were covered with prints of Matisse flowers and dancers.

Nora, barefoot, wore old jeans and a sweater.

"You look terrific," she said. "Like someone on vacation."

"Going out to dinner is vacation. Without Jay."

They had jasmine tea, and faced each other on the mattresses. Through old blinds, sun dusted the room.

"Are you on probation?" Nora's hands ran in and out of her hair.

"It's more like I've dug my way out of a cell. Blind. Through muck."

"No mud shows."

"The mud's in here," said Hanna, touching her left breast.

"That's nice mud," said Nora.

There was something both tense and easy in this pillowed room, a Turkish air. Hanna felt airy, afloat, yet cloistered, marooned. "I feel high."

"Free," said Nora. "Or maybe hungry. You hungry?"

"Just for air."

"It'll have to be tea."

Hanna brought her cup to the stove. Nora looked at her, her eyes, then her blouse, and put an arm around her waist. Hanna put hers around Nora's shoulder. They leaned forward and kissed.

Nora undid Hanna's blouse and bra. Undressed, they lay down, looked at and stroked each other, then, aroused, became more intimate.

It was, thought Hanna, like making love to oneself. There was the sense that Nora knew her body from inside. It wasn't especially exciting. It was almost a form of reconnaissance. Nora, no stranger in this country, was able to go further.

To be companionable, Hanna pretended thorough satisfaction.

4

It was midnight when Nora drove her back. Jay had read her note, which told him to read her diary so that he could understand how troubled she was by their marriage.

"I don't think I can live with you," said the note. "Not now. It doesn't mean I don't love you. Whatever that big word means."

Jay read the diary, more and more infuriated by what he regarded as its insensitivity. "Why couldn't she have opened up to me? It's those damn creeps. She had to find something, to keep up with them. If they're not in a mess, they don't know they're alive. Is life supposed to be paradise?"

He found a few dollars and ran down to the all-night liquor store on Sixty-Third Street, bought a quart of vodka, and by midnight had drunk half of it.

Hanna came upstairs and saw him marooned in his sad, magic circle (the silvery bottle filling in for the vase of Sanka). "Well?"

"I'm potted."

"You read the note?"

"You bet."

"And the diary?"

"I followed all instructions."

He sat in liquorousness like a fish in an aquarium—apparently the same, but altered by the tiny ambience of his new situation (of which the booze was but an element). Yet he looked beautiful, wounded, extravagant, baffled, and—to her surprise, for she'd had some experience of liquor—sexually excited. Even more surprising, she felt a responsive excitement. The signals crossed; discussion was shunted to the side.

For the second time that evening, she took off her clothes. They did not even bother to go down the hall but made love on the floor beside the apple cores and vodka.

Yet, Hanna told herself, half an hour later, awake while he snoozed off beyond troubles, she was in the jungle with Vanessa and Wanda and Clover. Energy, talent, and hope warred with her life; no relationship and no institution could help. She had the isolation of a pioneer in the circumstance of a soap opera. The only ax she had was the knowledge she was in trouble, that she was down there with the others.

Dr. Cahn's Visit

How far is it now, George?"

The old man is riding next to his son, Will. George was his brother, dead the day after Franklin Roosevelt. "Almost there, Dad."

"What does 'almost' mean?"

"It's Eighty-Sixth and Park. The hospital's at Ninety-Ninth and Fifth. Mother's in the Klingenstein Pavilion."

"Mother's not well?"

"No, she's not well. Liss and I took her to the hospital a couple of weeks ago."

"It must have slipped my mind." The green eyes darkened with sympathy. "I'm sure you did the right thing. Is it a good hospital?"

"Very good. You were on staff there half a century."

"Of course I was. For many years, I believe."

"Fifty."

"Many as that."

"A little slower, pal. These jolts are hard on the old man."

The cabbie was no chicken himself. "It's your ride."

"Are we nearly there, George?"

"Two minutes more."

"The day isn't friendly," said Dr. Cahn. "I don't remember such—such—"

"Heat."

"Heat in New York." He took off his gray fedora and scratched at the hairless, liver-spotted skin. Circulatory difficulty left it dry, itchy. Scratching had shredded and inflamed its soft center.

"It's damn hot. In the nineties. Like you."

"What's that?"

"It's as hot as you are old. Ninety-one."

"Ninety-one. That's not good."

"It's a grand age."

"That's your view."

"And mother's eighty. You've lived good, long lives."

"Mother's not well, son?"

"Not too well. That's why Liss and I thought you ought to see her. Mother's looking forward to seeing you."

"Of course. I should be with her. Is this the first time I've come to visit?"

"Yes."

"I should be with her."

The last weeks at home had been difficult. Dr. Cahn had been the center of the household. Suddenly, his wife was. The nurses looked after her. And when he talked, she didn't answer. He grew angry, sullen. When her ulcerous mouth improved, her voice was rough and her thought harsh. "I wish you'd stop smoking for five minutes. Look at the ashes on your coat. Please stop smoking."

"Of course, dear. I didn't know I was annoying you." The ash tumbled like a suicide from thirty stories; the butt was crushed into its dead brothers. "I'll smoke inside." And he was off, but, in two minutes, back. Lighting up. Sometimes he lit two cigarettes at once. Or lit the filtered end. The odor was foul, and sometimes his wife was too weak to register her disgust.

They sat and lay within silent yards of each other. Dr. Cahn was in his favorite armchair, the *Times* bridge column inches from his cigarette. He read it all day long. The vocabulary of the game deformed his speech. "I need some clubs" might mean "I'm hungry." "My spades are tired" meant he was. Or his eyes were. Praise of someone might come out, "He laid his hand out clearly." In the bedridden weeks, such mistakes intensified his wife's exasperation. "He's become such a penny pincher," she said to Liss when Dr. Cahn refused to pay her for the carton of cigarettes she brought, saying, "They can't charge so much. You've been cheated."

"Liss has paid. Give her the money."

"Are you telling me what's trump? I've played this game all my life."

"You certainly have. And I can't bear it."

In sixty marital years, there had never been such anger. When Will came from Chicago to persuade his mother into the hospital, the bitterness dismayed him.

It was, therefore, not so clear that Dr. Cahn should visit his wife. Why disturb her last days? Besides, Dr. Cahn seldom went out anywhere. He wouldn't walk with the black nurses (women whom he loved, teased and was teased by). It wasn't done. "I'll go out later. My feet aren't friendly today." Or, lowering the paper, "My legs can't trump."

Liss opposed his visit. "Mother's afraid he'll make a scene."

"It doesn't matter," said Will. "He has to have some sense of what's happening. They've been the center of each other's lives. It wouldn't be right."

The hope had been that Dr. Cahn would die first. He was ten years older, his mind had slipped its moorings years ago. Mrs. Cahn was clear headed, and, except near the end, energetic. She loved to travel, wanted especially to visit Will in Chicago— she'd not seen his new apartment—but she wouldn't leave her husband even for a day. "Suppose something happened."

"Bring him along."

"He can't travel. He'd make an awful scene."

Only old friends tolerated him, played bridge with him, forgiving his lapses and muddled critiques of their play. "If you don't understand a two bid now, you never will." The most gentlemanly of men, Dr. Cahn's tongue roughened with his memory. It was as if a lifetime of restraint were only the rind of a wicked impatience.

"He's so spoiled," said Mrs. Cahn, the spoiler.

"Here we are, Dad."

They parked under the blue awning. Dr. Cahn got out his wallet—he always paid for taxis, meals, shows—looked at the

few bills, then handed it to his son. Will took a dollar, added two
of his own, and thanked his father.

"This is a weak elevator," he said of one of the monsters made
to drift the ill from floor to floor. A nurse wheeled in a stretcher,
and Dr. Cahn removed his fedora.

"Mother's on Eight."

"Minnie is here?"

"Yes. She's ill. Step out now."

"I don't need your hand."

Each day, his mother filled less of the bed. Her face, unsup-
ported by dentures, seemed shot away. Asleep, it looked to Will
as if the universe leaned on the crumpled cheeks. When he
kissed them, he feared they'd turn to dust, so astonishingly
delicate was the flesh. The only vanity left was love of attention,
and that was part of the only thing that counted, the thought of
those who cared for her. How she appreciated the good nurses
and her children. They—who'd never before seen their
mother's naked body—would change her nightgown if the
nurse was gone. They brought her the bedpan, and, though she
usually suggested they leave the room, sat beside her while,
under the sheets, her weak body emptied its small waste.

For the first time in his adult life, Will found her beautiful.
Her flesh was mottled like a Pollock canvas, the facial skin
trenched with the awful last ditches of self-defense; but her look
melted him. It was human beauty.

Day by day, manners that seemed as much a part of her as her
eyes—fussiness, bossiness, nagging inquisitiveness—dropped
away. She was down to what she was.

Not since childhood had she held him so closely, kissed his
cheek with such force. "This is mine. This is what lasts," said the
force.

What was she to him? Sometimes little more than the old
organic scenery of his life. Sometimes she was the meaning of
it. "Hello, darling," she'd say. "I'm so glad to see you." The
voice, never melodious, was rusty, avian. Beautiful. No actress
could match it. "How are you? What's happening?"

"Very little. How are you today?"

She told her news. "Dr. Vacarian was in, he wanted to give
me another treatment. I told him, 'No more.' And no more
medicine." Each day she'd renounced more therapy. An un-
spoken decision had been made after a five-hour barium treat-

ment which usurped the last of her strength. (Will thought that might have been its point.) It had given her her last moments of eloquence, a frightening jeremiad about life dark beyond belief, nothing left, nothing right. It was the last complaint of an old champion of complaint, and after it, she'd made up her mind to go. There was no more talk of going home.

"Hello, darling. How are you today?"

Will bent over, was kissed and held against her cheek. "Mother, Dad's here."

To his delight, she showed hers. "Where is he?" Dr. Cahn had waited at the door. Now he came in, looked at the bed, realized where he was and who was there.

"Dolph, dear. How are you, my darling? I'm so happy you came to see me."

The old man stooped over and took her face in his hands. For seconds, there was silence. "My dearest," he said; then, "I didn't know. I had no idea. I've been so worried about you. But don't worry now. You look wonderful. A little thin, perhaps. We'll fix that. We'll have you out in no time."

The old man's pounding heart must have driven blood through the clogged vessels. There was no talk of trumps.

"You can kiss me, dear." Dr. Cahn put his lips on hers.

He sat next to the bed and held his wife's hand through the low rail. Over and over he told her she'd be fine. She asked about home and the nurses. He answered well for a while. Then they both saw him grow vague and tired. To Will he said, "I don't like the way she's looking. Are you sure she has a good doctor?"

Of course Mrs. Cahn heard. Her happiness watered a bit, not at the facts, but at his inattention. Still, she held on. She knew he could not sit so long in a strange room. "I'm so glad you came, darling."

Dr. Cahn heard his cue and rose. "We mustn't tire you, Minnie dear. We'll come back soon."

She held out her small arms, he managed to lean over, and they kissed again.

In the taxi, he was very tired. "Are we home?"

"Almost, Dad. You're happy you saw Mother, aren't you?"

"Of course I'm happy. But it's not a good day. It's a very poor day. Not a good bid at all."

Dying

DREBEN's first call came while Bly was in the laboratory. Mrs. Shearer's pale coniform budded with announcement: "He says it's urgent."

"Can't come." Watching the smear of kineton coax soluble nitrogens from the right leaf bulge, a mobilization of nutrient which left the ravaged context sere, yellow, senescent. "What kinda urgent?"

"Wouldn't say. An odd one." Her bud, seamed, cracked, needful of a good smear itself, trichloro-hydroxyphenyl, petrolatums, lipids: a ChapStick; or lipstick to mask its aging.

"Get the number." Eyes on the ravenous patch of leaf. Molisch, Curtis, and Clark had shown that mobilizing forces were strongest in flowers and fruits, less strong in growing points, still less strong in lateral buds, weakest in roots. Bly was checking on partial senescence, revving up one section of a tobacco leaf at the expense of another.

Two hours later, he drew the yellow Message Slip from his box: Name: F. Dorfman Dreben; Number: Bl 6-4664; Message: Please return call; Message Taken By: LES.

He knew no Dorfman Dreben, needed nothing from Bl 6-4664. The yellow slip floated toward the wastebasket.

The second call came that night while he read one of President Kennedy's favorite books—he was going through the *Life* magazine list one by one—*John Quincy Adams and the State of the Union* by Samuel F. Bemis. "Professor Bly?"

"Der spricht."

"Professor Bly?"

"I am Bly."

"F. Dorfman Dreben, F. Dorfman Dreben Enterprises. I called you at 2:40 this afternoon."

"My boss wouldn't let me go to the phone, Mr. Dreben. What can I do you for?" Bly held the receiver a foot away, six pockmarks in the auditing cup, six at the center of the speaker's circular rash. A great machine. From the solitary six, as much of F. Dorfman Dreben as could be electrically transmitted from Voice Box A to Ear Drum Y appealed. "It was your poem in *Harper's*, right, Professor?"

The forty-fourth poem he'd written since high school, the eleventh since his appointment as Instructor in Plant Physiology, Division of the Biological Sciences, The University of Chicago, the seventh reproduced for public satisfaction (cf. Raleigh *News and Observer,* December 1954, "Blackie! Thy very name meant life!"; the Wake Forest *Lit,* "Sonnet on Your Easter Bonnet," Fall, 1956, and four others in the same publication) and the only one which had brought him money ($35.00) and fame (notice in the Chicago *Maroon,* a call from the U. of Chicago Public Relations Office resulting in six lines in the Chicago *Sun-Times,* four comments from students, bemused, pleased, uneasy, mocking, even, stupefyingly joyous responses from colleagues, one letter from a lady in Milledgeville, Georgia, declaring the poem "the most beautiful I have read in years," requesting a manuscript copy for the Milledgeville Pantosocratic Society, and today, one, then a second, call from F. Dorfman Dreben, F. Dorfman Dreben Enterprises). "All mine."

"A great poem," said the six pockmarks. Seven lines unrhymed, iambic tetrameter with frequent substitutions, title, "In Defense of Decrepitude," epigraph, "A characteristic consequence of senescence is the occurrence of death," theme, "Oh death, thy sting is life." "Which explains, besides congratulations, my call, Professor."

"You're too kind." 2 cubed plus 4 squared equals my age, the square root of 576, a dayful of years.

"Not kind, Professor. Needy. I need your help."

You? And I, and my tobacco leaves, and Plant Physiology, students, the University, *Harper's*, girls—mostly unknown— children—unconceived.

"Though perhaps it will be of help to you too, Professor. Your helping me."

And the greatest of these. "Explain, Mr. Dreben."

"Easily. Here is our situation. My mother, may her soul, lies on her deathbed. A week, a month, who knows, a day, will no longer be with us."

"I'm very sorry." His right eye, nose bone, and right cheek leaked—not sorrow—upon a curl of purple violets (*V. cucullata*), filling a six-by-eight print, glassed over, above the phone, a retreat of flesh toward hollow, though not sorrowful, limpidity. He was mostly eye. Bly the Eye. Eye had mobilized the nutrient that might have fleshed his flesh, made him at twenty-four husband, father, householder, mortgage payer, Assistant Professor of Plant Physiology ("Get a loada Bly. Claims he looks like a violet.").

"Thank you sincerely, Professor. I can tell you're a man of feeling. It showed in the poem, and that's why I call. Because more than a man of feeling, you're a master of words." No. Master of Science, Doctor of Philosophy, but no M.W., except honorary, University of Dorfman-Dreben. "We are in need. Sister and I. What we want to do is to put on mother's stone, already purchased, a short verse, original in nature, only for her. For such a verse, we are inaugurating a contest, prize two hundred dollars. I am officially inviting you to enter the contest with a verse suitable for permanent inscription." The *cucullata* smeared its fuzzy purple into his small jaw, bruised his neck. He was being mobilized for the assault on stone. Bly the Eye reporting. M.W., O.N. (Original in Nature). "A month ago, I wrote this Robert Frost. Saw him on the Inaugural Day. One month and haven't had a line from him. Not even a 'no.' Once they get into politics they're through."

"Through?"

"Poets. Two weeks ago, I wrote Sandburg. Same result. Negative. They're not interested in a businessman's dollar. I tried writing one on my own. Failure. My sister tried. Also. Then my sister saw your poem in *Harper's*. 'Right in Chicago,' she said. 'A sign.' "

"I was in politics," said Bly. Treasurer of the Arista, Binyon High School. John Quincy Adams, defeated by Jackson, turned to poetry. *Duncan Macmorrogh* or *The Conquest of Ireland*. Epic in four cantos.

"If my mother could have read it, she would say, 'This is the poet for my stone.' "

Bly's mother, "Mother Bly," as his sister's husband, Lember, the John Bircher, called her, had carried the sonnet "Blackie" around in her wallet until its shreds had married those of the Brussels' streetcar stub, souvenir of the European week which was the product of her mother's death and legacy. He had sent his mother neither a copy of *Harper's* nor notice of his poem's presence there; evil communication corrupteth good parents. The viper generation that sent no sign. But he could use two hundred dollars, no doubt of it. The summer at the Oceanographic Institute at Wood's Hole was stale for him. He wanted his own week in Europe. He wanted to marry—girl unknown —though he had his nourished eye on a couple in Plant Physiology 263. A new suit. A car.

"Just a short poem, Professor. Maybe four lines. Rhymed."

"Rhymed'll cost you two-fifty."

The pockmarks paused. "Who knows? I'll expect to hear from you then? F. Dorfman Dreben, 342 Wacker Drive. Bl 6-4664. Any time, day or night. Messages will be taken. I'm very grateful."

Bly sat down under the violets, took up the telephone pad, and wrote nonstop:

> Claramae Dreben droops like a leaf.
> Her chest is still heaving, her boy's full of grief.

He pushed the eraser laterally on his forehead, once, twice.

> When she is nothing but dried skin and bone
> Two hundred smackers will carve grief in stone.

Two errors, "Claramae," odds against, one in two thousand, and "Two hundred smackers," which would not buy Bly's rhymed lines. No, a third error: the whole thing.

Bly threw the quatrain under the couch and picked up *John*

Quincy Adams who was thinking of going into Congress despite his son's assertion that it would be beneath an ex-president's dignity. An hour later, in bed, he thought first of the kineton smear and the alpha aminoisobutyne acid he would apply to it tomorrow, then of Miss Gammon, a wiry little number in Pl. Phys. 263.

He didn't think of Dorfman Dreben until the third call, five days later. He was home eating the Tai Gum How he had sent up from Sixty-Third Street twice a week. "I called you last night, Professor. Failed to get you."

"Forgive me."

"F. Dorfman Dreben. Mother is sinking."

"I was out, Mr. D." The weekly meeting of the instructors in zoology and botany, papers read, discussion, a good meeting.

Bly sat down under the *cucullata,* the Tai Gum How crawling with porcine force up his stomach cavity. "Mr. Dreben. I must have led you astray. I'm no poet. I've written very few poems. Even if I were a poet, I couldn't take the time to work on a poem now. After all, I didn't even know your mother. Not even her name."

The pockmarks were silent. Then, softly, "Clarissa, Professor. A beautiful name."

Bly got up. Almost one in two thousand. A sign. "Yes."

"You are a poet, Professor. No doubt of it. We are not looking for epics. A simple verse, original in nature. Any minute will be her last. I could feel so comforted telling her her resting place will be honored."

At lunch, a joke about the Irishman on his deathbed, sniffing ham cooking in the kitchen, managing to call to his wife for a piece, being refused. "You know better than that, Flaherty. It's for the wake."

"A simple verse at fifty, maybe sixty-one dollars a line. That's not a bad rate in any business."

Cottonwood brushed against the wire screen, the fluff comas breaking off, falling. Behind a violet shield of cotton cloud, the day's sun bowed good night. "Maybe I can try, Mr. Dreben. But listen, if you don't get a note from me this week, you'll know I couldn't do it. I'm not much on elegies. Not exactly a specialty of the house." Tai Gum How/Hot off the sow/One man's meat/ Another man's Frau. Dermot O'Flaherty, Epic in Four Graves.

"You'll try then, Professor?"

"I'll try, Mr. D. If I send it on, please remit the two-fifty by certified check. Also, my name is not to be signed to or be associated with the verse. The Division might not approve. And finally, we must never communicate again."

"Wel——"

"Not *au revoir* but goodbye, Mr. D. You either will or will not hear from me within a hundred and sixty-eight hours." The pockmarks chattered as the receiver plunged.

That evening, Bly sat back in his easy chair and thought about dying. In some ways, he was an expert. There was dying en masse, annually, dying deciduously, dying from the top—tulips, spring wheat, Dean Swift—dying from the bottom—he, Bly, nearly died there from the need to live there five or six times a week. Molisch in *Der Lebensauer der Pflanzen* showed that the century plant (*Agave americana,* L.) is a centenarian only when it can't become reproductive for a hundred years. "The most conspicuous factor associated with plant senescence is reproduction." The nutrient was mobilized into the fruit, and the rest suffered. Clarissa Dreben had conceived and spawned F. Dorfman, and who knows if it didn't kill her? Filial sentiments of a matricide. He, Bly, would at times have sold ten of his dayful of years for a few hours with even Mrs. Shearer's dying buds. People dying, Drebens dying. What to say? "Nuts." (Indehiscent, polycarpellary, one-seeded fruits, woodily pericarped. "Fine examination there, Bly.")

He picked up *The State of the Union,* then put it down, ran around the corner to the Trebilcocks and suggested that there was still enough light for a quick badminton game. He and Oscar tied the net cords to the apple trees, laid out the boundary stones, and whacked the birdie till the dark wouldn't even let them guess where it was. He told them his assignment, and, telling it, laughed at its absurdity. The next day, he told it at the physiologists' table, elaborating it with echoes of the Flaherty story. That was it. May passed, and thoughts of the dying Clarissa died with it. Teaching, the study of senescence, the preparation of a paper to be given at the June meetings of the American Association of Plant Physiologists, and then Phyllis Gammon, drove the drebitis from his system.

He had traversed the difficult teacher-student chasm between "Miss Gammon" and "Phyllis." There'd been coffee,

then Tai Gum How, then intimate conversation, then amorous
relations with the wiry young physiologist from Cumberland,
Maryland, who herself remarked about, and thus arrested, the
humorous notice of hot gammons and Cumberland Gaps. A girl
after if not Bly's heart, at least his mobilizing centers. Even the
thought of sacramental union entered his orderly mind without
disordering it. Not that there had to be a crash program. Phyllis
was no raving beauty, no sexpot. Her discernible virtues were
not those prized in the Bedsheet Derby. She was his, more or
less for the asking, a splendid alteration in his life.

He was playing badminton with her at the Trebilcocks when
Dreben showed up. A June Sunday that squeezed heat from the
stones and thickened the air with summer sounds. They played
in shorts, Bly shirtless, asweat. The apple trees were misty with
green, their branches wild with the coming weight of the rosy
balls busy now sucking nutrient from the sap. The yard ran with
children, four Trebilcocks, five Grouts, assorted derivations
from China, Ireland, the Baltic, Africa, a running sea of life,
rising in the trees, covering the flower borders, drifting through
the Jungle Gym and miniature geodesic dome in the yard. Bly
and Phyllis—a little wiry for shorts but a great pull on him—
whacked the feathered cork over the net while Trebilcock and
his wife poured a gallon of Savoia Red back and forth toward
their glasses. Bly and Phyllis swigged away between points, so
that by the time the dark, bald, bespectacled man in the
houndstooth winter overcoat strode through the yards, through
the quieting children, Bly was drunk enough almost to disbe-
lieve his presence. "Professor Bly?" Bly saw the black eyes scoot
up and down behind the spectacles, and the thinking, "This? A
professor? A poet? A sweaty squirt slapping a piece of cork at
a sweaty girl, boozing on a run-down lawn. What gives?"

"Yes, I'm Bly. What can I do you for?" though he knew it was
Dreben.

Hand out of the houndstooth sleeve, shaken by Bly. "F. Dorfman Dreben, Professor. You remember. A month back. Excuse
my bothering you here Sunday. Your landlady directed—"

"Over here, Mr. Dreben," and Bly led the man by the
houndstooth elbow to a corner where a rickety bench leaned on
an elm. "You want to talk with me about the poetry, even
though I told you that silence meant inability to bring back the
bacon." His bare chest, both narrow and puffy, a snake of hair

winding sweatily down toward his shorts, did not enforce the harsh chill of voice, blue eyes, nostrils shivering with hauteur.

Dreben's rear sank to the bench, the dark, bald skull lowered to the houndstoothed sternum. In the Renoir blaze of yard, he was a funereal smear. Sobered, easier, Bly said, "I'm sorry, Mr. Dreben. If I could have done the job, I'd have done it. Has, is—?"

"Two weeks ago. Smiling." Spoken to his bright oxfords. "She rests under two thousand dollars' worth of granite. Bare. Waiting the expression of our love." The head was up, spectacles catching the gold thrusts of light.

"What can I do, Mr. Dreben? I don't have time. I'm a full-time physiologist." He spread his hands, or rather one hand and one badminton racket. Then, blushed for the latter, and for the guzzled Savoia, for the lawn, for Phyllis, for—as a matter of fact —life. "Except for sheer physical relaxation, every now and then, I don't have the thinking energy for poetry, and poetry takes energy and time. Took me eight works—I mean weeks— to write the one you read."

The head, a darkly golden Arp egg, appealed. "Please," it said. "We know you're the one for us. Two hundred and fifty dollars, a prize in a contest, permanent commemoration on granite."

He'd almost forgotten the gold. On the grass, wiry legs folded against each other, strong knees raised toward an assuredly pointed dickey, straw-head apple-rosy with its own and the sun's heat, his hot gammon. Two hundred and fifty would give them a hot little week or two up on the Michigan Dunes. "In the mail by Tuesday, Mr. Dreben. Something will be in the mail. You send the check by return mail."

Dreben was up, houndstoothed arms churning, off. Not a word. Was silence a contractual ceremony? At the net, he ducked, head deploying for a half-second stare at the three staring guzzlers, then sideswiping half a dozen racing children, he disappeared.

Five hours later, in Michener's Book Store, Bly skimmed a volume on burials and funeral customs. He learned: that in common law, one is responsible for persons dying under one's roof; that corpses were considered sinfully infectious by Persians who placed them in dakhmas, "towers of silence," where birds defleshed them; that West African Negroes wear white at funerals; that the Roman funeral dresses—black—were called *lugubria;* that Patagonians interred horses, Vikings ships, Hindus and Wends widows, and the Egyptians books with their dead. Books, thought Bly. This was about where he came in with Dreben. Though for the Egyptians, the books were for the dead's guidance, whereas his poem was for display, the display of expensive devotion which could summon something "original in nature," a freshly created obect to bury with a freshly uncreated subject.

Bly walked home in the hot streets, past the humming student taverns, the boarded storefronts, the wastelands of the Land Clearance Commission, the crazy blue whirl lights of the police cars, the cottonwood elms sighing in the heat. Life, such as it was, mobilized in the growing points. In Michener's he'd been down where the forces were weakest, in the roots of custom, history, meaning, the roots of death, where only an odd Dreben, dark in his houndstooth winter coat, mobilized for them.

Out of the gashed window of what had been, three weeks ago, a Tastee Freeze Bar, the idea for his mortuary poem came to him.

"Systems in internal equilibrium approach states of perfect order as the temperature lowers toward absolute zero." The third law of thermodynamics which Oscar Trebilcock was using as base for research into frozen protozoa; out of the defunct ice creamery it slipped and made for the granite above Clarissa Dreben. "Yes," said Bly, Master of Science to Bly, Master of Words. "Death is perfect order, life disorder." Dodging a lump of dog dung in the cracked pavement, Bly, the Word Master, thought,

> Clarissa Dreben, know at last,
> Your disorder's been and past.

He stepped off a lawn signed "No dogs. Grass chemically treated," and finished:

> Showing others why they die,
> Under granite, perfect lie.

A great breath in his small chest and a proud look at the prinked-up sky. He'd done it. He ran up the block, up his stairs, called Phyllis and recited it to her. Her response did not dampen him; she was no flatterer. He typed it out on Department of Plant Physiology stationery, just stopped himself from putting an air-mail stamp on the envelope, and ran downstairs and two blocks to the Fifty-Third Street mailbox, pickup at 6:45 A.M.

He must have lain awake till pickup time, drenched in thoughts of gods and death as perfect systems, the former discarded by his mind's razor, Occam's, the latter retained, warmly, the spur to research, poetry, the ordering of disorder. His President's hero, Quincy Adams, filled volumes dodging the subject. That's what one did. One wasn't dragged by the beast; one saddled it and rode elsewhere. He was grateful to Clarissa and F. Dorfman, and went to sleep thinking well of them, the sun firing itself through the soot smears on his window.

The next week he gave his Senescence paper at the Plant Physiology Meetings in the Palmer House. A minor triumph which brought him two job offers which he brought to his department chairman for squeezing out a raise and promotion. He saw no one but physiologists and Phyllis, the latter at supper, though one supper extended to breakfast.

At the end of June, the Trebilcocks left for their yearly month in Wisconsin, and Bly remembered the Michigan cabin that he'd planned to rent with his Dreben money. It had not been sent, nor had there been any word at all from F. Dorfman. "Call the man," said Phyllis from the bed, where she lay, covered with his sweat and her own. He didn't have to look up the number. Bl 6-4664. He dialed and reached a message service, left his name, number, and any hope of getting through to Dreben.

Half an hour later, though, the phone rang.

"Hello, Mr. Dreben. I called to find out why I haven't heard from you."

"Yes. I was going to call. We've been considering the entries until just this afternoon, Professor. We've reached our decision. I was going to call. As I said. I'm afraid that the decision has gone against your fine poem."

Bly held the phone off for two or three seconds, the six pockmarks whirling in the heat. "What are you doing, Leon?" Phyllis in white socks, the bare remainder curved toward him like an interrogation mark.

He said, "You'd invited other—there were other poets writing verses for you?"

"Two others, Professor. Baldwin Kerner, editor of the Township School yearbook, a fine young poet, and then a dear friend of my sister's, Mrs. Reiser."

"Which won?"

"I have only one."

"Who won the contest?"

"Baldwin. His poem was not quite so forcibly expressed as yours, but it was beautiful and true to nature and Mother. Of course, he knew her."

"Is there a second prize?"

Pause. "Yes. You won honorable mention."

Bly lay the phone on the tiny rubber towers, reached behind him to touch Phyllis, who reached around to touch him. No plant in evolutionary history had ever contrived such mingling. Then the animal spirits mobilized in the reproductive centers, and he and Phyllis faced each other.

Idylls of Dugan
and Strunk

1

On a hunch, Strunk took the check over to Dugan in the hospital. "Is this your baby?"

Dugan's head is mummified, chin to scalp; the cola-colored eyes peer over damaged cheeks. "Lire. The rat." He passes the check to Prudence, sitting in the armchair.

She reads. "Six-point-seven billion lire. Who's this princely Corradi?"

"A Beinfresser holding company. What is it in dollars, a million?"

Strunk says he makes it a million-two. "No lagniappe."

"Not from your aunt," growls Dugan. "It's nothing."

Beinfresser was his discovery, he'd been after him over a year, and though he'd worked harder and come up goose eggs, he'd never wanted to hook a prospect more than this one. Ten days ago Strunk's girl had shown him how. Well, this was only first blood. The Beinfresser Library. The Beinfresser Student

Village. But lire. "If computers fell in love, I'd call it an accident."

"Maybe that's the way the Holy Ghost dishes it out." (The check was drawn on the Banco di Santo Spirito.)

Early spring light off the Midway. April 12. Roosevelt's Death Day in Dugan's calendar. Lucky it wasn't his own. *University Aide, Ex-White House Assistant, Casualty of King Riots.* He was stupid, but maybe now, after a terrible year, he was getting lucky. He had Beinfresser's first installment, he had Prudence —who could also be charged up to Beinfresser—and he was going to walk out of here more or less as he was a week ago.

But was Beinfresser pulling something? Lire didn't leave Italy. Maybe he was just thrashing around—angry that Dugan cornered him—twisting an arm to make a nickel, making the University pay for conversion of his spare lire.

The glooms and twists of fund raising. Strunk had laid it out for him the first day, three years ago. "Philanthropy's a Circe. Makes brutes."

Dugan had spent four years shepherding fifty Midwestern congressmen through three hundred billion dollars of appropriation; he did not take to the chicken feed of university donors. "They don't have to give."

Younger, gloomier, kinder, an endless generalizer, Strunk said, "They smell our interest in their death. Makes 'em mulish. It's not like plucking taxes from Topeka. You're head-to-head with these dollars."

Which was so.

Donors were coaxed over soufflés, in swimming pools. One studied their habits, wishes, connections. One knew one's rivals: strayed sons, forgotten cousins, Boy Scouts, Heart Fund, Bahai. One learned the seasons of donation: seeding, watering, bloom, the stems of resistance turning brittle, dropping into the basket. Even then it wasn't over. In three years Dugan had already been ambushed by devious wills, consumptive litigation.

Meanwhile, despite his pride at taking no guff, he ran errands, commiserated sniffles, confiscatory taxes, the moneyed nature of things.

His first year, he'd gone once a month to the Cliffhanger's Club for cheese soufflé, apple pie, and the discourse of Lynch, the bond man.

Out of the Georgia scratch country into the Chicago grain market, then, after the First World War, sensing the shift in Chicago big money from goods to paper, Lynch started the first great bond house west of Manhattan. A bachelor without apparent ties, a fund-raiser's dream, he was worth at least seventy million. Gray, froggy, his vague eyes hung from a large, warty head; a real beaut. Subtle, cold, autodidact and pedant, he was mad for discourse and learning. Yet never bought a book. University fund-raisers borrowed requested titles from the University Library and read them, preparing for the lunches.

In Dugan's time, Lynch was wound up in violence. Carlyle, Sorel, Lenin, Sartre, Fanon, the *Iliad,* and the Old Testament were piled by gold spores of soufflé to be grabbed, leafed through, quoted in refutation. "Got you, Dugan."

Dugan lost himself in dispute and took no guff. A New York street battler, a wounded Korean vet, he had authority in the old bond man's eyes. "Not that your rutting dogfights changed the world that counts."

What counted was dedicated violence, the violence of purification, a strike, Watts, Algeria. "I bring not peace." Lynch was wild about Stokely Carmichael, "a new Lenin," and was driven up to the University to hear him. His Negro chauffeur, Henry, sat beside him, "so you can hear what a great black man sounds like." But Stokely's cold rage roused old cracker blood. Lynch wrote out a question and told Henry to ask it: "Spose, suh, that rev-ole-oosh-n-erries is moh crupt den ex-ploiders?" Bird-head jeweled with sweat, Carmichael ran sad eyes up and down the little chauffeur. "You're wearing your master's livery, and you ask me such a question. Who wrote that out for you, brother?"

"Answer the question," croaked Lynch. He meant Carmichael, but Henry pointed to his right and said, "He did."

The *Tribune* photographer took a picture, the only time Lynch's face appeared in a Chicago newspaper. This "outrageous impropriety" was his excuse when Dugan popped the long-suspended bubble of his philanthropic intentions. "You see what happens when I stick out my neck. I get smeared all over the newspapers. Can't afford that kind of thing. I'm the diocesan financial adviser. Imagine what the Cardinal thinks. You'll have to wait."

Dugan's complexion was curd white, the pallor of repressed

fury. The old man, scared, blinked, then covered, asking if they could try Carlyle's *Frederick the Great* next time. "Hitler's favorite book. Goebbels read it to him in the bunker."

"We'd better cool it awhile, Mr. L." Dugan would eat no more soufflés.

A step, which, back at the University, he double-checked with his boss, Erwin Seligman, the Provost. "Absolutely. Tell him to shove it." Intense, elegant, baldly handsome, a tongue-holder and aristocrat. "I'd rather go under than dangle from that four-flusher's whims."

Said Strunk, "It's the beast of flirtatiousness. They dangle their dough under your nose like Elizabeth dangled her stuff for the ambassadors. The whole universe is a come-on. Djever see a two-month-old kid tug a blanket over his eyes?" The bachelor talking to the father, the ex-father. "My God, even flowers do it. Folding with the sun. And rocks. Those winking crystals. The Principle of Uncertainty. Sheer flirtation."

They worked facing each other, their desks by the trilobed, iron-ribbed Gothic window, one of hundreds in the educational Carcassonne along the Midway. "Americans live in a historical rummage sale." Strunk's blue-shirted, gorilla arm waved at the useless crenellations, culverts, contreforts. "Midway Gothic. And jungle," the arm over the slum miles under the University's architectural eyebrow. "Mies glass, Saarinen concrete, Pevsner topology. And behind, the American behind. With our *rejecta*. And here," the great arm over their slanting nook, "our little museum."

Sure enough. Back of Strunk's head was Dugan's two-dollar Pissarro print, woods, sky, fishermen, tow path, a pond doubling and confusing the rest. Behind his head, *Playboy*'s Miss March, "lasagna-loving, sitar-strumming Lisa Joy Sackerman, M.A. in Slav. Lit." Tacked beside Miss Sackerman's pale watermelons was *The Thoracic Viscera*, lungs, the central clutter, the muscular baggage of the heart, the screw-ribbed pole on top, the trachea, the crewel-stitched pole beneath, the descending aorta.

On their Indiana maple desks, amidst bank reports, Olivetti and Dutch Royale typewriters, Florentine blotters, Swedish letter openers, were Dugan's souvenirs, the quartz chip from a Mayan palace, pink limestone from the tower where Roland had supposedly blown out his warning and his brains, a conglomerate sliver from Injon which, with a quarter-inch of Pekinese steel, had been removed from Dugan's left elbow in 1951.

"Fossils, sediment, souvenirs, imports, hand-me-downs. Historical junk shop. And what am I doing now? Setting up a transatlantic telecast on genes with Crick, Perutz, Watson, and Burkle. Those little human museums." Strunk meant the genes.

Dugan was on Strunk's wavelength, liked him immensely, and though he seldom saw him outside the working day, knew he was the one he'd call in a pinch, had, in fact, after his son's death and his wife's breakdown.

They sat across from each other day after day, never quarreled, seldom felt disparity, though Dugan was fifteen years older, a hard-noser, athlete, fighter, a little man, and Strunk was huge, soft, a pacifist and do-gooder, a fantasist who wanted to alter the world and make himself heard doing it.

Strunk's reveries were violent, formed out of Eric Ambler and James Bond. He daydreamed himself in Park Lane tweeds carrying lethal pencils through chancellory gates, kidnapping presidential grandchildren to force changes in policy (infantile fingers mailed, one a day, with menacing but high-minded notes), organizing guerrilla wars on Burmese borders, convening world revolutionaries, himself and the late Guevara the only white men. Then, tanned and hardened, converting twelve-year-old Thai maidens into sexual H-bombs, riding herd on the aligned golden backsides of Santa Monica, sipping at the True Beloved's clitoral brim.

In daylight, Strunk outlined salvationary schemes, discerned threats to civic harmony, leaky valves, closed doors, defects in thought and state which he called to the attention of congressman, policy maker, theoretician, and physician in newspapers, magazines, letters. A new, unknown Voltaire, demi-poet, demi-artist, urban dreamer, reader, raised in Manhattan, educated in Chicago, a bachelor who'd not been east of Long Island or west of Oak Park, M.A. in Eng. Lit., University functionary and one-course-a-year lecturer in the English Department.

Whereas Dugan, born in La Guardia's New York fifteen years earlier and two miles southwest of Strunk's birth house on West Eighty-Second Street, fighter, traveler, ex-father, ex-husband, daydreamed pastorals. His life as violent as a legal, urban, burgher life could be, Dugan had no utopian thoughts. The University was the closest waking life he'd come to his reveries, and he believed this even after his fourteen-year-old son was stabbed to death on a Hyde Park street.

Dugan celebrated his fortieth birthday in October, 1967, "the two-hundred-eighth anniversary of Georges Jacques Danton, French revolutionary figure's birth," said the All-News Station WNUS. WNUS remembered Danton, no one remembered Dugan. Burkle, the Development Office's hope for the next Nobel, told him that after thirty-five, fifty thousand brain cells a year were irreplaceably destroyed. "Not a large fraction of ten billion," but, at forty, Dugan figured a quarter of a million lost cells no joke.

He'd birthday-treated himself to a color television set. Feet up on the old black-and-white one, drinking his nightly bottle of dollar German wine, he watched the shifting Renoirs of the Cronkite News. A scientist found that plants registered human antipathy. Hooked to a polygraph, they sweated anxiety when threatened. What next? Rocks? Matter itself? Unneutral neutrons, shocked electrons? The whole universe a sensorium?

So why not gloom for Dugan? Fifty trillion cells fired into feeling by ten billion (minus a quarter-million) neural triggers. "Enough neural combinations," said Burkle, "to register everything in the universe." Let alone Dugan's troubles: the war, the gripping stink of sulfurous air through the window, the cells dying in his four-decade-old head, his stubborn prospects, the birthday without his son, his wife cracked up in Oswego.

2

What other woman would unerringly find the wrong manhole, and falling, fallen, be saved, and how but by "dese tings." Her "bosoms." There in the middle of Clyde and Diversey, he, Strunk, and the Burkles walking to the restaurant, and no Lena, or only her head, which was screaming, "Omigawd." A black-matted cauliflower yelling in the manhole. Unlikely. (As it had been from the first day in the Amsterdam Avenue Library. "Scuse me, mister, could I take a look at that book you got there? I never in my life seen such a big book.") Hauled out of the manhole, groaning, she ate her way through clams, ribs, and shortcake, now and then hefting her bruised beauties, "Omigawd." Scene Ten Million of Lena's Theater.

Pain or pleasure, it never ended: chasing rock throwers off the fence, "Don't gimme that racial shit, boy, you're a rat, black or green. Toss another of them rocks, and you get it right inna mouth"; piling the Appalachians' mattresses into the Rambler ("Miz Dugan, you one fiuhn person"), shouting at the Subcommittee hearing, "He's a goddamn liar, Senator. Don't tell me, Smalley. I moved you in them five rooms myself, what you givin' these senators that shit for?" With Javits saying, "Now, look here, let's keep it calm, please, Miss." "Miss! There's ninety pounds of son out of this Miss, Senator. This man is lying. I moved him in myself. He is just milking you guys. Right, Smalley?" "Hell, Miz Dugan, ahm jis tryin' to git these senators tuh see the kiuhnd of thing, ya know," and Kennedy said, "O.K., Van, take down what this woman has to say."

Those first weeks in New York, she was the country mouse, no question, up from Simsbury, Ohio, nine hundred people, five Italian families who got together every month to sing opera, the kids taking parts, the factory money going into the pizzas and red wine from her father's *'storante,* people driving over the bridge from West Virginia or even the mystical sixty miles over the hills from Pittsburgh. (When someone had to go up there for X-rays, the families would see him off as if to the moon, he'd return with stories of the terrible roads, the turns, the black fog.)

It was from Pittsburgh their troubles came, Domenico Buccafazzi with the gold watch to be raffled for the Poor Widow with Seven Children Whose Husband Drowned in the Oak Grove Brook, and next month Papa asked him, "Who won the watch?" and it was someone over in Branchtown, and a month later, it was another watch, and this time it was won by a Mrs. DiBaccio, a Crippled Lady in Oak Grove, and Papa said, "I don't believe," and drove the pickup over the hills, and there was no Mrs. DiBaccio in Oak Grove. And one day Luccio, the fruit man, came in the house and told the kids to get under the beds, and said to Mama, "Don't go downstairs, whatever." In the street was a black Imperial with curtains down on the windows, and they all knew only They could own such a car, and Papa went into it, and was gone three days, they thought he was never coming back, and Mama said to Luccio, "I'm going to the FBI, I'm an American," but Papa came back that night; though not the same inside.

At night, the old people sat in the room with red wine, she would close her eyes on the couch and would hear how the little Oak Grove vegetable man, Cucciadifreddi, who'd Brought Over his sister's son and taken him into the store, had been forced by Them to Show the Sign and shot the boy himself and threw him into the river. She had gone to the funeral with Mama, and when people wondered how such a good swimmer could have drowned, she had said, "But, Mama, he was shot," and Mama had stuffed the rosary beads in her mouth and said, "Where you hear that? Who tell you that? Milena, please don' say tings like dat."

In Tampa, staying with Cousin Franco, who ran a club on the Gulf, she'd gone to a party, there were racks of fur coats, and the ladies' heads jerked toward them every other minute (as they had been gotten, so could they be got), and Franco came not with Cousin Mary, but with a pile of hair-mink-and-diamonds, Margarita, who invited Milena for a sail on her boat, till Cousin Franco said, "She don' visit." She had helped out at the tables, serving whatever it was that passed for Cutty Sark or Johnnie Walker, when the ladies started grabbing their coats, and there by the dance-floor palms, like a George Raft movie, stood the iron-eyed men with guns out, cursing.

Her brother Louie whizzed through law school and the bar exam. Every week, he'd be taken to New York or Chicago, and lapped it up, thinking what a card he must be. He hadn't finished the exams a month when a man whose picture she later saw at the Kefauver Hearings showed him a list which said, "Louis Masiotti, Judge of the Circuit Court," and Papa said, "We're moving," and they'd gone north, but one day the man showed up and asked Papa, "What happened to that son of yours? I showed him the list. Is he crazy?" And Papa said, "You know kids, he went on the bum. He is a restless kid."

Lena's cousins from Oak Park invited them to a party, Milena and the Irish husband who'd worked for President Kennedy. They were jeweled and furred and talked about their children. One of the cousins had blue streaks on her face. Two weeks before, her husband had been gunned to death in his bed, the blue marks were powder burns, and she was drinking with the wife of the man who'd made them.

Dugan told Strunk, who said, "Sure, but they're getting these guys now. Giancana has to live in Mexico, Genovese is in the can. With this immunity thing, they can't take the Fifth. Anyway, television is killing it. The kids don't care about the furs and nightclubs and fixing horse races. Watch. In fifteen years, there'll be no Mafia," but when they found Mikey bled to death in the street, though it was the Apostles that stabbed him, no question of that, Strunk believed it was the Mafia and wanted to have all of Lena's relatives hauled in till one of them broke down and confessed.

But by then, she'd started to break; one look at her face zipped Strunk's mouth, and he took care of the coffin, the service, the grave, the newspapermen, got Lena into the hospital, and sat with Dugan till he could manage by himself.

Though, thought Dugan, in a way Strunk was right, the Mafia was guilty, for wasn't it that crazy theater in her blood that not only made her heroic but made her force Mikey into the squad car and ride up and down the streets fingering the boys who'd forced the white boys to climb the ropes in gym and push them off? And wasn't it in Mafia towns, Tampa, Newark, Buffalo, Youngstown, Chicago, that government rotted and ghettos burned?

Misery fogged his mind. What did the cause of it matter? The kid was dead, one of the best ever, the only thing he'd come close to being lost in with love.

And the second thing, Lena, was as good as dead.

In the cold-temperature lab, Dugan had watched a professor dip chrysanthemums into superchilled nitrogen. Out they came, apparently the same, but crystalline. So Lena went through the funeral, apparently unaltered, only slightly abstracted, but within, the motion was gone. Strunk took her to Billings, and from there she went to Oswego.

3

Dugan discovered Beinfresser in the Periodical Room. Once a month he speed-read through thirty or forty periodicals in four or five languages. The gift of tongues, found out on Ninth Avenue among Puerto Ricans and Poles, developed in Brooklyn College, Korea, Washington. In *Der Spiegel*'s series on "The New Breed of Tycoons," he learned Beinfresser had not only gone to the University, but regarded himself as a "true offshoot [*ein echter Sprössling*] of Chancellor Tatum's reforms." It was during the Depression ("a moneymaker's good times are other people's bad times"), he'd cornered the dormitory coal and laundry concessions, made twelve thousand Depression dollars a year, and won a special farewell from Chancellor Tatum at the graduation ceremony: "You're the model of the student this University exists to eliminate."

In 1946, out of the OSS, he showed up in civilian clothes in Frankfurt/Main with enough of a stake to pick up the war's usable junk: tires, rifles, mess kits, soap, iodine, antibiotics, boots, condoms, airplanes. He had a work force made up of DPs, deserters, cripples, quislings, *Staatlosen,* Krupp foremen, Undenazifiables. They peddled his goods door-to-door, unfroze the assets in widow's mattresses, socks of gold sovereigns, wedding silver, unworked pig farms. Twenty years later, "this great coiner" [*"dieser grosse Münzer"*] was "the Daedalus, Ariadne, Theseus, and Minotaur of the largest corporate labyrinth in Europe." *Der Spiegel* listed "a small fraction" of the companies, "Uganda Ores, Buttenwieser Computations, Banque Nationale de Ruande, Walsh Construction Toys, Fahnweiler, Peyton Shoes, Tucson Metals, Weymouth Investment and Mutual Fund, Corradi, Sempler, Cie., Montevideo Freight and Shipping, Foulke-Arabo Petroleum Products, Meysterdam, Wrench Ltd., the Hamburg *Presse-Zeitung,* the Nord-Suabische Rundfunk, and *Peep, A Weekly."*

With the help of Alfred Somerstadt and Jean Docker of the Business School, Dugan followed the Beinfresser trail. Section 60-735A of the 1959 Internal Revenue Code was called by the author of *The Great Treasury Raid,* "the Beinfresser Provision," tailored by Beinfresser lawyers to his mutual-fund operations and inserted in the bill by Representative Templeton (R.-Ariz.) "without opposition." Mrs. Docker had done a dissertation on mutual-fund manipulations, but Beinfresser's were beyond her grasp. "He's just another social tapeworm."

Somerstadt was more useful. A jolly little fellow, tycoons enchanted him. He'd written a three-volume work on Diesel, Heinkel, and Bosch; these were the true forces of German history. "Hitler," said Alfred. "What is that *Schwein* but an economic splinter." Beinfresser was something else. Each day Alfred discovered some other refinement in the corporate geometry. "This fellow's an artist. Not a Bosch—he's no scientist —but money. Money he understands."

"Does he have money to give?"

Alfred's generous lip puffed out that absurd irrelevance. "What's that going to do for him? He wouldn't give a quarter to a daughter."

"He's got a daughter?"

"Of course not. Can you see him putting *Geld* into baby shoes? This man is pure. An economic saint."

Dugan had enough of the celebrant's mass. He needed a lead-in, but didn't spot one till Tatum showed up in Chicago for a speech to Midwest Philologists.

4

The ex-chancellor was a man who relished distant views and noises—droning, humming—the genuflection of furniture, all heights, pulpits, platforms, theater boxes. He was built to be looked up to. Tall, muscular, his face loomed with northern contrasts, salt-white hair combed into waves, blue eyes deep in deep sockets, cheeks red at the bone points, and creviced with years of public sufferance of fools. His voice was rough, scraped, his hands thick veined, a farmer's except for the nails, small reflectors which, as he talked, mooned around for emphasis.

Dugan, a sniffer of snow jobs, had to fight off a giant one. Tatum, like a great clown, made himself life's butt. He told Dugan how FDR had seen through him. "Ickes and I were after the Vice-Presidency. Roosevelt handled us like counterfeit fives." He went back to Chicago, defeat in his face. Failure was infectious. Soon he couldn't handle trustees, other university presidents, the faculty. "Those opera tenors did me in."

The eyes stayed on Dugan's, a weight of assessment. For *Harper's*, he'd written, "Kennedy's death scattered a flock of loyalists over the country, rough Irish trade that cleared the trail of his political flop and called it gold dust."

"Good fighters only remember their losses, Mr. Tatum. That's the way with you. And probably that billionaire graduate of ours, Beinfresser. He's always talking about you."

"Oh? What's he say?" Tatum never objected to hearing himself quoted. Though he had a fine clipping service and had seen the piece in *Der Spiegel*.

"He mentions what you said about the University existing to eliminate types like him. Yet, you know, he thinks of himself as your disciple. You're probably one of the few living people he's showing off for."

"Absurd. Except for an annual Christmas card, atheist Jew to atheist Baptist, I don't hear from him. Just an annual touch of spiritualist Esperanto."

"Maybe," said Dugan, sticking in, "but types like him are after some kind of championship. What they need is someone to crown 'em. Like Napoleon needed the Pope. I think it's why he sends you Christmas cards, makes references to you. I'm convinced all he needs to know is you're still behind the University. One letter from you, and I'd bet in a year or less there'd be money for a building. Named after you. The Tatum Cryogenics Laboratory."

Said Tatum, "I thought whatever the University was like now, it had good technicians. As usual, I'm wrong. The technicians are just romantic poets. Mr. Dugan, this man wouldn't notice if my corpse were left in his bathtub. As for the University, it wouldn't name a baboon's toilet after me. I enjoy a bit of Celtic twilight, Dugan, but at eleven o'clock in the morning, even my eyes are usually on the objects in front of them."

"You know your powers better than anyone, Mr. T."

Something went on in Tatum's face, a small anxiety. "Power is something men understand very differently. I've been around too many sorts to reconcile them."

"Some sorts are unquestionable, aren't they? Something comes off, or it doesn't. In public life or private. I was around Washington for two Cuban crises. I know the difference between bringing something off and not bringing it off. You can tell the difference in people's walks, the way they eat, when they joke, how they go to bed."

"Public failure intensifies private relationships, Mr. Dugan."

"Not mine, Mr. T. I can't operate anywhere with failure in my system."

"I think you'll come to feel differently. Even about the relative failures of your Mr. Kennedy. I think he was a fairly strong man after the Bay of Pigs. The admission of stupidity is strength. As for that Missile-so-called-Crisis, that was a sporting event, whipped up for personal redemption. Those silver calendars, JFK to RSM or whatever, they were boys' trophies. Banana-state dramatizing. Look at the Sorensen book, with all its theater talk, 'roles,' 'postures,' 'antagonists.' Crisis was just drama for your sportive ex-bosses. They'd burn up the world for a good show.

"I say the hell with all these strutters. Everyone quotes Acton's maxim, but how many believe it? I do. Stay in power long, and the concrete turns to smoke. You can't handle it. You can't tolerate opposition. And you exhaust your own aides. Look at the married life of a powerful man's subordinates. They're emasculated by him. He sets the schedules, tells them when they can go home to their wives. And if he wants, the wives will sleep with him. In their dreams, half of them do.

"I'm not speaking out of inexperience, Mr. Dugan. I stayed much too long at the University and nearly ruined it. And I was one of the few in America who knew what it was all about, knew, for better or worse—and you know it's worse—it was going to be the center of action.

"The best-intentioned become posers and tyrants. You don't want a letter from me, Dugan. You know the rich. You don't pat them at a distance. They want the dogs to come to their hand for the bone. I've got enough trouble finding a little meat for myself."

"That old queen," Dugan told Strunk back at the office. "One lousy letter. I should have beaten it out of him."

5

Leonard Strunk had bad luck with girls. This after an adolescence that, as that tunnel of horrors went, was a tunnel of love. From fifteen to eighteen, Strunk was almost continuously in love, and although he did not "lose his cherry"—as the touching expression of those years went—till his junior year at college, the body hugging, tongue kissing, and digital probation of a good lot of pretty New York and Chicago girls fed masturbatory pleasure, sometimes, blissfully, on the unclothed belly of whomever he'd brought up to his room to tune in on Amorous Brahms. Now, in his late twenties, masturbation remained Strunk's chief sexual relief.

As a good part of Strunk's life was determined by what he read, any shame about masturbation was allayed by select readings in twentieth-century novelists. When a Norman Mailer condemned it, Strunk sulked. "Why," he complained to Dugan, "the writer who strokes himself more publicly than any writer since Whitman should have this terrible bug about the most economical of pleasures, this old economist knoweth not."

Dugan disliked such subjects, had to force hearty interest. "When a man's work is done to corral nookie, and Mailer must get plenty, he's naturally going to crow over poor lugs like you beating their lonely meat to Judy Collins. If he ate shit, he'd be knocking hamburgers."

"It's more complicated than that. The guy hates solipsism. That's masturbation. It's why he had to give up fiction, how he saved himself from the loony bin by reportage. See that piece on the Pentagon in *Harper's*? Mailer's our Henry Adams. Explaining America's sewers and cathedrals for the East Hampton feebles."

Masturbation wasn't Strunk's unique source of sexual joy. There was also Mrs. Babette Preester, a thick, sometimes ardent divorcée, secretary to the Committee on New Nations, who shared herself with Strunk three or four times a month after a suitable dinner and what she called "downtown entertainment." (Shows, movies, concerts, good or bad, as long as they got her into the Loop.)

In addition, a student sometimes brought her problems to him in such a way that his fear of endangering a small hold on the English Department was overcome, and, at least for the duration of the term, he enjoyed more or less steady sexual joy. There were occasional windfalls elsewhere: a hat-check girl at the Astor Towers had, to his delighted surprise, winked at him; over Babette's low forehead, he'd made an engagement with her when retrieving his coat, and she'd come to his place on Dorchester a few times, though it was clearer than it was with Babette that she and Leonard shared nothing but each other's parts, clearer that long-term interests could not be realized or envisaged in Leonard's bare-floored, scarcely furnished, book-and-paper-laden bedroom-kitchenette.

Much of Strunk's spare time was spent concocting schemes, plans, suggestions, and criticisms, which were written up in letter form and sent to people of appropriate authority and influence. More and more, the correspondence absorbed his spare time and channeled his large energies. Sometimes, though, he thought his letters might be the static of a mind that was otherwise not getting through. Weren't letters a substitute for real writing? Toil without test? Yet how else be effective? It was better than writing on toilet walls. Though, God knows, more expensive.

Strunk bought stamps by the hundred sheet, and when postal rates were upped he suffered an economic crisis. In addition, he used fine stationery, Pott-sized, creamy rag paper with his signature, O. Leonard Strunk, engraved in six-point golden Mauritius off left center, his home address, in smaller script, off right.

He wasn't vain about his correspondence, nor did he consider it in capital letters as a life's work of commentary and reportage in the manner of Walpole and Grimm. Strunk thought of himself as a small conduit of serious ideas and humane complaints, a Voltaire without genius. Unlike Voltaire, he wrote no intimate letters, no mere expressions of wit, gallantry. He wrote to aldermen about potholes in the street, to the Bundy and Rostow brothers about Southeast Asia, to thinkers and scholars about their discoveries and specialties, and, after Christmas, wrote to the foreign artists who'd painted the finest UNESCO cards. He exchanged letters in French with Papa Ibrahim Tall about the problems of African carpet makers, in German with Willie Fenstermacher, the skiologist of Lech-am-Arlberg, and in English with Vuk Murkovich, the poet, about the bards of Montenegro.

In addition to corresponding with Private Persons, as his account book labeled them, Strunk wrote to newspapers and magazines over the world. His account book was covered with red dirks for Unacknowledged and blue skulls for Unprinted letters, but it was a bad year that saw fewer than a hundred in American newspapers alone. The Chicago *Sun-Times,* the Des Moines *Register* and the Santa Barbara *News-Press* regarded Strunk as a Steady, and their Letters column was instructed to use one Strunk a month.

In the spring of 1966 Strunk began writing to someone who became his single most important correspondent. Miss Elizabeth Schultz had been a student in his "Lyric from Wyatt to Berryman," and was now a researcher for *Newsweek*. She had begun the correspondence by writing Strunk what she said she'd meant to tell him after the course, that it was one of the finest she'd taken at the University. Strunk had replied in grateful acknowledgment, but, as his epistolary impulse was not so easily slaked, he wrote a longish response. What would interest her? He couldn't remember Miss Schultz by looks or intellect (though his record book showed he'd graded her A). He settled on a disquisition about the functions of news magazines, the perils of their simultaneous obligation to entertainment and comprehensive authority. To his pleased surprise, Miss Schultz wrote back an account of the transformation of her research (she worked in the Business Section) by the editorial and writing staffs, and related this to those fashions and conventions in lyric which were, "as you showed us in class," the key to many of the finest poems in the language. So delighted was Strunk that he wrote back an account of structural transformations in neurosis, kinship, language, and religion as he had intertwined them from pages of Lévi-Strauss, R. Barthes, J. Lacan, and N. Chomsky. Miss Schultz replied, after a week "spent on the texts," and her answer generated a full-scale epistle on the relationship of PERT ("Program Evaluation Review Techniques") to such other "self-generating systems as musical scales." Miss Schultz slid by this epistolary iceberg, waited ten days, and discussed the attempts by Wright and Breuer to overcome the "tyranny of New York property rectangles, perhaps another system of self-generation." Her gentle caution evoked in Strunk a tender flow of ideas which, in a few days, found epistolary form in a discussion of the relationship of basic forms to basic concepts. ("Is not the triangle inevitability, the pentagon authority?")

In short, Miss Schultz became Strunk's Interdisciplinary Recipient, his steadiest pen pal. In a year and a half, they exchanged more than fifty letters.

Strunk began to wonder more and more about her. One August day he decided he would take his pre-fall-quarter vacation in New York, but the afternoon mail brought him Elizabeth's reflections on Mini-Art and the Warhol Strategy, with a postscript which said that she was about to spend two weeks with her parents on their farm south of Little Rock. It was the first personal note since Letter One. His Interdisciplinary Recipient was a farmer's daughter. She, a daughter, could have a daughter. Not now—she was a Miss and no East Village hippie-mama —but the potency was more than likely there.

That evening Strunk reread the letter and felt the grip of loneliness. What to do? He telephoned Mrs. Preester, but was told by a baby sitter she wasn't expected till late.

He put on his summer suit, a pale gabardine he'd bought five years ago in Field's basement, and went over to the Oxford Lounge, from which, three or four times, he'd extracted a girl for a horizontal hour in his apartment. Tonight, however, the Kansas City Athletics were at the hotel across the street, and there were no spare girls.

Strunk walked to Fifty-Fifth Street, east to Jackson Park, and through the underpass to the lake. Out on the Promontory, black girls in bikinis stomped and curled to the isolating music of flutes and bongo drums. Coals under hibachis, beer bottles and cans shivered with fire and moonlight. From the vaporous green lake rose Elizabeth Schultz, long and softly ropy. Each nude tendon, each sweet transit from curve to curve, sped him to her. "Open, open," begged Strunk.

The next day, he wrote to Arkansas.

> Dear Elizabeth,
>
> The study of autism (Mahler, Fuère, Bettelheim) reveals the connection between excrement and the sense of self. The autistic child identifies with her excrement; a throwaway, she becomes excremental to save the last vestige of her self.
>
> Elizabeth, I must interrupt the train of thought. It is warm here. Mercilessly. Perhaps it is time to bring up (not as ejecta, let alone excreta) a matter long on my mind. I have been in hopes that you and I might be able to enrich our epistolary mutuality. It would, I mean, be a great pleasure for me to see you. To spend some time talking with you.
>
> I had thought of going to New York now, but you are not there. Before the beginning of the autumn quarter here— that is on Oct. 1—I have several free days. Would you perhaps consider reserving a room for me at a hotel not far from

your apartment? Yours is no longer a neighborhood I know
well. In my boyhood, it was one to be shunned in fear or
approached in trembling. At any rate, perhaps you will think
of this proposal and decide what is best. I sign off, then,

In cordial hope, in hopeful
expectancy, but, in any case,
immer dein,

Leonard S.

Post scriptum: Please forgive rude brevity. Much to tell you
anon re. cultures which prize excreta (Shakes's father;
post-Mongol Near East—cf. treatise of Ibn-al-Wahdwa);
sewage, drainage-ex-aquaria (Med. Lat. *sewaria,* sluice of
millponds), thoughts of Rome and Knossos, the Austro-
Germany of outcast (excretum) Freud, Protestantism (cf.
N. Brown on Swift, Luther), money as dreck in 11th-cen-
tury Europe. But, dear Elizabeth, all this can perhaps save
till we come together, hopefully, dare I say, in new phase
of our relat.

Y,

L.

6

The Thursday before his flight to New York, Strunk was too
skittery to write any letters at all, couldn't read, couldn't do
more than pack and repack, deciding which two of four suits
he should take, and which of the two pack, which wear.
Strunk shopped with the finesse of tornadoes, in with a head-
low rip, hand riffling Forty-Two Longs (though his arboreal
trunk and arms needed Extra Long), then choice, change, fit,
and out. He had one tailor-made suit. In July, 1967, a Lebanese
tailor from the Loop, in deep water after the Arab-Israeli war,
took his stuff up to the Windermere Hotel and offered bar-
gains to Hyde Parkers. Strunk disgorged a rare hundred and
fifty dollars and emerged with a "Mediterranean blue-green
double-vent glen plaid" that made him look like an Aegean
Island. Said Mr. Dalah toward the Strunk-filled ballroom mir-

ror, "Downtown you wouldn't walk out of here for under three-fifty."

The plaid was cut too squarely for Strunk's hulking shoulders, and Mr. Dalah had surrendered too soon to his extensive rear, but the suit was still Strunk's best, and thus hung over the closet door for Elizabeth's first 'sight of him.

That morning he took twenty minutes passing the electric razor over his face, inspecting and practicing expressions, trying for leanness in his generous cheeks, for depth in his puddle-colored eyes, length in his too apish jaw.

No beauty, Strunk, but after all, Elizabeth knew what he looked like, he had not put on more than ten pounds in the years since she'd been in his class, there were still elements of good looks that could be assembled by good will. And her letters bore no sign that Manhattan had raised her standards of masculine beauty beyond Strunkish reach; he might pass, especially in these days when even monsters were thought beautiful.

He ran in place, shoulders back, stomach in, great legs high. The razor cord twisted around the faucet, the razor pulled out of his pumping arm and crashed on the sink. The white plastic cracked, the buzz castrated into whine. Twenty-six dollars.

"Vanity," he told Dugan later. "There I was metamorphosing into Gregory Peck, and Matter Itself rose up against me. I ought to tear this up." His ticket.

Dugan said any woman who passed up a hunk of male glory like O. L. Strunk would be too thick to penetrate with human weapons. He drove him to O'Hare for a final buck-up. "I expect to see you back totally unhumped. An April carpet."

"Poor thing's probably in a wheelchair."

7

New York.

When he was a boy, Third Avenue was bums, pawnshops, bars. Lexington was the limit of the habitable world. You crossed to Third with fear. Now it was a gold-flecked pleasure tent converging downtown in fifty-story glitter. Here, at Elizabeth's corner, were restaurants, antique shops, tailors, cigar stores, butchers, a mailbox. The box which held Elizabeth's letters. No hand behind any light but one could write those letters.

She lived two doors east of Third above a frame shop, closed but lit. Ten names on the mail slots, girls from Teaneck, Hartford, Greensboro, and Mason City who came down the old steps for buses and taxis to ad agencies, dental offices, brokerages, *Newsweek.* Strunk pressed E. Schultz, 3C.

Telling Dugan as much as he wanted to a week later, Strunk confessed that the first look was a shocker. Here was this girl of questing intellect, of voice liquid with kindness, and, at the doorway, greeting her admired instructor, her mind's correspondent, her future lover, there was . . . Slob. Sheer Slob. And not even the Slob of Inattention—mind elsewhere on difficult matter, Thales tripping on the dungheap—but Conscientious Career Slob. Blond hair wild, hip-huggers uncomplimentary to big bottom, shirt stained, middle buttons misbuttoned so hole showed torn brassiere (a bit of tug there). She wore black glasses, had a yolk-tinged smile. What, he had wondered, was this self-presentation supposed to mean?

The place was not quite in motion, but looked as if the order of creation had just been sent in. Clearly the elements had not been able to get into shape on their own. Skirts, newspapers, *New Statesmen,* bridge scores, glasses, packaged-gravy envelopes, cracker cylinders, toothpaste caps, stockings, record jackets, manila envelopes, socks, panties, exhausted ball-points, piles of anything.

"It's a little crowded here." Said easily, liquidly. "I don't know what to throw out. My consumer mind. But here you are. The best item in the place." With an arm-shove, clearing a wounded couch. Then opened a labelless bottle of soybean-colored liquid and poured into glasses which many, less fastidious than Strunk, would have refused to touch. "I tell you, Dugan, at that point, I thought the old leaning tower would fall. Yet, I dunno. Somehow, in the room, she had that wine at her mouth, and there was this sweetness in her smile. Terrific. And she had the loveliest, clear jawline. I love jawlines. And an out-of-this-universe cream-and-fruit complexion. I tell you, she just came together for me. In that sewer of a room. Maybe that was the reason for it. A dung setting for the queen pearl. So I stayed. The whole week. The bedroom wasn't bad. And she's a heartbreaker. I recommend letters."

8

In Geneva, where the Rhone debouches into the Lake by the Quai du Mont Blanc is the Hôtel de Pologne, eight stories of angel-food-cake limestone, its lake-front windows shaded by purple awnings which, from the excursion boats docked below, appear the proper regal flourish of this most republican town.

Barney Beinfresser occupies the top three floors of the hotel. Six years before, plaster walls were knocked down, and, in the tripled spaces, walls of mirror and satin put up. Persian beds, Murano chandeliers, Roman chests, Empire beds, Brussels tapestries, French fusils, Danish desks, and American business machines were lifted by exterior cables and installed through dismantled windows. Fifty of the prettiest girls in the canton followed to answer phones and press buttons.

As is well known since the rise of capitalism, money will give a cripple legs, a bald man hair, a faded woman skin of rose and silk. Barney Beinfresser's money put gloss in his monk's crescent of black hair, exercised and massaged his flab into muscle, tanned his short body (and, in shoes, subtly elevated it), shaped his face away from his persimmon nose, educated sideburns over his great ears, and polished the very air around him. Girls genuinely lusted for Barney and told themselves—as well as him —that for richer or poorer they would be his.

Barney had horses and Barney had planes, Barney had assistants whose assistants had horses and his assistants had planes. And all this he had earned himself.

After a couple of head-bashing years in which he'd used up the stake he'd accumulated as a student-businessman at Chicago, Barney converted small Yiddish into German and became a denazifier for the OSS, a role which had him, a sergeant, outranking colonels. He worked out a technique for uncovering concentration-camp guards masquerading as inmates: a key question, a five-hundred-watt spotlight in the eyes and a punch under them; his confession rate was tremendous. He lived in a Rhine castle, commandeered cars, concerts, wine, and girls.

Meanwhile, he prepared.

He crated gargoyles off cathedrals (some fallen, some helped to fall), picked up dinner services of Meissen and Rosenthal china for cigarettes, and trafficked heavily in enemy souvenirs.

He had an OSS colleague, Corporal Vincenzo, who was attached to the Committee of National Liberation for North Italy. Vincenzo was in the Piazzale Loreto on April 29 when the bodies of Mussolini and Claretta Petacci were hauled in from the hills. Before they were strung up, Vincenzo cut off a few square feet of their bloodied garments and took pictures of the excisions. These, cut into square inches and mounted on inscribed plastic with the demarcated picture attached to the bottom, brought in fifty thousand dollars from collectors in New York, Paris, and Beirut. On May 1, Vincenzo and Beinfresser just missed a ride into Berlin, where they hoped to convert the remains of Hitler into inventory. It was one of their few failures.

In June they drove their crates in half-ton trucks into a Dolomite village and laid low till October. Vincenzo caught pneumonia, Beinfresser confused the antibiotic dosage, and Vincenzo died. Barney dug him a deep grave.

Two weeks later, Barney had his first office, a cellar room in the bombed-out Röhmer section of Frankfurt/Main.

9

March, 1968.

Beads of mist from Mont Blanc hang across the Petit Saleve over the beautiful lake and the gray Old Town. Strunk would have shivered with historic delight, but Dugan is too busy to shift historic furniture. His quarry is very present tense indeed, hairy-wristed, claw-eyed, clumped with terrific force, empty of courtesy.

Dugan and Beinfresser. They sit in an anteroom of an office Dugan will never see. Dugan is sure every word here is taped, there's probably a camera in the gold doorknob.

He has opened up with a conclusion: Beinfresser is a distinguished graduate of the University, his wealth is reputed to be considerable, he, Dugan, wishes him to become a permanent part of one of the great institutions of the world. "What endure at universities are the contributions of the faculty and its graduates. And what houses them. Everything else is transient. We hope a Beinfresser Library or Laboratory will be a fixture of the scene."

"I'm not much on sarcophagi."

Beinfresser's hands are at ease. Only small movements in the arms under the tan cloth suggest that he is not just waiting for Dugan, that he too is heading for something.

"If the next century's Shakespeare and Einstein walk out of the Beinfresser Library, nobody would call it a sarcophagus."

Beinfresser is annoyed at Dugan's shoes heeling his ten-thousand-dollar carpet. Nineteen-dollar shoes. The universities better get with it. They send men after money who look as if they don't know what it is. But Dugan seems a tough cookie. Why is he hung up with a third-rate enterprise? What's lax in him? Where's he been broken? He tells him a new Shakespeare won't need a new library. "Electronics is making an oral culture. Tribal. Nobody ahead of anybody else. Nobody storing it up in files or banks."

What a nerve, thinks Dugan. The *ancien régime* keeping the farmers down on the farm. "Anyway, I'm not thinking about plays I'll never see, Mr. Dugan. I'm only at the *Titus Andronicus* stage of my own life. Shakespeare worked with stories, I with money. I can't bury what I work with. You're not talking to the old Rockefeller now. He was," and Beinfresser pointed a thumb past his ear toward the old city, "a Calvinist. 'Money is the sign God knows I've acted right.' Pretty notion, but sheer balls. I may have been a lousy student, but in Tatum's day, even mules like me found out how to read old rocks. I'm no Calvinist. Money isn't sacred to me in any way. It's just what I work with. Not for. With."

Dugan held back from anything but a look of absorption.

"If I give money, it has nothing to do with Band-Aids. When I give it, it works for me directly or indirectly. It buys me something, or it puts odor-of-rose instead of wolf in someone's nostrils."

Dugan gave him a cold nod, old man to naughty boy; such a big bad wolf playing Machiavelli.

"I don't hide much, what's the point? I'm not even beating around your little bush. You got in here because I have a feeling. That's all now. A feeling the University and I may have something in common besides my degree. It may be certain studies that can be done that I'd, as it were, pay for. Or some property we both can use. I don't need to tell you the University has a tax advantage over even a well-lawyered businessman. Mostly, it's information I need. Maps. I want to know what's going to happen. And I don't want my maps to change too much.

"The universities are making all sorts of excitement. They're spilling over their containers. That changes the maps. My notion is you've got to get better containers. Things change, but rational men must see how they'll change.

"I've operated in junk heaps and ruins. Better than most. But that's over. I'm miles away from that part of my life. I don't want my factories in smoke. I've had that. I was booted out of Iraq last year without an ashtray. I don't like that. I want to get out before the pot boils. A good university's an information center. Maybe even a generator. I might be willing to pay for a plug-in.

"But don't expect anything by next Tuesday. Don't expect anything at all. And don't dun me. I don't forget. You're on my docket. There's a fair chance you'll profit the way you want to profit. But, let me, as they say, do the calling. This isn't a brush-off, Mr. Dugan." He was up. Dugan, in rage, followed.

"I can't have lunch with you. But there's a delightful girl, Mlle. Quelquechose, who said you caught her eye as you came in. She would enjoy your company. And there's always an excellent lunch for people with whom I do business.

"It's been a pleasure, Mr. Dugan."

10

Living as he had for three years in a place where most people systematically deformed their appearance in the interest of that higher appeal which disregards it, Dugan was exceptionally pleased by those who looked as if they'd studied how to look splendid. So the girl who sat on one of the gold couches of the lounge which spooned off the corridor of Beinfresser's anteroom converted the weight of the moneyman's assault into air. Mlle. Quelquechose was quite something.

A small girl, a pert beauty, hair cut boyishly like Mia Farrow's, a nose that started for blueblood hauteur, then buttoned off, blue eyes clear in liquid brightness, a small chin, nectarine cheeks. A miniature beauty, but then, for surprise, for erotic drama, within the red-sweatered suit, an almost Lena-like affluence of breast, and, out of it, what Dugan especially treasured, splendid legs, longer than the shortish body promised, the length emphasized by the nyloned inches north of knee to red miniskirt. The legs pointed his way, crossed like a man's at the red pumps, and an almost male, a gruff little voice came from the red-corollaed throat, "I'm Prudence Rosenstock, Mr. Dugan."

Beinfresser combed more than the Swiss cantons for his flowers. Prudence was Miss Western Michigan, 1962, a model for the Sears Roebuck catalog who'd saved to try it with Galitzine in Italy, hadn't lasted, and had been found by a Beinfresser man in the Milan Galleria cadging emergency income.

The autobiography unrolled in a Fiat 125, "a nervous car," said the Hertz girl, herself a likely enough candidate for the Beinfresser offices. Beinfresser allowed the girls a thousand Swiss francs, and a couple of hundred miles. Prudence suggested they drive into the mountains. Dugan, surveying the map, lit on Vezelay. He'd never been there, never been in Burgundy, and the idea of having the rest of his three days in Europe with Prudence, Burgundian cuisine, and medieval marvels was a powerful draw. Each expectation advanced the other. In fact, allowed it. Dugan was not the sort to enroll in Beinfresser's Fuck-Now, Kneel-Later business. He had to have at least the illusion Prudence was part of a Larger Scheme of Pleasure. He would not even let her charge the Fiat to Beinfresser.

It turned out he could discuss it with Prudence. "I may be semiprofessional, but it sure doesn't suit me. I'm like a nun there. I mean, I live in the hotel," she pronounced this charmingly in Dugan's ears, HOE-tel, "and I go upstairs to the office, and when there's no work, I go shopping with the girls or fix my hair or read, which is O.K., I love to read, but," and she tipped around in the corner to coax Dugan's look from the terrible twists of the Jura roads, a marvelous, novel animal in her round beaver collar and toque, a fur bloom on the red suit coat. "I mean, where's the Struc-ture of my life? I mean, what does it lead to?"

She got lots of good advice from her business acquaintances. Lying, bare, in the Gritti or the Paris Ritz, looking out the

windows at the Salute or the Place Vendôme, she'd posed the
problem many a time, and had received numerous if unvaried
solutions. "Flowers shouldn't worry about their future." Occasionally a job offer. "Sure, more reception whoring, and I had
a year at Olivet, bet you never heard of it, but it's a good school."
An occasional marriage proposal, "but I'm only twenty-four, my
looks are the type that last, if you don't drive us over the cliffs.
I didn't have it as a fashion model. You know they want these
pieces of pipe that can fold themselves up six or eight times and
still come out taller than me. I used to tie ice cubes against my
cheeks. A girl told me if you did that long enough it would make
them look as if they had caves in them. These big houses love
those caved-in cheeks. The more money you spend, the more
starved you're supposed to look. You're thin, you're spiritual. I
mean, the human body has so few variations, people go after any
crazy detail. Next year they'll be looking for girls with hair on
the lower lip."

They ate a lunch in Beaune that was so regal in detail and
strength, they decided to take a room in the hotel, and there,
after half an hour to digest and play with each other, they
snoozed, alternately cozying each other's backsides in their
semilaps.

That night, after hours in town and a dinner served like a
mass, Dugan told Prudence *his* troubles. Trouble-telling was a
fine superstructure for love. The tongue was an eloquent penis,
the ears generous receptors. Trouble-telling preceded every
deep relationship, as trouble itself deepened, then ended it. The
resistance of flesh to flesh, earth to cultivation, donor to beggar,
fact to system, this was proper scene for the few great human
moments. Dugan lay beside the soft beauty in the lumpy bed in
the Hôtel de la Poste, muttering his wounds, salving them in her
soft bowls, her soft hills.

The next day, in Vezelay, he bought a post card of the most
beautiful of the church's capitals, a dreamy stone man pouring
stone grain into a stone mill, an amazed stone man holding a
stone bag to receive the stone flour. The Guide Book explained:
Moses pouring the Old Law into Christ, Saint Paul receiving the
purified text. "Like experience," said Prudence. "You go
through the mill, so next time you do better."

Thought Dugan, Beinfresser has poured this crude beauty my
way, but what we have done together has refined her into what

I won't do without. There she curled in the Fiat, gob of American melting pot, white German, white Celt, taught letters in a PWA high school, lovemaking by a second-string guard, Western Civ. by a nail-biting doctoral candidate from Ann Arbor, ambition by movie magazines and the "Tonight Show," found useful by Beinfresser and now found crucial by Dugan.

11

The day's letter from Leonard was hardly more than telegram length, and then that evening, his telegram arrived with more or less the same message, but spelling out which plane she should get on this Thursday.

Ever since Elizabeth had read *Allegory of Love* and found out that love, like the spinning jenny, was an invention, she'd felt reborn, for if love was something patented in eleventh-century Provence, then so was every other conventional feeling somewhere or other patented. In Bi. Sci. 2, she'd read in Darwin's *Expression of the Emotions in Man and Animals* that musculature developed for one purpose was used by evolved creatures for another: hair bristling to frighten enemies became, in men, expression of their own fright. Thus she could make the motions of love without being in love. (By 1967, every urban girl in the world knew that.) But more, you could think without having to accomplish anything with thought, could run without going anywhere. You could do anything without having the reasons you were supposed to have when you were first told to do it. Wasn't this what existentialism was all about?

She'd come to define her life by accident as much as anything. The apartment mess, which Leonard hadn't caught on to at all, hadn't started that way. She'd been a more or less automatic tidier, as, in adolescence, she'd been an automatic slob, but one day she'd buzzed up to the apartment a guy who'd tied her up, and went through the place like Sherman through Georgia. He didn't get a nickel till he'd raped her. Not the worst, and she naturally took Enovid the way Englishmen take their brollies. A runty, thick-headed, white brute, he asked where the money was. Right in her purse, which she took from the icebox, and

handed him one of the two fives. He laughed and left, a handy-
man paid after a good job. She started to pick up the mess, but
stopped. No. There was no point. Who decided what was Mess
and what Order? Let her chips fall.

In a month, the habit of old order was gone; she'd disciplined
herself to disorder.

For Leonard, she'd actually compromised. Compromising
was something like accepting disorder. Don't buck it. Born a
farmer's daughter, with old attachments to natural order, she
knew there was no point in making life a series of funerals over
old habits. Disorder could include a few of these. Another stage
of liberation.

When, in college, she'd spotted her prototype spelled out in
novels (the Marquise de Merteuil, Lamiel, Hendricks), she realized her contribution to the new woman could be softness.
There was no need to be hard about altering woman's fate. She
didn't often feel hard, or mean, hadn't been pushed around
enough to be resentful or vengeful. Searching her own feelings,
she decided that her independence would be unaggressive, unlike her fictional ancestors', and if not consciously benevolent,
at least along her own reasonably gentle grain.

As for Leonard, he cared about everything. He cared who ran
for President, he cared who won. He cared for her and he cared
for going to bed with her. Old-line, he needed to put the two
together; or, at least, didn't bother thinking that they didn't
have to go together. He "wanted children," but couldn't separate the curiosity and egoism of having his own from the pleasures of having pretty human miniatures about the house. She
said, "I'm for solving population problems by adopting my
kids." Which annoyed him.

Which annoyed her. For she didn't like to annoy anybody
much, certainly not a dear old wise-foolish boob-brain like
Leonard. But she had no curiosity at all about seeing what her
genes came up with. They weren't her invention anyway. She
was just another transient hostess. It would be a grace to retire
them. Now that the world's submerged were poking their noses
out of the swamps, there'd be genius enough around to pester
the whole universe, let alone this planetary crumb. Such, at
least, was the view of E. Schultz.

She checked with United, and telegraphed Leonard she'd be

at O'Hare at six-forty-six—he was queer for numbers. She had a present to bring him from the *Newsweek* morgue about this Beinfresser he and his pal Dugan were after. The researchers hadn't been able to check this item and hadn't used it, but as a student of medieval literature she'd lit up at it. The source— an Italian World War II partisan—claimed Beinfresser got his start by selling relics of "Fascist saints" to American soldiers in occupied Germany. He'd gotten Mussolini's death suit, cut it into bloody strips, and sold them for a hundred dollars apiece. He had likewise—claimed the source—disposed of a suit of Hitler's underwear and Goebbels' clubfoot shoe. Whatever ghoulish use Leonard could make of this exemplary anality, she didn't know, but, if nothing else, he could see her ease of living as relief from it.

She also brought a bottle of the wine he built his courage with. If the gifts didn't stem from love, at least they came from thoughtfulness and caring. Shouldn't that serve even so antiquated a dear as Strunk?

12

The friendly skies of United buckled in the thermal troughs of early spring. In addition to which, the friendly plane was more than woman's flesh could bear, computer salesmen, grandmothers, rusting hostesses trying to enlist you if they were under twenty, eyeing you out of existence if you spotted them a few years. And the anal supper plates, subdivided by Cornell engineers, packaged by Michigan State. The eggs laid, the hatching skinnerized, the feathers plucked, the feet sliced by orderly metals, the contentment quotients laid out on statistical maps. Elizabeth hated airplanes.

Leonard's freighted little head rose half a foot above five other greeters. He was working to diminish his grin. She leaned over the rail and kissed it. "Cheers, love." Two hundred pounds of smiling butter.

He drove Dugan's Dodge, badly, a form of disorder she didn't relish. "I hate cars."

Was it the reason he didn't watch the others? Eyes on the pop-pop flashes of north-bound lights. The Loop huffed up, the traffic narrowed, slowed.

Leonard aimed for and missed the Ohio Street cutoff, went onto Congress Street at thirty miles per, ignoring horns, glares, fuck-you gestures out the windows. On the Outer Drive, relief. It was the only stretch of road he drove easily, the Magikist lips, the Standard sign, the Donnelly plant, the lit-up Douglas pillar, the Drive motels. Relaxed, he waxed. "It took the eighteen-twelve war to warm Jefferson to cities."

Liz, liquidly: "Why so?"

"Saw the country couldn't depend on Europe for manufactures. The anti-city strain is deep in America."

" 'Our alabaster cities gleam undimmed by human tears.' "

Leonard turned off the Drive at Forty-Seventh, drove past the wasteland fringe of the Southside slum, braked by a field of cinders, and kissed her. "I love your learning, Elizabeth."

Less than most men was Leonard made for automobile loving. Nor did Elizabeth relish the Dodge's mechanic breath, the double-parking yards off the express drive. How much dumbness could go with so much doll? "Preserve it then," pointing at cars screeching around them.

He got his hands on the wheel, started off, gears clashing. (If you can't find it, grind it.) "The Vedas are anti-urban, but the city's made for love."

"They do all right in the country. Sometimes with corncobs." Liquidly.

They drove around the high-rise twins islanded in Fifty-Fifth Street, turned up Dorchester without pausing for the stop sign, taking horn fire at the rear.

"The Vedas didn't have urban prescriptions. Buddha did. Like Jesus. The preaching was to the cities. And city people got him in the end."

They were not upstairs ten minutes when the phone rang. Prudence, Dugan's new girl, calling to ask them over for a drink.

Odd foursome of love.

13

In the fall of 1964 Dugan campaigned in California, half for the President, half for Pierre. Nothing big, answering phones, pushing noses out of keyholes, pacifying, procuring, buttering, counting, but it got him out of shepherding his congressmen, and his boss, Bronson Kraus, said he could gather the index figures and feed them to the President once a week.

Which he did, taking a day to gather them, and five minutes to show them to the President and listen to him repeat them without looking at the sheet of paper.

One day, after the session, Dugan told him that he'd been thinking about a guaranteed national income and would like to do something about it.

The huge executive forefinger rammed Dugan's breastbone. "When I need a shoeshine, Dugan, I'll git me the shoeshine boy."

Dugan was transferred to a closet in the Executive Office Building. Kraus found a place for him with the Archives Division declassifying material for release. Dull work for Dugan, who hated everything about history but making it. A Chicago congressman steered him to an opening at the University; there he flew, and there he stayed.

But Dugan's three weeks in Archives had traced a few grooves in his memory. When he and Prudence drank Bloody Marys with Strunk and his pleasant, ham-flanked, not unbeautiful Slob, Elizabeth, her little Beinfresser item ticked into the groove of an Italian Front cable about one Corporal Henry Vincenzo of the CIC, who, after being seen and photographed in the Piazzale Loreto the morning of Mussolini's death, had disappeared and not been heard from since.

As the others drank, Dugan's groove deepened and widened. Then he leaped up and wrote a letter which released the grip of fury Beinfresser had held him in since he had gone to see Chancellor Tatum at the Drake. The letter, most of it based on Dugan's infuriated guesswork, went as follows:

Dear Mr. Beinfresser:
   I want to thank you again for the fascinating talk. I will respect your wishes about not mentioning the subject I broached to you in Geneva. I only wish to tell you that the description of your possible relations to the University Campaign Fund is one which I understand.
   I write primarily of another matter which has come to my attention. I've recently been interested in the case of a Cor-

poral Henry Vincenzo of the Counter-Intelligence group which worked with the Liberation Front of Northern Italy (Audisio et al.). There is some evidence that Vincenzo played a somewhat amusing but discomforting role back there. It had to do with the acquisition and sale of some Fascist relics. I need not bother you with the details. What interests me is that the corporal disappeared in May, 1945 and has not been heard from since. His family assumed he had been killed by German sentries in the last days of the war, then stripped of his identification and buried somewhere. It occurred to me to write a number of men such as yourself who were in various Counter-Intelligence groups and might have gotten to know Corporal Vincenzo. If something about his habits were learned, it might lead authorities to him so that his family could be comforted about his last days (if such they indeed were). Did you perhaps know the corporal?

Chicago is on the edge of spring. My neighbor's tulip shoots are making their debut.

Miss Rosenstock, one of your former employees, joins me in sending regards.

Sincerely yours,

Hugh Dugan
University Development Office

14

By the time Beinfresser's response came, Dugan was in the hospital. Another consequence of his unhistoric regard for perturbation. For it was he who suggested that they go, the afternoon of Martin Luther King's funeral, to Sixty-Third Street; worse, he who had misinterpreted an informative gesture as a belligerent one, had let rage blot out his good sense, and had waged bitter struggle in the street.

It would be too much to blame him for not knowing that Beinfresser's donation had as much to do with these same events as with his clever letter, for Dugan is an old-fashioned man. That Beinfresser is ever alert to those perturbations which alter the values of property and chattel is something Dugan knows only theoretically. (The Beinfresser Computer Center, built largely with federal funds—and supplied by Buttenwieser Computations—began rising on Sixty-Second Street in 1969.) But our idyll does not really care for finance, only Dugan and Strunk and the girls with whom they will spend years. Beinfresser may make huge gains in Southside property, but Dugan and Strunk prosper in other ways.

This is an idyll.

A final section, then, about the troubled days after the murder of Martin Luther King in Memphis, which occurred the evening after Elizabeth came to Chicago for her first visit with Leonard Strunk.

15

In the monkish beauty of Strunk's apartment, Elizabeth woke. What was that ahead, Notre Dame? No. Slant light transmuting a window shaft of a Mies high-rise into a medieval tower.

Behind her, in the three-quarter bed of which he took two-thirds, her good monk, who, last night, had labored so sweetly in their common cause.

No common cause held together the troubled city of Chicago. Rumors burned, and then blocks.

Sunday, she and Strunk, Dugan and Prudence, drove downtown. At Madison Street, beyond the yellow police barricades, clouds of flame-edged smoke swelled, buckled, and broke.

That night the National Guard came into the city. The four lovers watched them—on television—land in planes, take to jeeps and half-ton trucks, then, driving into the city, saw them posted on avenues where stores were shuttered with iron X's, where other windows showed stalactite jags of glass. Smoke from dying fires snaked, flattened, and floated against the ancient walls, less than fifty years of age, but older than Pompeii if measured by cumulative degradation.

Again on television they watched concentrations of violence that made what they had seen even more desperate: a sibling conflagration in Washington, Robert Kennedy talking in a Cincinnati ghetto about his brother's assassination, grieving men who had been with King, the Memphis motel and the room from which the unknown assassin fired. Black leaders spoke direfully, bleakly, menacingly; the President read a hasty message. He had not had a week of martyr's pleasure after his great moment of renunciation. Undercut, as always, by the world's Ks.

Sunday passed, and Elizabeth changed her reservation. She called her office Monday, said she'd be in Tuesday; but Tuesday saw her head in Leonard's lap, watching King's funeral on Dugan's color television set. Strunk had a Xeroxed copy of King's dissertation on Paul Tillich. "God in the streets," he described it. "Mad the way these myths won't stop. You can see King spotting his death in the stories, but how does Judas know he must take the part?" Great nose and lips gilded with the weird light of the set, the rest of the upside-down head obscure to her.

Dugan, in a chair, hand on Prudence's head, feet up on the green casing of his discarded black-and-white set, pointed to Nelson Rockefeller in the packed church rising from a seat to stand with Mayor Lindsay of New York against the wall. The Rockefellers, said their instant historian Strunk, were quick learners. "And probably the only white Baptists in the church." The sermons, the hymns, the mourners in white ("an African carry-over," said Strunk), the smallest King girl asleep against the veiled mother, a bored Senator McCarthy high over his rival, Kennedy, candidate Nixon leaning over to gab with Mrs. John Kennedy, getting frozen, beating a quick retreat into difficult self-absorption: the white-power reef in the mahogany bay within the Ebenezer Baptist Church.

When the casket was put on the mule cart, the lovers went into the kitchen for hamburgers, which Prudence incinerated on the frying platter. "Two weeks, and I can't get the hang of it."

Dugan suggested they go see what was happening on Sixty-Third Street.

Strunk thought it would be dangerous, though there'd been comparatively little activity on Sixty-Third after Saturday night.

They got in the Dodge and drove down Cottage Grove by the smashed acres of urban clearance. "Better put the headlights on, Hughie": Prudence. Dugan pulled them on. South of Sixtieth Street, every car's lights shone against the sun.

Elizabeth said she thought the soldiers would be out in force. At Sixty-Third, under the filthy iron of the elevated tracks, they waited to turn left. A clot of teenagers looked across the iron-pillared, El-shadowed street. The light changed, Dugan went forward and waited for the north-bound cars to make his turn. Behind him, a horn sounded, and kept sounding. They looked around. "We allowed to turn here?" asked Prudence.

"Why not."

The horn yowled on, they made the turn, and Dugan looked around. A black man of thirty or so, leaned out of the window of a scarred Pontiac and yelled something.

Dugan felt his old street fighter's click. Perhaps it had to do with the misery of his last year. Who will say? He stuck his fist out, and yelled back, "Who the hell you think you ARE?" And pulled up, front wheels to the curb.

"Jesus," said Strunk. Prudence and Elizabeth could not speak, could hardly breathe, their mental preparation nothing in the dark of this stupid minute.

The Pontiac stopped in midstreet, cars pulled around it, the driver got out, Dugan's size, a lean man in a green sport shirt. Strunk could see a block down the pillared cavern. Guardsmen in olive green, spread ten yards apart, holding their rifles. A comfort, but Dugan was out of the car, in the middle of the street, flecks of light coming through the crossed rails, the teen-age boys moving off the boarded stores through the smashed glass on the sidewalks. They circled Dugan and the other driver. While the girls called Noes, Strunk got himself out of the car. Dugan and his new enemy faced each other, arms raising into pincers, faces stiff with rage. "No," yelled Strunk. "No more." The Pontiac driver stared at the white whale Strunk. Veins split his neck. Then, oddly, astonishingly, his head snapped toward the iron El tracks, and he yelled.

Terror.

Dugan, a statue, absolute marble in the brown street, shook loose, and then, madly, struck out. And was swarmed over, windmilled. Strunk, fear and terror drowned by necessity, called, "Soldiers. Police." Dugan was standing, slugging; six or seven others were slugging, kneeling, there was flash, teeth, blood. And then, from everywhere, people, women, girls, ulu-lating, and the soldiers, up the long street, running, bayonets out. And Strunk was hit in the back, the head, the side, oh God, his insides, his skin, arm, chest, nose, he covered up, the soldiers

were there, cars were moving, cars were stopping, and then
crashes, smashes, glass, a tavern window, bottles, boys running
up the street, and there were rocks and bottles in the air smash-
ing against cars and pillars, and a low boom, and a flower of fire
grew from the smashed store, and then a thick twist of smoke,
and the street was a blur, though Strunk, leaning on the car, his
shirt out, face bloody, saw over his arm a small girl and boy,
hand in hand, eyes chilled with fear, still as flowers on the
sidewalk, the sidewalks themselves a frieze, noise turned off,
and then sirens and blue whirl lights and black policemen and
two jeeps and a half-ton truck with soldiers, and men and
women flooding east and west in the flare-spiked shade, and the
fire bloomed, glass shivered, and a thin, old, bearded black man
in a burnoose raised his arms, and Dugan, face broken, body
filthy, welted, stained, and bloody, was picked up and put in a
jeep and was gone, and the old man said in Strunk's ear, "Better
git, mister," and then a rifle butt bent his side, and Strunk saw
the scared-and-scary face of a blue-eyed Guardsman behind the
gun, and got to the driver's seat in front of a whimpering,
shrunk Elizabeth and a collapsed, unmodeled Prudence and
with unepistolary uncontrol drove wildly through the iron cavern, dodging the pillars, turning north—wrong—on Drexel,
winging by glaring incarcerated eyes toward the light, toward
the open green and light of the Midway, toward the gray University towers.

Gardiner's Legacy

GARDINER lived and died in such obscurity that the revelations of the last twenty years seem particularly, if somewhat peculiarly, vivid. And now that Mrs. Gardiner is dead, one wonders whether the revelations were peculiar in a way which will affect our view of her great work. The textbooks have it that she was a simple woman inspired to great deeds by two things, the loving memory of her husband and a heroic commitment to history and literature. Who can say now? One knows that she began almost immediately after the funeral—if one can use a word which suggests a far more complex ceremony than Gardiner enjoyed. At any rate, it couldn't have been more than a month after the city put him in the earth that the news of the first two posthumous volumes appeared in the *Times*. And then, within six months, she'd found *Weatherby's Version* packed away with old clothes in the attic, and Gardiner vaulted from the status of a footnote in the second edition of Spiller and Thorpe to someone who rated a chapter alongside James and Melville and Faulkner.

That first year, it looked somehow unnatural, a hoax of some sort. Someone even suggested that Elinor had written the new stuff herself. (As far as I was concerned, all the better. More would have been forthcoming while she lived.) But such suspicion couldn't last long, and didn't. Elinor was, well, no fool, but nothing could have tapped Weatherby from her, let alone the journals and letters. No woman born of woman could have written it, at least no woman whose imaginative power did not equal, say, Sappho's plus Jane Austen's. And no one has yet accused Elinor of imagination. What was there, she saw, and saw well, which makes the final discovery even stranger.

There she sat in the midst of it, twenty years of brilliant commemoration, copying, collating, editing, managing the swelling estate, selecting playwrights and producers for the adaptations, corresponding with translators, scholars, devotees, newspaper people, a mammoth job, an enterprise that amounted to several millions of dollars, and more, of course, to a new image of action, character, and life.

For that's what Gardiner turned out to be, a Stendhal, a Dostoevski, someone who'd created a new sensibility. And there she was, giving it birth in the very act that betrayed her. Every commemorative motion, every discovery, ripped off her skin and flesh, broke the bones, ground them down, and blew the dust into space—and there she sat, getting photographed next to the bookshelves, apparently blooming, intact.

Can she really have remembered him? Certainly, the man she discovered was not the one she'd known, had lived with forty years. Surely he must have seemed like someone out of a dark age and she a literary archaeologist stumbling upon and then recovering the singular preservation. But forty years is forty years, and she'd never had anything but him. Hatched in some Dakotan province, pushed into Bismarck and then Milwaukee, slaving like a fellah to keep flesh to bone, seeing nobody, reading nothing, hardly dreaming, one gathered, and then, at nineteen, meeting the unlikely boy ushering in the movie theater—and that was it, until she was sixty and began reading what had happened in the interim. Happened while she kept him alive, working in the twenty cities that they lived in, clerking in stores and offices and markets, moneychanger in the subways, elevator operator, waitress, railway

checker. A long list, now more or less immortal with the rest
of it.

And he writing, occasionally with luck, with money, so that
it wasn't always grind. She did see half the world, although twice
the local embassies had to bail them out. (It's been reported that
once in Rome she prostituted for him, but this sort of thing will
only come out from now on, now that they have finally stuffed
her into a monument next to the corpse of whoever it was they
decided was Gardiner.)

Apparently she did the jobs and everything else with relish.
He was always, almost always, "nice" to her. Which of course
makes it worse. Years ago, on some television interview, she
said, "We never quarreled. He was astonishingly acute about
my feelings and always knew how to adapt his mood to mine,
to work a harmony. I would have done, I did do, everything I
could for him because it was precisely what I wanted to do. His
will was my will. And yet I don't think that he mastered me as
Catherine Blake was mastered by William." (She was almost a
learned woman a few years after their marriage. That was something else she got from him.) "I was never his instrument. On
the contrary, he completed me, or made me feel complete,
made me, I believe, a real person, and, if you'll forgive a possible
blasphemy, I had never existed before. He created me." A typical utterance. And this after she had taken the measure of his
loathing, knew how he detested her spirit and her flesh, mocked
at her with his women, put her remarks into the most disgusting
mouths in modern letters, knew that he kept her around him
as a reminder of Hell (he capitalized it, for he turned out to be
a kind of secular theologian, if one may risk the contradiction).
There she was for forty years, "the hair shirt," "the Adversary
and the Primal Sin in one," these a couple of less picturesque
and vehement examples of his view of her. All of which now
appear in the last work of his she put her hand to, the three
volumes of his *Elinor,* as she called it, the thousand pages of his
loathing drawn from forty years of reflection. Drawn by her
from journals, stories, and the first drafts of letters—"He never
paid a bill without making a draft of it first," she joked about him
once—most of which were indicated in the earlier volumes by
the once mysterious "E" followed by asterisks. The most fantas-
tic of all posthumous exhibitions. Consider the sheer bulk of his

hatred. Apparently, he had written about her from the beginning, from the very first meeting. "A lump of dung in the
lobby": this the gallant initial entry. He married her "to marry
Lilith," and he called the union "the marriage of Heaven and
Hell." Yes, I suppose that one could trace her public utterances
and find that every noble sentiment had been triggered by
reading some viciousness of his. There are numerous examples,
although systematic study of them would be work for a tough-
minded man.

It'll be done, as will everything else to resurrect that barba-
rous union. Gardiner and his wife will turn on the spit in history
as they never did in life. Every pounding which he never gave
her will be given, and every one she suffered after, because she
never suffered them directly, will be given too. Yes, like Stendhal and Dostoevski, he will live next to his works, a sample of
conduct as rigorous as a saint's, if dedicated to obscurer ends.
One must marvel at him, the superb restraint which never once
revealed its source.

One wonders of course about much of their married life. That
they had no children doesn't matter. The notebooks tell us what
children were to him. (It's reasonably clear that he forced at
least ten of the women to have abortions.) The sexual life, however, undoubtedly proceeded on normal lines—whatever it
meant to him, and what it meant was in the nature of research.
(The chapter "In the Adversary," from his version of Crébillon's
Sofa, may be consulted here.) As much as we know—and we
know a great deal about the sheer domesticity of their lives,
about their bed and bathroom, the kitchen table, incidents with
carpets and toothpaste, walks, swims, shopping, all transformed
by his malicious vision—we will never really know what it was
like. Fifteen thousand days they spent together, or fourteen,
say, when one discounts the excursions with his women, his
eighty-six women, the already famous gallery of his amours, the
women who composed a wholly different universe of delights,
the forty women of his Purgatory, the forty-six of his Heaven—
yes, he was the oddest of American lovers. It will not be so great
a surprise if some of these partners deliver up attics of material
to feed the mills of curiosity for another half-century.

But no material will ever mean what Elinor's has meant; none
will draw up the fog which will forever, I suppose, obscure her

contribution. Every penetration of that fog reveals a different structure. It is as if this was what he calculated from the start.

Or could it possibly have been her scheme? One can hardly credit it, but what else explains so much that is dark now, her amazing ignorance of the others, of his true feelings, his immense perversity, she who saw so much so clearly. Elinor was a brilliant human being. Her reconstruction of his work alone marks her a startlingly able scholar, an editor and bibliographer of enormous knowledge, acumen, and sensitivity, an immensely able woman of affairs, a powerful and subtle diplomat. And all this is as nothing when one estimates the emotional complexity behind this mastery. So great is this complexity that I have wondered if it might not have been there from the beginning.

Is it possible that she was the great mover all along, that she made him *living* as she later made his legend? Who discovered whom in the lobby of that theater? What did she bring with her from the Dakotan plain, what instruments to have managed so huge a legacy?

She did not write the books, nor the journals and letters. No, but the universe within which they were written, did she not provide that, shape that? And did he perhaps see her rightly all along? "In the Adversary." Was his work perhaps as much report as vision? This is the oddest mystery of the legacy.

In the Dock

1

I'VE cut lots of corners. Dochel's Nail of the Month claims I do little else. Her delicate point is that I've wasted my talent.

I take indictment seriously. Oddly enough, I still want to make gold in my soul. Has tranquillity undone me? I sit on my beloved back porch watching pumpkin-colored leaves fall into the tiny courtyard. I've got the stereo turned up: a soprano sings *"Mein Herz schwimmt im Blut";* after that, Ella Fitzgerald will sing the Gershwins. I lie back in a lounge chair smoking a cigarillo, drinking an Alsatian white wine. Bliss. Or it should be. But I am ashamed of my tranquillity. I ache with heart cramps I am too Nietzschean to call love and pity for the vague billions who surface in the news, the insulted, the broken, the deprived, the sinking and the sunk, those exalted in the Beatitudes and damned by the Genealogist of Morals as sneaks, counterfeiters, and masqueraders in ascetic pomp.

Ella sings, "You don't know the half of it, Dearie, blues."

Wouldn't you know. (These leaves will probably turn out to be subpoenas.)

2

Sylvia.

Seldon Dochel, my old tennis partner, wanted me to meet his Nail of the Month. "She's one of your admirers."

"My money or my beauty?"

"She loves your editorials. All that Let's Consider crapola. She thinks you know everything."

"A woman of discernment. That's a first for you. What is she? A chemist? A V.P. of Ill. Bell?" Since he left his wife, partly to escape what he charmingly called her Gobi Desert loins, partly because his sick daughter's groans and glares were unbearable, Seldon has suffered—and caused his friends to suffer—his woman trouble. "So-and-so is two steps off the street. I've got to have some human response. It was like hammering a nail into the wall."

"You have no patience, Seldon. Court them a bit."

"This is the twentieth century. I don't look like you, a dog's muzzle." His long face glitters, hypomanic blue eyes pop toward his glasses. "I should have the cream of the cream."

His new friend is a lawyer. "She did some work for Texas Instruments. Someone lent her an article from your rag. Despite what I told her about you, she still thinks you're the cat's meow."

Of course this was malarkey. Seldon just wanted to guarantee the worth of his acquisition.

I spend enough time with him, ninety minutes a day, six months a year, laced to his furious forehands, feeble backhands, crippled, mis-hit, or totally missed overheads. Except for an hour after our Sunday game, when we have juice and muffins at the Plaka, I don't see him socially. "Be glad to see her."

"Bring Emma, too."

That's another story. "She's in bad shape," I say. "She's looking for a new place, and she's just started a new course at Loyola."

"All right. Another time. It's you Sylvia's interested in."

A week later, leaning over the little table at the Café Procope,

Sylvia said, "Tell me, Cy. Why have you wasted your life editing other people's words?"

3

Seldon said, "You're going to get on with Sylvia. She's a terrific lady. Sensitive as grass. Knows what you're thinking before you do. And not trying to get her name in the *Penthouse* Forum. Nothing spectacular there, just nice old-fashioned chewing-and-screwing. Not like those camels I led around the Sahara. She's the reason I've been so sharp lately. The way she makes me feel I could run Borg's heinie out of Wimbledon. Not even your junk can throw me." Seldon goes mad when I dribble shots over the net, then lob over his head after he's made his tankish forward charge. I enjoy seeing him backpedal on his thick pins, windmilling wildly, the yellow ball hitting him on the head. But I have to be careful. Sometimes he'll stop in the middle of a point and glare hatred across the net at me. The big teeth clamp, the veins bulge, he may slap his forehead or his thighs. I've seen him stamp his own foot. He may say, "Your junk is killing me." He walks off the court to the black bag that contains his equipment and analgesics (antibiotic paste, tape, bandages, Valium, cans of cold pop, gut strings with tools to insert them, a carton of high-tar cigarettes). It's these last painkillers he needs. He lights up, inhales to his toes, and discharges the smoke of his hatred toward me. (He knows I hate smoke.) His innards roar. There is no restraint. The air fills with his body's foulness. His day has turned black. What is there for him? A life of abstract wheat and abstract soybeans. What's that for someone who hates the earth and its products? "I'll be death on the Floor today. I won't be able to make a bid." Moan. "I can't take your junk. Your excuses. 'Oh my, the sun got in my eyes. My racket's strung too loose. The wind. The noise.' While it was *me* that passed you clean, asshole." The cigarette arcs toward my face, his head goes in his hands. Sob. "I'm sorry, Cy. I'm a bum, Cy. I wasn't raised for competition. The Skokie nerds sent me to lousy fellow-traveler camps. The only games we played were cooperative. We were taught to be afraid of winning. The only way I can beat your brains in is to think of you as IBM."

In the tranquil little Plaka, among fishnets, wreathed harpoons, blue-and-white posters of Delphi and Epidaurus, the Sunday brunchers are familiar: O'Flaherty, the aristocratic bookseller, at the *Haupttisch* with his harem; Mme. de Forsch, the optometrist's widow, waving the tips of her fingers at us; the *NY Times* readers; the weekend lovers; the policemen. Only our table blasts. "I had you in knots today, pal. Oh, you looked ugly. Where was your junk today?" (Seven tables away, I see O'Flaherty look coldly at us. Josepha, our waitress, told me he wants us seated as far from him as possible.) Or, in despair, cursing his life, his ex-wife's omnisexual flings, his daughter's degenerating nerves, the disasters of Pit and Bedroom, Seldon beats his fists on the table, spills our juice into our muffins, wipes his face with our water, belches, groans, and passes his foul wind as if he were the only sentient creature in the place. Once a cop leaned over the partition and told him where the Men's Room was.

Emma can't bear him. He embodies what she hates, sexual boasting, unearned authority, unstoppable egocentricity, male tyranny. I tell her he's actually the most innocent fellow alive. "Under all that noise and swinger talk, he's really sweet and courteous. He's just got to show everyone he's not the good-hearted patsy he was raised to be."

"I'm not interested. I don't like his mouth. I won't be part of his therapy. I won't meet the unfortunates he drags into the sack."

In her anger, she writes slogans in silver eyebrow pencil on the immense red heart she painted above her bed. "Dochel to the wall." "Dochel, *lupus feminorum.*" "*Ecrasez* Dochel." "*Mange merde,* Seldon D." "Dochel *delenda est.*"

At the Café Procope, Sylvia, a fierce, heavy-shouldered sportive, brilliant-eyed woman, informed me very quickly that my life was a series of evasions. Smiling, she took her sport assessing —i.e., damning—my life. Sloth, it seems, was the heart of my character. I, who'd hung from deadlines since I was twenty, should have thrown such facts—and a left hook—into her face. Didn't. (Not immediately. Not exactly.) She told me, "Your work's a form of sloth." As was fatherhood. "You've made a second noncareer of that." We were at my old table, a dozen yards away from where I used to sleep, eat, and work. "Why have you spent all these years doing what someone with half your brains could do as well?" What a question from anyone, let alone someone I'd never laid eyes on half an hour before.

I tried to defend myself. "I can't be wrong about everything."
To that her response was, "Wrong again, Cy."

4

I was halfway through a bottle of house Chablis when Seldon
and Sylvia showed up under the blue awning. He was decked
out, admiral of the civilian fleet, in a volcanic blue blazer and
Gatsby flannels. Beside him, shoulder to shoulder, was this powerful, smiling woman in a frothy, lemon-bright dress. In the
queer end of daylight, she seemed lit up, bright blue eyes,
bright cheeks, bright—Seldon-size—teeth. "A merry lady," I
thought, as they walked over.
Dochel did not so much introduce us as point out two well-
known Dochel landmarks to each other: "Cy, Sylvia." As if our
names marked divisions of his life—his bed and battlefield—and
it was now time in the Dochel Scheme of Things that we be
aware of each other.
Sylvia and I shook hands. At least, she picked my hand up,
gave it a couple of probative strokes, and let it go. I was already
judged. I said it was nice to see her. She said social formula
didn't interest her, she did not think of herself as a scenic attrac-
tion, I'd better wait before I decided anything was nice or not
nice. "A pettifogging word anyway." That took care of "nice."
I let this rearrange my notion of what the evening would be like.
She gripped the neck of the Chablis. "They shouldn't be allowed to call it Chablis. They can't tell a Chardonnay grape
from a Muscat in the Napa Valley." I said I couldn't either,
perhaps I shouldn't enjoy the wine as much as I did. She tipped
the bottle over the glass pear on our table and doused the small
flame coming from the red candle within. "I can't bear coziness." Then, as if to show she could give as well as take away:
"Enjoy what you enjoy." I resisted thanking her; after all, I was
here to please Seldon. I said, "There's still daylight. I don't know
why they light them. Let me get better wine for us. They have
decent Italian stuff. Bardolino, Verdicchio, Orvieto."
"I'm here to meet you," said Sylvia. "I don't care what I drink.
As long as it doesn't fog my perceptions."
"They haven't fermented dynamite yet," said Seldon.
I laughed, but that was as much a mistake as the small pleasan-

try. Sylvia registered both by temperature only, five quick degrees of frost in the area between eyebrows and lower lip. She poured what was left of the bottle in our glasses, her own last, and said, "All right, let's get to know each other. Seldon told me you live ascetically. You don't dress like a monk."

I had on my summer outfit, blue pants, seersucker jacket from Field's basement, blue shirt, paler blue tie. "Thank you, I guess. I thought Seldon thought of me only as a backstop for his forehands." This advanced the conversion of Seldon from producer of the show to third-personned scenery. Why not? He deserved it. He'd loaded this cannon, and he was still all grin, Teddy Roosevelt teeth thrust over the table. "I've done my job," said the teeth.

At this point—nine o'clock—the baldies who supply the Procope's music struck up with "Amapola, my pretty little poppy . . ." They usually plucked their way through the tunes of the twenties, thirties, and forties, then worked up or down to the owner Sonny's favorite Puccinis and Donizettis. "Did Seldon tell you I used to live here, Sylvia?"

"Seldon's a mine of trivia." This with an imperial smile, one emperor to another, right past the ears of the described serf: what could such low-life make of high wit, the judgment of people who knew the world? Sylvia had sensed my opposition —and my resentment—and that made us equals.

Of course, it was she I resented. On sight. My *Weltanschauung,* my *Menschanschauung,* did not tolerate such shoulders in women, such arms, such power. Even as I admired the big smile, the handsome eyes, the jolly cannon of a nose, something else worked in me. Desire and resentment fused. I admired the eyes, but felt an excess in their lucidity, felt her will stoking the brightness.

Did she sniff my resentment? Yes, probably. She'd spent her life sniffing male resentment. So I rationalized for her even as I steamed.

She'd turned around, *swiveled,* and there was her rather beautiful neck under the expensive irregular cut of her hair. That too was interesting. The color, ratty brown, but worked by subtle oils till it glistened. And that neck, strong and long but somehow fragile like a souvenir of her gender. I've never socialized with women who head states or corporations, but about

those I read or see on television, I have similar feelings, the
subtle, imperial, but confused charmers like Mrs. Gandhi, the
fluent, frizzy mistresses of state like Mrs. Thatcher, Betty Boop
flirts and scowlers like our own Jane Byrne. Celebrity augments
desire. We know celebrated women so well, we have to force
ourselves to remember they don't know us. Of course, my lines
are drawn: Mother Teresa doesn't rouse me; nor did Eleanor
Roosevelt. And physically I draw the line at those rolling-flab
fatties Fellini and other Italian directors—it must be southern
notions of abundance—use as sexual initiations. No, I'm roused
by powerful women like Sylvia, challenged by their—to me—
ambiguous anomaly: the fact their bodies don't exist to satisfy
mine but—like mine—to satisfy themselves. Face to face—face
to body—with a Sylvia, my rational, tolerant, ERA-supporting
crust disintegrates.

What Sylvia was doing was giving the place the once-over:
drain spouts, waiters, lyre-backed chairs; kumquat-colored tables; the royal-blue awning with the loopy script—*Café Procope*
—the cedar tubs which the owner's father, my old neighbor
Guido, had filled with roses and which now held hardier, brass-
ier-looking, questionably organic shrubs; the waiters in their
dollar-colored cummerbunds; the strumming baldies; even the
blacktop roof outside my old windows. (Those days I climbed
out every evening for a drink at the very table we sat at now,
keeping an eye out for the occasional drunk wandering off the
café side of the terrace toward my open window—"Men's
Room's thataway, buddy.") As she swiveled back to us, she said,
"I spot fourteen code violations just from here."

"I'm sure Sonny pays off plenty," said I. "He's made a fine
place, though, don't you think?" I went on as her lips opened
for "No." "In time, they won't dare make trouble for him. There
are a couple of aldermen here right now." Like most Chica-
goans, I'm insouciant about the ubiquitous payoffs which oil city
life, proud as the next noninsider about the city's reputation:
frauds, clout, Rat-a-tat-tat, Fast Eddies, Bathhouse Johns, Need-
lenose Labriolas, Don't-Make-No-Waves. Chicago's the country's real Disneyland, Oberammergau with real nails. For us,
California's just Polynesia on wheels, and the Sun Belt won't
hold up anyone's pants. Since Mrs. O'Leary, our writers have
been feeding this guff to the world, and to us. Even the best

Chicago politician knows he doesn't have a chance here unless he at least pretends to know this old score, winking and smiling, even if he never dreamed of taking an illicit nickel. "There are probably several people here who won't be troubled by checks. In fact, I used to be on that kind of take myself. At least, I had house rates on food and drink. Sonny wanted happy neighbors. He's a good fellow. Though I preferred his father, Guido. He had his barbershop downstairs where the restaurant is. Up here on the roof, he raised roses. Not easy. Imagine what it was like, six months a year, to walk out my window in the middle of Chicago and see a terrace full of roses."

"Yes, yes, very—"

I rolled on: the more from me, the less from her. And those roses were marvelous. "Pure contradictions," I told Guido, out of my beloved Rilke's epitaph. "Strip their petals to discover their heart, and they disappear." Guido may not have appreciated this, but he appreciated my appreciation of his flowers. We sniffed, caressed, admired those beautiful secretive cupfuls of gold and ivory, scarlet and pink. The day after Richard Nixon pulled his festered self out of the American hide, old Guido—a Nixon diehard—fell dead out here. I picked him out of his compost heap. (Winey pomace, fish scraps, and God knows what, I can smell it now.)

"We may see Sonny tonight. I'll introduce you."

"Don't b—"

"Little dark guy, with *eyebrows.* Looks like a pasha. In his way, he's a scholar too. Named this place after the first coffeehouse in Paris. Run by a Sicilian named Procopio. He also told me that Michelet, the historian—"

"I know Michelet. You don't—"

"—said coffee was behind the French Revolution. I suppose he meant it roused the wine-soaked brains of the *lumières.* As good as any—"

"As bad as any. Totally moronic. I hope the man's reputation rests on something better than that." I couldn't keep it up. Sylvia would eventually break through. And I was worn out. I'm a listener, not a talker. My guide, the great Genealogist of Morals, thought women used weakness, invented weakness, to excuse themselves from life. *Erfinderisch in Schwächen*—inventive in weakness—was his phrase. He

198

didn't know women like Sylvia; his Cosima Wagner and Frau Lou were pussycats.

"I told you I was here to understand you, not revolutions, not cafés, not local hoodlums and fifth-rate Frenchmen. Not Chicago, about which I know sixty times more than you, Cy. I don't work shut up in a room. I'm in the courts, thirty hours a week, and cleaning legal latrines the rest of the time. You can't bullshit me." She propped elbows on the table, rested her manly chin on raised palms, and tried to hook my eyes with hers. I was in the witness box. "I want to understand you. Cy, the editor. Cy, the poppa. Cy, the lover. Cy, the smart guy who holes up in his nowheres turning out a very fine *News-Letter* read by—what? —eleven hundred souls?"

"Thirty-eight hundred," said I. "Sylvia, don't waste analysis on me. There's not enough to understand. I wish there were."

"That's Point One, Cy. I don't think you do."

"I don't get that. Why shouldn't I?"

"That's what I want to know. My suspicion is when a man buries his talent, he's afraid of it. Or he's hiding from something outside."

"Maybe so, Sylvia. I'm not introspective. Still, I think I'm far more ordinary than you suspect. Maybe that's what I'm hiding. All right, maybe I'm an ordinary intellectual. But that's it."

"I don't believe in the ordinary. I spend my life quizzing supposedly ordinary people, jurors, witnesses, clients. Not one of them is ordinary. So how could someone like you be? You digest difficult advanced research, you make sense of it, you write it up for laymen. You run on a double track, scientific and literary. That itself is extraordinary."

The words were sympathetic, the tone harsh. Like those blue eyes, fine, but overly keen, impatient, full of thrust and hunger. The nostrils, too, looked hungry. Air wasn't enough for them. They weren't simple conduits, but portals beyond which waited an avaricious, maybe even a desperate, intelligence. I felt my heart knocking. "You're *making* me seem extraordinary. What I do is simple. I get contributors to spell out research so I can understand it. Then I put down more or less what they say. I'm not a scientist, I'm hardly a writer. At best, I'm a steward of talent. A warder of my sty. I'm not even getting any better at it. You'd think I'd get more sophisticated, be able to take more shortcuts, but I don't."

Sylvia seemed absorbed by this. I couldn't tell if it was genuine absorption or courtroom practice. In court, nothing was incidental, everything was part of the battle. "Perhaps it's time for you to do something else with your life. I think you're wasting your talent. You're doing what you're doing because of inertia. Or sloth. And for peanuts. Is your name in the papers? Never. I have to ask myself what's going on. What's with Cy Riemer?"

"You're a quick study, Sylvia."

"That's my job."

Tusks of smoke grew from Dochel's nose over the table. I looked his way. "She's got your number, Cy. No wool over these baby-blues." Reaching over.

The baby-blues shot him a look that stopped that. "I'm not after Cy's number. I'm interested in him as a human situation. You brought me here to meet him. I assume that didn't mean seeing what color his eyes were."

"Forgive, forgive. I'm just enjoying."

"Enjoy," said Sylvia again, but as if it were "Die."

I was finishing the second bottle of Chablis. (There were no other marines on the beach.)

"I know you have a whole raft of children."

"Only four," I said. "One for each bedpost."

"What's that mean?" Her head on its fine ivory neck base looked Roman to me now, Caracalla's, Caligula's. The ratty, lucent bangs parted in opposite directions on the forehead. I also noticed a crimson wart on the left flange of her nose. Had the interrogative steam worn down her makeup?

"I suppose I mean the four supports of my life. Like 'Matthew, Mark, Luke and John, Bless the bed I lie upon.' " The sun said goodbye now, plunging behind the six flats. Little plugs of gold pinged against the glasses and ice buckets. One lit Sylvia's wart. "Does that make sense?"

"Everything makes sense. If you spend time making sense of it. Very interesting sense. I gather your children are more important to you than—I can't remember the name of your young companion."

"Emma," said Seldon.

"I wouldn't say that," I said. "I don't think of affection as a pie to be sliced."

"I'm sure you have more of it than most." The tone suggested I had little or none. "Seldon tells me you hold her hand, cook her supper, bind her wounds, wipe her ass."

Seldon added his ha ha to this jewel. I said, "I inflict more wounds than I bind. I wonder what I've told you, Seldon. I'm ashamed Sylvia has this view of me."

Dochel made it's-not-my-doing gestures.

"Nothing to do with Seldon. I'm testing the perimeter. I could guess you'd have a Mutual Tyranny arrangement with a woman. To reinforce your retreat from life. These relationships are never one-way. The weak party offers weakness, the strong strength. Both equally useful."

"You know lots about relationships, Sylvia."

"Not personally, no."

This got me a bit and softened what I said. "You're probably right, there's some soft Mutual Tyranny in most relationships. But Emma and I are more a Mutual Aid Society. You can call it love, if you need a name."

"The most useless word in the dictionary. You love Chablis, Seldon loves tennis. The question is, 'Are you doing each other any good or just sustaining each other's weakness? Are you being held back from something better?' Most relationships are just excuses for not getting to the depths. Love, as you call it, work, fatherhood. They can all be forms of sloth. Doing violence to your nature. What do you think, Seldon?"

She would have asked the table if Seldon hadn't been there. It was a cushion shot, that's all. The destination was me. Well, it couldn't last forever. In an hour, I'd be with Emma. She'd have saved up jokes from Johnny Carson to tell me, she'd hear my report on Seldon's latest debacle.

Seldon said, "Cy's basically an artist. A Bohemian. He likes all this." He waved at the rooftops, the candle-lit tables—only ours dark—the light-popped darkness of Old Town. "Shabby cuteness. That's Cy's world. He's a little enclave of high thinking. Not your average fifty-year-old failure. And the little Mimi who warms her hand at his candle is lucky."

I said, "Thank you, Seldon. That wraps me up now."

"Oh no," said Sylvia. She pointed the waiter to our empty

bottle. "We're not at the end of the rainbow yet." She was merry; a Cossack merriment.

I tried to look at us from outside. From the street. Here we were, a jolly corner of a jolly constellation of tinkle and glitter. What did it matter in the grand scheme of the night what Sylvia said or didn't? "Come on, Sylvia. What the hell. What about you? Husbands? Children? What's your story?"

She raised her left hand my way. The fingers were oddly fine, long and soft, strangely beautiful at the end of her big forearm. "No ring, Cy. So no children."

"There can always be a slip-up. Many of us started as amorous leaks."

"Very pretty. But I'm a careful person. Not a hole-in-the-corner philoprogenitor like you."

Below, the street lamps popped on, the lit iron musketry of the night. I loved that moment. Usually. I tried to hold it, to keep down what was rising. "I'm sure I did like the progening. And you're right, it wasn't done in public. And the progeny, I love them too. Most of the time."

"You're a lucky man. Maybe I was wrong about you. You've worked out your life. I've certainly met richer and more influential people less satisfied with themselves." I let this go. "Still, the big question is there." And here she put her unringed fingers on mine. I forced down the shock. (Fury? Excitement?) "Why does a gifted man confine himself to the narrowest possibilities of his talent?"

What a question. From anyone, anytime. The fingers were actually holding mine down now. She must have felt the agitation. I could see a sort of rosy triumph in her face. I pulled them away. My heart was in my throat, I was dizzy, I could feel pressure in my chest, my arms. "You know, Seldon, you're my pal. I've seen you taking lots of punishment for years. It's pained me. Though I know you require a certain amount of suffering. But do you need this much? I mean what are you going to get out of this lady? If America were between her legs, Columbus would have turned around." I put my palm over Sylvia's opening mouth. "This is a *mouth*." I took it away as her teeth came down. "It's going to tear you apart, Seldon. It's going to bite, and swallow what it wants and spit the rest of you into the street." I managed to get my wallet out, found a twenty-dollar bill and laid it on the table. "For your services, lady. If anyone pays you a nickel more than that for anything, he's out of his mind."

Confrontation is not—as they now say—my number. When I see it coming, I head for the alleys that lead away from it. As for the wildness of others, I usually swallow it. Why not? Even at Sylvia, I'd only half-blown my stack.

Still, half of it had blown, and I remember how infuriated I thought the scarlet fleurs-de-lis looked on the tiles of the café floor. Before I knew it, I strutted the almost unstruttable ten asphalt feet to my old window. I bent to climb through, puzzled at its being closed. In the window, I saw white eyeballs in a black man's face. "Oh, Lord," I called through the glass, thinking even then, I remember, the man would hear, "Oh, Lawdy," and think I was mocking him. It was like one of those Stepin Fetchit movies of the thirties. (Was everything I did tonight a fall into an abandoned tense?) I made excuse-me motions, right hand cupped to heart, left one to the sky, eyes lifted in puzzlement. As I did, there was laughter. Not from the frightened tenant of my old quarters. From the terrace.

It was then I blew. I felt the way lit phosphorus might feel, rage and humiliation burning. I had to walk past those laughers, past Seldon and Sylvia, whom I would not look at, only sensed as I went by them. I don't believe they were laughing, I had done them to a turn. Nor did I look at the guzzling, crowing, ignorant preeners to whom I'd given a little comic moment. What else did they have but vacancy and zero, waiting for someone like me to occupy them, give them point? Zeros waiting to un-egg themselves into sheer holes. Only their arrogant shells made them think themselves substantial, shells without even the mineral consistency and tenacity of functional shells. The little bald guitarist and the skinny bald bass player plucked away, sweating in the moonlight. I remember thinking, "At least they sweat, they keep time, they know how to read little squiggles on a page; not total nothings." Though what was the point of their old Italian plucks? To let these guzzling zeros hear each other confess their zeroheit. Better the frozen gases in a trillion miles of dark. At least out there there was no pretense. Gas, ice, mad wind, dark. The whole universe, a cough of dark.

That's more or less how I felt as I made my way past the tables, under the awning, down the stairs, round the lit corner to the parking lot into my old Malibu.

Sylvia had struck where it hurt. Even so, I might have swallowed it, if she'd not talked about Emma. Loyal, generous, darling Emma. The other side of the sexual moon. I was on the Outer Drive now, heading south, home, or not home, to Emma's. Out over the lake, out of the fumes of city light blurring the sharpness of the stars. That's what I should concentrate on. And the glistening, bronze cylinder of Lake Point Tower. And the bridge over the light-encrusted shaft of the river banked with mystic glass and steel, the murderous S-curve, and then straight south toward the imperial, deceptive—two dimensional till you were within yards of them—columns of the Field Museum.

Emma was asleep under the silvery slogan she'd looped on the red walls (painted over the cream base into the shape of a great-valved heart or grand, tiny-cracked buttocks): KONG LOVES FAY. Her nightgown twisted about her waist, her mouth was giving out some sleepish Esperanto. I lay naked beside her, home, and happy there in the familiar sleep-heat, the familiar fragrance—lavender and minty. My body touched the twin interrogations and gave them the male salute. There was a squirm of welcome from the faraway dream country. I slid off, the lieutenant still saluting, though now, in confused loyalty, it was saluting another body, the powerful, Seldon-occupied, Sieglinde Fortress that was Sylvia.

A Short History of Love

WE'VE been together four months now and—it's really silly—
but I don't even know your name." He didn't say anything so
she went on. "I'd never even noticed something was wrong till
a day or so ago."

"Oh?"

"It's not been necessary really . . . and then all the usual ways
of knowing haven't mattered here."

"What do you mean?"

"Letters and things. You get the letters in the morning—if
there ever are any—nobody could write me so I don't care—and
then you must come home just about the time of the afternoon
mail."

"I do see the postman quite often."

"And you take care of us at the stores, the passports and
identity cards. You know my name, don't you?"

"It's Rose or something, isn't it?"

"That's it. Rose. A rose in an open plain if that's possible. Just
two things, a plain and a rose and they differentiate nothing else

but each other. The plain nourishes the rose, and the rose gives meaning to the plain."

"That's quite beautiful," he said, and wondered if he'd interrupted her.

"Is it?"

"Yes, yes, it is."

"That's what I mean . . . the kindness of you. I know that you're the one for beauty. You're the one that makes beautiful things, knows what's beautiful in the room, in the park. Of course, I don't really know if you make beautiful things. I said that because you must. Do you?"

"Well," he said. "I don't really make things."

"I don't know what you do."

"Don't you?"

"We talk about the office and have jokes about Feldman and Gordon, but you're apart from them as if you weren't in the same office, or even had an office of your own. Designing things. A small office, a sort of grand closet filled with things you've made over the years."

"I can't say that it's like that." He raised an index finger to his head as if to push back a hair, but, being bald, the gesture only stood for a time when he had hair.

"I like it," she said, "your being bald."

"I don't mind it."

"It was one of the first things I knew about you. There was a shock right at the start. Your eyes were so bright one expected a tumble of blond hair when you raised your hat—and then there was nothing."

"You're a generous metaphysician."

"Metaphysician?"

"I used the word badly," he said.

"You do nothing badly."

"You're too kind."

"No. No, I'm not. I don't even know if you mean that. Like you telling Grimm what fine work he did, and he kept on, never knowing how ridiculous he was."

"He wasn't all that bad, was he?"

"He botched everything. Yet he kept going on what you told him. I'm afraid that I'm doing the same thing."

"I do hope you won't think that, Rose. Even if Grimm were completely without gift, that would have no bearing on us."

"No, I suppose not. Actually, I love you for telling him what you did. He was so small and lonely. Where did he come from?"

"I don't know. I'd imagined he was English."

"Yes, like you, I think." He said nothing. "I said that of course to find out. I've thought you were English, but you might as well be American, or Dutch."

"I was born in Sydney," he said.

"Sydney. On the other side of the world?"

"Yes, I suppose it is."

"But that's incredible . . . though I don't know why. You might tell me that you were Zeus, and I wouldn't have much more reason for saying 'incredible.' How did you come here? I mean, in a boat . . . and when . . . why?"

He went to the sink and ran the cold water, saying something which she did not hear.

"When? I couldn't hear you."

"I've been here for a long time. The business in Sydney was something temporary for my father. We came by boat, I believe."

"You believe?"

"I was very young. There was some sort of transition that I associate with the ocean."

"I came by boat. Six years ago. You know where I'm from, don't you?"

"It's America or Canada, isn't it? It's been weeks since we used the passports. The trip north."

"Yes, the trip north. The most beautiful, the only beautiful trip of my life. There was nothing wrong, not even the trains. We brought nothing and found everything. Those hills, and the fishing villages. Was it Sondeheym where the rocks were, and we drank that green wine and opened the oysters? It seems further away than sailing from New York. I wonder if we'll ever take another like it?"

"We were very lucky. Perhaps we shall be again. Would you care to see the radio concert tonight?"

"You said that differently. I don't know why, but you've never said anything like that before."

"We're both tired. A concert might be the thing to revive us. They're playing Corelli and some early Germans."

"What's your name, darling?"

He looked at the window, then turned and washed his hands

in the sink. As he wiped them on a dish towel, he said, "It's Charles, my dear. Charles Page."

She began to say, "How inappropriate," but then, looking at him, the long bare head and the thin artist's hands in the white towel, she seemed to see the name issuing from him like fog, and she raised her hands as it moved toward her, gray, lethal.

Milius and Melanie

1

THEY were to meet at the Wollman Memorial Rink in Central Park. A stupid idea, his, and in the unbalanced sentiment of reunion, agreed to by her. If they had even heard each other's voices over the phone, they wouldn't have gone through with it, but no, they had transmitted the proposals and confirmations through Tsvević; it had been Tsvević who'd spotted her in his painting, Tsvević who'd told him he must see her again, and Tsvević who had put in the call to Tulsa. "You must transform your emotional *situation.*" Tsvević, an intellectual straggler who compensated in ferocity for modishness, was undergoing Sartre; *situation* had nothing to do with its banal English uses; no, it stood for fixity which choice would shatter.

Tsvević gleamed with false wisdom, his dab of nose, popped blue eyes, and ice-colored lips mere service stations for the gray-topped mental apparatus which ran the Language Schools and, for thirty years, no small part of Orlando Milius's life. What counted even more in Tsvević was the maniacally tended flesh whose terrific muscles bulged clothes into second skin. Every morning, in sneakers and sweatpants, Tsvević ran four laps around the Central Park Reservoir, a character known to policemen and taxi drivers going off late shifts, and to the thugs who worked the West Side Eighties and Nineties. None had ever held him up: out for gain, there were nothing but gym clothes and flying feet; out for mischief and violence, there were those muscles. Such confidence muscles gave small intelligence, thought Milius, who, seven inches taller and fifty pounds heavier than Tsvević, was soft, had always been soft, and though not weak, for he walked a lot and lifted furniture at his wife's frequent command, had none of the confidence of size or strength. Milius would never appear in the park after dusk, he crossed streets with caution and swiftness, treasured all uniforms and the pacification they promised. A civic coward. Yet it was he, not Tsvević, who had almost a hero's record in wartime, had worked in the hills with partisans, had, if not shot, been shot at.

But he had not had the confidence to telephone Melanie Booler in Tulsa, Oklahoma. Indeed, lack of confidence had hidden his feelings about her for twenty years, and, even now, when he had at least recognized something in his painting, timidity had slurred identification; she had just looked familiar, an ideal woman, too beautiful and wise for him to have known.

Tsvević had spotted her at once, and, great fisher of feeling, had drawn Milius's old longing from him. "That's your Melanie."

Of course it was. Naturally. Melanie. Who else? On the floor in his loft, looking up at the canvas pinned in light, Milius saw her skating inside the smashed cobalt arcs and gorgeous polygonal blots. Once again the pilot had brought him in safely.

Safely, yes, but into harsh country! Up the corridor, Vera's cabbage soup steamed in on little Hannah's flatulent tromboning; and, in Milius's wallet, reposed the villainous paragraph from the *Times Literary Supplement* clipped out by his London publisher, daggered with a red question mark, and airmailed across the Atlantic.

Now, zippered to the neck in his old orange suede jacket, an overturned keel of black lamb's wool on his gray head, Orlando Milius diverts his nerves from the noon meeting by focusing on the brilliant New York scene. The Skating Pond blares pink and white; little frozen sea, fleshed over by sweatered, jacketed, scarfed, and capped New Yorkers twirling under the stony smiles of the great hotels, Plaza, Pierre, Essex and Hampshire Houses. Sunday morning, mid-December, yet a Floridan sun has softened the ice to a green scurf which permits no skating distinction but awkwardness: tots skitter, goosey girls shriek, corpulent swaggerers crumple.

Twenty-four years. She will not know him. Or worse, he will not know her. The crowds will rush on and off the ice at noon, and they will be lost in the rush. "To the left of the gate by the railing" wasn't sufficient direction. Had the railing even been here? It was surely not where they used to meet. No, they would walk together from Columbus Circle, skates around their necks, Melanie darkly golden, her body, so shy and full, turned military by a thigh-length leather jacket out of which stuck her beautiful, stubby legs, black in woolen stocking pants. Large-eyed, quick, shy, but never anxious, while he walked in fear that Sophie would catch them in the park, righteous in illegitimate posses- siveness, picking them out with that look which boiled needles off pine trees.

When Vera, quieter than Sophie, but with a fierceness disci- plined in wartime hills, learned what he had done, the ice under the skaters' blades would not be cut as often as his heart.

Learned?

Was he confusing Melanie and the *TLS*?

No, they were of a piece. There was meaning to the conver- gence. Vera would spot the common treason. Yet her father, dear old Poppa Murko, would have understood. Did he not want his turgid, scholar's versions of the Chinese tales put into clear English prose? Those beautiful chunks of Ming erotica which he had mined from Zagreb archives. And which now, for the price of a bottle of aspirin, transmuted the amorous encoun- ters of Nebraska salesmen into sensuous pageants. What had he, Milius, done, after all, but clean Poppa's Serbian gunk from these Oriental diamonds, polish them up, and put them into American settings? With no thought of large profits or glory. Just to make enough for paints and canvas, to keep Poppa's daughter in cabbage soup and his granddaughter in trombone lessons.

Yet he was not wholly innocent. No, he had made one mistake: he'd hinted at the Chinese sources of his books, but had never mentioned Poppa Murko. And perhaps a second mistake: he'd yielded to Benny Goss and Americanized the books: Mei-ling Fan had become Dora Trent; Ch'o Tuan, the eager scholar, was Roderick Peake, the lascivious topologist. "Now we've got us something," said Benny Goss. Yes, Benny, a dagger. Any minute the phone would ring, Benny would see the paragraph clipped from the *TLS*, and, with the rage of the cornered pornographer, he would throw Milius to the wolves. To Vera.

To Milosovich and Krenk. Twin canines, he remembered them, sharp, torpid, yet turbulent men, dark and ugly, he could not distinguish their features, or disentangle them. Spittle lickers of Mihailović, they'd sold out to the Germans, and he, Milius, had had to cut out for the mountains with Vera and live like a block of ice for a year while Milosovich and Krenk drank slivovitz in Gradisti. After the war, they'd surfaced in England with fish in their teeth (red-brick Chairs of Serbian Studies), and now, behind the anonymous authority of the *TLS*, they did their poisonous survey of Serbian Oriental studies, straying just far enough to include "the vulgarized, baroque renditions of Professor Murko's versions of the *Jou-p'u-t'uan,* the *Ching-P'ing-Mei* and the *Ko-lien h'ai-ying* made by neither a Serbian nor an Oriental scholar, but by a third-rate American writer, O. Milius."

A day, a week, and Vera would learn that he'd stripped her darling Pop of his rightful possessions, and she would turn him into soup. Ah, Melanie.

Yes, out of his need, as out of the broken polygons of his painting, came the dear love of his life, surely that, his Beatrice, his Laura, his Stella. Yes, noble Sidney's precious star, he knew those lovely poems: Stella sees the very face of woe, painted in my clouded face, how she will pity my disgrace, as though thereof the cause she know, and some heart-rending, bull's-eye ending, "I am not I, pity the tale of me." Yes, he was Milius *Pictor,* not Milius *Auctor Plagiarist Thief.*

Dear God, what the artist had to become in America. Poor Edmund Wilson hiding out from the income-tax men to sip his champagne in peace; the poets all mad, spiked on their own dreams, exhibited like Cromwell's head for public delectation; the painters smashed up in automobiles fleeing the ravenous curiosity hounds, poor Jackson, dear Joey. And who flourished but museum directors, gallery owners, publishers? Business actors all, bearing their expensive agonies for cocktail-hour inspection, or, lacking the gift of gab, for fifty-dollar-an-hour confessors. The artists looked normal, jovial, quiet, only occasionally stabbing a wife or doping their veins, the only workers left, and what happened? Milosoviches and Krenks. Mindless teeth, snapping at air, coming up with artist hearts. *O tempora, o mores, senatus haec intellegit, consul vidit, hic tamen vivint. Vivint?* They strut in Bedford Square, shine in the *Times,* these critic-heroes, full of hatred or wild, mad enthusiasm, consumers, editorial powers, dressing themselves in the snot of kings, rejecting, accepting, declining, appraising, and we, weak-willed artists, we follow, we succumb, we bend, we take them at their own worth. Astounding them. And they eat us. Oh, Milosovich, oh, Krenk, shoot me here, shoot me.

And Milius, lost, pushed his hand to his head; his hat, little upturned lamb's wool boat, scooted to the ice, and a tiny skater, unable to stop, ground into it, and smashed her tiny nose on the ice; blood and screams flowed over the green scurf, and Milius found himself gripped by fierce hands, shoulders shaken by a ferocious little man yelling into his face, blissful in his hatred, grateful for his daughter's blood so he could bite the world's throat, and Milius, trying to shake loose, called out, "Little girl. Darling. I'm so sorry. Forgive me. How are you? Little sweets, take a soda with me. At the Zoo Shoppe. Come," and he pushed his yellow gloves into the wild man's chest and, punched in the ribs, began to punch back, what was he doing, here on a Sunday bringing blood out of a child, punching, and then a stout, gray-haired woman in a cloth coat rushed between them, picked up the child, thrust her into her father's arms, stooped for Milius's hat, put it on his head, and said, "Orlando. Orlando, dear. Are you all right? It's me. Yes, Melanie."

2

The Obiitelj, the Family, that was Tsvević's name for the fifteen, then twenty, then seven or eight of them who met day in and out at the old Tip-Toe Inn on Eighty-Sixth and Broadway or in the creaky three-story brownstones of the upper Eighties and lower Nineties of West Side Manhattan. They used the Serbian name, abbreviated to Obiit, because Tsvević, a Serb, was the organizer. The others came from all over the Balkans, Willie Eminescu from Moldavia, Veronica and Leo Micle from Bucharest, the mathematics student, Panayot Rustchok, from Sofia, and from Pest, their great success, Béla Finicky, assistant professor of Oriental Studies at Columbia, who introduced his most confused and beautiful pupil, Melanie Booler, of Tulsa, Oklahoma. The Americans in the group were usually transients, pupils in Tsvević's Language School, Tip-Toe Inn acquaintances or sympathetic types who hung around the Soldiers-and-Sailors Monument on Riverside Drive. It was by this classical preface to the mausoleum of General Grant a few miles up the Drive that Tsvević's pupils met on weekends, here that Milius first saw Melanie. He had already come to understand that what held and stamped the Obiit—Balkan core and American accretions —was failure. Other New York groups, formed at the same time out of similar drifters, foreign and domestic, somehow acquired the motor power which drove them through the Depression and the war into various triumphs, artistic, theatrical, publishing, and publicity, but the Obiit foundered in eccentricity, quixoticism, sheer inability to make headway. Milius had thought about it many nights. Why was it? Lack of ambition? No. The Obiit members were full of schemes, personal, civic, worldly, universal, timeless. Lack of tenacity? Perhaps, in part. But more, it seemed that American life wasn't ready to absorb these unassimilable bits of the unassimilated Balkans, these fragments of fragments. The Obiit, like their native lands, were the shuttlecocks of established powers. You'd think these people, ancestrally alerted to overreaching ambition and toppling regimes, could have adjusted to American life. But no, hardly a handful survived—Tsvević, Eminescu, and Milius himself. Though he had never been a true part of them. He'd come to earn a living and stayed for Melanie, but always, his persistence, insularity, and, yes, hardness, had held him to his painting, and this in almost complete isolation from the powerful temperaments already making themselves known in New York—Pollock, Rothko, Klein, Hofmann, de Kooning. They were unstoppable, and after the war, they constituted the field, their critics, friends from WPA days, preceding them with brilliant manifestoes, their gallery sponsors alert to the importance of abstraction in the opulence, anxiety, hedonism, and skepticism of postwar life.

By then, the Obiit were scattered beyond reassemblage. The war had assigned them, fed them, broken them; even their bodies, oddly enough, had strange chinks through which certain war and postwar diseases found ready and fatal admission—hepatitis, lupus, erythemic myelosis. By 1948, ten of them lay in the cemeteries of Queens. Who, watching the dark, gorgeous, noisy energy held in the corner booths of the Tip-Toe Inn could have foreseen such decimation?

In 1935, when he first met Tsvević, Milius, aged twenty-eight, was living in a bedroom-kitchenette apartment with Sophie Grindel, a severe, sensuous Latin teacher at Stuyvesant High School on Fifteenth Street. Sophie and the monthly hundred-dollar check from the WPA Arts Section were his support. Sophie had forced him into the project. "If you couldn't daub a barn, you've as much claim on the funds as those bums at the Municipal Building." She got her cousin, Sasha Grindel, a painter by virtue of talk and possession of an easel, to sign his form. "That sulky Dutchman dreaming of Ginger Rogers, and that galoot Hammerslough reading Trotsky while the other bums swipe at the walls. Roosevelt stands in back of them, he can stand in back of a real American like you. Talent or no."

Sophie was no admirer of his painting. He was income supplement, bedwarmer, audience, and chef. While she corrected *fero, ferre, tuli, latum,* Milius broiled carp, made matzo-ball soup, tried out pasta dishes. Why not? He stayed home. He went out only once on a project, drove Sasha's jalopy through the Holland Tunnel to a New Jersey post office, and painted what he thought would be a fit mural for this center of Washington's struggling colonials, an ocean of English red and black out of which coagulated shivery red, white, and blue streaks. Up on the ladder, he bore the catcalls of the Philistine post card buyers. During Christmas, he did part-time work dressing Fourteenth Street department-store windows. Most of the year, he just painted at home or on the walls of his friends' apartments. Indeed, it was learning to use this diseased skin of cheap apartments which opened his eyes to his screen techniques and led him to think out his notions of accident-proof painting. The apartment walls were his Paris and his Provence. Smoke and brick dust now, they were no more durable than the spaghetti alle vongole of some Tuesday prewar dinner. Less memorable to that great eater, Sophie. In the morning, when she left, the six square feet above their bed would be a mean green grime; at four, she'd return with her quizzes to a thick garden of color, and would barely nod at it. Was this what Cicero, that canny sybarite, had taught her?

Sophie was not harsh or mean, only intense and fierce. Powerful, nervous, silently demanding, Roman-nosed as her authors, her features dominated the narrow flesh of her face, the subtle lips whose underflap was gripped by powerful teeth when he had troubled her, straight hair the color of a Moselle white wine, full of rich gleams, though sparse; and the eyes like hot chocolate, steaming. They'd seen each other first through an Ohrbachs' window he was decorating with sugar frost and holly, she checking out a pile of cashmere sweaters with the volatile, chocolate eyes that soon fixed his. Her underlip drew into her teeth, and, behind the glass, in shirt sleeves, Milius had felt a shimmer of heat. That night he'd gone home with her—there was no nonsense anywhere in Sophie—and, the next day, he'd removed his clothes in a paper bag from his brother's Bronx apartment and moved into her two and a half rooms down the dying street from the high school.

Sophie had no friends, and Milius was too absorbed in painting to visit his old friends in the Bronx. They saw almost no one but Tsvević, a substitute German teacher in the school system who, at Stuyvesant, tried to pick Sophie up. When, one day, he succeeded, he found himself brought home to Milius. A shock, but for Tsvević's disciplined system, one activity could substitute for another without noticeable abrasion. Lust stymied, Tsvević orated, planned, organized. He was beginning to roll out schemes of language schools. Urban man was in trouble, flabby in mind, flabby in body. "Tissues feeble, issues trouble." Tsvević's passion that year was Quintilian. "Perfect Man is Man Speaking." Exercise would build up the tissues, recitation of great poems and speeches would do the rest. There'd be no overhead, classes would be in the open air, "*Mens sana in corpore sano,* eh, Miss Grindel?"

Over the next months, they worked out the Scuola Quintiliana; notices were inked on the back of laundry cardboards and put in windows along Broadway. The first meeting was to take place on Saturday, March 21, at the Soldiers-and-Sailors Monument. The day came, but no pupils. Only Tsvević, Willie Eminescu, and Milius, the instructors. For forty minutes they shivered in a trough of Arctic air, then adjourned to the Tip-Toe Inn to regroup their forces. It was decided to delay the opening for a month, change the name to the Mens Sana School, and alter the curriculum to instruction in foreign languages, beginning with words for parts of the body, words which, as the new notice had it, "would be riveted in memory by overt motor activity. $2.45 per week."

Oddly enough, this notice brought out eight men and women on an April Sunday. The next week, fifteen enrolled, and, finally, about thirty people, mostly young men and women whose schooling had been doused by the Depression. They met every Saturday and Sunday for instruction in Serbo-Croatian by Tsvević, Roumanian by Eminescu, and in his family German by Milius. The first month, Milius did no teaching, but was instead a nonpaying and phenomenally able member of Tsvević's Serbian class. The pupils ran along the Hudson River framing Serbian slogans, bent low to address gruff vocatives to the stones of Riverside Drive, exhaled declensions toward the coppery cliffs of the Palisades.

Milius began his German class in May, four men and women he could not remember and Béla Finicky, who knew German as well as he, but who'd been converted by Tsvević to the cult of verbalized muscularity, and who thought it a good way to be with his pretty young student from the West, Melanie Booler.

Milius fell in love with Melanie during her first push-up. A modest girl, Melanie was not the sort to suck beauty out of the mirror. Her expressions, untrained by vanity, were striking smiles and laughs, the dark-gold head flung suddenly back. Intoxicating. That first day, she wore shorts, sneakers, white socks, a loose white blouse. When she lowered herself for the first push-up, Milius saw her cloth-capped breasts enjoying their little motion. Eye snared tongue; correcting her stance, instead of *"Man muss die Beine* [legs] *ganz gerade halten,"* he'd said, *"Man muss die Brust* [breast] *ganz gerade halten."* Professor Finicky, at the summit of a push-up, caught the error and divined the source; his eyes fixed hard on Milius, but, too late, Milius was lost.

Walking up Ninetieth Street to West End Avenue, he'd touched Melanie Booler's bare arm. "You are so beautiful, Miss Booler," he said. "I find *ich bin schon ganz entzückt von* you."

3

By the seal pool, an arc of fish flew by their heads. Chow time. The great commas waddled, honked, panted, dived, and then such grace, delight, and marvel. Melanie Dube laughed quietly. The powdered, grandmotherly lumpishness disappeared into smile lines. Under the specs, the periwinkle eyes, within the gray hair, deep gold shadows. (Ah, thought Milius, Melanie in his mind, the seals in water.)

They walked by the wolf cages, the gnus and ostriches, then north along the chunky feldspar wall which split avenue from park. Melanie talked of Jack, her brilliant son, a wanderer, guitar player, dropout and C.O., Milius of Vera, Hannah, and his books, of which she hadn't heard.

Out of breath a bit, yes, but inside, Melanie and Milius felt musical, joyous. What were years but signs for outsiders? They were insiders, and, an hour later, over English muffins on a couch in Melanie's room at the Hotel Bolivar, Milius, awkwardly, but not upset at the awkwardness, took up her unringed left hand and kissed it.

How could it be? Thousands of hours had not dispersed, but only screened his feelings. Anonymous, cautious, sidelined, he felt singled out, magnified. Orlando Milius, hero's name on a coward's heart, oddity cloaked in oddity, he had not looked into his feelings for thirty years. A painter, his feelings were absorbed by the techniques of appearance. No wonder his paintings were strange. Yet one didn't choose the strange, one fell into it. Like birth. (What to do but breathe, cry, suck?) Or the war. There he was, four thousand feet over the iron river, the ocher shack on the lip of the copse, and Vera, Djovan, little Vuk, and Poppa Murko with his wooden trunk of papers. Alone, he had felt all alone, and there was Vera, intense, tiny, her cartridge belt across her breasts, her black hair clipped under the astrakhan, and old Murko, dear snaggle-toothed coot, sitting on those Oriental grapes. Ah, it was hard. Old Murko could draw roses from a rock garden. At night, above the icing Sava, he read the manuscripts aloud, and Vera's face, touched by the steaming raka, flushed in the sudden, masculine silence. Yes, Poppa knew his stuff. He had learned plenty from the wily Mings, knew his lungs weren't going to last another winter in the hills; and provided for his manuscripts and his daughter. That was the way life went: those who knew their hearts arranged the lives of those who didn't. Was it too late? For him? For Melanie?

For Melanie, no. Not from the first minute, seeing Milius punched and hatless, her sweet Orlando, so blotted a mixture of subtlety and confusion, so intricate and awkward. Despite Dube, dear Dube, as far out of the mainstream in his way as Orlando in his. She'd fitted around his oddities all these years, she would not pain him now. But he floated on those depthless oddities, she was only another one along with the white wool socks he wore to bed summer and winter, the collection of snakeskins, the rooster imitation. Poor Dube. His puzzlement underwrote her week in New York.

She had never tried him beyond puzzlement, but she was ready now. Not that she had ever been one to force things. *Wu-wei.* That's what she had learned from Béla Finicky in Chinese Thought. *Let nature take its course.* Sails, not oars; the stirrup, not the whip. It was her nature, as well. Rivers bit away at old beds, and formed new ones. (Did that mean old beds were abandoned?)

Milius walked home through the park at Eighty-Fifth Street. Provence. Purple vineyards, silvered olive trees, Renoir gardens, Monet ponds, Cézanne mountains freaked with jets of gold. Oh, such beauty. His hands in the yellow gloves tensed and perspired, he knew the sign, he walked fast, he must get home. At Fifth he hopped a bus over to Second, then ran down the block, stormed up the stairs past Vera's call, "Orlando," and, in the loft, dived for his paints.

But Vera's cry was not to be shut off, and guilt amplified it in Milius's ears. He dropped his brush. "It's happened." At last. She's found out. Down the hall she'll come, a pot of steaming water in those partisan's hard hands. Benny Goss, Milosovich, Krenk, Hannah, Sophie, the ghost of Béla Finicky, Poppa

Murko, and the lustful Chinese scribes would sup on his souped-down flesh. It was over. Provence? Hah. The butcher's knife. "Orlando," called Vera, and then another cry, "Brat. Brat Lando." Another voice: baritone.

The door whirred. A great slab of man grabbed Milius in his arms as if he were cardboard, whirled him dizzy, kissed his cheeks. Hannah and Vera cooed and leaped at his flanks.

It was Vuk. Cousin Vuk.

He'd flown in today, hadn't Milius been reading the papers? There was to be a reading at Madison Square Garden, the only poet ever to read there. "Not one word publicity, and the house is sold off in two hours. Tickets skulped for fifty smockers."

Vuk the Bard, Tito's greatest export, life's king, subsidized for singing what Djilas was jailed for saying. At eighteen, he had told Stalin to his face he was going out of his mind, and the old iron man, with the Georgian worship of the poet-seer, had taken it deeply to heart. So dissolved the world's miseries in that Shark's face with the wise, ice-blue eyes.

Now Vuk was, as usual, suffering. Heartburn, cramps. He raised his sweater, shirt, and undershirt, put Milius's hand against his rib cage. "Feel, Lando, feel," and in a loud whisper to both protect and excite Hannah, "Weemens is keellink me." Rome, Brussels, London—"incredible"—Paris, Barcelona—"estupendo"—even Dublin, two, three a day. And drawing a pack of Gaulois from his corduroys, "Plus fumigottink mine lunks." The hard, narrow flesh devoured by little Hannah and Vera till the shirt dropped. Then, in Milius's ear, "But waddya hell, us Communist mission is focking capitalists." This the shy rail of a boy skiing the hills with his bag and shotgun, bringing back the snipe. Now, in Serbian, he stuffed them with that great cake which was his life: tiger hunting in Nepal, swimming with La Cardinale at Porto San Stefano, strangling a rabid camel in Kabul, debating Rumli in Vienna, frugging in a Siberian igloo. And the erotic Niagara roared: one-legged beauties in the Pescadores, tree loving in Zambia, a flower bath in Oahu, and heart-cracking loves with an Israeli sergeant, an Amarillo cattleman's wife, a florist's assistant in Kuala Lumpur.

But Vuk, seismograph as well as earthquake, spotted uneasiness in Milius's laughter. "Enough. Let's walk, Lando. I must get some New York gas to my lunks," and took Milius off to Central

Park, where Milius, content to be Vuk's oyster, opened up his troubles.

For Vuk, though, Milius's troubles were unrecognizable as troubles. How could sheer possibility, whether for love or hatred, be anything but good? Vuk was delighted about Melanie; it looked as if one could go on a long time. For Vuk, life was a trail of eggshells. That a shell should suddenly churn with new life was a wonder. "And where is this nymph of yours, dear Lando?" He must see her, this wonder of sixty-year flesh.

As for Milosovich and Krenk, he would grind them. If he could face Tito, Stalin, Khrushchev, and Mao, it would be an eye's blink to crush Serbian scum into nonexistence. He would read them out of the world in Madison Square Garden, pop them into dust in Chattanooga, St. Louis, Winnipeg, and L.A. He would pull them out of literature like decayed teeth, and he could celebrate Orlando's beautiful erotica—though personally he didn't care much for fancy smut—that was no trouble, but first, they must see Melanie, "your neemph."

Vera?

Vera would understand, appreciate, adore his being refreshed for her. "Like dugs, weemens love sneef of other weemens on bones." As for leaving her, well, that was perhaps too much. Life was no coffin, each day a nail, one must move after one's heart, but leaving, leaving was much trouble. He would not dream of leaving his own wife, she was his mother, sister, lover, nurse, why should he leave her, she knew nothing—hah, thought Milius—about his other focking, why should she, she was brilliant, beautiful, had a life of her own, was strictly faithful to him, who would need any more? With his shark's smile, insistent, innocent, powerful.

At the Bolivar, Melanie was celebrating reunion with Tsvević.

Reunion?

Tsvević was putting it on the existential line: hot coffee and cold turkey. In detail. (Serious advice could not be capsular, look at *Being and Nothingness,* look at *Saint Genet.*) He had hardly warmed up, did not relish the entrance of Milius, let alone Vuk. That a Tito stooge, a ninth-rate versifier, a publicity gorger and narcissist should preempt his platform was a bit much. Seldom calm, Tsvević grew into a frenzy of calm. His sentences lengthened, his face grew polelike under constraint, the madly exercised body quivered inside the grimy tweed. He was disturbed, yes, dismayed by their indecision. Life called to them, the very earth suspended its course so that they could come together again, yet here they were, locked in bourgeois fears, corpses of life.

4

Ah, well, perhaps, but not that afternoon, that dusk, that evening.

For Milius and Melanie are in the Paris Theater swept by the love story of a racing-car driver and a widowed script girl, melting as the difficulties of the thirty-year-old French beauties blot into their own.

While Vuk—at Madison Square Garden—dedicates his reading to that great artist in prose and paint, his old friend and comrade-in-arms, Orlando Milius, assailed on the left by vicious Serbian cannibals, on the right by silence and poverty.

And while Vera Murko Milius lies on a velvet ottoman, head aburst with Leo Tsvević's story.

Tsvević stands in front of her, a sword, vague eye on a print above her reeling head, a Byzantine Christ whose head lies shipwrecked on its reef of shoulder. "Serbian agony," he growls. "Smash these icons."

"Darling Poppa."

"No regrets, Vera. No bitterness. Bourgeois gloom saps vitality. Look up at Leo, darling." Vera looks up. "Liberate Orlando. And you liberate Vera." An iron hand grabs hers, draws her up, they are nose to nose. "You have camouflaged *une mauvaise situation, chère* Vera." His great eyes swim in the red-veined net.

Milius and Melanie drink Cherry Heering in the Bolivar Room, go upstairs, and, in the dark, take off their clothes. Sympathy performs its magic fusion. The clumsy, creaky bodies understand; they are lovers once again.

Ten-thirty, and Milius takes the crosstown bus, in his hand a cellophane sack of chocolate kisses from Whelan's.

In the tiny living room, Vera Milius rises, fierce and silent. The chocolate obols are laid on the ottoman. Minutes eat silence. Then Vera begins, quietly: the historical introduction, the Balkan histories of treason, epic stories, the long fight for national freedom, the wars, the Bulgars, Turks, Austrians, and Huns, the traitors, Djuleks and Mihailovićs, who dog Serbian history. She should have been alert to treason. She should know the grain of the world. Like Milos and Brankovic, Orlando is infected. That her darling father had seen him as a son, that she should have been his prize was spice on the legend. Yes, even as she was, the years of her fullness given to him, Ganelon, Djulek the Bimbasa, Judas. Robbery. He had robbed his only heir. What price was it to come into the world the child of Milius? Sixty-two years of age, treason took a new turn here. And with what? A sugar babe? A gold digger? A baby doll? No. No, beauty she could understand, flesh she understood, but such treason, no. To salt his treason, his rebuke, he took a woman older than his wife, a rag discarded years ago, a Western American woman, with dental plates, white hair, hard of hearing. Was this the madness of abstract artists? That they had no touch with life, the world? Was this the meaning of his treason, that it went against the grain of flesh as well as family? If he'd brought a filthy nag, yes, literally, a horse into his bed, she would have only more clearly seen the insanity of his treason. My God. And he brings me sweets, chocolates, Judas kisses.

Vera, small, dark, blunt nosed, solid, pours her survey on his head. Powerful, analytic, a great moment, and in English, her second language, her father would have been so proud. Justice, intelligence, wisdom, passion employed to describe, correct, chasten. She ended in a great breath, rose, as high as a small woman could, he imagined her with the bandoliers across her breasts, the fur hat, the knitted gloves in the mountain ice, Vera, the great soup maker, enduring here his few dollars, making her own world amidst the aliens, back now alone on her mountains, a heroine of family life, out of the sagas. And he, a swine, thief, two-timer.

Milius sat alone in the parlor, heard the toilet flush—Vera allowed herself the privileges of being natural—he crushed a piece of candy, the stain was beautiful, he would put it on canvas. He sat brooding, and, then, bored and tired; but there was only the other side of their bed. Did he dare?

Yes.

He went in. She was, of course, awake. (Could pain advertise itself in sleep?) He took her breaths as whips, undressed, ashamed of his body's ease, put on his pajamas, did not dare empty his bowels, only allowed himself to urinate, ashamed even here of relief, brushed his teeth so his breath would not add offense, crept around to the other side of the bed, undid his pajama string for more ease, slid under the quilt. "Forgive me, please, dear Vera. I'm so weak a man. Please forgive me."

She had often rebuked him for ease of sleep while her ears seined the city's riot. He tried not to sleep before she did, but once again, his body triumphed, and he snored, terribly. Vera then could sleep herself, certified by the criminality of his noise.

5

The next morning brought great changes. Via a telephone call at six-thirty. A reporter, then another, then the Yugoslav Embassy, then the State Department.

It was Vuk. But by mischance. Life had caught up with him. The cake had its worms. He was in Lenox Hill Hospital, skull crushed, sure of recovery, but in a bad way. Reporters were chronicling his New York day. The feature seemed to be one Orlando C. Milius, American painter and author, whom Vuk had visited in the afternoon and extolled at Madison Square Garden a couple of hours before he had been mugged, slugged, robbed, and left for dead.

For most of the day, Milius smoked in the blaze of contemporary publicity. Pen, mike, and camera elicited every available piece of his body, every cent of his income, every stage of his life. By noon, he had watched himself on television and read about himself in the early editions with the happy puzzlement of a child seeing a drop of water under a microscope. "So this is Milius, this mass of warts, this lump of crystals, this strange being who has been given my name." He was described as "handsome and distinguished," "faded and undistinguished," "a youthful sixty," "an elderly man," "a famous painter," "an unknown poet," "a war hero and scholar," "an unemployed language teacher." He could not wait to cart his new lives over to Melanie.

She, unaware of his fame, had sat all day at her window, watching a veil of cobalt sleet lift from the city, seeing the dendrite ache of Central Park trees, daydreaming the strange turn in her life. Orlando, my dearest, no sleet with you. Our autumn is harvest time in dear New York, sweet nature's town.

Milius, arriving at six, was almost an intruder. She had to shake herself from the day's cocoon, face up to his excitement and great news. The Willeth Gallery had made overtures, his first show in a major gallery; Benny Goss, voice full of gold instead of rage, had planned new editions, translations, campaigns for awards, critical conferences, the literary works.

Night edged dusk, Orlando wore down. Too much. The variety and speed were too much. Their embrace was static, the amorous focus blurred. "We must go out," he said. They studied the movie section. *Blow Up* had just opened at the Plaza. "That's our dish."

In his fine chesterfield, bought years ago in the Gramercy Thrift Shop, riding downtown beside his lovely Melanie, holding a newspaper which carried his own picture, Milius felt like a man whose rich personal life was of public concern.

In the dark of the Plaza, watching the two chippies wrestle each other naked on the purple backdrop paper, Milius had an erection. And simultaneously, a tremendous idea. He would paint screenlessly. He would lay clear, intricate blocks of space events directly on canvas. No subtle schemes of indirection, only direct interrogations of matter, unambiguous shafts through surface forms.

What joy.

He turned Melanie's head toward his and, in the dark, kissed her lips. Nature had its seven ages, yes, but each generation altered their dynamics and duration. He and Melanie were vanguardists of the sexagenarian revival.

Yet, an hour later, eating at a Second Avenue steakhouse, there was another relapse. The peppered vodka-and-bouillon drinks, the adolescent hamburgers and onion, the noisy, gaseous, glittery night of Second Avenue, were not the backdrop for resurrected feelings or revolutionary passion.

At the Bolivar once again, holding each other, eyes closed against the sad circumstance of their bodies, loving but spent, half-querulous, half-amused, Milius and Melanie separated in the labyrinth of desire.

6

Artists, Milius knew, were hypersensitive to their cycles, emotional and social, intellectual and sexual. According to Françoise Gilot, Picasso had a daily rise and fall: her job was weaning him from noon blues to the two-o'clock assault on canvas. Milius's friend Praeger, the poet-obstetrician, had a yearly cycle: a fine, productive spring; a frenzied, coruscating summer; then an autumn and winter of uncheckable misery. He himself, thought Milius, had an elephantine cycle: his works took years to come to anything; his passions were lethargic as glaciers, his discoveries immense, but molasseslike in realization. The discovery in the Plaza Theater had led to a week's thick-headed absorption in paints. Now, his insight come to almost nothing, he surfaced for air. Melanie was gone, gone and he'd hardly noticed. His last hours with her were more nostalgic than amorous, scarcely a backdrop for his painting. For a moment, he couldn't remember if he had taken her to the plane. He hadn't. He had moled it in the attic, refusing phone calls, not speaking to Vera or Hannah, forgetful that he had been, unaware that he was no longer, a public figure. Now fog throttled dawn light at his attic's glass wimple. Worn-out, stained hands on his long face, Milius was carved by his ache for Melanie. Seven-thirty. He'd been up since six.

He put on his chesterfield and astrakhan, kept on the lumberman's boots in which he painted, and went out. He walked by the great, silent museum which showed no Milius, into Central Park, up and down the unshaven little hills, across the empty bridle paths, between great rocks befogged into Rhenish ruins. He walked northwest to the reservoir and waited. A runner passed, another, and then, chugging slowly, lined, gray, pullover limp over his knickers, Tsvević. "Leo," called Milius softly.

Tsvević stopped, took breath, stared in fright. "Who? Where? What's up? Oh, you, Lando." He jogged in place, panting, eyes popped and veined. "Something wrong?"

"I'm so restless. I had to get outside."

"All right. I'm finished. Let's go home."

For years Tsvević had had a woman friend who cleaned his

apartment. She'd died a year ago, and Tsvević had not touched a broom or picked up a newspaper since. The place was clogged with candy wrappers, socks, shoe rags, empty tubes of Bufferin, exhausted inhalators, copies of *Horoscope* and the *Balkan News-Letter;* the rugs were plots of dust; months of burned toast and bacon fat hung in the light motes.

It was a little better in the kitchen. Tsvević brewed tea, cleared the table, poured into clean blue cups. They sat at the window which gave on a coppery well of light in the apartment-house courtyard. Tsvević regained confidence. "It's worked out badly, Lando. Who would have guessed that Titoist monkey would turn you into a public freak?"

"A freak? The picture in the paper? That was nothing, Leo."

"You're wrong. It was everything. Kings have lost thrones with less exposure. You're fortunate you lost only Melanie."

"Melanie didn't leave because my picture was on television."

"Your picture was on television because of the dislocation in your life."

"What are you saying, Leo? Make sense. Don't talk like a foolish mystic."

"Mystic? We mustn't be so quickly contemptuous, Orlando. The world has mysteries beyond the scope of J.-P. Sartre. Have you not read Teilhard? Matter has its mysteries, and the spirit is not insensible. All conditions are enchantments, Orlando. The mistake may have been in forcing the situation. Acceptance, Orlando. Our lot is good." He tossed his soaked tea bag toward a garbage pail; it missed and spread its tiny leaves against the porcelain side of the stove.

7

Nine-thirty. Milius walks across the park as he had come. The Queens factories have sent their fumes into the risen mist; *café au lait.* The rocks are lit in the hollows where the crystals mass. At Madison, Milius goes into the drugstore and changes ten dollars into quarters.

In Tulsa, it is only seven-forty. Dube answers the phone. "Hell-o." Milius's throat fills, his heart thuds on his ribs, he can't speak. "What's this?" says the voice. "Jack? Trouble?"

Milius tries to say, "Wrong number," but can manage only phlegmatic clearance. He hangs up, wipes the perspiration off his forehead with the sleeve of the chesterfield.

Two weeks ago, the failure would have thrown him off for a month, if not permanently. Not now. Now he will wait two hours and phone again, person to person. The operator will get Melanie to the phone, then he, Milius, will manage the rest.

Losing Color

THE last thing that had color of the old sort was the penknife. Pearl ponds in snowfields. I'd lifted it from a surgical coat in Mulligan's office.

Mother looked youthful. Suppressed fury had given her good color. (Which I did not take in as color.)

Mulligan said, "Why not wait out the hour?" (He'd seen the nick on my wrist.)

The hour was controlled. That is, as long as I was in slippers and pajamas, I'd be allowed in the corridor and Quentin's room. When I changed into the hospital smock, I'd be restricted to the other room.

I wanted as much time with Quentin and Cammie as possible; yet Cammie had left. I'd hardly noticed it.

We'd come here for Quentin. I was an unexpected dividend. Quentin would be leaving soon. In his smock, he looked like a miniature Roman senator. There was new intelligence in his eyes. (Those blue eyes that evoke the evolution of protection from northern ice. Since the rest of us are brown eyed, I'd wondered if an iceman had paid Cressida a visit.)

"All right?" he asked.

"As rain."

"Is rain right?"

"It is what it is."

This wasn't much, but it was all I had. With what was left, I looked at him and received what he returned. I think he knew he was to pass what there was to Cammie.

Mother waited in the white corridor while I changed into the smock. (I did feel the grace of this propriety.)

"It's surprisingly easy," I said.

"Not for me."

Perhaps, but what I could make of her looked vivid.

In the corridor, whitish things moved here and there. I was certainly not their center of interest. (And hardly my own.)

Now Mulligan is at the door. He shows his palms, as if he's apologizing for a poor gift.

What strikes me at the border is its boundlessness.

Lesson for the Day

Kiest, with lots of time on his hands—his wife had a job, he didn't—had fallen for—that is, couldn't wait to get in the sack with—Angela Deschay, a pie-eyed, soft-voiced, long-legged, frizzily gorgeous assistant professor in his wife Dottie's department. Dottie and Angela were soaring together. It was WE—Woman's Era—in the universities. Every department had to account to Equal Opportunity Boards in the University and in Washington for its minority-hiring practices. Humanities departments had long since run out of qualified blacks and Chicanos. The few in these fields were more precious than natural gas strikes, but there were still good supplies of women. "Not enough to have a representative or two," rumbled Kiest. "You have to represent the whole miserable spectrum, pouters, grinner, thumpers, grunts. And then you can't fire'm. Fire a slit"—he'd borrowed that term from the misogynist Ty Cobb—"and you've got a fire on your hands. They get a new job Wednesday and sue you for the one they lost Tuesday. Lost purposely, so they can collect double."

The rumbling went on, mostly to himself or to his three- and one-year-old sons who did not exactly tune in to it. It was just Dad going on.

What else did he have to do? He'd been done out of his place by the world's women. In fact, it was Angela Deschay who filled the slot he'd have filled here in Madison. The slit in the slot. His lust for her had been blocked and then ignited by the injustice.

"What leg can a man stand on?" This to Dottie over the repulsive Cheerios he bought—of course, he did the shopping —because she detested them. "The one in the middle? That's the one that does us in." Thin, bespectacled, mild and innocent-looking despite his rage, Kiest threatened her with transsexual operations. On her, on himself. "I'll turn slit and give you a run for our money."

Would she even notice? She rushed off, she rushed in, flew to conferences, interviewed, was interviewed, formed and chaired committees, got job offers, salary raises. At this publication-insistent university, her only postdissertation work was a bloody attack on her own dissertation adviser's swan-song book on George Herbert. (So veiled with fulsome praise that only Kiest and the victim knew what went on. Dottie herself didn't know. Her aggression was just hearty instructiveness. "He wouldn't respect me if I didn't point out a few things. He's the last man to want friendship to shackle scholarship.") The tigerish assault was pronounced "brilliant" by senior professors who otherwise couldn't justify Dottie's unstoppable rise.

Kiest foresaw their life: Dottie as Chairperson, Dean, Provost, President; board directorships, a cabinet post, and who knows then? He would be Henry Lucing it after her—with the difference that Henry Luce had been Henry Luce, whereas he had never been allowed to be more than just Kiest.

What had he done? Well, he'd written a dissertation on the great and terrible John Wilmot, Earl of Rochester. At graduate school, he'd done far better than Dottie, and yet he could not find a job within a hundred miles of hers. She'd been wined, dined, grabbed for, prostrated before, you'd have thought she was a fusion of Madame Curie and Marilyn Monroe. She was only an enthusiast, a worker, a prettyish, big-bottomed, strait-laced, no, slightly unlaced girl out of the bleached Calvinism of

Dutch Reform Michigan. They'd met at the Yale Graduate School, drawn together in dislike of the critical virtuosi there. The literary pantheon at Yale didn't feature Shakespeare, Milton and Wordsworth but the versions of them offered by H. Miller, H. Bloom, G. Hartman, and S. Fish (whom Kiest rebaptized as Grinder, Wither, Thrombosis, and Carp). Each day, he and Dottie watched them lash, hash, and hack *Lear, Comus,* Browning, and Blake into puzzles of hamburger. "The texts we live and die by," said young Kiest. "And over in Romance, the Barthes-Derrida swine are fusion bombing Balzac and Stendhal. Who'd dare to write a poem in New Haven?"

Not Kiest. It had never been his ambition. All he'd wanted was a chance to dig into the grand old texts. There were plenty of first-rate meals to be made out of those ingredients.

Dottie was saved by languages. At Olivet, she'd majored in classics; at Yale, this was her redoubt, a pocket of antique resistance to the critical buzz bombs. Fresh-faced, pop-eyes agleam with untouched availability, she wrote the thick, paratactic, unnecessary-to-read prose that was called wonderful writing in the academy.

He, Kiest, had come out of the Garden District of New Orleans with ever-thinning Southern speech. His father had been pastry chef at the Commodore Palace Hotel, he became an early observer, then a master of aristocratic ways. Adolescent, he found the bookstores in the Quarter, and, by senior year, was enough ahead of his classmates to win a fellowship—"they'll change it to 'pal-ship' "—to Tulane, and, after that, a fatter one to Yale. Ascent was written all over him. Dottie, with innocent hunger, grabbed him. How could she know she'd grabbed a lemon?

Or did she? Had she known even then she'd need a Kiest at home for kids, for chores? He wasn't sure. He accused her of "unisexing" him. Even then, she knew both the unimportance and the necessity of his complaints. She'd become one of the least passionate twenty-eight-year-olds in America, but, in complaint-time, she could slide into brilliant sexual parody, so that tumbling on her pale rear, or bouncing the bud-nippled chest, complaint melted away. Being home so much did fierce things to the sexual appetite.

Which is how Angela Deschay filled his head.

The Deschays lived across the grassy street. Angela too was a rising star, not in administration, but scholarship. She published complex articles on Revenge, Power Hunger, Persiflage and Dominance in Restoration Comedy. Before she'd come to Madison, she'd looked up Kiest's dissertation (thinking that the Kiest on the roster was Mervyn L., not Dorothy M.). They were on the same intellectual frequency. Her husband, Jimmy, was in the Divinity School, one of the hip new preachers, full of pop cultural garbage spaced tediously by spiritous infusion of Barth and Bultmann, Troeltsch and Tillich. Eyeglassed, helpful, huge, eager, Jimmy was full of soft causes, soft politics, and frequent soft furies which exhausted, sometimes paralyzed him. "How could she have married him?" groaned Kiest to little Myron, Baby Dan. Madisonians—he knew—asked the same question about Dottie.

He and Angela walked their kids along the lake and talked about the seventeenth century, university politics and, after a few awkward skirmishes, sex and marriage. She knew his views deeply, they were in his dissertation. Kiest spelled out his own failure in Rochester's. The bitter entertainer, pimp and jester to the monstrous king, was a rioter, hater, *débauché,* an actor and counterfeiter who disguised himself as tramp, porter, mountebank doctor. Hobbesian apostle and poet of Nothing, Rochester knew that the difference between con man and banker was that the banker's credit lasted one day longer; that coward and hero differed because the day the coward had to put up, the hero didn't. His couplets lashed everyone from crowned king to two-crown strumpet. Aged thirty-three, burned out by japes, revels, punks, liquor, and disbelief, he was converted by Bishop Burnet, and died in the arms of wife, children, debts, and church.

Kiest, five years shy of Rochester's deathbed age, had had no king, only dream queens, no career of make-believe, only a noncareer of it. His debauches were oneiric. Home, after a first spring-day stroll by the sail-white, passionate lake, he put the kids down for naps, and took out the two hundred and forty bound pages of his dissertation, *Rochester, the Burning Counterfeit.* Its harsh prose seemed beautiful to him, he mouthed the great Earl's poems. Angela's legs and breasts, her thick-glassed green eyes, mop of twiny, glittery, leaf-gold hair, her long back with— surely—its generous dip into the beauteous twins, oh what a woman.

> Naked she lay, claspt in my longing arms,
> I filled with love, and she all over charms,
> Both equally inspired with eager fire,
> Melting through kindness, flaming in desire.

For all her dutiful distance and careful amiability, Angela—he was sure—burned for him. She was the right age, the hot late twenties, and she'd seen around, through, and over her hefty, dull divine.

> With arms, legs, lips close clinging to embrace,
> She clips me to her breast, and sucks me to her face.

Angela, Jesus, Mary.

> The nimble tongue (love's lesser lightning) played
> Within my mouth, and to my thoughts conveyed
> Swift orders, that I should prepare to throw
> The all-dissolving thunderbolt below.

Kiest turned on the bed, piled pillows stiff with Sears floral print into an Angelac body.

> In liquid raptures I dissolve all o'er
> Melt into sperm and spend at every pore.
> A touch from any part of her had done 't,
> Her hand, her foot, her very looks a c—t.

Done 't.

Lips on pillow, Angela's and more, more. Other women. Dottie. Angela and Dottie together, hugging, kissing, grinding into porno flicks. His weapon, abused on the rough florets, clumped with generative sap. Window light poured rebuke: "So, Kiest, this is your career. What a great man you are. Life seized by the throat. Another great day, Kiest. Sculptors are itching to get you down in bronze."

Jimmy Deschay was making his preaching debut. More final exam than ministerial vocative, but no matter, it was a large event, and the Kiests were asked to swell the congregation that was part of it. The sacred tryout was in the First Methodist

Church of Springvale, twelve miles west of Madison, fifty feet off the Interstate. Kids had been bunched with a single baby sitter. Kiest drove the Deschays' nine-year-old Dodge Dart, sitting beside Jimmy, whose terror dominated fierce silence. The preacher's hands were in and out of his hair, cut into shaggy bangs like Robespierre's. (Every few months, he adopted another antique revolutionary style: ponytailed like young Jefferson, curled like Simon Bolívar.) His eye sockets, lips, and chin cleft dripped; cheekbones, forehead, and chocolate-kiss eyes shone liquidly. The radiant April Sunday darkened in the car. Dottie made talk but was shushed by the Lord's frightened bridegroom. Angela, bareheaded, jouncy in her orange-flower dress, tried comfort, and was likewise shushed. Jimmy needed all lines clear for late words from on high.

"Is he trying to drum messages from his scalp?" thought Kiest, furious at Jimmy's contagious frenzy. "That great Vidal Sassoon in the sky? Damn sheepish shepherd."

In church, he sat between the ladies. What a position. Never, never had human appendages so moved him. Under the flocculent orange balls bent the superb, unstockinged, untanned legs of this scholarly charmer, this—please God—sluttish slit. They straightened for hymns, for prayers, up, down, arms, sides, raising and lowering hymnals, fifty, seventy small contacts. She knew, surely, the warmth he generated, the feel of his suit sleeve, the tensed communication of his arm. The holy place, the holy occasion covered the awareness with unthinkability. "But," thought Kiest, "She is thinking. She *knows.*"

> Rise up, oh men of God.
> Have done with lesser things.

No music reader, Kiest fumbled toward the notes behind Dottie's authority, Angela's warble. Hymnals bounced to the thin tune, hymn-booked arms rocked, parted, touched. Down they sat, arms and sides sending and receiving.

"Here we go," thunder-whispered Dottie.

Jimmy was up, black robed, huge. Sheets of light spread from the great windows over sixty worshipers. An electric moment. "Dear friends," dove Jimmy. "The lesson for the day is Matthew 26:23. 'And he answered and said, He that dippeth his hand with me in the dish, the same shall betray me.' "

"Mother Mary. Does the bastard know?"

Kiest's thought was not just his. Air spiked between his sleeve and the bare arm beside it. The power of words.

"God," said Dottie. "Something's wrong."

The ministerial tower tilted. From the top, vowels bassooned into each other, "Aarch, eeech, uuueeeshhh." Black wings rose, sank, rose; the left wiped the ministerial brow.

"Jimmy." Angela, hands fisted, sent useless strength his way. "Oh please."

Whereupon, not God but Kiest came to the rescue. Small and straight, he walked the little nave and joined the stunned divine. Jimmy's face, red as if strangled, widened fishily. "Mr. Deschay," said Kiest to the assembly, "rose from a sickbed against his doctor's warning in order to preach today. It's clear he shouldn't have. With his permission, and yours, I'll read his sermon for him."

The colors of humiliation and terror countered those of surprise, relief. Jimmy touched the shoulder of his substitute, then sent the flock those eloquent gestures which would in future decades be seen in the smaller congregations of southern North Dakota. Back in his seat, hands folded, he gave perfect attention, as if he were the benign appraiser of his rescuer.

Kiest looked at the typescript, and gave it his fervent all. "Is this betrayal story the essence of Jesus' last Passover? I think not. Grand as the grand story is, deep as it touches our sense of fair play, the betrayal, necessary prelude to the great sacrifice, is not the ultimate meaning. No, dear friends." His eyes found the thick glass behind which were the astonished, excited, decision-taking green eyes of the stricken fledgling's wife. Rescued from her own sympathy and humiliation less by Kiest's stunning move than by the moronic complacence with which her bedmate accepted it, she showed in her look an invigorated sense of the author of *Rochester, the Burning Counterfeit*. And, sure enough, pondering this new acquaintance, she heard clear substitution in the laborious text: lines from the wicked Earl's "Satire against Mankind," surely never before or after heard from this pulpit.

> Birds feed on birds, beasts on each other prey,
> But savage Man alone does Man betray.

Pressed by necessity, *they* kill for food,
Man undoes Man to do himself no good . . .
For fear he arms, and is of arms afraid;
From fear to fear successively betrayed.
Base fear the source whence his best passions came,
His boasted honor and his dear-bought fame . . .

"So," said Kiest over nodding, scratching, shaking heads, "as Reverend Deschay tells us, the betrayal in the midst of the celebrating feast is the essential savagery of man which, in hours, Jesus will die to redeem. So, on this second Sunday after Easter, do not lose yourself in the savage ecstasy of spring, fine as it may be"—small, wild rustling below—"without remembering that amidst your feasting self the unredeemed beast trembles in readiness. And here Reverend Deschay bids you turn to Number 29 in the hymnal, 'There is a land of pure delight where saints immortal reign.' "

That evening, while Dottie was out with her Sunday play-reading group—playing Regina in *Another Part of the Forest*—Kiest put his sons to bed, and then, from his door sill, sent brainwaves of imploration across the forty feet of grass to Angela.

Surely she'd managed to drug her preacher into sleep. The ass had covered his debacle with Kiest's excuse for it; so well had he mimicked chills and fever that he suffered them. The car ride back to Madison had been filled with his sniffles. Kiest and Angela had not looked at each other. That was the sign: she knew, he knew. What more was necessary? Knowledge embraced need, need the invitation to requital. *What was holding her back?*

Gold shadows thickened, purpled. A fat moon sat in the oaks. The lights burned at the Deschays', but that was all. Kiest's expectation became anxiety, then misery. Ten o'clock. He threw in the towel and headed for the armistice of bed.

The phone. "Mervyn," said Angela.

"Thank God."

"No, *you*. Thank *you*."

"All right, come thank me."

Crucial silence. "Papers."

Papers.

Of course. End of term for the full-time assistant professor. Wife, mother, assigner of papers, reader of exams, there was hardly time for sleep, let alone . . . *let alone.*

"I need, I want, I must." The unuttered conjugation of Kiest's hunger. He put what he could of it into "Angela."

"Yes, Mervyn." Slowly, softly. It was something. Then, probably faking, "Coming, Jimmy. Goodbye."

Coming, Jimmy. The counterfeiting slit.

Kiest went into the terrible spring night. The moon hung in it like an ulcer. *What to do?*

Headlights in the oaks, and a professorial Dodge pulled to the curb. Dottie. Hot and rosy with self-gratulation: "Bye-bye. Thanks, again. See you next time. Bye-bye."

Kiest slipped inside, doused the bed light, took off his clothes under the blanket, closed his eyes.

"Asleep already, baby?"

"No longer."

"Sorry, lambie. Had to tell you. Zack said he'd do it at the Repertory if I'd play Regina." Off with the square slacks, the fuchsia turtleneck. "If I didn't have to chair that Curriculum Revision." Into the bathroom, front and rear nakedly abounce, splash, scrub, towel, and tinkle, she never closed the door, and back to the dark bed in her grim, dust-colored pj's. "What a day." The bed light shriveled Kiest's eyelids. "Sorry, sweetie, I've got a Special Fields on Coleridge at nine. Won't take me long. 'Frost at Midnight.' "

"You said it."

"Want to hear?" A specialist in metrics who couldn't find an accent with a Saint Bernard, Dottie sometimes treated him to a reading.

Why not? The day had supplied everything else. Coleridge was the one romantic poet he understood from inside: idler, dreamer, opium guzzler, fragment heaper, a mothering father, isolated, sex starved, pent up with the wrong woman, dying for another. "Read on."

But Dottie, racing, underlining, scribbling, was almost done and could only cap this day of counterfeit and despair with the final wintry lines: " '. . . the secret ministry of frost/Shall hang them up in silent icicles/Quietly shining to the quiet Moon.' "

A Recital for the Pope

1

I N 1567, Carlo Lombardo built a palace for Prince Aldo Lanciatore on the site of the Porticus Linucia which in 110 B.C. had been raised by the Consul M. Linucius for the distribution of corn to the Roman plebs. In the late seventeenth century, a master of less altruistic distributions, the papal banker Giorgio Fretch, bought the palace from the Lanciatore family, and summoned a pupil of Borromini, Fulvio Praha, to remake the façade into one of the aimlessly turbulent extravaganzas of Roman baroque. For years now, tours of Roman *palazzi*, on route from the Cancelleria to the Farnese, have stopped to heave a few laughs at the combination zoo, arboretum, orchard, and mythological wood which Praha's workmen churned from the warm yellow tufa rock and its protective stucco, but in the seventeenth century, this blast at Vitruvian chastity excited the cupidity of numerous Roman families of whom the Quadrata were the most insistent. They purchased the Lanciatore and held it in their possession until the First World War erased their line.

A month after Mussolini was installed in the Palazzo Venezia, the Lanciatore was bought for a song and his Spanish whore by Elisha Borg of the Standard Oil Company of Indiana, who, converted by the woman, left it surprisingly, not to her, but to the Dominican Order, on condition that it be established as an institute where well-bred American Catholic girls could become yet more refined under the tutelage of the sisters and the amorous frescos of Domenichino, Guercino, Albani, and Lanfranco.

Each June since 1951, eight American girls paid three thousand dollars apiece for a year's board and room, joined in artistic community by two somewhat older Spellman Scholarship Students, one of whom always came from Europe. In 1962, the American Spellman Scholar was a poet from Providence, Rhode Island, named Nina Callahan.

Nina knew Dominicans: her brother had joined the order at twenty, and, at twenty-one, had been able to let her in on the Dominican strategy of humbling the sharpies and exalting the occasional nulls who'd crept into the fold. The sharpies would find themselves peeling onions in Kansas kitchens while the nulls would be living it up in European palaces.

The four Palazzo Lanciatore nulls were Sister Clara, a withered thirty-year-old blonde who ran the kitchen ("into the devil's throat," said Nina to her one friend among the girls, Sibyl Taylor); Sister Mary Pia, a terrier-faced woman whose self-imposed duty was waiting up for the girls coming back from Rosati's and the Veneto hangouts with the local counts, princelings, and other loafers, discouraging manifestations of affection, and insinuating improprieties; Sister Louella, an immense, gentle lesbian whose pleasure it was to see that the girls never learned anything which would further liberate what she regarded as their inordinately free persons; and Sister Angie Caterina, a moronic dwarf assigned to the maintenance of the musical instruments and art supplies which the girls were supposedly utilizing in their direct encounters with the Roman muses.

The nulls were bad enough to sour Nina's first weeks in Rome, the girls and their luxurious idleness disturbed her slightly more, but what chiefly coiled her insides was the desecration of the real magnificence which had been accumulated behind Praha's façade in the four centuries of the Lanciatore's existence: the plastic Standa lampshades on the bronze Renaissance lamps, the dangling rips in the Licorne tapestry, the peeling Bassano landscape which sweated over an unsheathed radiator, the Lipton tea bags which daily sank in the chipped gold cups, the paperback detective stories which lined the cypress panels under the begrimed cherubs of the quattrocento cantoria, the ceiling's smoked lunettes, the crumbling egg-and-dye friezes, and the courtyard where weeds overran patterns and tumuli fattened in the lawn: a general squalor of ignorance such as Nina, in years of living from hand to mouth in cavelike rooms from Dublin to Vienna, had never encountered.

In her third week at the palace, Nina secured Sister Clara's careless permission to draw on the bulging maintenance fund for supplies and repairs. Before the sisters woke up to what was going on, she had summoned gardeners, masons, plasterers, painters, carpenters, electricians, and a piano tuner, ordered a thousand dollars' worth of books for the library, another thousand dollars' worth of art supplies—there having been not a piece of armature wire or canvas in the studio, which was used exclusively by the girls' dressmakers—and spent two weeks supervising the workmen and cruising the Via Babuino for a few indispensable replacements.

At the very point of triumphant conversion, the sisters' dull awareness was, not shocked, but penetrated by the reparatory swirl. Recoiling from the signs of sodomic luxury, they traced them to Nina and confronted her en bloc to tell her that she should let them attend to "the housework" so that she could take full advantage of her unique opportunity to live in splendor.

Shaken to tears, Nina could think of nothing to say but that in Francis L. Callahan's house one never found a paper napkin by one's plate nor month-old stains on the tablecloth. Though even this was not said aloud. Nina had no use for fruitless rebellion. The one response in her stay at the Lanciatore which even hinted disrespect followed one of Sister Louella's rebukes that she was not paying attention to the news broadcasts which gashed their every dinner hour in the interest of "keeping up" both Italian and knowledge of the world: "Sister, my mind is not good enough for current events."

Nina was a pixie of a woman, small, finely built, cup jawed, flat nosed, merry faced; only blue eyes showed the ire which followed such trampling on her passion for rectitude and beauty. Had it not been for one thing, she might have headed back to Paris then and there. But the one thing was a great temptation.

Each September, after the Pope's return from Castel Gandolfo, he received the girls of the Palazzo Lanciatore in private audience. Indeed, each girl was alone with the Pope for three minutes, and then joined the others for a group photograph. Framed in Standa's rhinestoned squares, the papal photographs lined the central hallway into the music room.

Nina craved those three minutes. She admired, even loved the round little pope, discerned a translucence in his peasant's vulpine face which marked a sympathy of the highest order. He was clearly someone who responded to the finest human notes, perhaps as much or even more than his elegant predecessor, Pacelli (another favorite of Nina's). She could endure eight weeks of the nulls for this.

As if to mark the time, she undertook another reclamation project, that of the chief human rent in the Lanciatore. This was the year's European Spellman Scholar, Černva Grbisz, who'd come from Cracow with a cardboard valise to pursue her violin studies at the Conservatory. Černva's valise contained neither toothbrush, comb, nor bar of soap. Černva was fetid. Her hair was a knot of greasy filth, her teeth a gangrenous yellow, her breath a reek of garbage. She owned two dresses; both bore sweat marks, armpit to hip, bloody purple on the dark dress, grainy chestnut on the light. When she entered a room, occupants gulped, swallowed, took off. It was this which began to perturb Černva enough to consult her fellow Spellman Scholar. Why was it, she asked, that others did not take to her? Didn't Americans like foreigners? After all, she was a Spellman Scholar, chosen for her adaptability as well as her mastery of English.

Nina made a quick, a "Catholic," decision. Yes, she told Černva, she was sure the girls would take to her in time, they were slow to make friends with people overseas, and, by the way, wasn't Roman heat terrible on one's hair. "I used to have to wash mine every single night." She took up a bottle of Dop. "Except I found this stuff in Prima. You only have to wash every other day with it. You take this one. I've got another bottle."

"I don't have no hair trouble," said Červa.

"Try it anyway, I'll bet you'll have the same luck I did."

"Your hair don't appear different to me."

Nina did not give up. With Elizabeth Arden soap cakes, Pepsodent toothpaste—"A new American product, worked out in a laboratory for Roman women"—cologne water, eyebrow tweezers, nail files, combs—"specially designed for the Roman summer"—and then with the dresses, skirts, blouses, and cardigans which the girls actually tossed into wastepaper baskets after dressmaking and shopping sessions, Nina tried, but although Červa relaxed once or twice into taking something, it was only to appease Nina, for neither her skin, hair, teeth, nor wardrobe were exposed to the menaces which so ruffled the little American.

Červa cared for only two things, the Church and her music. She could barely contain her joy in the forthcoming audience. As for the music, she treated the girls to a sample of it during an afternoon tea while Sister Clara lunged accompaniment at one of the Lanciatore's newly tuned Steinways. Face lit with religious and musical fervor, Červa ground a Tartini sonata into such excruciation that only Nina and Sibyl survived *in situ;* and Nina survived only by resolving to end her futile attempts to gild the weed. It was high time to return full time to her own work.

Nina's work, the core of her life, was the realization of a plan she'd mapped out when she was sixteen. The plan was to become a major poet. This meant she had to study the poetic accomplishment of the race. In eleven years, three in the United States, the rest in Europe, Nina filled almost all time not spent earning dinner and rent money tracking the great achievements of poetry in eight languages. In New York, Chicago, San Francisco, London, Dublin, Madrid, Paris, Berlin, Vienna, and then Paris again for the last two years, Nina scrounged for the eight or nine hundred dollars a year she needed to live by guiding, nursing and accompanying tourists; waiting on tables; drawing caricatures; playing piano in bars, clerking; helping in art galleries; begging; borrowing; and when really necessary, stealing. Waking without knowing where the day's meal would come from, far from dismaying, cheered and stimulated her. She thought of herself as a citizen of time, not space. Her country was Poetry.

The Spellman Scholarship was another of the things into which Nina fell. Her Dominican brother had sent her name and book of poems in to the selection committee. Although she was the only applicant who had so exposed herself to the public, it was decided to take a chance on her. Nina had qualms about leaving Paris, but was talked into thinking the award a sign of special grace and came with an eagerness that only the nuns dimmed.

In mid-July, she went back on the schedule she'd mapped out eleven years before, mornings in the library, afternoons seeing things, evenings writing. The schedule was pleasant habit, not constraint. Nina never hesitated to alter it for friends, concerts, or laziness. After breakfast at the Lanciatore, she walked as fast as the rising heat allowed across the Tiber to the Vatican Library where she stayed till it closed at one. She was working on a Plutarchan comparison between the poets of the *Greek Anthology* and the early Italian poets from Ciullo d'Alcamo to the *dolce stil nuovo,* using the *Volgari Eloquentia* as a guide. Her interest was in patterns of cadence, syntax, meter, diction, pitch, stress, junctions (she had also studied linguistics on her own), and the relationship of forms to topics. She did research into musical settings, one of her ambitions being to revive the *sagen-und-singen* techniques of the *Minne* and Provençal poets. It was exciting work. Leaving the library was as difficult as anything that preceded or followed it. She walked back along the rattling avenues to where her free lunch sat engulfed by Červa, the sisters, and the two or three girls who'd stood up their midday dates. Then, without siesta, she trolleyed around the city by the *circolare,* getting off at handsome prospects, museums, and churches.

Rome wasn't, however, exciting her as she'd imagined it would. There were wonderful things at the Villa Giulia and the Diocletian Museum, there were fine views and churches, but more and more the transistors and Vespas which blasted her ears combined with the punitive sun to give her massive headaches. Then, too, the imperial assertions of the embassies, the Bernini squares and Bernini fountains depressed Nina: like the aimless contortions of baroque churches, they proclaimed their egomania. It was as if the sisters had governed Rome since Bramante's time.

At night, dinner behind her, Nina's life came into focus. Looking over the Campo dei Fiori, the odors of the day's market still afloat, Nina's mind sought the precise articulation of thought, feeling, memory. In the dark solitude, old accomplishment married novel expression. Not even Červa's violin wrestling devils across the hall ruined her meditations.

In late July, Nina found herself involved with Sibyl Taylor's problems. Sibyl, too, was discontented with the Lanciatore. She trailed along with Nina, buying beautiful piles of fruit and ice cream, discoursing on her problems with amorous Romans. Sibyl was extremely pretty, blond, pleasant, sensitive. Nina, who liked gossip as well as anyone, found her a great relief from the whistlers and pinchers who were the only people with whom she had any words at all when she went round the city by herself.

Sibyl's most recent problem was not with a Roman but an American named Edward Gunther who'd come up to her in San Pietro in Vincoli to explain Freud's theory about the Moses statue. This had led to an aperitif and talk, hours of talk. Surprisingly, Edward had forgotten to take her address, but the next Sunday, he'd shown up at San Clemente, the church to which the sisters took them every Sunday because it was run by Irish Dominicans. Sibyl noticed him when he'd snorted at Sister Louella lifting Sister Angie Caterina like a poodle into and out of her seat. Sister Clara had pinned him with a fierce look.

Edward was large, black haired, soft looking, lively. He'd been in Rome a month longer than Sibyl and Nina, had neither job, function nor plan. "I'm relaxing a sick heart," he said, but did not invite questions about it. Nina felt some sort of truth in that, but also felt it was a smoke screen. For what, she didn't know. In any event, Edward was a continuous instructor about things Roman. Instructing, his face flamed with eagerness, his gestures with illustrative fluidity. Nina interpreted all this fire and liquidity as more than pedagogy. She also realized that it was not meant only for Sibyl. That did not worry *her*. She'd handled far subtler propositioners.

One staggeringly hot day, they drove out to Hadrian's Villa

in Edward's Fiat Cinquecento. "Small but the motor's air cooled." They weren't. Amidst the ruins, they sweltered and Edward lectured. Quite brilliantly. He'd read up on the Villa and knew where in the white rubble everything had been, theater, atrium, the model of Tartarus.

After an hour, the sun mastered the master. Edward led them to a dead pool where filthy ducks cruised sullenly over the scum. He and Sibyl removed their shoes, put their feet through the disgusting veneer and rubbed them against each other's. Nina felt more superfluous than the ducks. She wandered off while Edward, renewed by Sibyl's feet, was engaged in a comparison of Hadrian with "those broken-down artists who become dictators, Napoleon and Mussolini—ninth-rate novelists—Hitler, a tenth-rate painter." She found a piece of shade under an umbrella pine. Heat-misted miles away, lay Rome. *Animula, blandula, vagula:* Hadrian's poem to his little jokester-companion. Jokester-companion. That was like her own role here. Those clumsy, at-the-brink lovers, playing footsie in the scum. Or were they clumsy? How would she know? Scholar-priest of Amor, she had heard the subtlest confessions of those apt in its words, Ovid, Gottfried, Ciullo, Cavalcanti. *Ailas. Tant cujava saber / D'amor, et tant petit en sai:* To know so much *about* love and know *it* so little. Nothing that she'd read had matched what she'd felt in the occasional Irish arms which held her in automobiles, on dance floors outside the half-mile limit of Francis L. Callahan's honorable home on Water Street. Not that she was a Louella, not that she had hormonic deficiencies, though, worried, she had gone to a doctor at sixteen and gotten a shot of estrogen to see if it would ease her ability to be gratified by the local pawers. It hadn't. There was always something askew, a psychological oxymoron, a gulf between desire and perception. Her body, shaped for passion, if she could believe the Providence locals and transient hotshots from Dublin to Vienna (or, for that matter, the mirror) had felt nothing more than an odd, erratic itch which, she knew, must never become necessity. No Edwards need apply. She had what she had, far more than scum-rubbing with a professional mouther. What was she doing here anyway? Here in the ruined villa? Here in Rome? Free grub three times a day? Not enough. She'd survived years without institutional handouts. Kroening, the nutty Swede, who'd corresponded with Tolstoi, had given her a cottage in Brittany; Hauch, the Berlin painter, shared his room and food despite her refusal to share herself; Mrs. Mackie had supported her in Dublin on her Guggenheim and taught her Celtic to boot. Best of all, Mademoiselle, whom she'd deserted, yes, it amounted to that, to come here, her neighbor for two years in the attic on Rue de l'Université. Mademoiselle Laguerre. Minute, aged, horribly poor, yet so graceful amidst the propped wreckage, drunks and shriekers of that attic, she was like a Benedictine among the vandals. The ideal citizen, articulate, curious, the happy frequenter of museums and libraries, the thoughtful reader of discarded newspapers, a preserver of all that was handsomest in her marginal past: the two eighteenth-century Limoges cups in which she served tea (cracks away from her guest); the lace gloves, one soiled (and so always carried in the other); the thirty books, read almost to dust. A purer version of Francis L., really, a man whom Nina had never seen in shirt sleeves, who governed six children by eyebrow and finger motion, by a high unmentioned honor which could have sustained her through two lifetimes of passionate temptations. Mademoiselle and Nina spent fifty hours a month talking about Indo-China, books, Debussy.

Three months before Nina left for Rome, Mademoiselle showed her an inventory of her possessions, cups, gloves, books. By each item was the name of the intended recipient, *"en cas d'une éventualité."* Nina was to get the books, the clothes were to go to the old lady who came upstairs twice a week for tea, her money—about sixty thousand old francs—was to go with her fan, a few daguerreotypes, and the cups to a distant niece. With the inventory was a receipt for a cemetery plot and funeral service in the 18th arrondissement. Nina took the papers and no more was said. A few days later, Nina came to Mademoiselle with news of the Spellman award. *"Oh, ma chère,"* said Mademoiselle, "I needed no confirmation of your powers, but I am thrilled. It is a sign of special favor."

Nina didn't want to leave. "They don't include the fare to Rome, Mademoiselle." Mademoiselle took fifty thousand francs from a drawer. "I feel so lucky to be able to do this, Nina."

Nina would have gone if only to accept the money. Now, under the umbrella pine, she felt the departure as desertion, and, worse, desertion into the falsity, show, and noise which art and Mademoiselle's life fought to the death. She'd go back, if she had to sell Červa's violin. She'd go back after the papal audience.

2

The Lanciatore steamed with preparations. Sister Angie Caterina's muttering swelled with the excitement she barely understood. Sister Clara attacked swatches of black poplin so that Červa would make a suitable appearance. The girls stunned their dressmakers with demands for spectacular simplicity. Each three minutes with the Pope was to be an indelible picture for him.

On the great day, four taxis deposited sisters and students in front of the Vatican apartments. They walked up marble flights, passed glittering salons, the girls ogled the piked Switzers, were themselves ogled by papal secretaries. Then they were ushered into an antechamber whose golden magnificence staggered even these young productions of Grosse Point and Winnetka.

They were admitted alphabetically. Nina came third. The corpulent little Pope sat in a green and gold room frescoed by the Caracci. He smiled at Nina's curtsey, held out his peasant's hand for her kiss, asked if she understood Italian, where she was from, how she liked Rome. It was very beautiful. Very brief. And Nina backed out, yielding to Červa, whose fear-worked sweat glands had already gone to work on her new dress.

When the last girl returned, the Pope waddled out to pose for pictures. He stood beside Sister Angie Caterina, who raised her eyes to his generous chin and babbled what he may have thought English but which the girls knew was the senseless litany of her ecstasy and terror. "We're ready now," said the good Pope to the photographer.

But not quite, for Červa cried out. "Papa, one moment, please."

"Of course, my dear. What is it?"

Červa went over to the sofa and, from under her coat, drew out her violin. "All my life I wished to play for you."

The Pope said that there was nothing in the world that would so delight him.

Červa raised her fiddle arm. Horrific stains released their

terrible aroma. Then out of the tortured fiddle struggled Gounod's "Ave Maria," perhaps never in the history of performance played with such passionate deformity. The Pope smiled unremittingly. When Červa's thick arm lowered from its musical slaughter, he said, *"Molto bello, cara.* I am grateful to you." He waved to the photographer, smiled for the flash, and disappeared.

3

The girls returned to the Palazzo, stunned, one and all, by the incredible conclusion of the audience.

Sister Clara announced that tonight there would be no permission to leave the house. Since the very concept of permission had been the invention of Clara's fury, it spurred a mass exodus. Nina had the sisters to herself.

Around the dining room table they sat, sweating in their wimples. Sister Angie Caterina still muttered the grim syllables which bound her dim memory to the great occasion. Into this low static, Nina said, "Sisters, I'm going to leave Rome tomorrow."

Sister Louella dropped her coffee cup on the Persian carpet.

"Mother of God," said Sister Mary Pia.

"I cannot do my work here, Sisters. I've got to leave."

Sister Clara rose darkly. "Ingratitude," she said.

"I'm afraid so, Sister. I hope you'll make my apology to the Cardinal."

"Lord God," wailed Sister Angie Caterina, driven to clarity by the word "Cardinal."

Nina went upstairs, locked her door, and packed her bags. For the next hour, the door was banged, scratched, knocked, and implored at. "Please, dearie." "You must." "Young woman, your scholarship." "Give us another try, Ninie dearie."

"No, Sister, what's left of my mind is made up."

Only to Sibyl did Nina open, and that to refuse an offer to get Eddie to drive her to the station. "I'm back on my own. I better start getting used to it," though that was only part of the reason. It was time to shake loose from nulls.

"I'd go pretty slow with that one, if I were you," she threw to Sibyl. (Though who could be less like Sibyl than Nina Callahan?)

In any case, it didn't matter. For Nina Callahan, it didn't matter who played *with* or who played *for* anyone else at all in this megalomaniacal city of nulls and Caesars.

Arrangements at the Gulf

In Lake Forest Mr. Lomax scarcely ever went out of his daughter Celia's house. Most of the day, he sat well wrapped up in the upstairs sitting room playing cribbage with his valet, Mr. Graves. After his morning broth, he read half of the *Tribune*, and, in the afternoon, after his nap, he read the other half. The only season he remarked was winter, which began for him when he saw the first snowfall coming down over the lawns. Then he would instruct Mr. Graves to begin preparations for the trip to Magnolia, the Florida Gulf town where he spent the last twenty-three of his eighty-six winters. A few days later, that third of his family whose year it was to see him off gathered round him at the La Salle Street Station and waved goodbye as his train moved down the tracks.

In his last year, Mr. Lomax was annoyed to find that all his family who lived in or near Chicago—and this was well over two-thirds of it—had come down to say goodbye to him.

Later, alone with Mr. Graves in his compartment, Mr. Lomax mumbled, "Like a golf gallery. Goggled at me like a golf mob."

Mr. Graves went into the adjoining compartment to brew some tea, but tea did not settle Mr. Lomax this evening.

He waved Mr. Graves away, saying that he would stay up till nine o'clock.

Mr. Lomax wished to stay up the extra hour in order to consider the annoyance which he had suffered at the station, to consider it with the shame he felt in remembering that he himself had been the cause of it all. Two weeks before, at the family Thanksgiving Dinner, he had said something out loud which formerly he would not have permitted himself to think. He had been served and was studying a white cut of turkey breast similar to those which he had for some years pretended to enjoy for the sake of the family. "They've given me an awfully big slice this year," he was thinking when his son, Henry, a priggish busybody and alarmist, asked him if the turkey didn't look quite right to him. Mr. Lomax, with the same effort it would have cost him to say, "Yes," said instead, "I think I'm going to die in Florida." The consequence of this irrelevance was that Mr. Lomax's leave-taking had been an informal rehearsal of his funeral. Now, shaking his head, Mr. Lomax made sense of the parting remarks which his children had made to him, Celia's "It's been fun taking care of you, Papa," and Henry's "I'm sorry about the business, Papa." As if he hadn't forced Henry out of the firm thirty-five years ago, and as if Celia had not regarded him for twenty years as an immense burden sufferable only because she owed it to him.

"A pretty thought," mumbled Mr. Lomax. At least, he reflected, his bachelor friend Granville had never had to put up with that sort of smallness. Thinking of Granville, as he would see him the next day waiting at the Magnolia station as he had every other year for the past twenty, Mr. Lomax revived enough so that he almost shuddered at the funeral pageant of which he had been cause and center.

It was very nearly always Granville, the thought of Granville, which pulled Mr. Lomax up in these last years. They were so different, they had done such different things, that the comparison of their lives—and this is what Mr. Lomax constantly made —was never exhausted. The comparison had roots in both pity and envy, and, even now, as his mind wandered, Mr. Lomax pitied what he felt must have been the loneliness of his friend's departure from Philadelphia, and then envied its self-sufficiency.

Mr. Lomax was rather proud of his friendship with Granville —Granville was an author—for although the latter was not well enough known for Mr. Lomax to be distinguished by their association, Granville's varied learning and energy had been the source of much pleasure for him, in conversation, contemplation, and in Granville's books. From the last, Mr. Lomax had learned a great many things, the history of investment banking and of New England Colonial preachers, the topography of the Gaspé Peninsula and the rivers of California. Granville's latest volume—the third he'd completed since his seventieth year— had come in the mail the preceding week, and, thinking of this, Mr. Lomax rapped on the compartment door for Mr. Graves.

"Is anything wrong, sir?"

"You might try me with another half a cup," said Mr. Lomax, handing him the cup although this was not easy for him, "and I think I'll look through the new book."

Mr. Graves opened a suitcase and handed Mr. Lomax the book and his magnifying glass.

"Never mind the tea, Graves," said Mr. Lomax. "I'd better not stay up too late." He had not wanted to bother Graves just for the book.

As usual, Granville had inscribed something on the flyleaf. It went, "For my old friend, Frederick Lomax, from his 'young' admirer, Herbert Granville." Mr. Lomax frowned. He disliked his friend's frequent allusions to the decade which separated them, for he sensed in them a possible reflection of the uselessness of his own last years in the light of his friend's striking productiveness.

The book was called *Givings and Misgivings,* and Mr. Lomax, who sometimes read little more of the books than was required for acknowledgment and compliment, could not guess whether or not it would absorb him.

After a bit, he decided that it would not. It was made up of disconnected paragraphs of advice and reflection held together by little more than the calendar: there were 365 paragraphs, each labeled, in journal fashion, by a date of the year.

The simplicity, the naïveté even, of this arrangement suggested so much of Granville that Mr. Lomax looked toward the dark window as if to see him standing at the station in his

English cap and knickerbockers, and, in this movement, he recovered the ease and self-satisfaction which his departure had taken from him.

He turned to the paragraph headed March 11, which was his birthday. It went:

> Nothing honest comes with ease; nothing dishonest brings ease. The pressures of life are life itself, as the pressure of the blood is our pulse, the pressure of lungs our breath. Birth itself is the pressure of new life on old. The people who tell you, "Worry kills. Don't worry," do not realize that they are saying, "Life kills. Don't live."

Mr. Lomax read this through twice and then rapped on the door for Mr. Graves.

"A pencil please, Graves," he said, and, when Graves was gone again, he made a star by the paragraph and another at the bottom margin, and, by the latter, he wrote, "Nonsense," and then his initials, "F.L."

If he could have managed the pencil, thought Mr. Lomax, he would have written a great deal more. The paragraph had seemed to him almost an attack, and he would like to have countered it with something like, "The words of a man whose sole worry in life has been whether it's his year to go to Florida or California, who's never done any work in his life but write books, and never had anything to do with birth except be born."

The imagined counterattack tired Mr. Lomax, and he leaned back against the chair and closed his eyes. Then he tried another paragraph, June 11, which was the date on which his first wife had died and that, a year later, on which he'd proposed to his second. This paragraph read:

> Now that glittering heavens and hot seas warm the blood with feelings deeper than all memory, do not turn away, feeling incapable of such beauty. If unfulfillment is bitter, unacknowledgment is bitterer still. It is men who deny the world, not the world which denies men.

Mr. Lomax shook his head and decided not to write anything after this paragraph. In a moment, though, he thought of something, and, taking up his pencil and making the two stars, he wrote after the bottom one, "I wish you could have had one of mine, Herbert. F.L."

When the train arrived in Magnolia the next evening, Mr. Granville in his white cap and knickerbockers waved as Mr. Graves and the conductor helped Mr. Lomax off the train and into the wheelchair.

"Hello there, Lomax," he called. "It's good to see you again."

Mr. Graves wheeled Mr. Lomax over, and the two old men shook hands. "It's good to see you too," said Mr. Lomax. "You shouldn't have come down to the station."

Granville and Bob, the man from the Inn, helped Mr. Graves lift Mr. Lomax into the station wagon.

"I took the train down this year, too," said Granville. "Just decided not to drive. My reflexes are as good as ever, but I just decided against it."

"Wise thing," said Mr. Lomax, thinking Granville must have had an accident driving back from California last spring.

When they arrived at the Inn, Mr. Lomax went directly to his room without greeting anybody but the owner, Mrs. Pleasants, who waited on the verandah to welcome him for the twenty-third consecutive season.

He slept through dinner and came out at nine-thirty, just as most of the other guests were going up to bed. Those who knew him stayed with him while he had his bowl of soup, talking about their trips down and inquiring about his.

When they had all gone up, Granville wheeled Mr. Lomax out to the long porch which overlooked the Gulf, and they sat there alone.

"Here we are again," he said.

"And very good to be here," said Mr. Lomax.

"Lucky as well, I think," said Granville, moving his head slightly in the breeze and wondering whether it was too strong for Mr. Lomax.

"Not you," said Mr. Lomax. "You have some claim on the years yet."

Granville smoked a cigarette, taking care to blow the smoke away from his friend's face. "Funny," he said, following the smoke off the dark porch, "I always think of you when I think of that. I mean, after all, you're here and well here. That's taken a lot of weight off my shoulders."

"I've got good shoulders," said Mr. Lomax.

Granville looked at his friend, small and humped in the chair, and he said, "Of course." After a pause, he added, "You make me envious too, you know, so I don't know whether you do me more harm than good. I sometimes tell myself, 'Granville, even if you went around the world, married a ballet dancer, and did God knows what, you still wouldn't have lived half the life Fred Lomax has.' "

"Work and trouble. That your idea of a full life?" said Mr. Lomax. He shivered a little in the breeze. "Never did anything with real thought in my life, and the consequence is I leave nothing worth thinking about behind."

"Children," said Granville, emphatically.

Mr. Lomax grunted. "There were twenty people at the station to see me off, and, except for three in-laws, not one of them would have been alive except for me. But that's all, Granville. Could have been any twenty people in the station, any twenty off the Chicago gutters, and they would have been as near to me as those. As near and as understanding. The virtue of children is a fiction of bachelors."

"Can you mean it?"

"Can you ask me?"

They didn't talk for a moment but watched the moon coming out of the clouds, lighting the palms along the porch and the boats down by the Inn pier.

"I don't regret being old," said Mr. Lomax, looking up at the moon for a moment. "I don't think much about what comes next. As for what I've done, I did it without much consciousness, so it was mostly painless as well as wrong. I think a lot about mistakes. That and the Gulf. I think a lot about sitting out here with you, watching the Gulf." After another pause, he said, "I miss you the odd years."

"Thank you," said Granville smiling. "I think of you often then, too."

Mr. Lomax's hand tightened on the chair. "Do you mind my asking why you go way out there now since your sister died?"

Granville got up to put his cigarette out in one of the sanded containers on the porch. "I don't know," he said, sitting down.

"It's very pleasant out there. Mostly, it's because I've worried about getting stiff, I suppose. Old in a bad way. Not like you, of course, but you've had so much more than I."

Mr. Lomax was getting very tired, but he wanted to say a little more. "I told Henry, by accident, that I was going to die down here."

Granville knew that Lomax wished him to say something, but he could not quite make out what. He stared at one of the buoys trembling in the moonlight.

"I'd been feeling that way," Mr. Lomax went on. "It wasn't to arouse anybody—even if I could at my age." After another pause, he said, "I'd like to die when you're around, Herbert."

"That's a funny thing to say, Fred."

"Well, it is funny, but not really. Old friends are true family, aren't they, and you understand me, don't you? More than they. You meet me in the right way, say the right things, the right way." Then Lomax asked his favor. "If it's not this year, it'll be next."

"I'll come down then, Fred," said Granville.

They sat for a while looking out over the Gulf. Then Granville wheeled Mr. Lomax into his room, and, contrary to their custom, they shook hands as they bade each other "Good night."

The Girl
Who Loves Schubert

Y NTEMA and Scharf didn't like each other, but whenever
Scharf came to New York—about once a year—they had lunch.
Scharf would have finished his business and seen his few real
friends, there'd be an open lunch date, why not call Yntema?
They'd known each other thirty years, fellow law students at
Ann Arbor, till Yntema dropped out, months shy of the degree.

During school, Yntema had gone with a girl, Marjory Spack,
who was, he said, "Not my type. Beagle eyes and bandy legs."
He introduced her to Scharf (who married her). A week after
the introduction, Yntema took off for New York, found work in
the Trust Department of the Chemical Bank and prospered.

Scharf was orderly, finicky, conservative; Yntema, erratic,
flighty, a lover of disorder. When Yntema asked Scharf what was
new, the answer would be something like, "I live like a plant.
How different can leaves feel?" That was enough for Yntema.
They could get down to his troubles, which were always rich:
perfect matter for his fluent, seductive narratives.

Scharf adored them. (They compensated for his dislike of

their hero.) Familiar as he was with their themes and tropes, there was always fine new detail. The themes were Yntema's father and his "endless declension of tarts"; Yntema's doubts of his masculinity, traceable, of course, to the paternal freebooter; Yntema's wives, girlfriends, and therapies (sun cults, Tarot packs, LSD, jogging, diets), sources of his latest burst of "inner peace."

Almost every year there was a new wife or friend. "How's Felicia?" On his one visit to Yntema's West End Avenue apartment, Scharf had had a glimpse of her.

"I'm sure she's getting along. Why?"

"So there's a new installation."

"I'm with a terrific girl. A brilliant, tough girl. I met her at the Midtown Club. Weight lifting. I started lifting in May."

"You're looking very solid."

"Three times a week at the Club. And at home, with Walter." Walter was Yntema's eighteen-year-old son. "It's quite a sight, the two of us grunting under iron."

Walter's moods, schools, clothes, analysts, and drug bouts were a subtheme of Yntema's saga. Walter was "an index to his generation," a sociological thermometer luckily found in Yntema's own medicine chest.

Yntema had an abnormally quiet but lyric voice. Its lilt was that of repression: repressed laughs, repressed boasts, repressed feelings of every sort. Marjory Scharf remembered it as "a fake seducer's voice. A meadow disguised as a minefield." Laughter was always swelling in it. Then something held it back, and out came snorts and melancholy honks.

Scharf, who'd run to fat and was gray at forty, marveled at Yntema's looks. For all the divorces, the self-doubts, the expressed and suppressed hatreds, Yntema looked much the same as he had at Ann Arbor. Fifty-one, there were scarcely any lines in his face; no gray hair, just less black, less curl above a face that looked like a mix of Byron and Pushkin.

Over tea and *sushi,* Yntema said that Felicia's successor, Apple Gruber, was "the girl who loves Schubert. Remember *A Handful of Dust*? The fellow trapped in the jungle by that lunatic illiterate who makes him read Dickens's novels aloud over and over? That's me. Except I only have to listen, and Apple's unfortunately literate. She has this dowser's gift of

knowing what I don't. 'Have you read this, have you read that?'
'No.' So it's lecture time. I might as well be back in Ann Arbor
with all that rigged knowledge. You know how these Sardinian
kidnappers always ask for just the amount of dough the guy's got
in the bank. They're in cahoots with the bankers. Who's in
cahoots with Apple?"

"You must give yourself away."

"The inner banker. Maybe. She gets intellectual crushes. Last
spring it was Leibniz. Our place turned into an Institute. Fer-
ney West. Optics, hydrostatics, pneumatics, mechanics, calcu-
lus. There was nothing the old kraut wasn't into. *La vraie
logique, l'art de calculer, l'art d'inventer.* Monads crawling
around. Four months of Leibniz. Until ten o'clock, November
27. We're at Lincoln Center listening to Fischer-Dieskau singing Schubert. And boom, zoom, out the room. That night, the
monads get the sack. Boole, Frege, Russell, Peano, all those
great Leibnizian logicians who'd battered my head since August, are out. November 29 I come home from work and halfway up the elevator I hear Fischer-Dieskau singing *Die
Winterreise.*" And Yntema sang, " '*Manche Träne aus meinen
Augen.*' On every chair, scores, albums, articles, biographies.
Apple, who's a terrific Amazon—you should see her, she's spectacular, it's like making love to the Brooklyn Bridge—she's—
what?—swathed, enshrouded in a cloud of tulle. A golden peig-
noir. My Viennese Alp. Muscles? They're out too. Hair—which
had been tied up in a nice lump—is a blizzard. A red blizzard,
halfway to Egypt. On the walls are watercolors, lithographs,
woodcuts. The Vienna woods, the Danube, the Prater, Metter-
nich, Beethoven. A week later, Schubert himself shows up. In
bronze. Eyeglasses and all. Six hundred bucks."

"On you?"

"Are you nuts?"

"What does she do?"

"Physical therapy for retarded kids. Riding and rowing. Rich
she is not. But what there is goes to Vienna. I live in a Schubert
Museum."

If anything, Yntema's apartment looked like a museum of
Radical Nostalgia. Yntema lived his idea of the thirties intellec-
tual, domiciled, but ready to go underground at the first knock.
His building's tiny lobby had a defunct carpet, puce walls, an

ancient elevator, dark corridors. Varnish scabs ribbed the doors. Yntema's apartment was the natural bloom of this shabbiness. Its walls were the same heavy puce as the lobby's—there must have been a paint sale around the corner—the chairs and the sofa had long since had it. When you rose from them, clumps of hair rose with you. As for décor, Scharf remembered a swatch of frayed batik tacked between an unframed map of Europe and a Woolworth-framed lithograph of the British Museum Reading Room. The room stank of pamphlets.

Why did Yntema live like this? Alimony, doctors, girls and Walter were expensive, but he made lots of money. If ever a place staged an idea, it was this one. The idea was, "The hero of a mental saga needs no scenery."

Yntema was living with Felicia Mellowine, a very long-necked redhead he'd "rescued from the turpitude of Gimbels. Decorative Accessories. Eight hours a day, no sitting down or leaning on counters. Eighty-five dollars a week." Scharf saw Felicia for about a minute and a half. (Though quite a lot of her, for she wore nothing but a blue dressing gown that had served some of Yntema's more careless companions. He tried not to stare at the navel and nipples which winked through the holes.)

"Who's Lawrence of Arabia?" The voice didn't do justice to the beautiful throat.

"Why?" asked Yntema. He did not look up from his can of Blatz.

"Kojak asked this cop who he thought he was, 'Lawrence of Arabia?' "

"President of OPEC," said Yntema.

"An Arab?" Above the neck, Felicia was mostly pout.

"Say hello to Ed Scharf, kiddo."

"Hi Ed. I won't bother you. I'm into a good show."

Were all Yntema's women—after Marjory, of course—such washouts? They were so vivid in his stories. Perhaps what counted for him was not the girl but what he could invent about her. The less there was to work with, the more he could invent.

Or was this *his* invention? Was he Yntemizing? Making his own Yntema saga?

After all, Yntema radiated intelligence and self-control. The quiet voice was sane and clear.

"A few weeks ago, Walter and I are lifting away, dripping, concentrating. You don't lift, there's a lot to it. The idea's to put every muscle against its pain wall, then drive through it. You have to concentrate every second. Otherwise you'll break. So we're lifting, and, all of a sudden, I feel something. A glance. A shaft. I've got a hundred and seventy pounds in the air, and I spot the *schöne Müllerin* leaning delicately on the wall. Looking. 'Do you boys know what you're doing?' Remember, this girl has *thighs, biceps,* she bench-presses a hundred and forty pounds. 'Is this what you really want? I mean, what's the *point*? Walter'—Walter's stretched out, he looks like a weather map—'Walter,' she says, 'do you know that when Schubert was eighteen he composed two symphonies, three sonatas, and a hundred and forty-five songs? Does that give you pause, Walter?' Walter's so proud of these muscles, Eddie. You know he's not a big guy, eczema's crawling over him, what does the kid have but these muscles? He's worked like a dog for them. I mean what does Walter have to do with some one-in-a-trillion phenomenon who sneezed music? Push Schubert downstairs, the stairs sang.

"So that's life *bei* Yntema. Not all bad. I like to learn. And the first ten times you hear the *Winterreise,* it's everything Apple says it is. But that's the thing about this girl. She doesn't have the usual appetite. No one who looks like Babe Diedrickson—plus Maureen O'Hara—can have a normal appetite. She can't stop with anything. And with Schubert, it's not the songs she wants, it's what they conceal. What they mean. We had to hear this *Winterreise* till she figured out how it killed Schubert."

"I don't get that."

"It's baloney. That is, pure Apple. Her Schubert had a terrific life. His family loved him, he had great friends, they had these wine-drinking parties where he sang his songs. He composed every day, studied scores, read poems. He was smart as hell, read everything, classics, Goethe, Fenimore Cooper, discovered Heine. And he knew he was great stuff. Then he read these *Winterreise* poems, full of drivel about a guy wandering around the snow, a kind of *lumpen* Lear, barked at by dogs and so on. He goes crackers and ends up with an organ grinder. Apple's idea is Schubert took every word of this drivel and turned it on himself: he had no one, no girl, no real friend, nobody to understand what he was about. Except Beethoven, who'd just died. Schubert went to the funeral, and that set him up for his own."

"He killed himself?"

"*Typhus abdominalis.* Same thing his mother died of. But Doktor Gruber, Professor of Viennese *Schwärmerei,* says it's 'essentially suicide. The virus sits around waiting till it gets a mental cue.' Then boom, zoom, out the room."

Within Yntema's stories, there were always others. His saga was not a mere odyssey of bruises. Every bruise meant something. Schubert meant something. Apple meant something. The real story was always Yntema's, and Scharf knew that he discovered it as he told the other. That was why Yntema relished their lunches.

"Are you waiting for Schubert to go the way of Leibniz? Is that where you stand?"

Yntema tongued some saki, very thoughtfully. "Don't you see?" Oystery light from the perforated brass shades touched his eyes, teeth, cheekbones. He was like a little festival of insight.

Yntema had his narrative tricks: he held back, called for the check, went through the rigmarole with credit card, receipt, signing, tip, and it was ten minutes—while they walked up Forty-Sixth Street in their topcoats—before Scharf pushed him toward the end of the installment. "I don't see what you think she was getting at."

"I don't either. Yet." Yntema stopped. They were in front of the bank. "At first I thought, 'She's trying to get rid of Walter.' But she likes him. If only as another listener. It's something else.

"Leibniz was a force for her, a mentality, not a person. Schubert's something else: a presence. A person. One she takes to. His fecundity, his modesty, his confidence, even his smallness— he was four-eleven!—reproach her. And enchant her. What does that make me? Superfluous. Three's a crowd. The question is, 'Is she *gunning* for me?' Not with a gun. An Apple doesn't do it with a gun. The gun she uses is *you.*"

"Me?"

"*Me!* She uses you against yourself. Like Walter's muscles. *Die Winterreise.* She's contriving a *Winterreise* for me. An internal boot in the ass. And out goes Yntema. Into the snow."

The sun blinds the glass skins of Sixth Avenue. "The U. S. of A., Eddie. Shining, stretching, pushing, remaking. 'Oh say, can you see?' No? 'Then move on. The frontier. Build the sonofabitch over. The Indians? Grind'm.' Apple—Christ! her name's Martha!—she's pure American. Apple pie. And I've eaten of the apple. I've gotta pay. So that's where it stands. Am I Apple's eye? Or her Indians?"

The annual installment often ended like a serial, Yntema dangling over a sexual cliff. But Scharf was in on it; it existed because of him. As if Yntema had troubles in order to have a new installment for their lunches.

There was some ill will here as well: if Yntema dangles, why not Scharf? Scharf knew that Yntema was more than puzzled by his steadiness. His self-deprecations—"I live like a plant"—"I'm a uxorious vine"—offended Yntema as patronizing superiority: "He can afford self-deprecation."

Scharf was happy. He loved not only his routines but the idea of them. That fact was beyond or beneath Yntema's comprehension. He resented such vegetal contentment as a worldly as well as a Scharfian fact. How could a human being who was neither prude nor dummy restrict himself in a world so rich with possibility? Scharf felt that Yntema must think he was lazy, or that his energy was low. A wife of thirty years must be a security blanket, a form of avarice or fear. "And maybe that's right," Scharf conceded. Still, the concession didn't disturb him. The fact that he could imagine Yntema's views protected him from them. Which was his equivalent of Yntema's technique: surviving trouble by recounting it.

Scharf got back to New York a year from the next January and didn't call Yntema till his last day there. Yntema's secretary said he hadn't come to work.

"All these years I've known him, he's never missed a day," Scharf said, not quite to himself.

"I'm afraid he's missed quite a few lately."

It would have been the third time in a quarter of a century that they hadn't gotten together. But there was a blizzard in Chicago, no flights were going in. Scharf called Yntema's home from LaGuardia. Any chance of their getting together, he'd tried him yesterday at the office.

"Why not?" said Yntema, thickly.

"You don't sound well, Sidney. Can I bring aspirin? Di-Gel?"

"Bring a few cold cuts. You know Zabar's."

The abruptness, plus the canceled flight, the changed venue of their get-together, and then the snow, which started coming down as he rode back into town, pushed Scharf toward depression. The ride was slow, the air heavy. Still, after checking back into the Westbury, he felt better. He taxied to Zabar's and hauled off twenty dollars' worth of corned beef, pastrami, Swiss cheese and Kaiser rolls.

Yntema's lobby sported a green-mold paint and, in place of the defunct carpet, a corrugated rubber runner. The elevator groaned worse than ever, the corridors were as grim, and the front door sicker of varnish than it was three years ago.

Yntema too was in bad shape. He limped, his eyes were dull, the black curls were stippled with gray, and his arms and shoulders seemed at odds with his T-shirt.

The living room was also the worse for wear. Neither map, lithograph, nor batik swatch festooned the puce walls. The room looked as if it had been in a fight. A leg of the coffee table was taped, there was a purple stain on the unhappy sofa.

Scharf followed limping Yntema into the kitchen—another piece of misery, though not a battleground. They unloaded the delicatessen onto poorly cleaned plates, and took cans of Blatz out of the only icebox with a spherical motor on top that Scharf had seen since World War II. "I've seen better days," said Yntema.

"I can see that." The room, Scharf realized, was bare of music. No scores, no albums, no bust of Schubert. "Apple taken up another subject?"

"Did she not, Eddie. Very bad scene here." Yntema's pitch was odd, and there was something askew in his face. "Not pleasant."

"Bit of a brawl?"

"Hell of a brawl. The bitch did for me. Christ, it's hard to manage these rolls." His teeth squirreled around the Kaiser roll.

Scharf looked closer. The fixity, the evenness, the whiteness of the teeth. Proud-mouthed Yntema had a denture. Still, he wolfed, pastrami bits falling on his jeans, the chair, through the slit in the Blatz can.

"I'm glad I stayed over. I wanted to hear how things were going."

To his surprise and pleasure, Yntema let out a considerable—
unrepressed—laugh. "Hear? Look!" He spread arms, pastrami
in his left hand, beer can in his right. "*Yntema Bound.* Act
Five."

"She really gave it to you."

"Nose. Teeth. Concussion. She threw the goddamn bust at
me. Which I'd tried to bust. If I'd have been two feet closer,
she'd have killed me. What an arm. She got my ankle with the
barbell. There's lots of Blatz." He hoisted his empty, and Scharf
brought him another, thinking, "There's no pleasure seeing him
so low." Which surprised him.

Was it that he was actually *seeing,* not just hearing about it?
It was just bruise, not storied bruise.

Story did come out, at least story matter. Slowly, and with
little verve. "Felicia started it."

"She came back?"

"Not to me. I saw her. On the street. Recognized her neck."

"Not *cut!*"

"Mink doesn't cut. And that little red nut of a head under
more mink. Standing outside Armando's. You and I ate there,
five or six years ago." Scharf nodded. "I called her. She turned,
saw me, her mouth flew open, and she got red as her hair. I
thought she was going to pass out. I had no idea. Then I see the
old bastard coming out of Armando's."

Yntema looked at Scharf, who picked it up. "Your father?"

"Dr. Tart-Eater himself. I don't know how she found him. Or
he her. I don't want to know. But there he was holding on to
the mink. He saw me, started to say something, I saw his mouth
twisting for it, but she pulled him off. Five years ago, he'd have
kicked her into the gutter. Now he's a thousand years old; he
just got pulled off. What a moment. I leaned against the menu
board. Asking myself, 'What does this say about my life? My
choices? Am I just a continuation of that pig?' " Yntema's voice
had more lilt in it now, and some dental clicks as well. "Every
time I've thought, 'He can't go lower,' he does. 'Pitched past
pitch of *pitch.*' And what about me? Where did he pitch me?"

Scharf pointed to the battered room, to Yntema's face, his
ankle. "I still don't see the connection."

"I took off, just walked uptown. I got home. Apple was out
rowing her kids in Central Park. There was this"—hoisting the

salted curls toward what was no longer there—"Viennese *merde* all over. Spectral *merde.* Musical *merde.* Bronze *merde.* I was so low. I felt like I was being played, like a record. Then I just let rip. I hit Franz Peter with the barbell. Right in the eyeglasses. Bashed them into the nose. Knocked a chunk of it off. I flattened him, then flattened his albums. Crazy, just crazy. In my whole life, I never got a drop of beer on a library book. That afternoon I tore them up. Scores, articles, books. Terrible."

"You didn't knock your own teeth out."

"I needed help there. You're sitting on my blood. Or hers. What a battler. But I busted her too. She came home to the wreckage and went crazier than I. Threw her damn Schubert at my face. When I came to, the two of them were sitting on me. Then the super came. Pacified her. They must've heard the racket on Broadway. A woman scorned is nothing. Smash a god, that's when you get fury. Imagine where I'd be if she'd been lifting weights all those months. As it was, I was two weeks in Lenox Hill. I just got off the crutches."

Scharf had to spend another day in New York—O'Hare was still closed—but there was no question of seeing Yntema again. He felt that he'd identified a body; the saga was over. Oh, Yntema was off crutches, there'd be a few more turns, more spills, another girl, and another, but what counted for Scharf was over. Ulysses had come home. To nothing worth singing about. (The only songs that survived here were Schubert's.)

That afternoon, Scharf, about to pass a record store, went in and bought the Fischer-Dieskau recording of the *Winterreise.* For some reason, he didn't bother working out, it seemed the right coming-home present for Marjory.

Wissler Remembers

Miss Fennig. Mr. Quincy. Mr. Parcannis. Ms. Shimbel. Ms. Bainbridge. (Antique, silver-glassed, turn-of-the-century-Rebecca-West face; at 22.) Miss Vibsayana, who speaks so beautifully. (You cannot relinquish a sentence, the act of speech such honey in your throat, I can neither bear nor stop it.) Miss Glennie, Mr. Waldemeister. All of you.

Do you know what it is for me to see you here? To have you in this room three hours a week? Can you guess how I've grown to love you? How hard it is for me to lose you?

Never again will you be a group. (Odds against, trillions to one.) We've been together thirty hours, here in this room whose gaseous cylinders emend the erratic window light. (Those spritzes of autumn the neo-Venetian neo-Gothic windows admit.) We have spoken in this room of Abbot Suger, Minister of State, Inventor of Gothic, have cited his "Dull minds ascend through material things." (Not you, never yours.) But did I tell you that I took a trolley to his church, Saint Denis, sitting next to a Croatian lady who trembled when I told her that just a week before I'd talked with the little salesman Peter who'd been, who was, her king? There's been so much to tell you, woven by my peripatetic memory to our subject.

The thing is I want to tell you everything.

Though I will see some of you again, will write many of you letters of recommendation—for years to come—may even, God knows, teach your children (if you have them soon), may, some day, in Tulsa or West Hartford, see you when your present beauty is long gone, I know that what counts for us is over. When you come up to me in Oklahoma or Connecticut and ask if I remember you—"I took your Studies in Narrative course nine years ago"—or twenty-five—I will not remember. If you remind me that you wrote a paper on Wolfram's *Parzival,* that you were in class with the beautiful Indian girl, Miss—was it Bisayana? and Mr. Parcannis, the boy who leashed his beagle to his bicycle, perhaps I will make out through the coarsened augmentation and subtraction of the years both you and that beautiful whole that was the class of Autumn Seventy-Seven, Winter Sixty-Two. But what counts is gone.

Teaching.

I have been teaching classes for thirty years. Age twenty-one, I had a Fulbright Grant to teach fifteen hours a week at the Collège Jules Ferry in Versailles. The boys, *in-* and *externes,* ages ten to nineteen, prepared for the baccalaureate exam. Four days a week, I walked the block and a half from the Pension Marie Antoinette and did my poor stuff. I was so ignorant of French, I had addressed the director as *Directoire.* ("I thought you were trying to get to a government bureau.") When I entered the classroom, the boys rose. A thrill and an embarrassment to an awkward fellow not born a prince of the blood. "Good morning, boys." "Good morning, Meestair Weeslair." Much sweetly wicked *ritardandi* of those long syllables. "Today we will do an American poem. I'll supply the French translation, you translate into English. Anyone who gets within twelve words of the original gets a present." Five of the twenty-five understand; they whisper explanation to the others. Blue, black, brown, gray, green eyes intensify and shimmer with competitive greed. (Every student is numbered by class standing and introduces himself accordingly: "I'm LeQuillec, sixteenth of twenty-five.") "Here's the poem. Forgive my pronunciation.

> A qui sont les bois, je crois le savoir,
> Il a sa maison au village.
> Et si je m'arrête, il ne peut me voir,
> Guettant ses bois qu'emplit la neige."

The next day I collect the English versions.

> To whom are that wood, I believe to know it.
> It have its house at the village.
> And if I arrest, it is not able to see me,
> Staring its woods who fills the snow.

"Not first rate, LeQuillec. *Pas fort bien.*" I read them the original. *"Ça vous plait?" "Ah ouiiii, M. Weeslairre. Beaucoup!"*

I see LeQuillec's dark pout, the freckles of Strethmann, the begloved, elegant what's-his-name? Persec? Parsec? who wrote me the next year in Heidelberg. "Dear Mr. Wissler. How are you? I am well. You shall be happy to know I am fourteen of thirty-one this trimester. How do you find Germany?"

Très bien, Persec. I am teaching at the University here. In the *Anglistikabteilung.* Two classes. For the *Ohrgeld,* four hundred marks—a hundred dollars—a semester. Not a great fortune, so I work for the Department of the Army decoding cables at the Staff Message Control. I have Top Secret clearance which enables me to forward the reports of suspected Russian breakthroughs at the Fulda Gap the coming Christmas Day. One week I work from six P.M. to two A.M., the next a normal daytime shift. My classes adjust to this schedule. *The American Literary Experience.* 1. *Prose.* 2. *Poetry.* The first assignment, James's *The Ambassadors.* American libraries all over West Germany send me their copies of the book. I give the class a week to read it. The class shrinks from forty to seven. I don't understand, they rapped on their desks for two minutes after Lecture One. Still, even students who apologize for dropping "because of schedule conflicts" come to me on the street, doff caps, shake hands. A girl runs up the Hauptstrasse to me, asks if I will sign a petition. "For Helgoland, Professor." "Fräulein . . ." "Hochhusen, Professor." She is nearly as tall as I, has hair a little like Ms. Bainbridge's, heart-rending popped blue eyes, hypnotic lips. "Forgive me, Fräulein, I don't think I can sign political petitions when I work for the American Army." Unlike students later on, she says, "I understand, Professor." What a smile. "Excuse me for troubling you." "No trouble, Fräulein. It's a pleasure to see you. I love you." (I do not say the last three words aloud.)

I teach the sons and daughters of soldiers whose bones have been left in the Ukraine and the Ardennes. I teach those who themselves fired guns, were prisoners, who received lessons on such scum as I. We read Emily Dickinson, Thoreau, *Benito Cereno,* Hawthorne (some of whose nastier views run parallel to their old ones). I talk of the power of blackness and try and connect it to the rubble of Mannheim, Ludwigshafen, Frankfurt.

The first poems we do are German: Goethe, Trakl, Heine. To show them what close reading can do for poems. They take to such naked delights like literary sailors ashore after months. *Sie sassen und tranken am Teetisch, Und sprachen von Liebe viel.*

American soldiers fill the Heidelberg streets, eat in special restaurants with special money. I live in a special hotel, buy food in the American Commissary. *The ambassadors.*

Fräulein Hochhusen helps me with my first German poem. "Will you check this for me, please, Fräulein? I just felt like writing it. I don't trust my German at all."

> Wir waren einmal ganz neu.
> Solange die Stellen brennen,
> brennen wir Heu.
>
> Once we were utterly new.
> So long as places burn
> we burn [make?] hay.

"It is not exactly correct, Professor, but very, how shall I say? *Eindrucksvoll. Original.* Original. And your German is beautiful, Professor."

No, Fräulein, berry-cheeked Fräulein with the burnt-hay hair, it's you who are beautiful. Give me the petition, darling Fräulein. Tell me about Helgoland. Will they test bombs there? And who owns it? Germany? Denmark? I want to know everything. Is my poem true German? Is it a poem? Do you love me as I love you? "You're much too generous, Fräulein. I feel so bad about the petition."

Herr Doppelgut, stooped, paper-white, dog eyed, had walked three hundred kilometers, "black across the border," yet manages to get whitely back to see his mother and bring me dirt-cheap books from East Berlin. When I go there Christmastime, with my visa stamped by all four occupying powers, I walk through thirty ex-blocks of ex-houses and ex-stores. Ash, stone *dreck,* half an arch, a pot, a toilet seat, a bicycle wheel, grimacing iron struts. Insane survivals. In front of the Russian memorial tank, a young guard holds a machine gun. From my new language text, I ask, *"Vy govoritny russki?"* Silence. *"Nyet?"* I think I see the muzzle waver. "Robot," I say, yards off. Gray ladies in beaten slippers fill carts with rubble and push them on tracks across the street where other aged ladies unload them. I go back to Thoreau's beans, to the white whale, to intoxicated bees and Alfred Prufrock, to Herr Doppelgut and Fräulein Hochhusen, to close readings of poems. Of breasts.

Yes, I cannot omit something important. In every class, there is another system of love at work. The necks, the ears, the breasts, the cropped hair of Ms. Bainbridge, the go-ahead green eyes of Miss Fennig, the laughter. There are more parts of love than a city has sections, theaters, parks, residence, business, Skid Row.

I move to Frankfurt. To take a higher paying job teaching illiterate American soldiers. A tedium relieved only by new acquaintance with the bewildered backside of American life: ex-coal miners, fired truck drivers, rattled welterweights, disgraced messengers, sharecroppers, fugitives, the human rubbish conscripted to fill a quota, shoved now into school for the glory of the army. I have the most beautiful single class of my life with them. End of Grade Four. There is a poem in our soldiers' textbook, "The Psalm of Life." *Tell me not in mournful numbers, life is but an empty dream, for it is the soul that slumbers and things are not what they seem.* We go over every word, every line. How they begin to understand, how deeply they know these truths. Sgt. Carmody whose boy is dead in the new Korean War. Gray-haired Private Eady who writes his mother the first letter of his life: "I am in Grad Too, Muther. I work hard every day but Muther, I think it is to lat for me now." Pfc. Coolidge, mouth a fortune of gold teeth, a little black man who joined up after being injured on the job—the Human Missile in Bell and Brother's Circus—and whom I summon to VD Clinic every Monday afternoon. "Dese froolines lak me, perfesser." Carmody, Coolidge, Eady, Dunham, Lake, Barboeuf. The class ends on your breathlessness, your tears, your beautiful silence.

Back home then, to Iowa, to Connecticut, and then here, to the great Gothic hive of instruction and research. Hundreds of classes, hundreds and hundreds of students. Themselves now writing books, teaching classes, building bridges (over rivers, in mouths), editing papers, running bureaus, shops, factories. Or dead in wars, half-alive in madhouses. *"Dear Mr. Wissler. I am in a bad way. No one to write to. There is nothing for me. Help, help, he . . .,"* the *lp* dropped off the post card (mailed without return address from Pittsburgh). "Dear Professor Wissler. *Do you remember Joan Marie Rabb who wrote the paper on Julien and Bonaparte in 1964?*" I do remember. For it was a paper so gorgeously phrased and profoundly opaque I called in the dull, potato-faced Miss Rabb to explain it. And with explanation— missed connections filled in, metaphors yoked to amazing logic —the potato opened into a terrible beauty. *"I married, Profes- sor. A ruffian, a churl. Children have come. Four, under six. I could not sustain the hurt."* "Miss Rabb, if you can ever put down on paper what you've told me in the office, you will write a work of genius. But for now, you see why I must give you a C." *"You liked the paper, thought it, thought I had promise. What I have done, with great laboriousness, is to transmute it into the enclosed poem. Will you see if the promise is herewith fulfilled? Have I a work which has at least merchandisable power?"* Fifteen penciled pages, barely legible, and when read, wild, opaque, dull. "Dear Mrs. MacIllheny. I look forward to reading your poem when the pressure of the term is over. Meanwhile, I hope you regain your health. With good wishes from your old professor, Charles Wissler."

At times, very few, thank God, there have been students who've rubbed me the wrong way. (How many have I antago- nized? Surely many more, but the standards of courtesy are so powerful, only the rudest and angriest breach them.) "I have never, never, never, never, never in my life had a C before. Is it your intention, Mr. Wissler, that I do not go to law school? Do you delight in ruining my *entire academic record*?" Terrifying calm from the plump, parent-treasured, parent-driven face.

"One C does not a bad record make, Ms. Glypher. Admissions

Officers know that anyone can have a bad class, an imperceptive instructor."

"Lovely philosophy, sir, but that does not change the C. It does not get me into *law school.*"

May I never be cross-examined by Sophia Glypher. "What can I do, Ms. Glypher? Can I change the grading system to accommodate your ambition?" A wicked stare from the not unbeautiful gray eyes. Since you are so clearly intelligent, Ms. Glypher, why is it that you don't see that my standards curve around sweetness, beauty, charm?

"I'll write an extra paper. Retake the exam."

"There are two worlds rotating around each other here, Ms. Glypher. One is the world of papers, exams, grades, degrees, applications, careers. That's a fairly rigid world." (Or unfairly.) "It is as strictly ruled as chess. Break the rules, you break the world. This is the world that's supposed to count. In the other world, there are no grades. In that world, you're not a C student. I don't know what you are. Or what I am." Ms. Glypher rumbles here on the verge of a discourtesy which might draw us into open combat. As it is, there is struggle. (Unequal.) "That world's one without end. I see my job more in that world than the one in which I grade you C." Even as I oppose her, wrestle within her magnetic hatred, I believe this. "In that world, we're equal. To some degree partners. Your accomplishment there becomes mine, mine yours. It's the world that counts."

"But not for law school, Mr. Wissler. I don't object to poetry, but I'm talking reality."

"Ms. Glypher, the whole point is that you aren't. You are so attached to the one world that you don't even see it clearly. The Admissions Officers happily do. They will recognize your talent even through what you think of as this stain on your record. If you like, I will put a letter in your dossier explaining my belief in your talent along with the reasons I graded you as I did."

"I don't think I'll trouble you to do that," says Ms. Glypher in her finest moment. One which tempts me to the drawer where the Change of Grade slips are kept.

Before, within, and after classes, the stuff of articles, books, lectures—San Diego, Tuscaloosa, Cambridge—East and West—

Lawrence, Kansas, Iowa City, Columbia, South Carolina, Columbia, 116th Street, New York, Kyoto, Bologna, Sydney, Buenos Aires, Hull, Nanterre, Leiden. Everywhere wonderful faces, the alert, the genial, the courteous (the bored, the contemptuous, the infuriated; but few). And everywhere, love, with the sexuality displaced (except in the instance which became Wife Number Three). That has been priestly excruciation.

Then pulling toward, docking at and taking off from fifty, I became conscious of the love that has been under all the others. I love individuals, yes, and I stay aware of clothes, bodies, gestures, voices, minds, but it is the class itself I love. The humanscape. The growth of the unique molecule of apprehension and transmission. From the first, tense, scattered day through the interplay, the engagements, the drama of collective discourse to the intimate sadness of the last class. How complicated the history, the anatomy, the poetry of such a body.

Miss Fennig. Mr. Quincy. Mr. Parcannis. Miss Vibsayana. Except for your colors, your noses, your inflections, your wristwatches, I can tell very little about your status. (You are from a warrior caste in Bengal, Miss Vibsayana. You wrote it in a paper. Miss Glennie, you were the brilliant, solitary black girl in the Harrisburg parochial school. You gave me hints of it in office hours.) But I know you inside out; would like to give you all As. (Won't.) All that part is clear, though Mr. Laroche won't know that the extra paragraph he tacked on his paper lowered his grade from B plus to B; nor Mrs. Linsky that if she'd not spoken so beautifully about Stavrogin, she would not have passed.

December. The last class. There is amorous ether in the room. (Isn't it what Alumni Organizations try to bottle?) Don't we all sense it this last time?

"There's a fine book by the French scholar Marrou on the history of education in antiquity. I recommend it generally, but mention it in this windup class because it was there I first encountered the idea that there are strikingly different notions of individuality. One sees this also in the first volume of Mann's Joseph series. People hardly know where their ancestors leave off and they begin. That might be straining a bit. Marrou speaks of family identity. Certain Roman families were known for certain sorts of generosity, others for sacrifice. That's certainly still true. Think of American families associated with philanthropy or public service. Even if an individual in the family feels it goes against his grain to go public —as it were"—smiles from Miss Fennig, Mr. Waldemeister— "he is still conscious of the possibility of public life. I don't say that makes it harder or easier for him." Miss Fennig's slim face is alight, her eyes floatingly green under her large spectacles. She runs her hand through her long hair, in, up, out, back. Mr. Quincy's urchin face is stippled—such pain for him—with hormone frenzy. He tries to sit where he can see Miss Fennig. The brilliant, troubled Ms. Shimbel is about to speak. I wait. She shakes her head. How she understands. (Speaking only on demand, resigned from so much, but who knows, perhaps already launched on some intricate enterprise.)

I talk more. I watch. Mr. Parcannis questions. Miss Vibsayana responds, endlessly, softly, the thousand bees of her throat discharging nectar into syllables.

"Forgive me, Miss Vibsayana, what you say is beautiful, but I'm afraid we must finish off."

Wonderful inclination of eyes, head. "Excuse me, Professor."

"Of course. You know how much I enjoy your notions. How much I enjoy all your notions. It has been a splendid class. For me. There is almost no future I think should be denied you. What world wouldn't be better led by you?"

I don't say that. Instead: "I will have office hours next week. If you have questions about your papers, the course, anything at all, please come see me. And come whenever you like next quarter. We haven't gotten as far as I'd hoped, but you've helped get us quite far. Goodbye and good luck to all of you."

We have no tradition of farewell—applause, rapping, waving. Still, the faces compose a fine comprehension of our bond. There is the sweetness of a farewell between those who have done well by each other. (It does not exclude some relief.)

In the hall, Miss Vibsayana approaches. "May I—I don't quite know how to put it, Professor—but I feel privileged that you permitted me to take this course."

"I'm grateful to you for contributing so much to it. Thank you."

Outside, darkness falling into the white lawns. The paths are mottled with clots of ice. The Gothic buildings shine beautifully under the iron filigree lamps. A half-moon hangs off the bell tower.

Bundles of cloth and fur walk home. Hellos, good nights, goodbyes. Talk of exams, of Christmas plans. Snow like hard meringue. Winter looms. And whoops, heart gripped, I'm heading down, hand cushioning, but a jar.

"Oh, Mr. Wissler. Are you hurt?" Miss Fennig. What an embarrassment.

"No, no, not at all." She bends, gives me her bare hand. I hold it and get pulled while I push up. "Thanks so much. My first fall of the year."

"I took two awful ones yesterday," she lies.

"I wish I'd been there to pull you up. Thank you again."

"Are you sure you're all right?" Green eyes, unspectacled, tender.

"I'm fine, thank you. I think it's wonderful that our last day should see me being pulled out of the snow by you. I wish you were around whenever I took a tumble."

"I'll try to be. It almost makes me hope you'll fall again."

"I will, Miss Fennig. And I'll look for you. Good night now."

"Good night, Mr. Wissler. Take care."

You too, Miss Fennig. You too, dear Miss Vibsayana. Mr. Parcannis. And LeQuillec, wherever you are. *Gute nacht,* Fräulein Hochhusen. So long, Sergeant Carmody. You too, Ms. Glypher. So long. Take care. Good night, my darlings. All of you. Good night.

Orvieto Dominos, Bolsena Eels

THE wind in Edward's lungs, stored up so long, now had American sails to fill. The white Fiat beetle was rattled as much by this release from his Italian captivity as from the ninety kilometers of the Via Cassia it consumed every hour. Vicky, however, was not much of a sail. Most of her morning's strength had gone into evading the Group. Once they were off in the blue bus, she felt like taking to her bed. After all, they'd had lots of warnings about being picked up, and though Eddy was an American, he *was* twenty-five, a man of the world, and clearly capable of international designs. But wasn't this secondary? After all, she'd come to Italy to see and learn, and Eddy both knew things and talked wonderfully about them. It was he who'd shown her that the Moses statue in San Pietro in Vincoli was not "the sign-bole of hanker," as the Guide put it, but something more complex, witness the hands, not "clenched in hanker" but only stroking the beard reflectively. Though Eddy admitted at dinner that it was Freud who'd first pointed this out, he had, after all, read Freud, whereas the Guide had probably never heard of him, unless a plaque on one of the tours indicated that Freud had gone to the johnny somewhere in Nineteen Ought Two. Anyway, if you started to ask the Guide a question in the middle of his lecture, he'd wave you away, afraid he might pick up in the wrong sentence, and leave the Group without the hot news that the Sistine's *Giudizia Universale* was painted thirty years after the Ceiling.

And then, it was so much nicer having your own car. Eddy hired the Fiat Six Hundred right after she'd agreed to come with him. He did things right. Though she could just see her father, laid up in bed after a fall from Sugar Belle—and thus with lots of time to stew—getting the news from the Group that Victoria had gone off to Orvieto for a night of God-knows-what with a strange man. Not that there was going to be any funny stuff. A little woo-pitching, fine, but, though she knew she must be passionate from the way she'd felt hundreds of woo-pitching times, Vicky knew also it was wiser to save *that* for when you had nothing else in life but diapers. In the Flower Market, just across the street from Portinari Drive-Yourself, Eddy had picked up a still creamy lily from one of the unsold hundreds thrown there by the vendors, and she had its curling flake in her wallet as a good-luck charm against the possible evils of the expedition. It was going to go all right.

"I'm sorry, I didn't get it, Eddy. I was thinking about the darn Group. Will they be surprised. They were going to Orvieto Thursday, though they never make up their stupid minds till it's too late to plan right. Last Wednesday, we were all set for Naples, bathing suits, towels, everything, and where did we end up but in Cerveteri and Tarquinia looking at Etruscan tombs. Not that they weren't great, but we didn't use our suits till Saturday. At Ladispoli. The sand was as black as your hair. Which is great for hair, but creepy to walk on. You had the feeling every dirty foot since the Etruscans had dragged itself on the beach."

"It's probably just the composition of the rock. Even the Tyrrhenian's forceful enough to launder a beach."

They'd planned to eat lunch in Viterbo, but Edward was so hungry that they turned off the Via Cassia at a place called Caprarola to find food. He pulled out the Baedeker, and, to his amazed delight, saw that the little goat town was the site of "one of the most magnificent chateaux of the Renaissance built by Vignola in 1547–59 for Cardinal Alexander Farnese." He read this to Vicky as if talking about an ancestor, so happy was he to have stumbled upon what few tourists would see, his Baedeker being sixty years old and this road fit for little more than goats and Fiat beetles. Theirs crawled down the hill in second, and, sure enough, high on the town, like a beautiful forehead, was a gray palace.

"Let's eat first," said Edward. "Though I'll bet there isn't even a *trattoria* in this metropolis."

Which seemed to be correct, though down at the bottom of the hill there was a café. They bought four gorgeous chocolate cakes shaped like the funny Etruscan tumuli at Cerveteri. Edward ate three of them.

Then they drove up to the palace courtyard, where, to their surprise, five large cars were parked. "Maybe the Farnese still live here," said Edward. He got out and ran around to open her door, getting what he wanted, which was a good view of her legs, which he had so happily stroked the night before and with which he planned to be in more intimate contact tonight in Orvieto.

The cars were not the property of the Farnese, but of an outfit called Royal Films which was, right-then-and-there, making a film about Napoleon's sister, Pauline. In fact, said the lady custodian, La Lollobrigida was in the garden at this very moment, with about a hundred other people, the implication being that they were trampling the lawns entrusted to her care by Rome. Edward's disappointment at this invasion of his discovery was mollified; he bought the tickets of admission ravenous for a view of the Lollobrigida.

For an hour, then, he and Vicky leaned against a wall while propmen arranged shrubs as a background for the cameras which finally ground away at a woman in green velvet and gold plumes cavorting on a tranquilized stallion over the undefended lawns. Edward's eyes strained with avidity, until a Napoleonic extra said the cavorter was only the Lollobrigida's *contrafigura*; the Lollobrigida herself was off in a corner where, indeed, Edward and Vicky saw her in a duplicate of the gold plumes, probably pining for nice company. But it was lunchtime, too late to satisfy her. Not until they were back on the Via

Cassia, Edward's stomach thunderous with hunger, did they realize that they hadn't gone inside the chateau.

In Viterbo, they ate in a vaulted *trattoria* called Spacca. "It means, 'split,' I think," he said. "I'm ready to," and staggered out under the weight of *lasagna al forno, vitello arrosto, piselli, patate, formaggio,* and *frutta.*

"How is it you're not fat?" asked Vicky, aghast at his large body heaving for breath under the black sports shirt, his head sweating from the working interior more than the roaring, stupefying one o'clock sun.

"Nature. I don't help it. It's great camouflage for gluttons. I'm really pretty hard," and he suppressed the afterword, "You'll soon see."

He asked directions for the Duomo, and they drove the closed-in, cobbled streets of the medieval quarter until they saw it in a fine little piazza, flanked by a *palazzo* with a Gothic loggia and a half zebra-striped campanile to the left. They parked in front of the *palazzo* which, said Edward, was where the people of Viterbo locked up the cardinals in 1270 to see if hunger would force them to end two years of indecision and choose a pope.

"Did it work out?"

"Gregory the Tenth. Hunger's a great persuader," and he helped her out, filling up again on her legs. "We're parked right where Hadrian the Fourth, the only English Pope, Nicholas Brakespeare . . ."

"It rhymes."

". . . made the Emperor Frederick the First hold his stirrup."

In the restaurant, Edward had reread Baedeker in the toilet and was more primed than usual. Though for sightseeing he was always primed. It was serious work if you did it right. The night before, he'd looked up the appropriate quotations in Dante and written them into the end pages of the Baedeker, starring them to correspond with the text. This was, in a sense, payment for Vicky's companionship, the entrance fee to what he would later guide her to, the self-discovery of lovemaking.

An old lady sitting on a chair outside the Duomo drew a six-inch key from her dress, opened the door, and led them inside. It was the first Gothic church Vicky had seen in Italy, and, after three weeks of baroque Roman churches, where every chapel, every inch, seemed to be straining for independent beauty, the stripped-down high, proud nave made her feel high and proud herself. Edward too was hushed, and forgot about Guy de Montfort stabbing Richard of Cornwall's son as the consecrated bread was being elevated at the altar. He followed the old woman, listening to her devoted, unmechanical talk about the dates of the church and the Mantegna frescos— uncovered by the bombing in '44—which looked like broken bodies issuing from graves for the Last Judgment. A believer in nothing, Edward was still a lover of churches, though like the Romans, who, the man at Portinari Drive-Yourself had told him, "manufacture the faith which is believed elsewhere."

On the way out of Viterbo, they stopped fifteen minutes at the Museo and looked at the Etruscan sarcophagi and pottery. "They're so calm about death," said Vicky. "Maybe that's what they lived for, to teach other people how to die."

Edward, a little annoyed at the rhetoric, said there were too many signs of the good life found in their tombs, and pointed to what she had missed, a couple playing with each other's nakedness, etched finely on the black back of a vanished mirror. "It's when you live to the full that you can die well," he said, preparing her for the evening with this rhetorical turn of his own.

Which she suspected, but the way things were, seeing so much commemorated life, she could take in stride what was to come. She would be calm and intelligent, equipped, like an Etruscan, with her curled-up lily corresponding to the little plate they carried in their stone hands on which there was a piece of stone fruit for the death god.

They'd planned to swim in Lake Bolsena, partly because of something in Dante, but Edward had missed the turnoff because he'd followed a sign to Montefiascone, and they'd gone up for a bottle of what Baedeker called "the best muscatel in Italy." The bottle had the "Est, Est, Est" motto on it, said Edward, because of a valet who'd been sent ahead by his master to test the best wines and mark "Est" on the inn doors where they were served. At Montefiascone, he'd written it three times, and his master stayed and died there.

It was a happy indirection: the main road to Orvieto could not have been more beautiful. All along the way there were trees soaked with gold pears and violet plums, trellises with huge blue

grapes, and, every kilometer or so, an arbor flooded with ambrosial magenta flowers, the like of which, said Vicky, she had
never seen. They were haying in the fields, and oxen drew
wagons full of the golden stuff along the road. Now and then,
they passed country versions of the papal loggia where people
talked and drank among white hens out of the sun. Vicky felt
queerly ashamed to be so free, so easily motorized, with no
mission but sightseeing and the diffused expectation of love.
The countryside felt intimate to her, familiar, filled with what
she had little experience of, but much feeling for, the gathering
of what had been sown, the harvest of labor, not the easy
moneyed harvest which brought the best, or at least the most
worked-at, transported, and refined products, to salivating
mouths.

Edward, too, was half enchanted by the heat, the wine, the
sense of this blond girl feeling it with him, driving easily through
the flaming, delicate hills cultivated to the last inch by a people
articulate not in the mouth, but in gesture and posture. Half an
hour from Montefiascone, round a turn, a couple of thousand
feet up across the huge valley, they saw the little walled city,
brown, contained, sunstruck. Orvieto. It disappeared as they
drove around the road, and reappeared at the next curve, disap-
pearing and reappearing again at each snaking curve.

Down the Fiat beetled, and then up, until it crawled through
the medieval, the Roman, the Etruscan walls into the skinny,
cobbled ways, going in second, dodging men, women, children,
past little open stores, into and out of little piazzas, by chocolate
and gray *palazzi,* and then, following the arrows, arriving at the
Duomo in front of the astonishing façade, gold, blue, rose, all the
colors of the road and fields, sculpted, assembled, "the most
beautiful polychromatic monument in the world," said Baedeker, a gorgeous face for the tremendous black-and-white-
striped body roaring in back of it.

"My God," said Vicky.

Among the other tourists and cars and buses and the post-card
shops, they stared at the dazzling front. Edward read out the
description in Baedeker, the commissioning of the church by
Urban the Fourth after the "miracle of Bolsena," the appearance of drops of blood on the bread consecrated by a doubting
Bohemian priest. "1263. The Feast of Corpus Domini."

"What, Eddy?" But dreamily, for what was there to say before this marvel with the incredible face and black-and-white body. She noticed that the black-and-white extended beyond the cathedral to the steps which led to the Piazza and to the doorways of some of the shops.

A great bell sounded in the square, five-thirty. Up on a tower, a bronze man was striking a bell with a bronze hammer.

"But how darling," said Vicky softly.

"What, dear?" asked Edward, touched.

She pointed to the bronze man. "Isn't this the nicest place you've ever seen, Eddy? I think I could live here forever."

"It is especially nice," said Edward. "Let's go see the Signorellis while it's still light," and he took her bare arm against his own half-bare one, and walked up the steps and through the central portal.

Inside, Vicky again felt the breath of wonder. The interior seemed huge, a divine, airy structure, great columned, uncluttered, leading far off to the beautiful choir. They walked slowly up the marble pavement, and saw, in the right chapel, people looking up.

"I thought it would be bigger," said Edward, who had a book of the Signorellis back home in New York. They went in, and he sat back under the portrait of Dante, his head against the signature "Mario e Domenicho '48," took out his black-and-silver opera glasses and studied one section of the great frescos at a time, smiling when he saw familiar figures, the young man with arms on hips, the prostitute with hand out for money, the woman riding the devil's back toward the pileup of the damned. Perhaps the same prostitute. The damned were twisted, their bones showed, their tendons and muscles were knotted, idolaters, lusters, killers, sloths, gluttons, doubters, whipped, choked, and wrestled by devils. Across the room, the saved were arched toward heaven, their bodies full, strong, and easy. Edward's favorite sections were those filled with the colors of life, the prostitute's blue shawl, the blue-and-yellow striped pants of young men, the plumed hats, the bulging brown money sacks. Edward's book was only black and white. It was the surprise of Signorelli's colors that thrilled him most, and the color was strongest in the narratives of life, the preaching of the anti-Christ, the final confusion before Gabriel's trumpet. On the side of the left wall was Signorelli himself, standing in black with the church's Treasurer, thoughtful and a little surprised at what he'd created. Never in his life had Edward been so absorbed by painting. He even forgot about Vicky, who, though very happy in the lovely chapel and particularly taken with the sweet, strong blues in Fra Angelico's sections, was getting neck-weary. She sat next to Edward, who, after a minute of not noticing her, put a hand on her knee and said it was wonderful, wasn't it, to which she assented.

"Michelangelo owes this man more than Piero," he said. "Fresco perspective, foreshortening, arranging all these figures, making some seem sculpted, some painted, all that."

"I think the light will be better in the morning."

"Ten minutes more," said Edward. "Why don't you see what's in the other chapel? And tell me, so I don't have to see it." And his eyes were back in the opera glasses.

As it turned out, Edward did not see what was in the other chapel, and did not see Vicky again either, except for the thirty seconds in which she ran in, breathless and wild, to whisper, shatteringly, "It's the Group. The Group! I had to tell 'em I came on my own, and I've got to go back with them. Now." And then, as his insides broke up, she blew him a kiss, and he watched through the opera glasses as his lovely blond girl joined the bunch of weary sheep following a dark, grabbing female up the great nave and out of the central portal of the cathedral.

Head in his hands, Edward shook it back and forth until he realized that he was becoming an object of touristic concern. He clicked shut the glasses and headed out after them. Maybe she'd get away. But where would they meet? The car? Or in the Signorelli chapel? She'd said the morning light would be better. But the night? The night. He ran into the piazza in time to see the fat, idiotic backside of the blue bus waddling off down the street. "Holy God," said Edward. "They're probably off for Siena." He touched some holy water to his perspiring head. "No. Not that. They're off to a hotel, and she'll be back. Yes."

With this, Edward felt a little better. Also hungry, nervously hungry. He asked one of the piazza-loungers if there was a decent hotel nearby, and got directed to a small *albergo* down the steps from the left transept of the Duomo. It was a fine little tower, three stories high, with a small garden at its front steps.

Edward got a room on the top floor, gave in his International Driving License, said he had no luggage at all—neither, unfortunately, had Vicky, except her bathing suit in the dashboard slot—washed, and then lay back on the beautiful double bed, the *matrimoniale* which would have been his night's paradise. Outside the window was the upper left transept of the Duomo, topped by a small bell, and peppered with five small gargoyles; beyond, in haze, were the violet hills of Umbria. It was the nicest hotel room he'd ever stayed in, eighteen hundred lire, three dollars' worth of irreplaceable niceness. Maybe he could make it for a night without Vicky. After all, he'd lasted twenty-five years without her. Considering that seven weeks ago he'd been at a desk thirty-five floors up in the thunder of New York, his head screaming with burdens, he had been pretty lucky, with or without her. He dressed and went out to find a restaurant. People were going home along the mocha streets, and Edward walked among them, taking the wall against the cars, bikes, and Vespas which snaked in and out of the road. Dusk came in like a man happy to be home from work, and lights flicked on in houses.

Orvieto. It had been a great city in the Etruscan League, Volsinii, and it did not die with calm Etruscan intelligence in the harsh face of Rome, but stayed great for centuries, though limited by what had been its strength, its wall-cinctured hills. Now it had nothing but lace, wine, post cards, and fifteen thousand people walking the chocolate corridors, smiling. Mostly smiling. The people at the *albergo,* the *padrona,* the waiter, the maid, all smiled with especial sweetness. Did the town make for sweetness? He was back at the Duomo, beautiful in an evening gown of spotlight. Its steps were crowded with soldiers—it must be a base—mothers and children, young men. Edward went across to a restaurant terrace in the Piazza, faced the façade, and ordered a mezzo-liter of Orvieto, pasta, eggplant parmegiano, and roast beef Bolognese. At the other occupied table, three soldiers gorged while he waited tensely for his own parade of marvels, which, when they came, he consumed in a frenzy of bliss under the rouged holy beauty of the crescent moon. The cost was two-and-a-half dollars: maybe one could spend a life in Orvieto. Did the Duomo need an up-and-coming, an up-and-been PR man?

After dinner, he heaved himself down the Piazza and across a strip of pines to the city wall and sat on it, looking out over the black basin of valley, barely defined by ten or twelve lights, a couple of which were moving, cars Edward tracked in and out of winding roads. Orvieto's perch didn't seem secure to him, though God knows it had lasted two thousand years longer than New York and beaten down God knows what invasions of the high walls on which Michelangelo had not improbably sat absorbing Signorelli's lessons.

A group of soldiers came along, singing, saying something or other about *ragazze.* Edward got up, turned left under a street arch, walked down a cobbled street into a square, passed a hunchback sitting on the edge of a street fountain, went down another street filled with the blast of a television set, came into a large square faced by two *palazzi,* climbed a staircase past an old man sleeping against the wall, and looked out from the balcony on the otherwise empty square. To the left, eighty feet in the air, two white faces of a great clock showed ten minutes to ten. Three young fellows ran up the stairs, shoving each other. On the balcony, they played some sort of hide-and-seek game, though there was no place to hide but behind one's own knees in the dark. Halfway down, Edward heard some loud talk, turned, and saw a huge spool of film feeding a movie projector. He understood only isolated words, *"strano," "amore," "man-giare," "dispiace."* The old man was still propped against the wall. A white cat walked by, striped by the bars of the staircase. Edward walked out of the square, down two still streets, then, in a third, saw fifteen faces, mostly old ones, craned toward a boxed light in a corner of a bar: Edward recognized the mock-heroic tune which introduced *Carosello,* Channel One's evening collection of commercials. Further up, four soldiers and two girls giggling at them. More streets, the same streets, and, now and then, the voices of *Carosello* crashing out of a window.

Back at the Duomo, there was no one in sight, but Edward heard music. He walked to the left transept and saw ten young men, four of whom were sitting on the black-and-white steps playing an accordion, a guitar, a cowbell, and a rattle. The song was called "Domino, Domino," and Edward thought the words were something like, "Domino, Domino, you're the one thing I have in the world, dear. Domino, Domino, there is nothing but you in the world, dear." In the middle of the song, the ten-thirty bells from the bronze man's hammer sounded, filling out a guitar chord. The six men around the musicians, mostly in sport shirts, were motionless with attention, their postures as fixed as those in the frescos fifty yards away from them. Edward went to the staircase that led from the Piazza toward his *albergo* and sat in the shadow, listening to the songs, looking at the stars behind the striped church, the Great Bear, the same stars in the same position behind the striped body for seven hundred years.

The music was soft, but very clear, the only noise in the square: "Jealousy," "*Volare*," "Begin the Beguine," "*Il pleure dans mon cœur*." Two of the young men broke the circle with "*Ciaò*s." Then two others. "Don't leave, boys," hoped Edward.

What else was there? Walled up in the little town, the three movies seen, tired of *Carosello*, without girls. Not unlike New York, really, except that there the noise disguised the situation. It was clearer in Orvieto, pathetically clearer. That was the difference. With another: in New York, there was no Duomo, and no Signorelli chapel saying, "It's been done, boys. We've reached it. Peddle your post cards, and go home." The town had stopped around "the greatest polychromatic monument in the world" and the "great milestone in the history of painting in Italy."

And what did Maitani's façade and Signorelli's frescos have to tell the boys? That they would be judged, here and now, before and later, playing "Domino, Domino," peddling post cards, driving Fiats, judged with everyone else according to the absolute, black-and-white standards of the *Giudizia Universale*. If there was a harmony of black and white in the universe, as in the body of the great church, it did not matter who would be judged only black or white. The harmony of black and white was beyond individual fate. Bell, accordion, rattle, guitar, the notes watered down and moved single file, like the cranes in Dante flying toward the Nile. The white faces of the clock showed eleven-twenty-one in the Roman numbers which could tell little more than time, lacking the power to express complex equations. The black-and-white body could not sustain worldly life. The musicians, the soldiers, Edward, needed Vickys, love, opportunity, cars, chances to get out of the walled-in city. Unless they were the one-in-ten-million already wise, ready to be judged on the selling of post cards. Signorelli painted himself in a black cloak, and showed his white hair streaming out of a soft black cap. The rest of his picture was finely colored, hotly for life, mutely for afterlife, but all colored. Signorelli worked in this little hill town, on his back, straining his neck like the wall-curved figures of his frescos, three, four, five years, needing nothing else after his days but bed, a bottle of the local wine, maybe now and then a girl. One in ten million.

When the guitarist got up, so did Edward. He went to his room, washed, and got into the *matrimoniale* as the great bell sounded midnight, followed by two dings of the cathedral bell, unsynchronized with it. "Vicky," said Edward. His body felt hollower than any bell. And hers? Was it waiting in some Sienese *albergo* for his body clapper to sound it?

A bad night. The watchtower clock, the bronze bells, and his need, unslakable by pillow. He didn't sleep till two-thirty, and then woke at six to the sound of a man delivering bread on a Vespa.

He got out of bed at seven, and went over to the Duomo to see if Vicky was in the chapel. It was closed, and Edward refused the porter's offer to unlock it. He went down the street to a bar for an espresso and pastry, paid his bill at the hotel, and drove dangerously through walkers, loungers, soldiers, children, down the mocha corridors, following the Duomo arrows in reverse, spun out of the great chocolate walls, around the hill, and out toward the Via Cassia for Rome.

Five minutes later, he was on the other side of the valley, looking back at Orvieto, small, contained, pathetically beautiful. "I won't see you again in this life, sweetheart." He drove off, his insides thunderous for food, and stopped at the first *trattoria* on the road where he ate six rolls, with butter and jam, and drank two cups of *caffelatte.* Then, replete, he was back in the white beetle and heading up the dazzling road toward the Lago del Bolsena where he'd take a swim before going on to Rome. Two nights ago, for Vicky, he'd written down the quotation from *Purgatory* xxiv about Pope Martin of Tours, transformed by diet more than any other of the canto's gluttons:

> Ebbe la santa Chiesa in le sue braccia;
> Dal Torso fu: e purga per digiuno
> L'anguille di Bolsena e la vernaccia.

Martin of Tours, who had the Holy Church in his arms, and now, in Purgatory, did without his beloved Bolsena eels cooked in white wine.

Edward was directed by a man on a donkey to the lake turn-off, went down a kilometer of brown dirt to a tiny beach where there were eight wooden cabanas under an arbor of the ambrosial, magenta flowers Vicky liked. He took his Hawaiian trunks from the slot, got a cabin for fifty lire, hung his shirt, slacks and underdrawers over a sign about swimming three hours "*dopo pasta,*" put on his suit, which his sister said made him look like a pineapple, and walked into the marshy, leguminous lake. Off to the right was the island where, Baedeker reported,

> Amalsuntha, Queen of the Goths, the only daughter of Theodoric the Great, was imprisoned in 534 and afterward strangled whilst bathing by order of her cousin Theodatus, whom she had elevated to the rank of co-regent.

Edward went in the water and swam his perfect, boy's-camp crawl, fifty feet out, or forty beyond the furthest Italian swimmer. To his left was the other island, where Baedeker placed King Donough O'Brien's surrender to the Pope in 1064. "That's not for me," said Edward. He headed for Amalsuntha's prison. Not more than four strokes further, he felt a fire shoot through his stomach. He grunted with pain, clutched his stomach, and doubled over. Cramps. Sweat poured off his head. He stopped moving, sank, moved a foot and an arm, tried to turn over on his back and failed, sweat pouring into the lake water, his head ripping. He let himself go all the way down, knees to his chest, was cooled by the water, touched the oozing bottom, stood on one leg, then hopped a step toward shore, doubled up again, sank, touched bottom, hopped again, sank once more, aching, straightened, and hopped once more, nausea rising in his stomach and throat, irresistible. He turned his face from shore, toward King Donough O'Brien's island, and vomited into the lake. His throat loosened, soured, he sank in the water, the pain lessening. He kicked, slowly, moved his arms, slowly, and slowly, his insides rancid, walking, hopping, swimming, his body emptied of pastry, rolls, the rotted gluttony of the days, he made toward the little beach.

After an hour's rest, he took off his trunks in the cabin where the ambrosial odors of the magenta flowers overpowered his own rancid ones. He removed the sport shirt and slacks from the sign about "not swimming till three hours after eating."

"Signs," he grunted. "I ought to pay attention to these damn signs."

Zhoof

1

THE man was Powdermaker's age, fifty, but grayer, eyeglassed, sharp faced, somehow not American. Somehow? Yes, there was some indrawn, hard-knot quality in that face, something older than the rest of him that said, "This is what we are, what we've been, what we'll be." It felt European to Powdermaker.

Retrospection? Well, yes, he was looking back, but Powdermaker prided himself on looking back clearly. He was no sentimentalist, no rhetorician of memory. For instance, he was systematic about classifying novelty. He located new faces on the spectrum of those he knew well. This man looked like Eph Weiss, the photographer. Not quite as sharp, or as innocent as Weiss. Eph looked like an innocent fox, much of the innocence sitting in the don't-tell-*me* green eyes. This man's eyes were lighter, more rigid, stony. "Maybe I'm going overboard here."

Initially, the fellow seemed all right. (Which made what happened worse.) "A man of the world. Like me." A comfortable, thrifty burgher in a sport coat off the rack, slacks, a dress shirt open at the collar, all more or less in synch, soft blues, soft greens. If anything, Powdermaker should have liked him.

Yet he was sure he hadn't. He remembered liking the wife. She had gotten out of the compartment at Chiasso to wait for the dining car. In his narrow, proud French, Powdermaker had talked with her about the weather, the train, the whereabouts of the car, and then, in his even narrower Italian, asked a workman standing in the rail bed when the diner was coming. The man pointed up the track, there it was.

It was then that the husband, standing at the compartment door, told his wife to come back on the train, he didn't want her on the platform till the car was linked up. Powdermaker remembered his surprise at the order, its specificity and sharpness. She must have been used to it. She said something which Powdermaker didn't get and stayed where she was, or, rather, walked further up the platform in the direction of the car coming their way.

Mostly, Powdermaker was hungry. The only thing he'd had since breakfast was a limp, Dali-esque burger in the Wendy's across the street from the Stazione Centrale in Milan. The restaurant in the Excelsior had closed at two, and everything else within blocks of the station was closed. (It was the Sunday of the Ferragosto weekend.) Wendy's, at least, was air-conditioned. Back in the station, he took his bag out of the *deposito* and ate the sack of gingerbread cookies he'd bought a week ago in Nuremberg.

2

It was his first time in Nuremberg. That's why he was there. Also, it was the last town in which he could leave his Eurocar without paying a drop-off penalty. The People's Express flight had landed in Brussels, and, twenty minutes later, Powdermaker was on the E-40's boring green fields flagged with some of the bloodiest names in European history: Liège, Malmedy, the Ardennes. At the border, he took a small road to Aachen; woods, hills, Teuton quaintness. The ancestral land of the Powdermakers—Pulvermachers—was not one of Powdermaker's

favorites. For one thing, the language was too tough, the verbs
waiting in ambush to shoot down the piled clauses. Outside of
simple declarative sentences, Powdermaker was lost in it. Oh,
with much flipping in his pocket dictionary, he could read the
newspaper and order dinner, but that was it. His accent was
good—he had that knack in all his languages—but when wait-
resses, salesmen or desk clerks opened up to him in idiomatic
German, he bowed out. Annoying. There was much that was
annoying here, but, as everyone said, things worked: the water
was hotly fluent, the radio full of Beethoven, Mozart, the Bachs,
the windows kept out street noise, the air conditioner labored
in silence.

In town was the rebuilt church in which Charlemagne had
been crowned and the rebuilt Rathaus, whose staircase was
lined with pictures of Adenauer, De Gasperi, Schumann, Roy
Jenkins, and George Marshall, the rational, decent champions of
Pan-Europa, men after Powdermaker's heart. Across the street
from St. Follain, "burned in the seventh century and again in
1944," Powdermaker took a picture of an immense wolfhound
drinking from a pool surrounded by seven fat-bellied, bronze
sacks of greed, bronze hands in each other's bronze pockets.
One bronze fellow, a thin, browless meanie, was instructing a
boy in the secrets of calculation. The sculpture's title was *Kreislauf des Geldes.* Powdermaker checked *Kreislauf* in the yellow
dictionary: "circulation." The Circulation of Money. Germany
mocking itself, as it had after every catastrophe it had inflicted
on Europe. Mockery was the outlet for national ferocity. Or so
—in the manner of Eph Weiss—thought Powdermaker.

3

The Autobahn was another outlet. No mockery here, and no
speed limit. Powdermaker floored his asthmatic Opel past slug-
gards and was himself flashed, honked at, and passed by Mercedes and BMWs. In an hour, his stomach was an iron knot, he
was soaked with sweat, his tie and belt were loose, his moccasins
off. *Gott sei dank,* the radio played Bach and Mozart; otherwise,
the Autobahn would be a river of blood. What was the ratio
between German music and German ferocity?

RICHARD STERN

4

The thirty-pfennig tourist pamphlet began:

> Certain thoughts always spring to mind when Nuremberg is mentioned: bratwurst, *Lebkuchen,* toys, Dürer, the Christmas Fair, and the famous soccer team.

These were not the thoughts that sprang to Powdermaker's mind. His thought was the album of *Die Meistersinger,* a print of the walls, towers, spires, castle, Virtue Fountain and Pegnitz River of medieval Nuremberg.

Now, on this infernal August day, there it was: St. Sebaldus, the Lorenzkirche, the Schloss, the Rathaus, "the wonderfully preserved fifteenth-century gentleman's residence" called the Albrecht Dürer Haus.

Three o'clock, the day boiling in gold. Powdermaker walked up the König and Kaiser Strassen, past fountains, bridges, churches, past flocks of unisex punks in hot black clothes, orange spiked hair, eyes agog in mascara moons. Here and there— punctuation in this reconstituted Hans Sachs town—were tramps, often with bottles in their hands; they soliloquized, boozed, bummed smokes: failure in the marrow of the insistent commerce of bargain tables (patrolled by tense, intrusive clerks). Powdermaker paid four marks, two dollars, for sixteen green grapes which he popped against his teeth and palate.

In the Hauptmarkt, a fellow in top hat and a girl in tights clog danced for an unsmiling crowd. A white poodle carried the hat around for coins. By a baroque fountain which jetted water from the bronze nipples of haughty ladies, a girl with an angry, pocked nose played the violin for no one. She played Vivaldi, terribly. Powdermaker crossed the square to listen, paying tribute to the idea of public music, and to her isolation. When she scratched out the end of a movement, he dropped three marks into the violin case. She did not thank him. He walked down the Kaiserstrasse and browsed in a bookstore; he liked to have a souvenir from every foreign town. Hot in a saleswoman's impatience, he bought a cheap yellow paperback, *Lyrik des Exils.*

Looking at it, he almost bumped a bearded man in a filthy brown suit. The man carried a wine bottle. To Powdermaker, he said, *"Erst brennen Sie uns, dann liefern Sie uns."* [First you burn us, then you ruin us.] In his blue blazer, his Italian shoes, French shirt and English tie, Powdermaker jumped aside, furious. What goddam nerve. Miserable, bomb-brained ruin, ignoramus, know-nothing. That he should say this to me, whose cousins could have been beaten to death by his uncles a decade before he'd been conceived.

5

Under chestnut trees was a pleasant-looking restaurant. Powdermaker ordered a *Bauernomelett,* a *Gemüse Salat,* and a carafe of white wine, lit a cigar, unfolded the *Nürnberger Nachrichten,* and relaxed with these sacraments of the good tourist. In the local news, a man celebrated his twenty-third birthday by knocking the books off the shelves of a local bookstore; the police found him in the bushes, laid on the cuffs and took him off. There was a wasp plague in the Rhineland. In Frankfurt/Main, a woman attended the murder trial of her daughter, a member of the Red Army Faction; the mother formed a group of RAF parents to see that the children were not abused in prison. "For instance, they supply no washcloths. The prisoners must use their handkerchiefs."

"Hast was zu rauchen?" Powdermaker looked up to an elderly, bald fellow speaking to him across the hedge which separated restaurant from street. "I don't smoke," said Powdermaker. The man's face grew red; he pointed to Powdermaker's lit cigar. "Filthy Yankee liar." The indictment went on, beyond Powdermaker's German, a high-pitched aria which roused Powdermaker's neighbors, some to laughs, most to anger. A waiter ordered the drunk to take a powder. The man cursed and shook his fist, then suddenly sank with hydraulic slowness to the ground. A police car pulled up, two uniformed policemen leaped out, lifted, held, cuffed and lectured the drunk. Bald head lowered to his chest, he was put in the back of the car. It turned Powdermaker around. "To be so singled out. So humiliated."

6

That night, tense and fearful in the *couchette,* worrying about kicking the bunk above, falling out of his narrow bed—he was in the middle of the left side of the double tier of three—holding back internal as well as overt noise and motion, peeking and trying not to peek at the girl on the upstairs bunk, choked with airlessness and human smell, then, opening a window, cold, and covering himself with his blazer, Powdermaker passed a restless, semihallucinatory night.

The desk clerk in the Hotel Veit had been so nice to him—looking up the train schedules from Munich to Milan, directing him to the *Bahnhof*—that it almost overrode the uneasiness he'd felt in Nuremberg. Wonderful what one decent person can do for you. This was a squarish, half-sunk, ordinary fellow with small spectacles on a small nose and mild gray eyes that seemed to have seen much, suffered much, and stayed decent. Eph might have said, "You never know. The guy's apartment walls could be covered with Jewish skin." Eph's skepticism, his humor, was as automatic as Powdermaker's benevolence and sentimentality. No, this was a decent man, and if, like all men, he'd done bad things, he was not doing them now.

On the local train to Munich he was amazed how much he had forgotten about Nuremberg. He was alone in the compartment, looking at the woods, the farms, the pretty *Dörfchen,* when he thought, "My God, I didn't see the Stadium, the Hall of Justice. I didn't think of them. Unbelievable." For the next few hours, in that train, on the platform, then in his *couchette,* chilled, tense and sleepless, he went over his Nuremberg lore. There was a lot of it. He'd seen films, he'd read books, he'd been in arguments about the modern history that stuck like poisonous spines to this town. Why had he thought only of Wagner and Dürer?

A decade ago he'd seen the great Ophuls film. It was shown in two evenings at the Art Institute—and he'd left the auditorium shaking like a leaf. The next day, he talked about it with Weiss, who for a month brought him books about the trials, the Nazis, and their state. Nothing was more fascinating than historical monstrosity, and there may never have been a historical monstrosity as monstrous as this one. Nuremberg was its heart. Powdermaker, a man who was bored to death with Holocaust talk, who could hardly bear to hear that word, who equally disliked anti-Semitic stories and stories about anti-Semites, found himself sinking with ravenous pleasure into the stories of Nazism. Awake in the *couchette,* he both remembered and contrived theories about it. Hitler had revived the Spanish craziness of the purity of blood, the *limpieza del sangre. Blood* was the touchstone. The Nuremberg rallies were consecrated by the touch of the *Blutfahne,* the flag bloodied by the martyrs of the *Putsch.* Hitler's speeches and Streicher's stories were full of blood: the syphilitic Jew whose sick blood sapped the national strength; the single cohabitation of Jew with Aryan which contaminated beyond salvation; the Jewish doctors who raped female patients under anaesthetic in order to corrupt the Aryan heritage. The Nazis were terrified that their own blood was bejewed. Maria Schicklgrüber became pregnant while working for a Jewish family in Vienna. They gave her a pension even after she married Johann Hiedler and passed her name on to her five-year-old son Alois. Unlike his peasant ancestors, Alois stayed in school and joined the Austrian civil service. His third wife, his niece Clara, became the mother of Adolf. Alois, a sadistic drunkard, whipped the mischievous and imaginative boy who hated him deeply. A Jewish doctor took care of Clara Hitler and saw her out of the world. In Vienna, seventeen-year-old Adolf stayed in Jewish houses when he was rejected for admission to the academies of painting and architecture. In Vienna too he contracted syphilis and left suddenly for Munich, before his preinduction medical exam. He served bravely in World War I, then returned in the ebb tide of humiliating defeat to a Munich bristling with every sort of hate doctrine. He met Rosenberg, Streicher, learned the anti-Semitic theories of Wilhelm Maar and read *The Protocols of the Elders of Zion;* he became his terrible self.

Then there was Goering. For a schoolboy essay about his beloved stepfather, Hermann von Epenstein, he was called on the carpet by the headmaster and forced to wear a placard around his neck which read, "My *Pati* is a Jew." And Hess's pal Haushofer had Jewish blood; so did Heydrich. For all of them, Jew-hatred meant self-cleansing and a Jew-cleansed Germany (plus all those shekels). Hitler's speeches, Wagner's music, torch lights, blond sex making blond chains. The Third Reich was turned into a bomb.

It was right that the trial of the bomb makers was held in Nuremberg. Powdermaker could remember the faces of the men who sat in the dock: the pale fat-cheeked contempt of Goering; the black-browed remoteness of Hess; the long, brutal, scarred face of Kaltenbrunner; the bald, obscene, childish fierceness of Streicher; Speer, Rosenberg, Dönitz, Schacht, Frick, Frank, Sauckel, who else? Oh yes, Ribbentrop, Jodl, two or three others. In the Nuremberg courtroom they sat in two rows, Goering at one end of the front row, Schacht at the other, like scornful brackets.

And none of this had he thought of for a single moment during the five hours he was in the town. *Morgenlicht Leuchtend, Morninglight Gleaming.* Walter's prize song which won him the hand of Eva and admission to the Meistersinger fraternity. It was morning now, shots of gold in the pearl interstices of the Italian hills. Blood and beauty, hatred and heroism, bashing, biting, cutting, stealing, twisting, easing the hatred and misery of life on the bodies of Jews, Poles, Gypsies, the old, the weak, the defective, the impure. Morninglight gleaming.

7

In the dining car, the couple sat in the last of four booths on the right side, Powdermaker in the first booth on the left. There was no exchange of words or looks. Powdermaker let others set the social tone; he was content to make a decent impression (and to take his own).

The waiter asked if he wanted a cocktail. "Just wine, please," and chose the second-least expensive white, then veal piccata, pasta, and salad. Across the aisle, the waiter asked the couple if they'd like to sit in the nonsmoking section. They rose and went into the back half of the compartment. "How about you, sir? Nonsmoking?" the waiter asked Powdermaker. "For me, too," he said and sat again in the first seat on the left as far as possible from the couple; he was not one to intrude.

In retrospect, he couldn't remember if it had been one minute or five before they made their move. He was looking out the window at the little villages stuck on the hills above Lake Lugano.

On their way back to the smokers' section, the couple passed him. The waiter followed, asking if anything was wrong. The woman said something which Powdermaker didn't hear, some sort of explanation. Still he felt nothing wrong, just faintly amused surprise. But it was enough to alert him, so that he heard the husband say, *"Zhoof."*

In a second, Powdermaker had spelled this out, *"jouf"*; and, in another, decided it was the harsh, pejorative version of *"juif."*

He'd never heard or read the word, but he knew with certainty that the man had called him, Powdermaker, the equivalent of "kike." If there was any doubt, it disappeared when the wife said, "Shhh," and something else, and the husband responded, *"Mais il parle italien aussi."*

Sitting with his cold white wine by the beautiful lake, Powdermaker felt as if his head had been sliced like a grapefruit and put on a plate. Everything cold in the universe poured into his decapitated trunk. His heart thumped, his hands shook the wineglass, perspiration rolled from forehead and cheeks to the white tablecloth. He felt himself flushing, paling, felt what he almost never felt, pure rage. He turned all the way around and stared, no, glared at the man's back. The wife forced herself not to look at him, he saw that, but she transmitted nervous awareness to her husband. Powdermaker's fury was registered, that he knew, and he turned back to the wine with some relief.

Perhaps he'd been wrong. Perhaps the word meant something else or was even part of another word. Maybe it had had nothing to do with him at all. "No," he thought, "I can't dodge this." When he'd followed them into the nonsmoking section, something had happened to the husband: he could not physically bear being close to Powdermaker. He'd dragged his wife away and given her the one-word explanation, *"Zhoof."* When she'd tried to quiet him and said, "At least, speak Italian," the man said, "He also speaks Italian." (He'd heard Powdermaker talking at Chiasso.)

The waiter brought Powdermaker's dinner. *"Bon appétit."* He tried to eat, to be calm, to enjoy the luxury of eating on a train moving through beautiful places. This was his last full day in Europe, tomorrow he'd fly back to Chicago. Why should a vulgar hater ruin things for him? He tried to lose himself in the beautiful last daylight, to become translucent, a slice of human scenery. After all, what did anything matter?

No luck.

The food was tasteless, the wine flat, the scenery was scenery. He turned again and sent all the hatred he could summon toward the man who hated him.

If he'd been stronger, more self-confident, even more gifted with anger, he could have walked to their table and said, "Madam, you have the bad luck to be married to a Nazi pig."

8

A year or two ago, Eph Weiss told him, "The reason travel's so important to you, Arthur, is that it gives you the illusion of being someone. It's tiring, you cover ground, and it makes you think you're accomplishing something."

Powdermaker had said, "It makes more sense than what I do here with you."

"You're a lucky fellow, Arthur. You don't see what's in front of you."

As he'd said this from behind his viewfinder, his green eyes aflare over the little porthole, Powdermaker thought, "A photographer's point of view."

For years, Powdermaker had lived by filling a gap in an advertiser's gallery: the faintly Jewish gentleman. His decent face could also pass for Spanish aristocrat, Italian waiter, golfer at the second-rank Jewish country clubs. He usually sported good but not tailor-made suits, three-hundred dollar watches; he drank Jim Beam, had a Piece of the Rock, a Harris Banker's attention, drove a Chrysler, dreamed of a Porsche.

Earlier, his range was wider. Pullover round his shoulders, tennis racket in hand, he leaned over convertibles driven by open-mouthed blondes. The year Manny Echevarria spent in Cozumel, he'd doubled as a gaucho, a chef, and, moustached and bereted, a Basque fisherman.

Son and grandson of assimilated German-Jewish burghers, his slogans were theirs: let sleeping dogs lie; don't cry over spilt milk. His father changed the name from Pulvermacher to Powdermaker. Young Arthur stayed out of school one day of two for Rosh Hashanah and Yom Kippur, but he was not bar mitzvahed. "Such nonsense isn't for us, why spend such money?" As for any

Pulvermachers who'd stayed in Germany, God knows what happened to them. No calls for help were made, or, at least, received.

At Wright Junior College, Powdermaker was spotted by the photographer Eph Weiss who needed a "nice-looking Jewish but not too Jewish model." For twenty-eight years, they worked together. Beverages, cars, garments, accessories, what purified, what amused, what glittered; for these products he posed.

When Powdermaker complained about the emptiness of his life, Weiss said, "We're indispensable, Arthur. We're making the myths the tribe lives by. We show them how to live. Without us, they'd burn down the Pentagon, shoot the presidents. Which they do pretty regularly, anyway."

But Powdermaker felt a professional hollowness. Only traveling fulfilled him: he was taking in the world, preparing for something that wouldn't be just appearance and pretense.

9

At the brief stopover in Bissone, Powdermaker dashed the hundred yards from the dining car to his compartment. It relieved and exhausted him. He felt swallowed by heat. In the compartment, he took off his clothes and sat naked by the window, bent over the vents through which cold air rose. At Lago Maggiore, mountains fell down greenly to the water; blue and white villages clustered around spires. How beautiful and neat Switzerland was; it was what it was supposed to be.

Zhoof. "Am I so clearly that? The eyes? The big nose? My walk? My open mouth—the Whiner's deferential mouth, the Ingratiator's smile? All that helpfulness with the train; damn eagerness to belong? Jewiness. *Zhoofheit.* Whatever the bastard saw, felt. And couldn't bear. Some yidstuff leaking out of me. The only thing that counted for him. Not tourist, not American, not fellow traveler. Certainly not fellow-man. *Zhoof. Disjectamembra.* Garbage."

10

He'd be coming back. Their compartment was three down, they'd walk past. Powdermaker could open the door, naked, and stare at them. The message would be, "You aren't part of that world which obliges me to clothe myself." He'd be in his own compartment, he had his rights. Or did he? There might be some railway code enjoining decency. Maybe he could say, "Madam, would you care to come in and have a nightcap? I can offer you more civilized company than you're used to." Even if ignored—of course it would be—it would make the point. Or would it reinforce their contempt for *Zhoofs*? Maybe a collision: he'd open the door as they passed and crash into the bastard. "Watch where you're going, you old bastard," while he kicked his ankle, kneed him, put an elbow in his eye.

Never in his life had Powdermaker done anything remotely like this. Was it time? He'd been insulted; men had fought duels for less than this. If he could only hold on to his anger, not weaken it with doubt, maybe he could pull it off, *do* something for a change.

11

The year before, Powdermaker had gone through the Guillaumin Collection at the Orangerie. Cézannes, Monets, Manets, Bonnards, Pissarros, the wonderful familiar crew who'd brought such happiness to millions. To Powdermaker, the Cézannes were special, an intelligence beyond beauty. You could look deeper and deeper into them. They touched the essential, they were essential.

Now in the compartment, with the door ajar, not just the compartment door but the one in himself, Powdermaker felt something in that untouched part of himself which had been identified in contempt by the man. *Zhoof.* It stood for the outsiders who had brought the message which linked the transient to the eternal. It said, "You, you by the road, criminal, coward, beggar, weakling, you're an absolutely essential part of what counts." That was the part Hitler couldn't stand in himself and identified in his sadistic father with the Viennese Jew who'd impregnated the upstairs maid.

Powdermaker had spent his life posing, and would leave behind nothing but a few images that persuaded people to decorate the surface of their lives. Now, thanks to a twisted fellow, he'd been forced into the part of himself that he'd covered over, one it was necessary to recognize, if not defend. Only that way did you earn the right to be on the same earth with the Cézannes, the deepeners and sweeteners of life. As for the haters, they existed, oddly enough, to rouse the drugged souls of the world's Powdermakers.

12

Powdermaker slept well. He woke to the porter's knock, opened the door and got his passport, put on his socks, shirt and pants, and walked down the corridor to the bathroom. While he emptied his bowels, he looked at the passport picture, as blank a one as he'd ever taken. Someone was waiting. As he zipped up, Powdermaker knew it was the *Zhoof* hater.

Why hadn't he brought a deodorant? The fellow would smell his leavings: a triumph of disgust. "Good," thought Powdermaker. "Let him choke." Another repertoire of violence flashed through him: elbow in ribs, knee in groin, door slammed in face. The fellow was probably stronger than he, but he'd have surprise on his side. He could at least stamp on his foot; no, he was in socks, more evidence of *Zhoofheit.*

He opened the door. There the man was, in shirt and jacket, face sharp and blank till it registered Powdermaker and turned icy. Powdermaker arranged his own face into amused contempt and looked into the fellow's eyes. The man drew back into a further state of blankness. Passing, Powdermaker felt him hesitate—could he endure being in a *Zhoof*'s toilet, the wood still *Zhoof*-warm? Powdermaker heard the w.c. door shut.

13

As the train pulled into Brussels' Gare du Nord, the couple stood behind Powdermaker. When he got off, he looked behind. The woman looked at him, flushed, almost pleading. He gave her a small nod, a sympathetic, a human nod. She understood.

Double Charley

PROFESSIONAL deformity: the dyer's hand, the blacksmith's forearm, the model's complexion, the lawyer's skepticism. And the songwriter's?

"Mindlessness," said Charley Schmitter to his longtime collaborator, Charley Rangel. "Empty mindedness. So your tunes don't bump into anything but my jingles. And vice versa."

Manifestly untrue, but Charley Schmitter never reconciled himself to "this degraded métier." "The Greatness of the American Musical Comedy" was not an admissible topic at Schmitter's table.

On the other hand, Schmitter gave no quarter to *official* poets. "Glue-eyed narcissists, licking the fat off their own bones so some acne-headed sophomore can have his quota of wet dreams. So some Bulgarian history major can think about something while she mouths his member. 'I wandered lonely as a cow / That chews the cud of Chairman Mao.' Ohhhh, soobleem."

Immense, passionate, mad for his own spiels and his own

learning, Charley Schmitter couldn't be contained by any métier.

At least, this was the sense of his old-time collaborator. "Soon
as he had a few bucks salted away, he could become what he
always was, a spieler, a schmooser." This to Maggie Moon, Rangel's off-and-on-again companion. "He's the most profoundly
self-contented man in the world." (Rangel himself was no slouch
in that department.) "He's got a tolerant, gifted wife, willing
tootsies, the constitution of Mont Blanc. And he doesn't need
more than ten or twelve thousand bucks a year to pay for his
lousy flannel shirts, Gallo Rhine, and egg foo yong. The greatest
pleasure he provides himself: schmoos. He only calls now to try
it out on me. When was the last time I had a lyric out of him?
Seven years ago?"

"Too long," said Maggie.

" 'Starved in Fat City.' His last trip out here. Six, seven years
ago. Just before your vanishing act."

Afraid that her irregular life was upsetting Chippie, her ten-
year-old daughter, Maggie had disappeared one morning, bag
and baggage. For three weeks, Rangel had had no word at all.
Then a one-line card from New York: "Chippie had to get away.
Love, M." (Which, thought Rangel, was the reason he didn't set
"Fat City"; never would.)

That had been dark-night-of-the-soul time for him. He'd lived
with Maggie five years, since he'd come back to Chicago.
There'd been no commissions coming in, jockeys weren't playing their songs. Only now and then would a "Golden Oldies"
play a Double Charley. So he came back to the apartment he'd
grown up in on West Armitage above the candy store his parents owned. (It was a Christian Science Reading Room now.)
Maggie had left her third husband, "the Casanova of cotton
goods," and was working in the Billing Office of Roosevelt Hospital. Rangel came in to complain and walked out with an invitation. His own wife had stayed in Santa Monica, was en route to
marrying the unit manager of a TV news station. The great
sexual switchboard had more links than Ma Bell's System, but,
sooner or later, everyone got plugged in, if only to his own
opening.

Rangel fell so hard for pretty Maggie, he wasn't bothered by
her marital record. "I just kept trying. It was a substitute for

B.A., M.A., Ph.D. I'm an expert now, Charley. And you're—
what's that Kern song?—'My Man.' "

"Pollack and Yvain," corrected little Charley.

For the first year, he'd been so charged by her presence in the
same apartment, he thought he couldn't think of anything else.
It turned out to be the best year he'd had in a decade. Schmitter
caught fire, and Decca took a flutter on a Double Charley
album. (Connoisseurs of the forties made room for it between
their Beatles.)

A largish girl, especially next to tiny Rangel, Maggie had the
complexion of an English milkmaid. Pretty to the point of unreality: a perfect bobbed nose and eyes so strangely lit by every
feeling, you could not concentrate on their color—a blue-
flecked verdure. When she put on weight—every six months or
so—it went to her face and marred the perfection. But such
distinctions were only for Maggie and such experts as himself.
Passers-by still kept looking back for seconds: quite a tribute to
a woman clocking at fifty.

Back then, though, her beauty and their passion were intensified by what she called "the condiment of guilt."

It was that, she said, that made her take off. Chippie, "disturbed by the irregular life," was stuttering. Rangel told her
many children stuttered. "Ignore the stutter, respond to the
meaning."

But Maggie, fearful of imperfection, rushed the little girl.
"Speak up, speak up." Of course, it got worse. Rangel begged,
ordered, threatened. For him, children were sacred. "The look
on Chippie when she tried to get a sentence out," he told
Schmitter, who'd come to Chicago for a work week. "It breaks
me, Charley. I never hit a woman in my life, let alone the one
I loved. But if she gets on that kid again, I may break her nose."

Did that message reach Maggie? In any case, within a week,
she and Chippie were off.

A month later, Schmitter telephoned to say he'd seen her, she
was working in the Billing Office at Lenox Hill. "Seems to be all
right, Charley."

"I don't care," Rangel had said. "If it wasn't for Chippie, I'd
hire a truck to break her bones. Every part of me that loved her
hates her. But I've even stopped dreaming of busting her nose.
God bless whatever physics does it."

Ten months later, he saw her in the Art Institute. "I don't believe it." She was gaunt, newly beautiful. "Why didn't you call me?"

"I thought you'd kill me."

She'd been back two months, had an apartment in Hyde Park with a librarian at I.T.T., Olive Baum. She worked in the Billing Office at Michael Reese. Chippie was at Kenwood, a good public school.

They began going out again, and then, after a visit from Schmitter and the consequent departure of Olive Baum, she and Chippie came back to West Armitage. Stutter gone, Chippie went to Francis Parker; Rangel paid.

"It's like leaves," Rangel told Schmitter between spiels. "Once the chlorophyll factories start churning out all that green, you can't see those gorgeous reds that'll kill them in the fall. She's back, we click, she's for me, it's green for go."

"Not bad, little Charley. Maybe I can work it up for us."

Rangel knew better than that. There'd be no more lyrics coming his way. Only happiness with Maggie eased the pain of it then.

"Why can't you write your own?" Maggie asked him.

"Did Gershwin? Did Rodgers?"

"How about Porter? Berlin?"

"I don't have it. I can't even work with anyone but Charley."

"It's not too late for that. Get the right tune in his head, push him with a title. Recerebrate him. And you'll have another Double Charley."

Not that easy.

Though every morning, breaking from sleep, ideas dribbled into Rangel's head. Sometimes he got them on the pad beside his reading light. Phrases, rhythms; six bars, eight. The piano sideboard piled with note cards, ideas enough for a Ring Cycle. But songs themselves, finished songs, that was something else. He couldn't work without Schmitter. Didn't know why. After Hart's death, Rodgers found Hammerstein. Weill had Kaiser before Brecht, Anderson and a host of others after. Mercer, Arlen, Youmans, almost everyone moved from lyric bed to lyric bed. Without difficulty, nostalgia or remorse. Only he seemed yoked to one writer. "I'm just a standard thirty-two-bar hack," went his self-deprecating line. "Charley's stuff transfigures me. Without it, I'm dry gulched. No charge in the battery. Pffft."

Maggie's suggestion was "Try a new style. It's not you that's yoked to Charley. It's your old success. You're yoked to it and call it 'Schmitter.' "

"Anyone else say that, I'd punch his nose. 'Success!' I hate those damn songs of ours. I hear one on the radio, off it goes. Antiques. Claptrap. Unbearable. But I can't feel my way into this new stuff. It sounds like recitative to me. *Sprechstimme.* And not such brilliant *Sprech* at that. As for the seventy-eight varieties of rock, they're demolition derbies for me. Lyric fission."

Not quite. Rangel was tempted again and again by the easy speech—"Nim Chimsky could sing it"—the unpushiness of the melodic line. "Into you before you know you've bitten it. But I can't feel it. Can't write it. It's not my line."

From New York, Schmitter telephoned bulletins of self-gratulation. "We're still a name at the Capers Club. Frunz"—their longtime agent who now took ten weeks to answer Rangel's letters—"overheard Steve Keith bawling out his latest jailbait the other night for not knowing who Double Charley was. Told her to listen to 'Slit Throat' if she wanted to know what a song was."

"Did he tell her he lifted six bars from 'Eat This Heart'?"

"That was flattery too, Charley, you know that." The telephone magnified Schmitter's wavery treble (a surprise for those who knew its immense source). "Did Beethoven sue Schubert for stealing from the 'Kreutzer'?"

"He was dead. Or maybe it killed him. I'da bloodied the little shit's nostrils."

"Nonsense, sweetheart. It's noblesse oblige. Keith has nothing to gain from puffing us. The point is, among cognoscenti, we *still count.*"

"He's made four hundred grand from our six bars, he can afford to pamper his guilt. He probably saw Frunz lapping it up in the corner, knew it would get back to us. More points for Keith."

"Bitter, Charley, bitter."

Why not? Could he live on third-hand compliments? Day after day, he was at the piano, music paper on the flowerless wooden trellis, notes making their way from keys to paper;

where they died. In the wordless, the Schmitter-less vacuum, they died. And nothing came from New York. "It's that cretinous broad you introduced him to," he said to Maggie. "She's dried him out. He always said he couldn't work around idiots. And now he pours himself into that mental Sahara."

"She's the sign of his trouble, not the cause. Charley's not young, lambie."

"Sure he is. At ninety, he'll have more sexual charm than Paul Newman. Bulk, bad leg, bronchitis, nothing derails Charley. Age is just a rumor to him. Sickness is for other guys. Stupidity. That's what kills him. He goes home to Agnes to get Olive's stupidity washed off him. I'd finance some babe through a doctorate if she'd play with Charley. He has to have his toke of baby nookie. Look at him."

Pointing. On the wall, in a mosaic frame, was Agnes's marvelous miniature of him. Agnes painted on enamel in the manner of the Persians and Léonard Limosin. Her portrait of Charley had won a prize in Paris. Before that, Rangel had told her he couldn't live without it, and he bought it on time, two hundred dollars a month for four years. There was the great black bramble of a head, the wild moustache ambling into the regal cheeks, Schmitter's bulk jutting over the enamel curve. Beside the figure in the six square inches, a fountain frothed minuscule lilac spray in solar glitter.

That such Flemish genius flowed from the florid, muscular, eagle-browed Agnes had been an art world secret for decades. Only with the Paris exhibition in the midsixties did Agnes Schmitter become the name behind those few, tiny works of refined genius. Till then, she was only what she kept on being, Charley Schmitter's passionate, tolerant, quarrelsome, adoring, bellicose worshiper. For years, she'd shut her eyes to the passionate geniality which poured sexual charm over New York ladies.

Not that Charley ever *came on*. He was just there, waiting with a rub here, a kiss there. His parts bulged in his corduroys. Of them, and anything else that was not controlled by the power of thought, he was magnificently careless. What counted was mental power. "It's why I work with Rangel," he'd said from the beginning. "Not just that he's a top musician. He could be twice as good, and I wouldn't work with him if he were a dope."

Maggie kept telling Rangel Schmitter would revive. "One day, you'll sing him a few bars, it'll be like a quarter in the jukebox. The machinery will crank up again. Olive or no Olive."

Rangel knew it was over, but possibility nagged at him until the last day.

That occurred one month after Charley's last telephonic burst of schmoos. He'd been, he said, reading the poet Jules Laforgue, "the kid Eliot stole the line about measuring out his life with coffee spoons from. Listen to this." And the wavery voice, tinier than ever, read in what seemed to Rangel perfect French, a few difficult lines of verse.

" 'Divers Flutes!' How does that enchant you? 'Mademoiselle who might have wished to hear the wood of my diversity of flutes display themselves a bit.' Can you imagine crooning that to a hundred, a hundred million people? And that's the source of modern mentality as they see it at Cambridge and the Sorbonne. Think Stockhausen could work up a tune for that baby?

"I'm glad we never worked that side of the street. That's for No-One-Caresville. We're down where people eat, sleep, love, and die. In tune with *this* world. We didn't go diving into waterless pools."

On the way to New York for the funeral, Rangel realized that had been Charley's memorial; and—who knows?—perhaps his justification for turning off the spigot while his partner still thirsted.

Two hours before the funeral, Olive Baum called him. (Maggie had given her his number.) She wanted a favor. "Agnes wouldn't let me see him at the hospital." She was crying. "He *wanted* to see me. She *told* me. She had the nerve to tell me. He couldn't speak, could only move his eyelids; and he blinked 'yes' when she asked him if he wanted to see me. She said she asked him twice, and he blinked 'yes,' and she didn't tell me till he was gone. And now she won't tell me where he's being buried. You tell me, please, Charley. You know we loved each other."

"I'll get her to let me tell you, Olive."

Rangel had identified the body for Campbell's; Agnes had been too distraught. In the coffin, ready to go, Charley was de-Schmittered: powdery, Roman, the black bramble head too grand for the wispy neck and the timid blue tie someone had put on him.

The funeral day was rough with January light. An icy day. Tiny Charley sat beside Agnes in the back of the limousine. (He'd always felt smaller next to her than he did next to Charley.) Her face was full of aquiline rancor, her black hair—"I suppose she's dyed it for years"—lay heavily on her shoulders. It smelled musty, sad. The limousine went up the West Side Highway heading for Mount of Hope Cemetery. To their surprise, Charley, great scorner of death, had, for forty years, maintained a plot there.

In the mortuary city, his coffin lay on the iced earth among the small gravestones. Below were the grander slabs, one-room marble mansions. While they stood, uncertain what to do, it began to sleet. Drops pelted the coffin. "Should have brought a Bible," said Rangel. "Or an anthology." No poems came to mind. He tried to think of a line from one of their songs. Couldn't. "I guess this is it, kid," he said. "God bless you."

With the soft sleet and Agnes's tears, this was Charley's service.

Rangel put his arm around as much of her shoulders as it could reach, then wandered down the slope looking at names, some familiar. On one marble slab, he read, "Billy Rose." Across from it was a one-room temple with ugly stained glass. "Agnes," he called. "Charley's in good company."

She looked through the sleet at the little man pointing to the sarcophagus.

"It's Gershwin. Wouldn't you know? Even here, we suck hind tit."

"Make sense, Charley."

Back in the limousine, Rangel looked at the sleet changing to drizzle and fog. The countryside was muffled in rat fur, the Hudson invisible. Rangel tried to think of Charley, the amputation of Double Charley. He took Agnes's hand. "Maybe you should have let Olive see him."

"What?"

"She was just a security blanket. I know that. Still, a sad dummy. Let her go up to the cemetery."

Agnes removed her hand.

"You were the only woman who ever counted for him."

"Hah."

"You were. The only one that understood him, that he could talk with."

"A lot you know, Charley."

"I knew him forty years, Agnes. No one but you better."

"No one knew the big stiff. Everyone knew parts of him."

"It's always like that. But we knew him most and loved him most."

"That's the truth."

"I wish he could have seen that dumb broad. She must have been something for him. At least, it was the last favor he could give anyone."

Agnes, florid, haughty, looked down at him. "That's what it would have been. The great favor-giver. The charm-distributor. That's where his career went. Everybody got his lyrics but you, Charley."

"I got enough. But Olive could have used one more."

Agnes picked at her heavy hair. (Charley moved away. Its odor was poor.) "She had no more business there than . . . Maggie."

"Sure she did. She was Charley's. For better or worse."

"And wasn't Maggie? Didn't she head out with him too? That was no great secret in New York. Why shouldn't she and sixteen others have been in the hospital room? He'd've found hands for them all. Oh God." Past and imagined wrongs clotted with her new solitude into a terrible bolus of feeling.

While she sobbed, Charley Rangel, arms out to hold what he could of her, felt his own head cracking. So that was the story. The stinking small grain of this world.

At Ninety-Sixth Street, the chauffeur made the fat turn off the Drive. Here in New York, Double Charley's last song began, the mean act of betrayal that was Charley Rangel's to set, to live with. "I'da punched his goddamn nose for him," he said. "I'd've bloodied the big bastard's nose."

Riordan's Fiftieth

RIORDAN'S fiftieth birthday. For three years, it had been waiting for him; and here it was, a day like another, up before everyone, a cup of Instant, a corn muffin with marmalade, the six-block walk to Stony Island, the ride to the bus shed. He said nothing about it; but every other minute, it was there. Lucky he didn't drive Big Bertha up a lamppost. And thank God he had Route 12, a bit of air, a bit of green. When Lou Flint was fifty, three years ago, his missus turned the apartment into a parade float, there was everything but Playboy bunnies, and, all over, paper banners with "Half a Century of Flint" on them. The old lady had come on with a cake in Flint's own shape—what a shape, not far off a normal cake. And half the boys from the shift were there, there must have been forty, plus wives, it looked like Randolph and State. What a racket, what presents, and they'd drunk till time to go to work, there must have been fifty collisions and a thousand road fights that day in Chicago.

That was the way to pack it up.

And here he was, George Riordan, fifty to the day, and on his way home he'd had not one greeting and didn't know if his own kids had been told, but knew if he got a greeting out of her, it would leak out of the side of her moon face and make him feel, "Who're you, Riordan, that anyone in the world should care you've weighted the planet fifty years?" The twins, ten years of Riordan spunk, would think it no different from any other day. They wouldn't remember that even last year they were making crayon pictures of cakes and missiles for him. "Happy Birthday, Dads," and big kisses, and she'd stirred herself enough to come up with a store cake, and Bill had carried it in and Joey had cut it up for them. She had refused her piece, though had not refrained when he was off on the route the next day, oh no, had put half the cake in her gut, and when he'd asked for a piece that night, she said it had gone bad, they made it with month-old eggs, she wouldn't buy any more A & P cakes, you bet your life, and, anyway, wasn't he a little long in the tooth to be stuffing himself with chocolate night after night, a coronary would clout him on the route, he'd kill a bus load if not himself and be hauled off for prosecution in the courts, he'd damn better watch his weight, he wouldn't be able to stuff himself back of the wheel. This from Mrs. Fat herself.

Not a civil word to him for a week, and then, in front of the kids, this mouthful of sewage if he bothered to answer would make him so wroth he'd haul off and fetch her a clop round the ears.

What had happened? Where had his tranquillity, where had his life gone?

Was she right, had it been a mistake from the start? One of her wild remarks that rang true. Four kids late. Why hadn't she stopped? God knows she had stopped the last years, he never even looked at her now, not that that slop of rump could get a rise from a three-year-old bull. A slob and a bad-mouther, this was what came of her, and the poor kids, living under this terrible roof with her leaking acid over them every day of their lives. No wonder Stan and Susie got out quick as they could. As if any other man could have stood her as long as he had without falling into a bit of comfort and sympathy. He hadn't moved a finger that way. Day after day, twenty-three years watching the birds climb on the bus, every shape and color of woman, legs climbing the steps, the skirts over the knees, let alone those skirts, where, practically in his eye, were thighs and more. And he had nothing but smiles and didn't know where to turn, only looking in the rear mirror and trying to steer.

What was it all about?

If the Cubs were warm in the race, at least there was something to look for; and in winter the Bulls and the Hawks, in the fall the Bears. All these animal teams he'd invested his heart in.

Not enough.

The folks were dead on the highway ten years now, Sis moved off to Detroit, and now the kids, Stan in the army, sure to go on to the lousy war, and Sue downtown calling up once a month, unable to hold her rage for his not sending her to college, her mother's tongue lashing him, who had been so dear a little girl, never a pouter, always fetching and kissing. As if he were Rockefeller. And she wouldn't even try the night course at Loyola or Wright Junior. Beneath her. No, above her, she never brought home the gold stars, the nuns said she was a dreamer, wouldn't concentrate. What did she dream about? The Beatles and worse. How did they fit her for college, even if he'd had the wherewithal?

There was a spoilage in this family. Maybe it was him. That was her view, he had that clear, though God knows short of lying around with a can of Schlitz watching the game, what was his life of luxury? Who had he made pay? Stan and the twins liked the games just like he. Every summer, he took them off in the car for two weeks, Colorado, Texas, Vermont, they'd seen the whole country, thirty-nine states they'd been in. And stayed in the best motels, it cost God knows what over the years; added up, it would have sent Susan to college, Stan too. But what were they to do, all those years, live like clams in the dark? You had to get out of the city. God knows he couldn't blame the blacks down in Woodlawn, Kenwood, Lawndale, penned into those streets summer and winter, year after year. He might bust out and club a few heads himself given that.

So here he was, fifty, Susan a stranger and Stan in the army because he wasn't in college, and it was a rotten war, not the way it was in Korea where if you weren't gung-ho you were daft, and if you froze to death in the hills, at least you knew you were keeping the Chinks from running the Pacific, and he hadn't lost so much as a fingernail. Perhaps better off if he'd come back minus an arm. Worse men than he were pulling ten thousand a year toting up figures at desks or bossing their betters in bottling plants and the white oil drums down in Whiting. Ten and fifteen thousand, and here he was, twenty-three years behind the wheel and finally making eighty-four hundred with three weeks in the summer. Plus the dread half your time you'd be hit on the head for the fares. He'd been damn lucky there, held up only twice and never been touched, knock wood. Now the fare box was locked, and the signs were up the drivers had no money, but there were heads and lushes all over, they stumbled up the steps with their dollar bills, didn't know or couldn't read, and one of these days, out on Route 10 or 11, one of them might slice him up for his shoes and his cap.

Not even the boys in the pool knew of his birthday. No loner, he just didn't shoot off his face. And wasn't close to anyone now. Two years ago, he'd dropped out of the card game. Elly could have made a scene if they'd come to the house; he'd said she'd taken sick, he had to stay and watch her. So no one said, "Happy Birthday" and "Keep it Flying, Georgie." They talked as they always did. It was the vote for Manager of the Year, and they'd passed over Weaver. "He only won a hundred and thirteen games and cleaned up the Reds in five." This from Powers. And he'd thrown in, wasn't that the way it always was, they always passed over the ones who did their jobs with their mouths shut and picked some flash with the bankroll behind him. "Like Durocher," said Powers, who grew up behind Comiskey Park and hated the Cubs. "No," he said, "Durocher took an armful of bums and kept them contending five years. He's loud but no bum." No point knocking good men. Though God knows Durocher showboated and mouthed.

The best of the day was the half-mile walk from Stony. Not the neighborhood it had been when they'd moved eighteen years ago, and, true, it got worse each year. But it wasn't as bad as Elly's complaints that he'd kept them here while the blacks took over, knocking everyone over the head, and she scared to walk to the A & P except in broad daylight and then with her heart in her mouth. Maybe, but at six, with the night coming on, it was quiet and out of the stench of downtown, the air was breathable when the wind was up, they were close to the Lake, what he'd've given for that as a boy, and there were a few trees.

Walking, he rolled. Cramped on a bus seat eight hours a day didn't slim you, and he started low to the ground as it was.

The streets still, small lawns in front of the stone threeflats, and, every now and then, a little home, the sort they'd aimed at for years, and if there hadn't been Stan's teeth, the surprise of the twins and the summer trips, that would be what they'd be living in now. Which might have kept her happy. Enough anyway to let him walk home tonight to a cake and his kids singing Happy Birthday over the candles so he could know he hadn't spent fifty years for nothing at all. So he was visible to someone. After all, his job was decent, he serviced more people in one week than most people in fifty, people of every type and look, and he went all over the city of Chicago, every four months taking the worst of its air—Route 7, where you moved up State on a Wednesday at noon at a mile an hour, the fumes of the tailpipes making hell in your lungs. And for eighty-four hundred a year while hamburger was seventy-five a pound. Oh Lord, this was wasting his mind on complaint. Here was a nice October night, the leaves falling, quiet in the streets, the air decent enough, he had four fine kids, he'd lived fifty pretty fair years, why fill the head with such garbage? Fifty years old, and inside no difference, no pains, maybe stiff in the back after the route, quicker to hit the sheets at night, but the same, and God knows if some decent woman, a widow like Mary Sears or a decent little cat-face spinster like Helen Whatshername—how long since he'd seen her, Easter Sunday at Holy Name—would say, "What about it, Georgie?" who knows if he mightn't take up the stakes and start for fresh. A woman, a real woman with sympathy and a body for his loneliness, and no more gaff and meanness. This sniping life while the boys looked on and ran off to the television to get out of the way.

Bad thoughts, and, at his corner, there was lead in his heart, his key was lead, and his legs, and up the stairs past the college kids and the widow, and then, ah well, his own door, scratched, the pattern of scratches as close to him as his signature, and the noise of "McHale's Navy" from the machine and the slab of light from it as he passed to hang up his jacket, and her kitchen noise. "Good evening, Elly," he called toward it, and maybe there was a "Good evening" back at him and maybe not, and into the living room with Joey and Bill in the armchairs, and his hands on their heads. "Hello, boys, how goes it today?" and got his "Hi, Dads" from Bill, the plugger, and a colder "Hi" from Joey, Elly's product, who rose to affection only when food was in his mouth. Though he loved them both equally, they were dear boys, he couldn't take offense at Joey's coldness, the boy didn't know what he did or why, and now and then, out of the blue, the boy would pop up and kiss his cheek. They were good boys, he hoped he could get them into a decent trade, or, who knows, maybe college. If the present crop of wild ones didn't burn them all down by then. What a world.

Washing up, his face looked strange. The eyes seemed loose in the sockets, and his face thinner, maybe it was the new fluorescent which trimmed it down. A pug's nose, a chin like a boat keel, and what was left of his hair a rubble color, ash and brown. No face for the movies. Just George Riordan on his fiftieth. His own birthday cake.

Too late for the TV news, he lay on his bed and listened to WGN. The usual garbage. They'd caught a hippie nut who'd killed a whole family out in the redwood country of California. The nuts of the world were everywhere. You were as safe in the middle of Chicago as anywhere. Nixon mouthed some guff to the United Nations, so fast you could hardly follow, if he wanted to speak why sound as if he didn't, the man was a phony, and this Agnew a showboat and mean to boot. And the wars, Arabs and Jews, and forty boys dead in Vietnam, and this the lowest count in years. But if one were Stan. Hundreds wounded, and they didn't tell you if it was sprained ankles, lost legs or worse. Maybe Stan would call. Last year he'd come home late, but in the morning he'd had a funny card from him. Signed, "From a fellow fan." There'd be no chance Sue would call. She would remember and make a point of *not* calling. Or she'd call tomorrow and not say a word. Elly had handed her tongue on to Susan. Poor thing, poor girl making life miserable for herself. Selling shoes was a decent job for a girl without training, why wail you'd been given the short end of the stick? Seventeen, she had years to look around and try other things. Her mother's daughter, and God help the man who fell for her apple head, though God knows he still loved her and wouldn't want her to spend her life alone selling shoes. Why was she such a weight on him tonight? What had he done to turn her from him? Was it only college she'd wanted?

In the morning, he'd climb in the bus, and Harry would give him the finger, and he'd come out of the pen, the great swiveling bus, and there would be that release, the roar and out in the morning. That's how the bus is. Years of it don't add up enough *to send you down to Loyola, and you didn't have the grades, my girl, for the nuns to set you up. What is it you want from me, darling? I wish I could give it to you yet.*

"Supper. Wash your hands, boys. Let's go."

The call that used to cheer his heart. He'd come into the roast after his day, the table set and the kids, four or two, and there'd be talk over the meat, and they'd pass round the chunks of potato and scoop out the beans, there'd be gravy for the beef and brown betty or ice cream for dessert, and coffee, ten or twelve colors on the table, and noise, and sometimes Sis and her husband, and sometimes no children, only friends, and, years before, Mother and Dad.

And now what was there for the twins but a house of gloom. No one came, and even Stan and Susan were gone. Elly would not have his friends, saw only her pal the Mouth during the day. What idea of life would Bill and Joey have? That it was a tunnel of gloom, best out of it quickly. With dinner a call to a graveyard of feeling, to argument or silence, the only noise that of plates or Pass This or Mind Your Manners.

Tonight at least there was noise.

Joey said Bill hadn't washed, Bill said, "You're a liar," and he'd come in with, "I'll take a look, and don't let me hear such stuff in your mouth, you're brothers," and Joey said, "You're husband to Mother, why do you fight?" and after a breath he got out with, "Older people have their differences over the years, and we're not the same flesh and blood, let alone twins, and keep respect in your mouth or I'll slap it there," and Elly said, "Let's forget talk of slapping, the both of you wash up your hands, you too, Joey, I can see the muck on them from here," and she sat down and put a breast of fried chicken on her plate and handed the platter down to him without a word.

"How's it go?" he tried.

"It went," she said. "You want to break down and try the peas?"

On his birthday, she cooked the one vegetable he hated. "I haven't eaten a pea in twenty-five years."

"It might be the making of you." Bare arms, red, chafed, and the moon head with a tent of brown fluff, some sight for a man, yet her skin was clear and the green eyes. Years ago, years ago it had been a face. Now bunched with anger, the nose, mouth, and chin crowding the middle. What waste.

The boys were back, Joey scowling. He asked them how school went.

"Same," said Bill. "Joey got throwed, oh well, never mind."

"Where did Joey get throwed?" from Elly.

"You mousefink. I'll get you, finko." Joey hot, and, before the other mouthed back, he said, "I've had it from you two. One more little love song tonight, and I'll haul off and clap you for good."

A grumble from Joey with "You and who else?" somewhere inside, but he took it as grumble. God knows he didn't want to break heads on this of all days.

"You can imagine where he finds his words," said Elly. "He don't need to read up in the dictionary. You might check your own mouth once in a while."

"Come on, Mom," said Bill. "Let's try it in peace." His plug-ging boy, a peacemaker at ten. Joey was into his chicken leg, grease over his face, lost. As if in a different part of the universe. Oh, life was a raw, strange thing.

"It's not me wants war," she said, and held up a forkful of peas in toast to him. The actress. A hundred and eighty pounds of ham.

He put his fork on the plate with a noise, lifted his fists to the table, felt the silence, and said, "Boys, you know what?"

"What?" said Bill. Joey stopped jawing the leg.

"Your dad's at a milestone today."

He could feel thunder down the table, could feel her darken, feel the resentment, he was putting one over her, she who should have been springing surprise for him. But that wasn't what he wanted. He didn't want that.

Said Bill, "What's a milestone?"

"A milestone. It's something that's important. You know on the turnpikes, they have the signs giving you the mileage every mile. They used to be on white stones. Well, I'm at a big white stone today, I thought you'd like to know."

"You been fired, Dad?" said Joey, scared, the chicken leg shaking in his fist.

"No. I'm fifty years old today. It's my birthday, and a big one, and I'm going to take everyone over to Thirty-One Flavors for dessert, and you can have three scoops or four, whatever you want."

"Yay, Dads," said Joey, and out of his chair with the chicken leg and kissed his cheek.

And Bill came up, and said, "Happy Birthday, Dads. Wish I knowed, I'd made you a card," and kissed the other cheek.

And from her, "It slipped my mind. I thought it was next Friday. I had a cake on the list for it. Well, here's looking at you," and she hoisted her coffee. It was something anyway. At least, for a minute. "And may the next fifty see you try harder."

"Thanks, Elly. The first fifty's the toughest."

"On who?"

There was no stopping her. It was like a child in her. Maybe the change of life would ease her. Let it pass tonight. What counted were these two, throwing them a lifeline, giving them a boost. Too late for her. Maybe for him.

She didn't go with them, but till they went, there were no more slams, and the boys didn't fight, they felt something, and it was good to get out in the dark, the day had counted for something. Back in the car, he told the boys of Mother and Dad and how they'd come so close to seeing them born and how loved they'd have been, and when they got back, Elly said, "Stan called to wish you returns of the day, he says he's fine," and there was a Hawks' game at eight from Maple Leaf Gardens, and Hull got the hat trick, first in the year. It was enough, more than he'd expected.

The moral was keep looking and waiting and maybe push it a little here or there, there's enough somewhere to celebrate, and maybe she was right, God knows, he could push harder the next fifty.

The Sorrows
of Captain Schreiber

1

AN American novel today, mademoiselle?" asked Schreiber,
craning around Goupin to see the paperbound book in the
pocket of Verité's pullover. They were walking home along the
Cher.

"So you see, Captain," and she pulled the book out so that he
could see the title.

"Le Loup de mer," he said. "I've never read him."

"London," said Goupin, also looking. He pronounced the
name in the French manner. "I'd thought he was English."

"You read a great deal here, I've noticed," said Schreiber.

"We are far from Paris, Captain," she said.

"Thank God," added Goupin, looking at his daughter.

"I wonder," she said softly.

"I had only two days in Paris," said Schreiber. After a pause,
he asked, "What sort of books do you prefer, mademoiselle?"

She raised her eyes to him and then beyond to the Cher.
"Would you think philosophy, Captain?"

"Perhaps," he said.

"I'll be getting to that soon, I'm afraid. There are only six novels left. Then only history and poetry intervene. Perhaps you have books I might borrow, Captain?"

"Verité!" said Goupin sharply.

"I should be delighted, mademoiselle. I'm only afraid my tastes won't suit you."

"You're right, Captain." She looked down again at the road. "One doesn't broaden one's tastes in a tannery."

"A rather novelistic remark, my dear," said Goupin softly.

His daughter made no response. Her pullover pinched her under the shoulders, and she was wondering if this was what made Schreiber stare at her, the bones bulging through the gray wool as haphazardly as potatoes in a sack.

They came to the side path.

"Will you come over this evening, Captain?" asked Goupin, easing his eyes from his daughter's squally hair to Schreiber's soft, blue-tinted face. "We still have two bottles of Calvados in reserve. What better way to celebrate the arrival of spring?"

"That's awfully kind, Goupin," said Schreiber. "May I accept for another time? The corporal is driving me to Bourges after dinner."

"Good things will wait, Captain. Perhaps it would be all right to invite the corporal as well?" He phrased it this way knowing the Americans were strange about Negroes.

"I'm sure he'd be honored," said Schreiber.

They parted with some ceremony, handshaking and bowing, and then Schreiber followed the beech-lined path to his billet while the Goupins continued on up the Cher road.

Verité always watched Schreiber move off down the path to her aunt's house. He was plump and ungraceful, and she felt that his movements were a fit mockery of his position as the local representative of the liberating forces. "It's the black corporal who has the soldier's posture," she said to her father, and then blushed, feeling that her father imagined she was really thinking of the other corporal, whom she had nearly forgotten. Without realizing that she said it aloud, she cried, "A German corporal's higher than an American one."

"Perhaps," said her father, "but they do not have the staying power." He found this amusing, but he did not wish to smile and cause his daughter embarrassment.

She did not have the energy to laugh or to answer him properly. "To him, I'm everybody's fool," she thought. "What's the difference?" and her eyes fastened on the brown dirt under her feet, the road she had walked so many times that she thought now there would be no other for her, ever, and that the most she could hope for would be to be swallowed by the oblivion of the habit and to leave it all as soon as God willed.

2

Schreiber lived in a two-story greystone house built around a cobblestone courtyard with a garden in the middle of it. There, in the garden, watering the blackberry bushes she raised there now instead of sweet pea and syringa, stood a small, square woman with straggly gray hair. When she heard the clacking on the cobblestones, she put down the hose, wiped her hands on her apron, and turned around.

"Good evening, Captain Schreiber."

"Good evening, Mme. Cassat," said Schreiber, and inclined his head to her, touching his cap.

Often, before dinner, he sat with her in the garden but tonight, although Mme. Cassat made the smoothing gestures which served as invitation to such occasions, Schreiber walked across to the door which led to his room.

"Have you seen my brother, Captain?" she pushed out, smoothing her hair and dress and sleeves.

"Just now, madame," replied Schreiber, half-turning from the doorway.

"I must tell him something about the radishes," she said, and blushed. She picked up the hose and, tightening the spout, concentrated the stream on the tiny shoots of lawn. "He wouldn't have been allowed in the parlor before the war," she grumbled, listening to him go up the stairs. The reflection warmed over the embarrassment of her improvisation with him and reassured her of her own permanent respectability.

Upstairs, Schreiber had started to type. Mme. Cassat listened to the clicking resentfully and, as her husband came out to the garden, almost snarled at him, "What's he chipping away at? All his papers and numbers and ugly American. Probably counting our china."

Actually Schreiber was engaged in more abstract calculations. He was doing a study of the villagers' evasion of certain censorship restrictions based largely on circumlocutions they employed in letters to avoid these restricted topics. He had begun the study as a subsection of his first administrative report on the village, but he had gotten interested in it and decided to pursue it on his own in a scholarly fashion. He had never before done anything so thorough, not even in law school, but he seemed to have an instinct for research, and it went very smoothly. Indeed, he found that the techniques of research were almost as pleasurable for him as the contemplation of the effects the completed study would have, the small, significant circles it would excite, and the delightful sensation of his own position at the center of them, the authority on this particular fragment of the world. The books piled on his desk, commandeered from the Library of Bourges and from Army Special Studies, pleased him by their bulk and solemn titles. The typewriter too was pleasing to him; its noise reminded him of tiny nails being hammered into meaningful junctions.

In the evenings, he usually typed out the results of whatever meditations he'd had on the walk from his office to his billet. Then he would read a chapter or two from two or three of the books and type notations on memorandum cards. All this went very easily for him. The thoughts came dreamlike, and he typed as if the mechanics of his wrists and fingers determined the conclusions themselves. As, on the walk, conversation with the Goupins was no hindrance to his private meditation, so part of his mind was detached from the work as he typed. Often the dull, rusty face of Verité Goupin appeared under the little black hammers of the machine. "Pitiful," he thought as he hammered a comma into one of her muddy eyes.

When the dinner bell sounded, he tapped a semicolon and went over to the basin, rinsed his hands, emptied the water into the slop jar, and went downstairs to the dining room.

It was this evening, as Mme. Cassat offered him the usual choice of *fromage à chèvre* or *port salut* at the end of the meal, that the feeling which had often come upon him as he deliberated the choice—the Cassats waiting with ridiculous intensity for his varying answer—became recognizable as the feeling that he was here, now, and for the first time in his life, at home. Before he'd come to France, four months ago in the fall of forty-four, Schreiber's preoccupation had been writing long letters to his wife filled with bitter analyses of the military life and alien manners. Two weeks after he'd been assigned to the village, however, he'd written her that he had time to write only the briefest notes and that she in turn should direct all her letters through the APO to his office. Now, he hardly ever thought of the squat, white house in Rye or his wife, and he could scarcely remember the color of his daughter's hair.

"Do you think the *chèvre* too soft this evening, Captain?" asked Old Cassat.

"Not particularly, monsieur. It seems quite good."

"One doesn't like it too soft, but when it's hard, it dribbles all over the floor. It's really only good in Brittany," said Cassat, as if reproaching his wife for keeping him here in Cher. He sucked the last curds from his gums, his dentures rattling with the effort, and took up a knife to take the skin from a fine Italian pear.

"Yes, I've been there," said Schreiber, staring at the yellow membrane spiraling delicately from the white meat, and thinking of Verité.

3

Tiberius lived with Mme. Verna Zapenskya just above her bakery two blocks from the Hôtel de Ville on the Rue Bulwer-Lytton. It was not his official billet, but there were only seven enlisted men in the village and Captain Schreiber did not worry them with regulations. In return for her favors and domestic provisions, Tiberius gave Mme. Zapenskya the double distinction of living with a noncommissioned officer and a Negro. In addition, her bakery was soon doing a lively trade in American cigarettes, chocolate bars, soap, underwear, and other valuable items from the PX in Bourges.

Mme. Zapenskya and her neighbors dreaded the release of her husband from the PW camp in Germany; as the son of a White Russian officer's *valet de chambre,* he was looked upon as inordinately jealous and vindictive. Numerous offers were available to Tiberius to exchange the comforts of the Rue Bulwer-Lytton for similar but less precarious ones. He had, however, a fondness for Mme. Zapenskya. She had a huge picture of Franklin D. Roosevelt pinned to the wall next to a mezzotint of the Virgin ("The Lady smiles but the American laughs," she said), and Roosevelt was one of Tiberius's personal idols. He persuaded her to add a somewhat smaller picture of another idol, Jack Johnson, and, under this trinity of images, he lived quite happily.

Tiberius had studied French at Bucknell, and, within a month of his arrival in the village, he spoke it better than Captain Schreiber. In this month, he became one of the central forces of the village, a judge of disputes and a counselor of difficulties; he also became Schreiber's most valuable source of information.

One night a week, he drove Schreiber in to headquarters at Bourges, and, on these drives, he gave him reports on the village.

Tonight, the most important news was Fougère's decision to close the tannery.

"What do you mean, 'close it'?" asked Schreiber. "It's been there fifty years. Doesn't he like us?"

"Probably that too, Max. In general, he's just had enough. In his pockets and of this place. He's going down to his daughter's in the Midi. 'No coal thieves there,' he says." Tiberius drove carefully over the bridge. "I guess you'll have to get that Goupin girl a job in the office."

"What about the others? There're five or six of them."

"They'll find something. Verna needs somebody. Metayer too. They'll find something."

"I'd like to take the girl in. She's a little slow but very nice. The old man invited me over tonight."

"She had a little German beau last year. A corporal, except corporal's a little higher with them." He stretched his arm under Schreiber's fat jaw, so close to it that the stripes on his sleeve looked like scars on Schreiber's neck. "There's the cathedral."

"We've seen it," said Schreiber, looking.

"They've got a lot of thirteenth-century glass stored away. You ought to put in a request to get it back in."

"I suppose it could still be shelled."

"Things are pretty well wound up, Max."

The major at headquarters worked at night, and he always

tried to keep Schreiber for drinks. Schreiber never accepted, but the major managed to delay him at least an hour with fatuous questions and quibbles. Schreiber was always worn out after the sessions, and he and Tiberius usually went to a bar outside of town for some Cinzano or Pernod to pick them up.

"They're starting to let the GIs out," said Tiberius when Schreiber got back to the jeep. "I drove over to the place, and they're swarming over it. MPs all over too. Guess we'd better go home."

"He murdered me tonight," said Schreiber. "I could really use one," but they drove back.

In front of his billet, Schreiber said, "She'll have to learn English, you know."

"That's not much of a problem. She's probably had it in school. Maybe you could help her a little."

"We'll see," said Schreiber. "She's a pretty decent girl."

The Goupins were talking with the Cassats in the living room when he came in. Verité was in the corner, head bent over a book.

"Have you heard what's happened, Captain?" asked Mme. Cassat, calling to him from the door.

"Fougère closes the tannery in three weeks, and Verité has no job. Like that," she cried, clapping her hands together sharply.

"These things happen, madame," said Schreiber, "and they are always difficult—but it so happens that I may be able to help. If mademoiselle would consider working with us, we've been needing someone for a long time. It's only a question of knowing a little English . . ."

"English!" cried Mme. Cassat. "Wonderful! She's studied it for years, haven't you, my dear?"

"That's very kind indeed, Captain," said Goupin. "Very kind."

"I could never speak it," said Verité.

"Nonsense!" cried Mme. Cassat. "Why it's quite simple. I re-member it myself, and it's forty years since I've said a word," and she said quickly, in English, "Good morning. Goodbye. What hour is it? Jolly good."

"I've never heard you speak English, Germaine," said Old Cassat. "It sounds elegant, doesn't it, Captain?"

"Indeed, monsieur. Mademoiselle shall learn it almost as well if she cares to try. I should be happy to spend some time helping her myself."

This statement produced some seconds' silence.

"That would be very generous, Captain," said Mme. Cassat softly.

"You will find me a difficult student, Captain," said Verité, looking up from her book.

"You learned German fairly well," said her father evenly, and there was another wordless interval.

"We can begin tomorrow evening, mademoiselle. In three weeks we should be able to do a good deal." Schreiber bowed slightly and said, "Good evening."

"We shall see," said Verité, and stared at Schreiber's back moving down the hall.

4

Schreiber told Verité that the north side of the river lay in an exposed position within two kilometers of the freight yards and that they would do better to hold their lessons on the south side.

"Of course, he doesn't mind our being blown up before or after the lessons," thought Verité, but, nevertheless, twice a week she walked with him across the bridge below her house and a mile up the river to a clearing in a beech grove. Here they had the lesson.

Goupin went down to his sister's after they left, and he could see them walking on the bridge, his daughter, a few steps in back of Schreiber, stooping till she was just his height. They didn't look at each other.

"I hope he will be as cautious as the German," said Goupin to his sister.

"This type always is, Axel. Anyway, more can come from it. Willy was nice, but he could bring only trouble."

"I suppose nothing much can happen to her," said Goupin.

"Only better. She will have a job, it will give her some amusement and," he laughed here, "she will learn American."

They stopped talking when Old Cassat came into the garden to talk about prices.

Despite forebodings about her adequacy, Verité learned English very rapidly. Schreiber was industrious and patient. After they left the house, he would ask her the vocabulary he'd assigned at the end of the preceding lesson. When they reached the grove, he corrected, in the last of the daylight, the sentences she had written out. The last hour and a half was devoted to conversation. Here Verité was brilliant. With a limited vocabulary, she could say, after the first lessons, almost anything she wished. She was in a sense more fluent in English than in French; it was as if the feeling of exposure which hindered her in ordinary conversation disappeared in the foreign idiom. Although most of their talk concerned natural objects or typical situations, Verité managed to infuse her talk with more of her own feelings than she had ever before put into words.

"You amaze me, mademoiselle," said Schreiber as they crossed back after the fourth lesson.

Verité, to whom the word "amaze" was new, fathomed its meaning and made it her own.

"It's very fine to amaze someone, Captain. One considered me amazing only for being so not-amazing. I am very disappointing to Poppa." She said *"trompante"* for "disappointing."

"We are nearly always disappointing to our parents," said Schreiber, hesitating over "disappointing" to let her learn it. "And they to us."

"Sometimes," she said.

Goupin, walking up the road, noticed they walked almost flank to flank now, and it amused him. He waited for them at the bridge and called in English, "Have you learned much this evening?"

"It comes slowly, Poppa," Verité answered in French.

"Your daughter is modest, Goupin. It goes very well."

"I'm glad. Come refresh yourself now after your labors, Captain. We have not opened the Calvados yet."

"Delighted," said Schreiber.

At Goupin's, Schreiber mentioned that his work was decreasing at the office and, since the weather was so nice, that they might hold their lessons more frequently.

"You take too much trouble, Captain," she said.

"An extraordinary kindness, Captain," said Goupin.

"It is you who do me the kindness, mademoiselle," said

Schreiber. The Calvados had warmed and exalted him, and, after he had said this, he wondered if it had sounded awkward. Later, walking home, he decided that it had, but that Verité had understood it even beyond its intention and had not disapproved.

5

"What was it like?" asked Schreiber when he met Verité at the bridge the evening the tannery closed.

"Sad," she said. "I'd nearly forgotten it was going to end. Fougère called us in at four and told us we could go home an hour early. He said he supposed he would never see us again. We cried."

"Europeans have very strong sentiments," said Schreiber.

They walked across the bridge, and, on the other side, Schreiber touched her arm.

"I ask myself sometimes if your wife is sad at home," she said.

He dropped his hand and said, "I don't know. I hear so little. She has much to occupy her time, but she may be sad."

"Americans have not such strong sentiments," she said.

"Some," said Schreiber.

"You are here," she said, "and are one of us here."

They walked to the grove and sat down. There were no longer any sentences to correct.

"The permission to hire you came from Bourges today. A week or two and the money will be—we say, 'allocated.' "

"I understand," she said. "I will enjoy working in your office."

"You'll really be in Tiberius's office, but I come in there often." She looked expectant, and he added, "The work is not difficult."

"Is it interesting?" she asked.

"You file—*classez*—letters. If you read them, it's interesting." She smiled at him.

"Will it go on much longer, do you think?" she asked. They both understood "the war" for "it."

"I don't think so. Perhaps."

They both thought of the war being over, and what would happen.

"It could go on a long time," she said. "The Germans are soft alone but very hard together. It could last for years."

Schreiber said he didn't think so.

6

Two days before the war actually ended, the report was broadcast that an armistice had been signed. Verité was in the office at the Hôtel de Ville—she had worked there almost two weeks —when Tiberius ran in with the news. Verité ran up to Schreiber's office, but he wasn't in. Then, like everyone else in the building, she ran outside.

The streets were filling. Over the village, people ran into each other's houses to announce that the end had come. The bars and cafés and the square in front of the church were filled with people. The priest rang the bells, and the people in the fields, hearing, started coming into town.

Tiberius was in the jeep shouting and singing. Eight people piled in with him, and they passed around bottles of red wine and American whiskey. They kissed each other, men and women, and waved to people in the streets.

Verité started running home. Halfway there she met the Cassats on the way to town.

"What's happened? Is it all over?" called her aunt.

"Yes, it's all over. The war is over."

"We must go to church," said Old Cassat.

"Yes, Poppa. You're coming too, Verité?" but her niece was running up the path.

"She should come," said Old Cassat.

Nobody was home. Verité waited.

In an hour Schreiber came. He had run most of the way from town, and he was gasping and sweating.

"Come," he said.

She took his hand, and they walked quickly to the bridge and over to the other side. They said nothing. In the shade of the trees, they slowed down. When they came to the clearing, they stretched out on the ground and held each other.

They were there about ten minutes when they heard a terrible noise far down the road on the other side of the river. They sat up and stared, and soon they distinguished the rasping horn of the jeep and Tiberius and the others shouting. They watched the jeep drive wildly over the bridge and turn up the path which led to the clearing. They stood up quickly and brushed off their clothes.

"Come on, Max," yelled Tiberius. "Climb aboard. Let the lessons go tonight."

Schreiber said nothing. He walked over to the jeep and pointed toward town. Someone spilled wine on his jacket. "Get back, Corporal," he said. "Get back on the double."

Tiberius looked at him. "Christ, Schreiber, it's all over," he said slowly. He spun the jeep around and drove back. The horn began sounding halfway down the path. They could hear it for two or three minutes.

They had sat down again, but now he started to get up. She touched his arm, but he shook his head, brushed off his clothes, and held out his hands to help her up. She took them, and he pulled her up and held her hands till they stopped trembling.

"Later, my dear," he said. "They might come back tonight."

7

People were not overly disappointed that the armistice report turned out to be false because the announcement of it was coupled with an assurance that the real end was imminent. The day after, the bells and cannon were heard from Bourges. In the village there was no celebration. People nodded to each other as if to say, "Well, there it is," and that was all. Those who had celebrated too wildly before kept inside as much as possible.

That night Schreiber met Verité at the bridge as usual, but this time they walked down instead of up the river. They walked for three-quarters of an hour before they found a place where they could be comfortable.

They talked little, in French, about what would happen. Mostly they waited for it to get dark.

They met every night for almost two weeks, staying out till three or four in the morning.

On the twelfth evening, Verité was at the bridge listening for the footsteps. When she heard the steps which were not Schreiber's, she said, "Now it's over."

It was Mme. Cassat. "He said you'd be here," she said. "He

gave me this for you." She took an envelope from her sleeve and handed it to Verité. It was one from his office and stamped with the legend, "Passed By Censor." "He came back for an hour to pack his clothes and papers. The black one calls for them tomorrow, but he left tonight. He gave me the letter and told me to give it to you, that you'd be here."

Verité was reading the letter. Mme. Cassat turned away. "These things happen," she muttered, smoothing her sleeves. She was rehearsing what she would say.

The note was in English: "They called me today, and I'm going to Germany. I'll be on my way as you read this. I'll get a leave (*congé*) before long. You know what I think about everything. We shall arrange things." It was initialed, "M." She had never called him Max, didn't even know it was his name till she heard Tiberius use it. It was this that made her cry.

Mme. Cassat turned around and held out her arms. "These things happen, my dear."

8

Schreiber was assigned to Mainz. He drove there in the front seat of an army truck; twenty enlisted men were packed into the back. They arrived at night and cruised around the center of the city looking for a building they could requisition to sleep in. There was almost nothing standing. Only the cathedral. Here and there smoke rose and water flowed in the streets. Nobody was awake. They saw a few people rolled up on the grass, and, down by the river, there were hundreds more. Women, children, old men, and cripples. Across the Rhine, they could see American barracks. Two bridges stretched halfway across it; they looked like broken fingers.

They went to sleep on the banks.

The disorder upset Schreiber. He tried to think of Verité, hoping her image would compose him to sleep. Instead, he could see only piles and piles of white cards toppling over on hundreds of desks. The vision made him feel sick, and he went down to the river. He threw up in the water, and then he washed off his face. He got up and saw that an old woman had been watching him. "I was sick," he called to her in French. She looked him over and said something in German. He nodded, smiling to her, and then suddenly he felt much better, and he thought how good it was that the war was over.

The next day, they began working, setting up headquarters, contacting troops, registering the populace, establishing market lines. Schreiber worked harder than he had ever worked in his life. He went to bed every evening as soon as he was off duty. Only when the French command took over the town did he have leisure, and then he allowed himself to think about Verité.

He wrote to her, putting the letter sealed into an envelope addressed to Tiberius. In a week he wrote another. His first letter was returned, stamped, to his amazement, "Absent Without Leave. Returned By Censor." Then he wrote directly to her. There was no answer. He wrote again saying that he would be returned to the States in less than six months.

It was nearly two months now since he had seen her or heard from or about her. Mystery revived and sharpened his passion. He began to think of her all day long. He considered taking his discharge in Europe, of never going back to the States, or only after the affair had run the course these affairs must run.

Finally, he requested a week's leave and got it. He waited two days for a ride to Strasbourg and there three days for one to Dijon. He was already a day late when he started for Bourges. In Bourges, for eight cigarettes, he hired a taxi to drive him to the village. It was seven in the evening when he saw the Hôtel de Ville. He told the driver to wait there and in an hour to drive up the road to Goupin's. He gave him another cigarette and fifty francs.

When he saw the bridge, he started trembling so much he had to stop. He sat down under a beech tree and gripped the bark. He held it so tightly his arms numbed to the elbow. Then he got up and ran to Goupin's. There were no lights in the house. He opened the door and shouted, "Hey." There was no one there, but he shouted twice more. He switched on the light and the first thing he saw was a great heap of books piled up in the corner. He went over and looked at them a second, then kicked at the middle of the pile. The books tumbled against the wall. Six or seven of them remained stacked; he picked up the top one, put it to his lips, then dropped it.

He ran out of the house down the road to the Cassats'.

They were sitting with Goupin in the garden. Mme. Cassat was frightened at the running and called, "Who's there?"

"It's Schreiber," he called, and he ran to her at the edge of the courtyard. He saw Goupin sitting with Cassat in the garden. "Goupin, where's Verité?"

"Come," said Mme. Cassat, and she took him by the sleeve to where the two men sat.

He started to say, "What's wrong?" but he couldn't summon the French for it.

Old Cassat said, "Mlle. Verité is gone, Captain, gone off."

"With the black one," said his wife. "No one knows where. Nearly two months."

Schreiber looked at them all and turned away. At the gate, he said in English, "A taxi is waiting for me."

He walked down the side path to the river. He didn't dare look at the bridge.

The taxi would be coming soon, he thought. He wondered if he should wait for it in the bushes, then slip under the tires. "I'm thinking of suicide," he thought. "Over love." In his pain, he was almost proud. He said, *Un peu ridicule.*

He wondered how deep the river was off the banks. "Not enough," he thought. He started to cry thinking of her, but also because he couldn't do anything to himself.

At the road, he sat under a tree to wait for the taxi. The ground was wet; his legs were cold. It seemed incredible to him that he was here. When the taxi drove up, he climbed in and said, "Back to Bourges." About halfway there he started to cry. He cried all the way back to the city, not caring what the driver thought nor about anything at all.

La Pourriture Noble

CHRISTMAS EVE, Chicago was dressed in its climate of martyrdom, deep freeze. Thirty-five years ago, Mottram's internal navigator had brought him to this gelid foreskin of phallic Lake Michigan. Every winter since, he'd cursed the choice. A man's defined by his errors. Mottram came to Chicago with the worst of his, Adelaide Haggerty. He'd not only picked the wrong place but the wrong companion. (He'd shed the companion.)

This Christmas, Chicago felt right to him. It was the right place, and freeze was the right climate for his solitude. Solitude, more, the sense that he'd been abandoned, was, in a way, his present to himself. He and Adelaide—ten years after their divorce they were friends—had waved their daughter Deirdre into the Alitalia flight to Milan. Junior year abroad. The first Christmas in twenty years without her. All in all, a relief. He need go through none of the Christmas hoops. Mottram's father was an Anglican clergyman. For him, Christmas was the hardest day of the year. Even atheist and skeptic parishioners often let nostalgia bring them to the Christmas service. "They come to recharge their contempt," he said. His Christmas sermon was a frightful weight, especially—Mottram learned this when he read his father's diary—as old Mottram was a hive of doubt: self-doubt, religious doubt, polymorphous sexual doubt. Some of this young Derek had sensed. At Christmas, it settled into the rectory; it was in the holly and the mistletoe, the Christmas goose, the wrapped books, socks, gloves, and sweaters the three Mottrams exchanged before Father carted off his sermon to St. George's.

Self-doubt was a Mottram trait. That and hatred for its generator, the Infernal English Class Machine (scoring off the skin of inferior, degraded Englishmen). More than anything else, it sent Mottram to America. It didn't matter that Mottrams weren't near the bottom of the pyramid: clergymen and successful tradesmen could snub as well as be snubbed. Three generations had gone to Oxford, they were certainly not bottom-drawer, but this didn't mean insulation from jokes, looks, ironies, exclusions, and, worse, implied, required inclusions. After Oxford, Mottram was apprenticed to a cousin's wine firm. He spent a year in Bordeaux—where an even creakier Machine ground out points—then grabbed the chance to come to America with the firm. Whom should he meet his third month in New York but one of the relatively few American girls savaged by the Machine.

Daughter of a chauffeur to one of the First Irish Families, Adelaide Haggerty grew up feeling invisible to those she'd been taught to believe were everything. Pretty, she felt ugly, smart, she felt stupid. Timid, sex-starved, stuttering Mottram made her feel beautiful and wise. If he stuttered, it was in Oxbridge English. That signaled social superiority to the Southampton chauffeur's daughter. She fell for his phonemes, he for her falling for them. Two months after they'd met at a New York matinee, he was offered a job in Chicago with Sellinbon Wine Imports.

Driving back alone to the Southside—he'd refused a dinner invitation from Adelaide and her husband—Mottram prepared for solitude. At Mr. G's he bought lamb chops, grapefruit, Häagen-Dazs, and Constant Comment; at the Chalet a slab of Brie and two bottles of Bushmills Irish; at O'Gara's a sackful of paperback novels. Martyrdom did not include starvation or mental blank.

Christmas Eve. Three-thirty. In his snug bay window, Mottram sat with the first whiskey of the evening. His apartment was the second—top—floor of Harvey Wallop's hundred-year-old brown-shingle cottage. Pinewood Court's two- and three-story bungalows had been put up for workers who'd built the Columbian Exposition buildings in the 1890s. Like Harvey's, some had been modernized or enlarged, others were molecules away from collapse. Harvey, a contractor, had modernized, renewed, remodernized and renewed every inch of his place. The floor gleamed, the ceilings were freshly painted, the porch was solid, the heat and plumbing superb. Mottram was Wallop's ideal tenant: no wife, no young children, few visitors, and a polite sufferer of alterations and repairs. The rent was low, the living easy.

Mottram watched night fall into the street. Lamps shaped like guillotines exposed cruel lumps of ice; now and then shadowy, thuglike nonthugs passed by, homeward, wayward. Some were leashed to dogs, some carried Christmas trees or sacks of packages. Here and there, tapered bulbs were strung on trees and wreaths; but mostly, on Pinewood Court, Christmas was invisible. Which suited Mottram. When the doorbell rang, it was as shocking as a fire alarm. (He hadn't seen anyone coming up the street.) There was no speaker system—Harvey mistrusted them.

Mottram kept the brass chain linked in its slot and opened the door. It was a tall, bearded man in a knee-length black overcoat. He carried a blue denim laundry bag.

"Yes? What can I—?"

"Derek. It's me."

Mottram looked closely and recognized him. "So it is," he said. "Denis. What in—? Come in."

"I walked from the Greyhound Station."

It would not have surprised Mottram if he'd walked from West Virginia. "That was intrepid of you, Denis. I couldn't imagine who it was. Santa Claus skips this house. I'm glad," he lied, "to see you. Give me your coat." He took the denim bag, then pointed to the coat till Denis got the idea, removed and handed it to him. It weighed a ton. He hoisted it over the brass knob and led Denis up the carpeted stairs. Denis had wiped his feet on the doormat. "You remember the way. What a surprise. What would you have done if I hadn't been here?"

"Waited for you."

Of course. Denis would have waited a month. The coat was probably full of peanut butter and Fig Newtons. "Well, we'll celebrate, tea for you, booze for me. Herbal, right? There's probably some left over from last time. It's what? Four years? Maybe there are some Fig Newtons. Petrified by now. We'll see. We'll scrape something together."

In the living room, Denis plonked himself in the red leather armchair in which he'd spent most of his last visit. "What's that?" he asked. *That* was Mottram's newest acquisition, a five-foot-high ficus tree in a lacquered rattan basket. "It wasn't here last time."

"It came a week ago. From Deirdre. She said she wanted something alive around here."

"Trees should be left outside," said Denis.

"I hope you don't mind if it stays inside."

Denis regarded its thin braided trunks and emerald leaves. "It belongs outside." But there were other enemies in Mottram's apartment. Indeed, he sat where he did to avoid seeing the painting over his head. It was Mottram's prize, a de Kooning–like swirl of rose and violet, in which lay a spread-eagled nude woman. Mottram had paid more for it than he'd ever paid for anything. "How is little Deirdre?"

"Not so little."

"She's a dear little girl."

Denis did not register much contradiction. "Where have you come from this time, Denis?"

"Missouri. The Lotus Foot Ashram. Outside Kirksville."

"Things didn't go well?"

"Things went very well. A fine place. Could've stayed a long time. No desire to leave. Had to. Not sure why. They gave me a bus ticket. Yesterday. Pulled me down."

"Pulled you?"

"I'd climbed up. A gazebo. Gold weather vane. Held on to it. They got a ladder. Took me off. The bird came too. Bad business. Nothing to do. I took the ticket. They knew I had friends in Chicago."

"Friends? Oh, yes. Of course." On a planet of five billion, somehow he, Mottram, had the privilege of being *the friends* of this pathetic gilk.

It was the third time in seven years Denis Sellinbon had come to him. The last time he'd stayed almost a week, the first time nearly as long. That first time, Denis's father had warned him Denis was coming. Walter called from L.A., where he and Eileen had moved after selling the business. "Denis is loose, Derek. I'd told him—I hope you'll forgive me—that in an emergency he could go to you. I'm afraid he might show up. He was with some Arkansas swami. If you could possibly take him in for a day or two, I'd be very grateful. Or just get him to a hotel. If he has no money—he usually has some—advance him a few bucks. I'm sorry as hell about this, Derek. I wish—"

Eileen's trombone snort filled the earpiece. "He's no trouble, Der. A good boy. Basically. You know that. Different, maybe. A stubborn bugger, but he doesn't need much. Place to sleep, the floor's perfect. He's used to floors. He eats anything, stale rolls, beans, whatever, it'll be better than what those monks give him. And he's a world-class faster. Let him clean up the place for you. If I know you, it needs it. He's good with brooms. Just watch out for lice in that beard. Get him to shave it. We're off to Tucson for a few days. If you have a problem, put him on a bus. He'll be fine. Look, he may not even show up."

Of course, he showed up. Eileen had told him to. Mottram got that from Denis. Denis had asked her if he could come back home, told her he wouldn't be any trouble. No, she'd said, no way, Dad's heart was on the fritz, Dad couldn't take any excitement. "I won't make any excitement." "You *are* excitement. You go to Derek Mottram. He owes your father everything." That's how Denis reported it. Whatever else he was, he was no liar.

Which, considering his life, as Mottram did, was odd. How could a child of Eileen Sellinbon not become a liar? But instead of small, constant lies, Denis constructed a labyrinth of which only he was Ariadne.

For years, he'd been able to live in two worlds. The Sellinbons sent him to a Montessori school. At age ten, he'd brained a girl with a block and had to leave. From then on, he always had to leave.

Eileen wouldn't hear of a shrink; Boylans and Sellinbons didn't go to medicine men. For loose screws, there were seminaries and monasteries. Priests existed to mop up spilled milk. Walter—the freethinker—had made a mistake not sending the kid to the nuns from the beginning.

In his first Chicago years, Mottram had known the Sellinbon household well. Walter did a lot of business at home, gave tastings and dinners for customers, salesmen, vintners, advertisers. Those first years, Eileen was under wraps. Even when she showed her crude stuff, Walter's kindness and courtesy compensated for it. But why had he ever taken up with her? Was his inner navigator as punch-drunk as Derek's or Denis's?

Like Adelaide, Eileen had been a sort of beauty. A big woman, but, in those days, both slim and voluptuous. Her hair was the brilliant red of danger signals, her eyes were ice-blue. In those days, her mouth didn't look like hell's gate. The thing was she didn't talk much in those days, though when she did—just saying hello, taking your hand, and welcoming you—you sensed her discomfort and aggression. Mottram didn't sense her genius for other people's weakness, her hater's need to display it. The first time she set eyes on him, she'd said, "I didn't realize your Englishman'd be such a dumpling, Walter." In time, her vulgarity became a domestic Van Allen belt against which Walter's kindness and gentleness shattered. Denis would have had to have the thrusting power of a rocket to break through unharmed. How terrified he must have been of her voice. Not that Eileen knew she shouted. She didn't even want to talk; it's just that she couldn't bear others talking. She hated other people's ease. (Why should they have what she didn't?) After those first, submerged, apprentice years, her tigerish self emerged. She interrupted, she contradicted, she overruled.

Only Walter escaped her tongue. Walter was the best of men, a wonderful lover, husband, father, a brilliant businessman. Eileen had been raised in a household of female deference. That part of her which didn't imitate maleness still deferred to it. So when the wine men—they were all men in these years—came to the house, Eileen buckled herself into her notion of femininity. That she had no taste for dress, makeup, charm, decoration, cuisine, or—Derek guessed—amorousness did not seem to bother Walter. That his Eileen tried so hard, that she went against what he must have known was her grain moved him. Only when she brought out what had been fermenting beneath did he realize that the business was imperiled by it. Her terrible voice blasted the old give-and-take of vinous dinners. The acme of her ruinous interference came the night a representative of Château Mouton-Rothschild, Alexandre de Bonville, came to the house. It was the night before the signing of their first contract with Sellinbon Imports. An arrangement with the firm of Philippe de Rothschild was very important to Walter. Perhaps it was this which roused Eileen. "I prepared for weeks," she said after. "Read my eyes out. I had Baron Philippe down cold, knew everything about him." No sooner was Bonville in his chair than she let go: "In this house, Alex, your boss is God. *Preemyay nay poos, second jay dikne, Mouton soos*." This was her version of the famous motto, *"Premier ne puis, Second je daigne. Mouton suis"*—"I can't be first, I scorn being second. I am *Mouton.*" Hearing it in her special brass, Bonville reeled, which was but prelude to her recitation of the rise of Mouton, its rejection by the Bordeaux vintners as a *premier cru* "after Phil took over," its acceptance in 1973. She went on to the annual labels, the change of name after "Paulette died, what a gesture," the rivalry with "your cousin's brew. You Jew boys know quality, just like us Sellinbons." Bonville was about as Jewish as the Pope, but shriveled in his chair as if he'd been an eight-year-old *shtetl* boy before a storm trooper. A red trumpet of flesh, Eileen ended with, "That's why we love doing business with you boys. Now, let's put on the nose bag."

They did not put on the nose bag. Bonville excused himself, and, after five minutes in the bathroom, emerged with regret: jet lag had caught up with him and was advancing a flu with which he did not dare endanger them.

The contract was never signed, and, from that night on, Sellinbon Imports began to sink. Walter, awake at last to his domestic swamp, began shifting all entertainment to the office. Too late. Three years later, Walter sold out most of the business to Félicien Trancart and moved to Los Angeles. Mottram turned

345

down Félicien's offer to handle Italian, Spanish, and Portuguese wines and retired on his share of the sale and the small means of his father's estate.

The day after Walter and Eileen had called, seven years ago, Denis had shown up. Gentle, polite, he asked little. Much of the next days he spent calling lamaseries, monasteries, ashrams. It was astonishing that there were so many, you'd have thought the Midwest was Tibet. (The month's phone bill suggested a hot line to Lhasa.) The rest of the day, Denis sat immobile in the red armchair looking into space. Two or three times, he went off to St. Thomas's for mass. The fifth day, after an epic call, he told Mottram he'd be off, he'd found a halfway house for alcoholic ex-clergymen in Ashtabula. Mottram walked him to the IC—the Fifty-Ninth Street Station, as Denis refused to believe there was one on Fifty-Sixth. When he got back to the apartment, he found Denis's present, a book of poems and essays by modern Russian poets. Who else in his life would have found, let alone given him such a book? It was inscribed, "For Derek, who, beneath his shroud, is pure. From Denis. See Page 74." On that page, Denis had underlined sentences of an essay by one Khleb-nikov.

> The word can be divided into the pure word and the every-day word. One can think of the word concealing in itself both the reason of the starlit night and the reason of the sunlit day.

This time, Denis had brought a present with him. "I painted a picture for you."

"How kind of you Denis. I didn't know you painted."

"I paint well. It's to replace—" and he tilted his head to indicate the painting over his head. "I don't think you want little Deirdre exposed to such a scene. And you may have other young visitors."

"Little Deirdre isn't little, Denis. She's twenty, and off on her own. To Europe." Almost adding that she might be revealing herself to some Italian contemporary in just the manner of the offensive painting.

Denis had removed from his denim bag a wrinkled square of paper which he unfolded, then shook out like a wet towel. He took it by the corners and held it up. "The wrinkles will iron out. But you can see, can't you?" What Mottram saw was a mess of tepid color, silvery blue with some reddish sticks leaning this way and that. There were also some grayish oblongs against what in a realistic painting might be a stormy sky. "I see you like it. I painted it last week, thinking of you here. Of course, it's abstract. I take Exodus 20 seriously."

"Exodus 20?"

" 'Thou shalt not make graven images, or any likeness of any thing in heaven above, or the earth beneath, or the water under the earth.' I believe one is permitted to suggest. Do you see Rockefeller Chapel, the ice skaters on the Midway? I knew it would please you, and I've used the colors of your rug. It's the size of—this thing." He held the watercolor above the splayed nude. "I see I misjudged it a few inches each way, otherwise we could just slip it under the frame. We'll have to tape it now. Have you got Scotch tape?"

There was no point in fury, but Derek was suddenly furious. The colossal nerve of this intruding nut. How dare he? His mother's son. Still, he managed to say, "I paid more money for that than I've ever paid for any thing, Denis. And I've been offered five times the amount I paid. I have an art historian friend who thinks it's a masterpiece. Deirdre appreciates it. It has pictorial value. I'm afraid if we subscribed to Exodus 20, there'd be no artistic culture anywhere in the world outside of Isfahan and Damascus. It is not something out of *Hustler* magazine. Not that I'm ungrateful for your painting. It's very pretty. I don't have room for it here, but I'll find a place for it. I'm grateful to you for thinking of me."

"If you had Scotch tape, I'd show you how nice it looks here. I remembered the colors of the chair and the rug. You see how I've used them, red and pink. Give yourself a chance. You'll learn to like them much more than . . . ." Voice trembling as the demonstrative pronoun died in his throat.

When Mottram got up for his six o'clock pee, he saw down the hall Denis's immobile profile by the emerald bush of the ficus leaves. He wore the black sweater, pants, and shoes in which, last night, he'd gone to his room. Perhaps he'd slept in them. Or did he sleep? "Sharks," thought Mottram, "don't." Instead of standing up, Mottram sat down on the oak toilet seat. What was he going to do with him?

One thing he was not going to do was spend Christmas watching Denis watch, or not watch him. He had an invitation he'd planned to ignore, had even mentioned it to Denis last night. His "out." "Félicien and Valerie Trancart's. He used to work for your father."

"Blond moustache, brown eyes, three cheek moles. Like Orion."

"Amazing, Denis. You can't have been more than ten when he left the business." Was there a smile-flick on Denis's hair-bordered lips? Yes. But were Félicien's eyes brown? Were there moles on his cheek? He'd check that out. "He got your father into those Perigord dessert wines. Montravel, Bergerac, Monbazillac. We put them into Chez Drouet, Maxim's, the Ambassador East. Cincinnati, St. Louis. We had a good order from New Orleans, the Commodore Palace. Monbazillac alone did half a million dollars for us. Then Félicien tried making it himself, got some Semillon and Muscadet cuttings and planted them into an Ozark hill. They never grew the right mold. *La pourriture noble,* they call it, the noble rot. That was a few years before your dad threw in the towel. Félicien took over half the business. He asked me to work for him."

"Why didn't you?"

Mottram was surprised. Denis was actually curious about him. It was as if the wall had said Good Morning. "Fatigue. Sloth. *La pourriture ignoble.* My father left me a little money. I'd put it in the market, done all right. And I had the share of Sellinbon your dear dad gave me. I thought I could just make it, and I have. Biggest expense is Deirdre, and that won't be for long."

"Little Deirdre," said Denis.

Eileen's call came as he was serving Denis a poached egg and an English muffin. Nine o'clock, seven A.M. in Westwood, she must have been prowling the floor all night after Denis's call. "Merry C., Derek. I hear Santa arrived. In the St. Nick of time. You boys having a nice time? Did he bring you a present?

Besides himself." And sotto voce, "Selfish little bastard." In normal roar, "A relief I got him settled. I take off tomorrow."

"I'm not sure what you mean by 'settled.' "

"We don't want him riding the rails on Christmas, do we? By
the way, you can take him to Félicien's today. I called."

"What?"

"Valerie, that little rat, began some French nonsense, I cut
her off at the pass, reminded her what her little hubby owed the
Sellinbons, so you boys won't have to be alone with each other."

"Very thoughtful of you. Where are you off to?"

"Paradise. Want to come? Tahiti, Moa-Moa, Samoa, Go-
Blowa. Six weeks in a white boat with, please God, rich, rich
white men. If I come back with the same monicker, I'll have
blown thousands. Two weeks on the fat farm, a suction job on
the boobs, I was stepping on them. You should see me now."
Mottram shut his eyes. "Young tourist at the Brentwood market
asked me if I used to be Kim Novak."

"Were you?"

"Too bad you're such a poor rat, Derek. Well, give that thief
Félicien my love. He must be rich as the Pope, I'm surprised he
wasn't on the *Forbes* list." So, thought Mottram, she's scouting
the world's four hundred richest; she's as deluded as her son.

"It's Mother?" said Denis.

"Right. Off on a cruise."

"Off," said Denis. "Always off."

That afternoon, the two of them walked a slippery half-mile to
the Trancarts' Kenwood mansion. Mottram had given Denis a
blue tie, otherwise he remained the arrow of death.

At Trancart's, a mob, neighbors and friends of the parents and
three children. There were log fires, holly and mistletoe; champagne, punch and Glühwein passed round on silver trays; hams,
roast beefs, cakes and cookies on the huge dining room table.
Denis faded into a curtained nook where he sat in a golden
armchair; his black-sweatered arms hung down its golden
flanks; the bearded head was tilted, as if receiving messages.

Every fifteen minutes, Mottram checked up on him. People
seemed to nod or talk at him, he seemed to respond, but
blankly. He was not a social creature. The space around him

grew as if people had discovered he was a George Segal figure of flesh-like material. Mottram felt a twinge of something. "But why? Let the bastard sink."

Mottram spotted a bottle of Monbazillac you couldn't get outside of Perigord and made it his own. He drank glass after wonderful glass. This was Paradise. Pretty women with red cheeks floated in the room on Bach cantatas. Faces, dresses, silver, mirrors, chandeliers, chairs, curtains, couches, the odors of good food, what a fine party. Mottram talked to a wine salesman, an obstetrician, a pretty professor of chemistry, the wife of a football player. The martyrdom of solitude leaked away. "Thank you, Eileen," he thought. "May you find your match in the South Seas, maybe a nice killer shark."

A woman's terrible scream speared through the jolly haze, followed by silence, as if the whole house had been hit in the stomach. Then another scream, and shouts, laughs. Mottram knew; he could not budge. "Get'm down," he heard. "Right now." The *r* of "right" was French, the voice, Valerie Trancart's. Mottram took four deep breaths, then managed to walk through people toward the curtained alcove.

There was Denis, beyond Mrs. Trancart's outstretched arm, high up the curtain, bearded head touching the ceiling, arms and legs gripping the golden curtain. Men had moved chairs and were now reaching for his legs, but he kicked them off. He was implored, tempted. There was also laughter, hearty and nervous. Everyone found some way to deal with what you were not supposed to deal with Christmas—or any other day—in Kenwood mansions. "Der-reek," called Valerie Trancart. "*Où es-tu? Viens vite. Mon Dieu. Le fou est en train de détruire la maison.*"

He was at her side. "Denis, it's Derek. Would you mind coming down, old boy? We've had our joke now. Very good. But we'd better get home. I'm tired." For a moment, he thought Denis responded to him, but if so, his was just one voice among spectral others. "Maybe we'd better get the firemen. Or an ambulance. We'll take him to Billings. Or maybe—do you have a ladder?"

He'd been anticipated. Félicien and a houseboy carried one in and propped it up, a yard from Denis. Félicien pointed to the houseboy and gestured toward the ladder. The boy shook his head. As for Félicien, he had the physique of a cauliflower; even if he could get up, what would he do? People looked around. Where was the football player? Not here. Mottram felt the heat of attention.

"Hold it steady for me," he said to Félicien, who held one strut while the houseboy held the other. Mottram, breathing hard, went up one, two, four, five rungs, till his bald head was within two feet of Denis's beard. "Denis," he said quietly. "Look at me, old fellow." And Denis, eyes enormous with fear, did look, and seemed to see. "Could you manage to slide down, old boy? Then we'll just go home. We'll walk back to the house. Could you please do this?"

For a moment, comprehension and agreement seemed to be in Denis's face, then this small social contract ruptured, and he was back in the wild place that had sent him there. Mottram heard a small buzz-saw sound, then saw what it was. Behind Denis's head a rip opened in the gold fabric, and, suddenly, like a terrible laugh, it went. Denis swung like Tarzan on the gold curtain, swiped Mottram, knocked him off the ladder and crashed on top of him.

Three days later, Mottram walked around Promontory Point. He'd been pampering his aches long enough. No breaks, no large bruises. Luck and thick Trancart carpets saved him. And Denis, too, had broken nothing of his own. (He'd had not only luck and thick carpets but Mottram.)

And he'd signed himself into W-3, the psycho ward. "To spare you," he told Mottram. "You'll have a ready-made explanation for them" (*them* being the Trancarts, the party guests, all who couldn't understand the "higher reasoning" behind his behavior).

Mottram had been too furious to listen to the higher reasoning (it had something to do with inner and outer facts), although it seemed that he was one of the few people capable of understanding it. Aching, angry, and humiliated by Denis, exhausted by the ambulance ride and hospital processing—thank God Denis had Blue Cross—Mottram was in no mood for Denis's loony flattery. Wheelchair to wheelchair, they waited for X-rays in the emergency room, and Mottram lectured. "There's no acceptable explanation, Denis. You ruined the Christmas of a hundred people. You ruined five or ten thousand dollars' worth of drapery. You're a troublemaker."

"I am. I have been. I may always be."

"You need help."

"All do."

"*You* need medical help. *You* need to-to-to-" For the first time in years, Mottram stuttered. "Get closer to the world in which you-you-you live."

"I wanted to get out of it. That's what I was doing."

"Up curtains? Through ceilings? Did-did you-you think you w-w-were Santa Claus?"

"I couldn't remember where the door was. People stared, expecting something. Wanted me to leave."

"S-S-so you were s-s-s-supplying a demand? N-N-No. You created one. They didn't want you to go till you d-d-did what-what you did. You harmed people. You harmed property. People will have to pay real m-m-money for the d-d-damage you did. You can't."

Beard against his chest, Denis sank in the wheelchair. A study in contrition. No, thought Mottram, he's not contrite, he's working out loony explanations, I can feel the heat of his concentration. It insulates him.

Denis had ruptured his solitude, forced him into—well, pleasure, and then had made him pay through the nose for it. He couldn't disavow him, he'd brought him. (As the hunchback brings his hump.) "They can hold you forty-eight hours, with or without permission. Sign in yourself, and you can sign out when you're better."

"I know these places," said Denis, quietly. "But I'll sign. You'll have peace of mind."

Home, without Denis, was indeed peace. Beloved solitude. Nothing to supervise, nothing for which he was responsible. Bliss.

The third day of it, he treated himself to the walk up Fifty-Fifth Street to Promontory Point. The sun was brilliant, the air frigid. Ice quilted the tiered boulders of the shore. The lake had carved itself into a zoo of almost-animals. Dazzling, beautiful,

solitary. Occasionally a jogger ran by, huffing smoke. Six miles
north, the black and silver cutlery of the Loop lay on the white
sky.

Mottram was still stiff, but it was the stiffness of years. Age
stiffened the cells as it loosened the moral seams. Bit by bit, it
seduced you into carelessness till you died in a heap of it. Careless. You didn't care. You took care—of yourself. Loosely: it
didn't matter how you looked, what—within limits—you did.
You weren't punctilious, weren't dutiful. Want to change a routine? Change it. The only boss was your body.

Mottram's father had been dutiful to the end, had asked the
right questions, displayed ministerial concern. His collar bound
him to obligation. Essentially, Mottram knew, his father was a
cold man. He'd read his diary. Again and again, the old man
beseeched the god in whom he hadn't believed for decades for
belief, warmth, feeling.

Mottram had, for years now, felt himself turning into his father. First his looks, the baldness, the gray eyes, the pinched
nose, the long cheeks and jowls. Five times, seeing himself in
shop windows, he'd said with surprise, "Dad!"

And now he felt his father's inner chill. (The burden of obligation. Martyrdom.) Coldness had sneaked into him, like ice into
water.

In the mailbox, a post card, from Italy. *Scaffolding over The Last
Supper.* Deirdre. He poured himself a glass of Bushmills and
read in the bay.

> Dear Dad,
> Exhausting flight. Milan freezing. Hotel horrible. Still, I'm
> *here*!! I guess there's no point in going to see this!! The
> Duomo is white. Crazy. Merry Christmas. xoxoxo.
> Signorina D.
> ta figlia

The girl who owned his father's eyes, her mother's hair, and
his two thousand dollars, the person who'd inherit his couch and
carpet, armchairs, kettle, paintings, every material thing including what she'd have to see into the earth.

Light from the street lamps slashed Pinewood Court. Four-thirty, the dark was holding off. The doorbell rang. Startling. What the hell? Down the stairs—legs aching, calling through the door, "Who is it?"

"It's me, Derek. Denis."

"Go 'way. You can't come here. You've given me trouble enough for a lifetime. I don't want to see you again." This is what Mottram wanted to say, came close to saying. Instead, he opened the door, shook Denis's hand, took his coat, hung it on the brass knob, and led him upstairs.

And here he watched him: slumped in the red chair by the fizzy green crown of ficus leaves, almost hammerlocked in the legs of the rose and violet nude, Denis dunked Triscuits in peppermint tea and recited, quietly, his "escape from the medicine men of W-3."

For all the blips in his genetic matter, Denis was as intrepid as Caesar. He'd pulled wool over a battery of psychiatrists, told them he wasn't used to alcohol, had had too much to drink, and then, before he'd known what he was doing, had pretended to be Tarzan to impress a pretty girl. He actually had been sliding down when the curtain ripped off its rings. Many people there had been amused by him, but not he—virtuous, sensible Denis —he was embarrassed and ashamed. Félicien had been his father's friend and employee, he'd never in the world have done anything to harm him. And he would pay for the damage he'd caused, if it meant sending the Trancarts fifty dollars a month for the rest of his life. (Slipping soppy Triscuits into his mouth, bits befouling his black beard.)

"You surprise me, Denis. So-so manip— worldly."

"I know such people inside out. If God stepped out of the Burning Bush, they'd use him to light their cigarettes. If I told them the inner truth, I'd be locked up for a year."

"I don't h-h-have your spiritual resources. I'm ordinary. I live among the ordinary. Why don't you accommodate to us? You understand us."

Denis thoughtfully rotated a Triscuit in his fingers. Part of it fell on him. "It's only those who understand who count for me. My teachers. You."

"I can't teach anyone anything. My life's modest, even poor, but I have a right to it. You have no right to change ordinary people. Even if you're saving us. Okay for Je-Jesus to bring swords instead of peace, but there's been only one Jesus. Maybe one too many."

"You're afraid they'll put me away. You're doing your duty. *In loco parentis* for me. You're a good person, Derek." He sprang from the chair. Mottram, frightened, got up too. "I'm going to show you something." He raced downstairs; Mottram, still fearful, started to follow, but then he was back, carrying a white cube. "Here," he said. He handed it to Mottram. "My book."

That night, Derek read himself to sleep in Denis's book. Or rather, he read at it; the most dogged reader couldn't have read it straight. There were eight hundred small pages—Denis had folded and cut ordinary eight-by-eleven bond paper into quarters—every other one of which was covered with tiny script. Denis had explained the arrangement. "It's a workbook. Every reader's a collaborator. Across from my ideas, his ideas. Next to my experience, his. It'll be a great success."

"So you have commercial ambitions for it?"

"Why not? Money's filth, enlightenment isn't. Everyone can be reached."

"I thought you only cared for cognoscenti."

"I don't know that word."

"People-in-the-know. Special people."

"The idea's to make everyone cognoscenti."

The modest title was *The World's Mind.* The dedication read, "To my teacher, Satyandi Purush, at whose Blessed Lotus feet I lay thought and life." (Under the dedicatee's name, another had been crossed out.)

As for the book itself, it was written in short, clear (and clearly borrowed) sentences. It began with the human progenitor, "Four-and-a-half feet tall, muscular, and black. Eve, traced via mitochondrial DNA. 200,000 years B.C." Millennia were skipped, and the author descended for a sentence to the prepaleolithic. Then the lower paleolithic: "The Clactonian worked with rough flakes. The Levalloisian worked with large ones." Mesopotamia: "4,000 B.C. The Al-Ubaid period features simple agriculture and painted pots." That did it for Al-Ubaid.

Asia Minor, Persia, India, Turkestan, China, and Siberia took another two pages. Ancient Egypt, "known as *Kemet,* the Black Land," was given a page of its own.

Modern history got personal. So the French and American Revolutions were important because Sellinbons had "come to tame the Indians." The famous mixed with the unknown, the private with the public. "The most important person in Nazi Germany was not Adolf Hitler, but my teacher Herman Schlonk." This was the only reference to either Hitler or Schlonk. An account of Philippe de Rothschild's life took up four pages.

Here and there, the book burst into reflection. So there was a discussion of leisure, an appeal to tycoons and politicians "to take more of it" so that they would "have less time to make trouble for the rest of us." Some pages were just lists of names, "Einstein, Mendel, Darwin, Faraday, Dr. Peabody, Whistler, Hudson, Chevrolet, Mayor Bradley."

"A history?" thought weary Mottram, "No, a listory."

He was too tired to turn out the light, but when he woke hours later in the dark, he thought, "Odd, I could have sworn." He stumbled to the bathroom, not noticing what he did when he awoke again at eight-thirty, that Denis's book was neither on the bed nor on the floor. He looked under the blankets, beneath the bed. Nothing.

The explanation was that Denis was gone too. Mottram found his note on the kettle.

> Derek. Was tempted to wait for goodbye, but the bus leaves at nine, and it's a ninety-minute walk to the station. What is goodbye between friends? I'm off to Brother Bull's Lamasery, near Oconomowoc, Wisc. Long talk with him last night. Seems right for me. A black man. (Blacks are the only Americans who still feel.) You're one of the few whites that has a good black heart. I want your opinion of my book. It will be a useful guide for schoolchildren, and high school students can use it to prepare for the SATs. I put the ficus plant outside.
>
> Denis

Mottram, part of whose frost had melted at this letter, finished it in fury. His plant. Deirdre's gift.

And that was nothing to his rage when he saw Denis's horrible watercolor Scotch-taped over the nude. "I'll kill him." He tore it off and stomped on it. That filthy, cretinous Eileen-spawn had bombed his life. Where did he get the goddamn nerve? Taken in like a crippled dog with nothing in the world to recommend him except the memory of his father, and he repays with destruction. Bitch son of a bitch mother, crawling in like the hound of death and pawing my sacred things. Where had he put the plant? Good God. Talk of exploitation, talk of power plays. These innocent killers, tuning up their harps while they rifle the eyes from your skull.

The ficus tree was freezing on the porch. Mottram ran down in his slippers and carried it in, the cold pouring off its bright leaves. The monster had killed it. "My poor ficus," he said. "I'll never forgive that bastard."

Two days later, the day Mottram did the laundry, he went to get Denis's sheets. Ripping them off—Denis had made the bed—he saw something fly into the air. It was a hundred-dollar bill. Incredible. The fellow couldn't even hang on to his few dollars. "I'll send it to Deirdre." Serve him right. But, of course, he put it into an envelope for Denis. When he got an address, he'd send it on. (Not to Eileen, she'd confiscate it.)

When a letter did come, four weeks later, he'd almost forgotten it.

The Lodge
Melvin, N.D.

Dear Derek,

Snow is part of my nature, but there's too much here at The Lodge. We're vowed to silence. At meals, the thoughts of Swami are read. So quiet. You hear the riprap of the river over the stones. Good for this restless soul of mine. Brother Bull's was good, but irreconcilable differences. I wish I had money to send you, but have only seventy-seven dollars. (Swami asks for the rest.) Please share it with Félicien. The author of Ecclesiasticus, Jesus, son of Sirach, says (approximate rending), "The world is a composition of fury, jealousy,

tumult, unrest, fear of death, rivalry, and strife" (the Jerusa-
lem Bible). I read the Prophets, Bantam Shakespeare, and
Kahlil Gibran (a Lebanese man who loved strong coffee,
cigarettes, never married, and eked a living from sketches
and writing). If you need music, train your ear on wind.
Practice drawing the light coming through the frost. One
day you and I can tour the US. Like Steinbeck and Charley.
It interests me to know if it is all there.

> Your friend,
> Denis

Mottram was a poor dreamer, but that night he dreamed
vividly. He was going into a church with Adelaide, but was
stopped by a powerful detergent smell in the nave. "Varnish?"
he asked. "No, it's george," said Adelaide. So, they waited outside, but inside was a full congregation. There a child cried. It
was little Deirdre. Who was also little Denis. He/she ran outside
into his arms, weeping, and he told her/him, "I'll never leave
you." In his body, he felt her/his sobbing relief.

When he woke for his six o'clock pee, the dream was with
him. He asked himself what "george" could have meant. It was
somehow important. As the yellow stream clattered into the
bowl, it came to him. "George" was his father's church in the
country which, so many years ago, Mottram had left for good.

Packages

As I was staying in Aliber's place across from Campbell's, my sister asked me to pick up the package. "I guess it's the acknowledgment cards." Our mother had died five days before.

Campbell's is a wonderful funeral factory. It does it all for you, gets the notice into the *Times*, sends for the death certificates (needed by banks, lawyers, accountants), orders the printed acknowledgments of condolence, and, of course, works out the funeral; or, as in Mother's case, the cremation and memorial service.

We'd held the service there in the large upstairs salon. Lots of flowers and few mourners: Mother's friends—who were in New York and ambulatory (eight octogenarian widows)—cousins, many of whom we hadn't seen in decades, two of my children, Doris's, and my father with Tina and Leona, the two Trinidad ladies who kept him up to snuff. A black-gowned organist—the closest thing to a religious figure in attendance—played some of Dad's favorites, "Who," "Some Enchanted Evening," and "Smoke Gets in Your Eyes" (this one a bit much in view of Mother's chosen mode of disintegration).

The package was wrapped in rough brown paper tied with a strand of hemp which broke when I hoisted it. "Don't worry," I said to the shocked Mr. Hoffman. "I'm just across the street." I held it with one hand and shook his with the other. Outside, limousines and chauffeurs idled—it was a slow death day in New York.

Thursday. Garbage collection on East Eighty-First. A massif of sacks and cartons ranged the stony fronts of town and apartment houses. No one but me on the street. Across Fifth Avenue, the Museum fountains poured boredom into the July heat. I left the package in a half-empty carton, walked to Aliber's door, then returned and covered it with yesterday's *Times.* Back to the house, key in the door, then back again to the package, which I unwrapped. It was a silvery can, the size of a half-gallon of paint; labeled. Curious about the contents, I tried to open it. No lid. Nor was it worth the trouble of fetching a hammer and wedge from Aliber's. I stripped off the label, rewrapped the can, and covered it with the newspaper. On top of that, I put a plastic sack of rinds and fishbones.

Aliber's apartment is dark, leathery, high ceilinged, somberly turbulent. Its walls are books. Books litter tables, chairs, sills, floors. An investment counselor, Aliber is really a reader. His claim is that all intelligence has a monetary translation. A cover for sheer desire to know everything. (He does better than most. Of the hundreds of Aliber books I've looked at, ninety percent bear his green-inked comments.)

There are hours to kill before Doris picks me up. I activate air conditioners and sound system and pick out some correct music. A cello suite of Poppa Bach. Naked on the leather couch, I listen until it overflows my capacity. You need weeks for such a piece. It should take as long to listen to as it did to compose. Or is the idea to reduce vastness into something portable?

A package.

I think I thought that then, though the notion may have come after I'd found *The Mind of Matter* in the wall behind my head. I read a chapter devoted to Planck's "famous lecture to the Berlin Academy in May of 1899," in which he described "that extraordinary quantity" which "for all times and cultures" made possible "the derivation of units for mass, length, time and temperature." Planck's constant. Not then called h. Only 6.625 $\times$ 10^{-27} erg seconds, or, by our author, "that stubby transmitter of universal radiance . . . Nature's own package." Little as I understood of this package, I felt some connection between it and Bach's and the one which held what was left of what had once held me.

Six weeks earlier, back in Chicago, I'd written a letter in my head. *Dearest Mother. Last Saturday, I unbuttoned your dress and slipped it off your shoulders. Doris undid your bra, and for the first time in decades, I saw your sad breasts. We put the gauzy, small-flowered nightgown over your head and pulled it down the bony tunnel of your back, your seamed belly.*

Before we taxied to Mount Sinai, Leona fixed your hair; tucked, curled, waved, and crimped it. (If her eight months of beauty school produce nothing else, they've been worth it.) It was your last home vanity. When we left you, sunk in the narrow bed, the piled hair survived. Your stake in the great world.

I finished lunch with my spring wheat man in the Wrigley Restaurant and walked alone by the Chicago River. Immense brightness, the Sun-Times Building a cube of flame. All around, the steel-and-glass dumbness of this beautiful, cruel town. *I noticed, then noticed I noticed, the bodies of women, white and black. Thank you, Mother, for my pleasure in such sights.*

A girl in leotards the color of papaya meat jumped around a stage in front of the big nothing of Picasso's metal gift—bloodless heart, brainless head. Huffing, she explained arabesque and second position to the soft crowd of municipal workers, shoppers, tourists. It's splendid being part of a crowd like this, letting bored respect for art muzzle the interest in the dancer's body. Bless such civic gifts.

There have been times I've wanted your death, Mother. At least, did not much care.

It was money. That noise. Curse me for it.

I've walked through slums, *bustees, barriadas, callampas, favelas, suburbios* (the very names a misery). *In a Calcutta dump, I saw a darker you,* forty years younger, everything in her life within her reach: pot, shawl, kid. *What should a man do with money?* Getty, the billionaire, claimed he wasn't rich, didn't have a spare—an uninvested—nickel. I'm rich. So what am I doing in these glassy dollared Alps—reflections annihilating reflections—the money canyons of your town and mine?

Unearned dough. *It came to you without effort; it filled your head. (Should noise fill heads like yours? Or mine?)*

Last week you said you wanted "to go," and you kissed me with the strength of goodbye. (Goodbye is what's left.) *Soon you'll be nothing but your purses, your spoons, your china, your sheets, your doilies. Your money. You'll be an absence in Doris; in me; a shard in Dad's head.*

After Mother's death—which he does not acknowledge: she is *out for lunch*—his head is in more of a whirl than ever. He shuts himself in closets, undresses at three P.M., goes, pajamaed, into the street (brought back by the doormen). One night, he appears naked at Tina's bedside. He says he wishes to do things with her. Disused parts hang from his groin like rotten fruit. Tina gets a blanket around him, persuades him back to his own bed. "I was *so* scared, Miss Doris. Doctor is a strong mon. Yesterday, he move the fuhniture round and round the living room."

Deprived of cigarettes—he sets clothes and furniture afire—and of the *Times*—there's a pressman's strike—his hours are spent walking from room to room, staring at Third Avenue, winding his wristwatch.

As the small shocks of his small world dislodge more and more of his brain, his speech shrivels to the poetry of the very young and old.

"How are you today, Daddy?"

"Rainy."

"What time do you make it?"

"Too late."

He lives by a few lines of verse which embody a creed and an old passion for eloquence. "For a' that and a' that, A man's a man for a' that." (We recite the Burns poem at his grave.) "Oh, lady bright, can it be right / This window open to the night?"

Decades of control slough off the frail body. He sits tensely in the living room. "What you doin', Doctor?"

"Waiting."
"May I ask what you waitin' *for*?"
"A girl is coming."
"What gull you talkin' of?"
"None of yours. Give her fifty dollars. A hundred dollars."
Tina has a grand laugh. (And laughs are scarce here.)
He is furious. "Out."
He waits an hour, then locks himself in the bathroom.
"You okay, Doctor?"
"Am I supposed to be?"
Doris calls Dr. Rice, who is not surprised. "It's the ones who've done the least who do the most now. I've known them to masturbate in front of people."
"Maybe we should get him a girl."
"I don't think that would do any good. And *he* certainly couldn't."
"What can be done?"
"An extra tranquilizer before bed."
Not a few times we would have liked to tranquilize him permanently. But senility too is part of life, one of the few remaining middle-class encounters with the Insoluble.
One afternoon, before I went back to Chicago, he came in while I was going over estate papers. He was in white pajamas. (The day's familiar divisions were no longer his.) "I have to talk with you, Son."
"What is it, Dad?"
He took a scrap of paper from his old billfold and gave it to me. "I want to go here."
"You are here. This is your address."
"No, dear. I want to go *home*."
"This is your home. No one else's."
"I don't think so."
And he was right. Home is where his wife lived. Or his mother —who died during the Spanish-American War.
The next day, his need to go home was so strong, we took a taxi four blocks to Doris's house. How happy he was. Doris was a segment of that female benevolence which had watched over him from birth, mother-stepmother-sisters-wife-daughter. They were a continuity of watchfulness. How he kissed Doris, and talked, until, noticing unfamiliar furniture, a different view, he

grew weary. We taxied home, and now it was home, the place where his wife would be coming after lunch.

In Chicago, I got the day's bulletins by phone. "He peed in the dresser."

"Jesus."

"I think he confused drawer and door. They both open. I mean it wasn't totally irrational."

"Bless you, Doris."

He became incontinent. "I never thought I'd live to clean up my own father. I couldn't let the girls do it."

"How long can it go on?"

"Dr. Rice says he's strong as an ox. There's nothing organically wrong."

"Poor fellow."

"He misses you."

"How do you know?"

"He lights up when I say you're coming. Can't you come?"

"I'll try."

But didn't. At Christmas, I sent him a check for a billion dollars. "To the World's Best Father."

"Did he like it?"

"I don't think so. He tore it up."

"How dumb of me."

"He's still a human being, you know."

"I hadn't forgotten." *Despite those reports of yours,* I didn't say. *Which convert him into a pile of disasters.* "I should have come. He knew I should be there. And knew I knew it." Unable to say it directly, he tore up the check.

His last paternal correction.

At the end of the beautiful novella which Proust plants like an ice-age fragment in his novel, Swann thinks how terrible it is that the greatest love of his life has been for a woman who was not his type. (This thought—like the piano music of Ravel—detonates the world's pathos for me; though consciousness makes it as beautiful as the music.) My mother was not my type.

A month after Dad's death, I dreamed that she and I were having another of the small disputes which disfigured thousands of our hours. "I can't bear your nagging," I said. As always, my anger silenced hers. She said she'd tell my father to speak to me. But when he came in, he was the old man who died, and, instead of his slipper, I saw only the sad face of his last days.

Then my dream mother said, "I hope you'll be coming back to New York next summer."

"This one hasn't been very pleasant."

"I haven't had a good one either."

I knew this meant the ulcerous mouth, the colds, the drowsiness which disguised and expressed her cancer.

I was about to tell her that I would be back, when this part of the dream became a poem. (My dreams often conclude in poems and interpretations.) On a screen of air, I saw lines from George Herbert's "The Collar." "Forsake thy cage," they read,

> Thy rope of sands,
> Which petty thoughts have made, and made to thee
> Good cable, to enforce and draw,
> And be thy law . . .

My dream interpreter here let me know that my cable had turned to sand because my parents were dead. I was free.

I've been a father so long, I didn't know how much I was still a son; how onerous it was to be a son. Now my "lines and life were free." "But," the poem continued on the screen of inner air,

> as I raved and grew more fierce and wild
> At every word,
> Methought I heard one calling, *Child!*
> And I replied, *My Lord.*

My response was not *"My Lord"* but *My Duty.* The Duty which had raised and formed me.

Only at the beginning of my life and the end of hers did I love my mother wholly. When her life was over—like a simple-minded book—I pitied its waste.

There was much intelligence and much energy in her. Yet what was her life but an advertisement for idleness. And how could such a woman have failed to be a nagger, a boss, the idle driver of others, an anal neurotic for whom cleanliness was not a simple, commonsensical virtue but a compulsion nourished by her deepest need? *Wash your hands. Pick up your clothes. The room is filthy. Eat up. Mary wants to go out.* (The sympathy for Mary veiled the need to have the dining room inert, restored to preorganic purity. What counted was setting, stage, the scene before and after action. What drastic insecurity underlay this drive toward inertness?)

Too simple.

Mother loved learning, going, seeing. She loved shows, travel, games. She loved *doing good.*

Nor is this enough. She was the reliable, amiable center of a large group of women like herself, the one who remembered occasions and relationships, the one who knew *the right thing to do.*

Her telephone rang from eight A.M. on. Lunches, games, lectures, plays, visits. Lunch was a crucial, a beautiful event. One went *out.* (But where? Longchamps—before its fall—Schrafft's, but which one? *Or shall we try a new place?* What excitement.) Whose game was it? Beasie's? Marion B's? Justine's? Bridge, canasta, gin, mah-jongg (the small clicks of the tiles, "One dot"; "Two crack").

A smallish woman, five-four, brown haired. (Gray for the last twenty years, but I always *saw* her brown haired.) Not abundant, but crowded with soft, expressive waves. (Expressive of expense; of free time.) Clear brown eyes, scimitar nose, narrow lips; a sharp face, once soft, fine cheeked, pretty.

She died well. "What choice do I have?"

Not bad; for anyone, let alone a monument to redundance. (Bear two children, *cared for by others,* oversee an apartment, *cleaned by others,* shop for food, *cooked by others*.) She died bravely, modestly, with decorum. The decorum of practicality. (Her other tutelary deity.) She made up her mind to be as little trouble to those she loved as possible. (Cleanliness reborn as virtue.) She set her face to the wall, stopped taking medicine (without offending the nurses she loved so in the last weeks), and sank quietly into nonexistence. The last hours, teeth out, face caved in, the wrestler Death twisting the jaw off her face, she managed a smile (a human movement) when I said we were there, we loved her. She lay, tiny, at the bottom of tremendous loneliness.

Packages

* * *

Doris and I wait for a taxi at the corner of Eighty-First and Madison. Seven o'clock, the tail end of the day. Traffic flows north. Buses crap plumes of filth into the lovely street (where —I think for some reason—Washington's troops were chased by British redcoats two hundred years ago). A growl of horns to our left. A Rolls-Royce honks at a Department of Sanitation truck in front of Aliber's house. The garbage men are throwing sacks and cartons into great blades whirling in the truck's backside. A powerful little fellow throws in the carton with my package.

"What's the matter?"

"Nothing."

"You look funny."

"Tell you later."

Goodbye, darling.

And: Why not?

You were a child of the city, born here, your mother born here. If I could have pried it open, I would have spread you in Central Park. But this way is better than a slot in that Westchester mausoleum. Foolish, garish anteroom to no house. Egyptian stupidity.

And it was the *practical* thing to do.

Wasn't it, Mother?

The following stories are reprinted from *Teeth, Dying and Other Matters* (Harper & Row, 1964): "Teeth," "Good Morrow, Swine," "Wanderers," "The Good European," "Orvieto Dominos, Bolsena Eels," "A Short History of Love," "Arrangements at the Gulf," "Gardiner's Legacy," and "Dying." The following from *1968: A Short Novel, An Urban Idyll, Five Stories and Two Trade Notes* (Holt, Rinehart and Winston, 1970): "Ins and Outs," "Milius and Melanie," "East, West . . . Midwest," "Idylls of Dugan and Strunk," "Gaps," and "Gifts." The following from *Packages* (Coward, McCann & Geoghegan, 1980): "Wissler Remembers," "Mail," "The Ideal Address," "Packages," "Troubles," "Lesson for the Day," "Double Charley," "Riordan's Fiftieth," "The Girl Who Loves Schubert," "A Recital for the Pope," and "Dr. Cahn's Visit." Of the previously uncollected stories, "Losing Color" first appeared in *Antioch Review;* "Zhoof" in *Formations;* "In Return" in *Encounter;* "In the Dock" in *TriQuarterly;* "The Sorrows of Captain Schreiber" in *Western Review;* and "La Pourriture Noble" in *Chicago Times.* Others of the stories were first published in *Accent, The Atlantic, Big Table, Chicago, Commentary, Epoch, Harper's, Hudson Review,* and *Partisan Review.* Many of the stories have been revised here, most of them slightly.